Down Daisy Street

KATIE FLYNN

arrow books

Reissued by Arrow Books in 2004

15 17 19 20 18 16

Copyright © Katie Flynn 2003

Katie Flynn has asserted her right under the Copyright, Designs and
Patents Act, 1988 to be identified as the author of this work

First published in the United Kingdom in 2003 by William Heinemann
First published in paperback in 2003 by Arrow Books

Arrow Books
The Random House Group Limited
20 Vauxhall Bridge Road, London SW1V 2SA

www.randomhouse.co.uk

Addresses for companies within The Random House Group Limited
can be found at: www.randomhouse.co.uk/offices.htm

The Random House Group Limited Reg. No. 954009

A CIP catalogue record for this book
is available from the British Library

Penguin Random House is committed to a sustainable future for
our business, our readers and our planet. This book is made from
Forest Stewardship Council® certified paper.

Printe

Katie Flynn has lived for many years in the Northwest. A compulsive writer, she started with short stories and articles and many of her early stories were broadcast on Radio Mersey. She decided to rite her Liverpool series after hearing the reminisc- ces of family members about life in the city in the arly years of the century. She also writes as Judith axton. For many years she has had to cope with ME ut has continued to write.

Praise for Katie Flynn:

'She's a challenge to Josephine Cox' *Bookseller*

'You can be guaranteed that if you pick up a Katie Flynn book it's going to be a wrench to put it down again' *Holyhead & Anglesey Mail*

'A heartwarming story of love and loss' *Woman's Weekly*

'One of the best Liverpool writers' *Liverpool Echo*

'[Katie Flynn] has the gift that Catherine Cookson had of bringing the period and the characters to life' *Caernarfon & Denbigh Herald*

For another Kathy: Kathy Nimmer of Indiana and her dog, Raffles – two of the best and nicest folk you could wish to meet.

Acknowledgements

Many thanks go to Rosemarie Hague, for her wonderfully vivid memories of Liverpool during the Second World War and to Alan Hague, who told me as much about the RAF in Norfolk as my tiny mind could hold. Also many thanks to the staff of the Great Yarmouth Library, who got me invaluable information about the Horsey floods.

As usual, many thanks to the staff of the Wrexham Library, who supplied me with books on the Second World War and, last but not least, thank you Bet Carter, née Douglas (affectionately known as 'Dougie' by her fellow Waafs) for all the information on barrage balloons.

PART I

Chapter One

1935

It was a fine September day and Kathy Kelling, neat in her new school uniform, was coming slowly along Stanley Road, swinging her satchel and enjoying the warmth of the sun on her back. A lad who was drawing level with her gave a loud guffaw as he caught sight of her and slowed his pace to amble alongside, saying as he did so: 'Who's perishin' smart, then? I'm a-goin' to call you Lickle Miss White Socks. Well, whazzit like then, your new school? Or are you too swell-headed to speak to the likes of me, eh?'

Kathy eyed the lad cautiously. She knew him, of course – all the flower street kids knew one another – but since he was two or three years older than herself, she could not immediately put a name to him. She gave him the benefit of a long, hard stare and realised after a moment that he was Annie McCabe's older brother . . . what the devil was his name? Johnny? Jimmy? Yes, that was it, Jimmy. He had a shock of soot-black hair and deep set, dark-blue eyes, and was wearing a faded check shirt and ragged grey flannel trousers. Though he had boots on his feet, they were so cracked and broken that she could see the greyish tinge of his skin through them.

'I'm not swell-headed, as you call it, Jimmy McCabe,' Kathy said, having placed him. 'And it weren't me who wanted to leave Daisy Street School and all me pals, it were me mam, just remember that!'

'Awright, awright, keep your flamin' hair on,' Jimmy said in an aggrieved tone. He squinted across at her, beginning to grin. 'My Gawd, even your bleedin' ribbon is a green 'un! I bet your bleedin' knickers are green an' all.'

Kathy felt her face grow hot. 'You cheeky bugger!' she said wrathfully. 'The colour of me knickers is no concern of yours, nor me hair ribbon, for that matter. Oh, gerralong home and let me enjoy me walk.'

Jimmy guffawed again. 'I'm a-goin' to keep you company,' he said grandly. 'Can I carry your smart school bag, Miss?'

Kathy was about to tell him roundly that if he laid a finger on her satchel she would beat him to death with it, when a welcome diversion occurred. A figure came hurrying along the pavement towards them, waving and calling out as she came. 'Kathy! Ooh, we did miss you, it were horrible in school wi'out you. But how did it go? I say, you look real posh. What are the other girls like? Do you have a best pal yet?' The girl glanced at Kathy's companion, raising her eyebrows interrogatively. 'Don't say you're sweet on our Kathy, Jimmy McCabe! Are you walkin' her home like they does in romantic novels, eh?'

If Jane O'Brien had searched for a year, she could not have found a better method of sending Jimmy McCabe on his way. He gave a loud, jeering laugh and spat into the gutter, then said: 'Bleedin' girls! I wouldn't walk a decent one home, lerralone a stuck-up little tart like Miss Kathy Kelling. I just stopped to tell her wharra fool she looks in that green jacket thing. Anyhow, she won't want to go around wi' you, Jane O'Brien, now she's at a posh private school, with a green uniform!' He looked speculatively at Jane. 'But if youse is short of a pal, now that Lickle Miss

4

White Socks has took herself off, you've gorra champion in Jimmy McCabe any time you say the word.'

Jane sniffed but Kathy saw that she dimpled as well. 'Oh, gerron with you! Buzz off, Jimmy,' she said dismissively, and the two girls watched as he loped off down the road, disappearing into the next side street.

The girls turned to each other and Kathy tucked her hand into her friend's arm, shaking it slightly. 'All boys are alike; they take one look at you and want to be pals,' she said. 'Wish I had curly yellow hair and dimples.'

Jane laughed. 'At our age, all boys hate all girls,' she said wisely. 'But in a year or two it'll be a different story and we'll both have fellers dogging our every move. Now come on, queen, tell me everything, right from the first moment you started at the new school. There ain't no point in me telling you, because Daisy Street School don't change, 'cept that it were mortal dull wi'out me best pal to have a laugh with.'

Kathy took a deep breath and began to tell Jane all about her day from the moment she had entered the large, airy reception hall until, with her bag crammed with strange books and her head with strange experiences, she had left her new high school. Looking back on it now, it had been an unusual, almost unnerving experience. She had started at the Daisy Street School at the tender age of four, nine long years ago, and knew everyone, both teachers and pupils, almost as well as she knew her own parents. She had been reluctant to agree to Mrs Kelling's suggestion that she should try for a scholarship to a school whose pupils would continue to matriculation level and beyond, but had sat the examination and had been secretly impressed both by the lovely old house and by the crowds of girls in their smart green uniforms. The fact that they were all strangers to her had worried her at first but when she got the letter saying that she had gained a place and inviting her to the school for an interview with Miss Beaver, the headmistress, she had decided that perhaps it was high time she knew more of the world than the restricted area of the flower streets. Furthermore, her parents' pride in her achievement had made her realise that they would be cruelly disappointed if she turned down this opportunity.

'It's the best chance you'll ever have to better yourself, luv,' her mother had said fondly. 'You'll make friends with girls whose parents are a good deal higher up in the world than either meself or your dad, because workin' in a corner shop like I do or in a timber merchant's yard, like your dad, aren't what you might call jobs which need brains or education. Your dad's never been bitter, but he were top of his class right up to the time he left school and should have gone on to do examinations and that, only by the time he were fourteen his dad had died and his mam needed every penny her lads could bring in. So you see, you're gettin' the opportunities that were denied to us and we're right proud of you. You shall have everything the other girls have, everything you need, even if it takes our last penny. Not that we'd let Billy go short, but he's a baby still and by the time he needs money spending on him you'll be earning.'

Kathy had always known that her father was clever. He had sometimes told her about his struggles in evening classes to catch up with other boys who had stayed in school a year or two longer, and she had always admired his tenacity and the quickness with which he had grasped subjects that were new to him. He was naturally good at mathematics but it was hard for him to get a white-collar job where he could work with his head rather than his hands. Managers were reluctant to employ someone who had left school at fourteen, but once the results of the examinations he took in evening classes were available he got his first job as a clerk at the sawmills, and from that position moved slowly but steadily up through the hierarchy until he was at the very top. In fact, by the time Kathy was in school, he was chief accountant at the sawmills and was justly proud of his ability to do the job.

Because of his own bad start, he had been determined that Kathy should have a good grounding in subjects additional to those taught at the Daisy Street School. But he had realised that any lessons he gave his daughter must be fun as well as instructive, and often their sessions would begin seriously and end in gales of laughter as Kathy, at his behest, tried to work out how long it would take twenty wasps to eat their way through a two-pound tin of golden syrup or how long it would take Mam to fill the wash boiler if she were only allowed to use a teacup, remembering that she had to take ten paces in each direction between the copper and the tap in the yard.

Kathy, who adored her father and thought him the best man in the world, now knew that fulfilling her parents' expectations was her responsibility and acknowledged that if she could not do so she would be letting Mam and Dad down as well as herself. So she had approached her new school with a certain amount of caution though this had speedily proved to be unfounded. She had been taken to her classroom and provided with a roneo'd timetable and her class teacher, Miss Ellis, had told her that in this school it was the pupils who went from class to class, rather than the teachers, so that one did not remain in one's classroom all day. This idea was a strange but pleasant one, and the fact that different teachers taught different subjects also meant that one was less likely to be picked upon. If a teacher disliked you, she only did so for forty-five minutes before one picked up one's bag of books and moved on to a new classroom and, of course, a new teacher.

A good many of the girls in her class had been at the high school since they were four or five, but they were a friendly crowd, eager to get to know the two new scholarship girls, Kathy herself and Isobella Newton. When the teacher announced that it was dinner time, Kathy and Isobella were already sufficiently friendly to join the queue going into the dining room together, where Isobella admitted, in a breathy whisper, that she had been warned of awful consequences if she dropped food on her clothes. Kathy, who had received an identical warning, suggested that they should tuck their handkerchiefs into their collars or simply remove their tunics and go into the dining room in their blouse and knickers. This remark had the pair of them so helpless with giggles that they earned the wrath of a senior prefect. She warned them that though laughing was not forbidden it was frowned upon in the dining room, and added that conversation should be restricted to such remarks as 'Please pass the salt'.

The morning's lessons had suggested to Kathy that she was not going to find herself left behind by the rest of the class and the afternoon sessions confirmed it. Though neither she nor Isobella had had a chemistry lesson before, they were intrigued by the information they were given and by the short experiment which Miss Webster, the teacher, performed on the dais. This lesson was followed by a period in the gymnasium, where Kathy really shone, for she was already an expert at such things as shinning up ropes and walking along walls, having done so ever since she was big enough to join in street games. To be sure, here one climbed ropes as thick as one's wrist and walked along a great wooden beam and not a crumbling brick wall, but the rest of her class clustered round her when they returned to the changing room, asking her, only half jokingly, if she had ever belonged to a circus. 'No, but I have walked walls and climbed ropes all me life,' Kathy had said truthfully. 'I like boys' games and anyway, in Daisy Street girls and fellers all muck in together.'

Someone sniffed disparagingly. It was a tall girl, with her hair braided into a long, fair plait, who had a habit of looking down her nose at people smaller than she. 'I don't see anything to be proud about just because a girl can behave like a monkey,' she remarked, in a rather drawling voice. 'But these scholarship girls are all alike, sharp as little monkeys but with no real intelligence.'

Several of the girls glanced at her with dislike and a round, fair, cuddly-looking girl, whose name Kathy already knew to be Ruby, said: 'What a disgusting thing to say, Marcia. It's stupid too, because when the end of term results come out I bet both Issie and Kathy will be placed higher than you. And you can't walk the beam or climb ropes either,' she ended triumphantly.

The taller girl shrugged. 'If I wanted to be mistaken for a monkey, I might care about your opinion,' she said nastily. 'Come along, Cynthia, let's cut along to

Miss Grimes's room so that we can choose our seats before the hoi polloi arrive.'

The two girls strolled off and the rest of the class straggled after them and no more was said, though Isobella whispered to Kathy that she rather feared Marcia had coined a nickname that might well stick. 'Do you mind if they call you Monkey?' she enquired anxiously. 'But perhaps they won't, because no one likes that Marcia much, do they?'

Kathy had replied loftily that she did not care what anyone called her but was relieved to find, when the girls congregated in the cloakroom at the end of the day, that she was still addressed as Kathy, even though the prefect insisted on 'Katherine' when she spoke to her.

The incident in the gymnasium was the one rather sour spot in a day which Kathy had otherwise thoroughly enjoyed. When relating her doings to Jane, she told her how unpleasant Marcia had been but ended, 'Though no one called me Monkey, after all, so I needn't have worried.'

'But you said you didn't care if they did,' Jane reminded her. 'An' anyway, practically everyone down our street has got a nickname. They've been callin' me Blondie for years!'

'Ye-es, but Monkey sounds so rude somehow,' Kathy said reflectively. 'Monkeys swing through the trees in the jungle and steal things and they're in zoos. I wouldn't mind being called Brownie, because I've got brown hair, but that's different.'

Jane admitted that it was and then said, half accusingly: 'But you've gorra new bezzie and now you've left Daisy Street I've got no one. Where does that girl Isobella live, anyroad? Is it near here? Only I know you've gorra have a pal in school and it can't be me, but – but I'm still your bezzie outside school, aren't I?'

'Oh, Janey, of course you are,' Kathy cried. 'As for Isobella, I don't know that she'll ever be my best friend, even in school, but we're both new and – and they keep telling you to get into pairs to go from class to class . . . as for knowing where she lives, I didn't ask her and she didn't ask me, but one thing I am sure of, we shan't be meeting up outside school.'

'Well, I dare say it's mean of me, but I'm glad,' Jane said contentedly, as they turned into Daisy Street. 'You'll want to go home right away, I expect, so you can tell your mam and dad everything. Can we meet up later, though?'

Kathy consulted the small wristwatch which had been her father's present to her for winning the scholarship. 'Mam works till six tonight and it's only half past four,' she said briskly. 'So if you want to come round and give me a hand, I'll get the tea going, like I do every night, so Mam can come in to a hot meal. Then I'll have to fetch our Billy; he's with Mrs Hughes in Pansy Street. I've gorra deal of homework to do, but I can whip through that after I've had me tea.'

'I've been home already since we finish school before you, so I know you won't find Billy with Mrs Hughes,' Jane said. 'She's taken her Phil to the dentist so she brought Billy round to my mam. Mam's had to go off to work, but your Billy's safe enough. Tilly's giving an eye to them, so they're all playin' in the kitchen, happy as pigs in muck. Do you want to go round straight away and fetch him? Only it'll be easier for the pair of us to get tea at your place if you leave Billy where he is.'

Kathy agreed wholeheartedly with this since Billy

had reached the age when saying no to everything was great fun and obeying a sister's instructions, even when the sister was a great deal older, was not nearly as amusing as simply shaking his head and tightening his lips. Tilly, Jane's eleven-year-old sister, was a sensible girl. She did her very best to help Jane to look after the younger ones and could be relied upon to see that a meal was prepared each evening provided that her parents had left her either money or ingredients. She and Jane were jointly in charge of the household whenever Mrs O'Brien was not available and, by and large, they managed extremely well, though Jane, being the older, had more authority.

Jane and Kathy turned into the back yard of the Kelling house in Daisy Street, as they had done so often in the past, and it was Jane who reached up to the lintel and pulled down the back door key on its length of string. She unlocked the door and the two girls entered, Kathy slinging her satchel down on the floor with a sigh of relief for it was simply bulging with books. She began to struggle into her mother's calico apron, saying as she did so: 'Mam's left the food in the pantry. If you'll just riddle the fire, I'll fetch the stuff through. She'll have left enough for you as well, Janey; going to come back later and have your tea with us?'

Jane often shared the Kellings' evening meal. Kathy knew her mother felt guilty about being the parent of only two children, when Mr and Mrs O'Brien had eight, and did her best to ease their burden by feeding Jane three or four times a week. On this occasion, however, Jane shook her head. 'Thanks ever so, queen, but not tonight. Mam's gorra job cleanin' in the Prince of Wales on Stanley Road, so Tilly and me is goin' to make the grub for me dad and the kids.' As she spoke, she was adding coal to the fire with the brass tongs, having already riddled it free of ash. She began to heave the ash pan out, then turned to her friend. 'So once we've got your mam's tea on the go, you might as well come round to number eleven and give a hand wi' ours,' she said hopefully, 'before taking Billy home.'

Kathy sighed. She hardly ever went into the O'Briens' house after school since it was like walking into bedlam after the quiet orderliness of her own home. There would be kids everywhere, the youngest two, bare-bottomed as well as barefooted; there would be a mound of potatoes to prepare for the pan, accompanied usually by a scrawny cabbage and pock-marked carrots, which Kathy always suspected had been picked up by Mr O'Brien, who was a porter at the St John's vegetable market, when the day's trading was finished. Some families, she knew, actually scoured the big bins into which the remnants of the day's produce were thrown, but people like that did not live in Daisy Street. Mr O'Brien earned a tiny wage and was glad of his wife's contribution to their income, though this was somewhat haphazard. Mrs O'Brien often boasted that she could turn her hand to anything and this seemed to mean that she never stayed in one job for long. Kathy's mother, who was fond of fat and friendly Mrs O'Brien, made excuses for her, but Kathy's father had been heard to mutter more than once 'Jack of all trades, master of none' when Mrs O'Brien's grasshopper boundings from job to job were drawn to his attention.

But the last thing Kathy wanted to do was to hurt Jane's feelings. 'All right. Once we've got our food on the go, I'll come round and gi' you a hand with yours,' she said. 'It'll be a good hour before Mam and

Dad are home and I'd sooner our Billy played with your little ones than came back and plagued me.' She was rewarded by Jane's beaming smile.

Mrs Kelling had left a pound of minced beef, three onions and half a dozen carrots, as well as a slab of Madeira cake, beside which stood a jug of milk and a packet of Bird's custard powder. Kathy's mouth watered as she began the preparations; minced beef stew followed by cake and custard was a great favourite of hers and she guessed that her mother had purchased these ingredients to make her first day at the new school a bit more special. However, quite a lot of work was involved in the creation of the dish. Kathy chopped carrots and onions with streaming eyes, fried them and the meat in a little dripping, added flour and water to thicken the gravy and then pulled the pan over the fire, keeping it to the edge of the flame so that it did not burn and stirring it with her mother's long-handled wooden spoon from time to time. Meanwhile Jane scrubbed the potatoes and popped them into a second pot, and then the two of them laid the table. When this was done, they damped down the fire, pulled the pans to one side of the stove and set out for Jane's house. Minced beef stew did not need long cooking; now it was on the go, it would need no more attention until the potatoes were pulled over the fire some twenty minutes before Mr and Mrs Kelling returned home.

Kathy shrugged off the calico apron and hung it on the hook on the back of the door. In the ordinary way, she knew she should have removed her uniform before beginning to work, but she guessed her parents would want to see her in it and anyway, since she was going round to Jane's house, the O'Brien family too would be interested in her new clothes.

14

Jane, however, looked at her rather doubtfully as Kathy slipped her arms into her green blazer. 'You don't want to wear that round our place, queen,' she observed. 'Suppose young Freddy climbs on to your lap and then has a pee? And all our kids are filthy as pigs in a midden. Tell you what, bring your mam's apron . . . but do leave that jacket thing behind.'

'Yes, you're right, since I'm supposed to wear the hat if I'm wearing the blazer and it's just like a bleedin' soup plate,' Kathy said, rather reluctantly removing the blazer and hanging it back on the door once more. 'And it's not a jacket, it's a blazer, you halfwit! Still, I'll take the apron. I don't want me new tunic mucked up, I'll grant you that.'

The girls set off for Jane's house, which was only four doors away after all, and crossed the filthy back yard. Kathy always took a deep breath and held it before so doing because the lavatory in the corner was used – or misused – by the whole O'Brien family and not emptied as often as it should have been. As a result, she usually arrived at the back door bright pink in the face and breathless. She sometimes wondered what Jane thought of such antics, since her friend continued to talk merrily as they crossed the yard and certainly did not hold her breath. I suppose she's used to the pong, Kathy thought resignedly, as they entered the kitchen. She let out her trapped breath as unobtrusively as possible, but four-year-old Teresa, giving a shout of welcome and hurling herself at Kathy's knees, said innocently: 'Did you have a nice day, Kathy? Did you run all the way back from the school to Daisy Street? Is that why youse face is all pink?'

'No, she's red in the face 'cos she don't like the smell of our lavvy and holds her breath,' Reggie said scornfully. 'Don't you know nuffin', our T'resa?'

'I know lots an' lots,' Teresa said boastfully. 'I bin to school now three days.' She turned saucer-like blue eyes up to Kathy. 'I can *read*,' she said triumphantly. 'I can read me letters. I'm cleverest in the class, me teacher says.'

Kathy laughed and rumpled the little girl's fair curls. All the O'Brien children were blond, curly haired and blue eyed; even the boys were pretty, though they did their best to dispel the good impression created by their looks by behaving as atrociously as they could.

Jane, crossing the kitchen in the direction of the knee-level sink at which Matilda was already scrubbing away at a quantity of spuds, laughed and tugged one of her small sister's curls. 'You can't read, you silly little dope,' she said affectionately. 'Why, you're not even sure of your colours yet. I heered you tell our mam you wanted to wear the red jersey to school and you've not gorra red jersey; you meaned the blue one.'

Reggie, who was six, crouched down and blew a raspberry into his small sister's face. 'Dopey, dopey, dopey,' he jeered. 'Who doesn't know blue from red, an' there ain't a brain in your head, you can't even tell the time of day, you might just as well be dead.'

Incensed by this uncalled for criticism, Teresa grabbed a building block from Tommy, the youngest O'Brien, and clouted Reggie with it. Startled, Reggie stepped back, his bare foot landing heavily on Tommy's hand. Tommy let out a squeal like a pig, then launched himself at Reggie, and fastened his teeth in the older boy's calf. In two minutes, a full-scale war was being waged on the dirty kitchen floor, in which little Billy Kelling joyfully joined, screaming with excitement, and Jane and Kathy had their work cut out to be heard above the din.

Such fights were not unknown in the O'Brien family and Kathy knew from experience that as soon as someone began to cry the brothers and sisters would sort themselves out, pet the injured party and forget their differences. But on this occasion what stopped the fight was the sound of a heavy thump, upon which the shrieks were cut off abruptly and silence descended.

Kathy took one shocked look at the mêlée and stooped to snatch her little brother up from the floor. As the fight had rolled over him, Billy's head had come into contact with the edge of the fender. There was an ugly wound on his forehead and blood was streaming down his pale little face, whilst a huge bump was growing before Kathy's horrified gaze.

Jane, who had joined her sister at the sink, turned to see what the silence was about and gave a scream which rivalled a steam whistle. She did not ask who had inflicted the blow, knowing at once that it had been an accident, but flew across the room with the dishcloth in her hand and began tenderly mopping the little visitor's bloodstained brow. Kathy, still clutching Billy to her breast, swung round so that Jane was forced to cease her ministrations. 'Don't touch him with that filthy cloth,' she said fiercely, tact forgotten in the anxiety of the moment. 'Don't you remember what they told us at Red Cross? You mustn't touch a wound with anything dirty because of germs. Besides, he's knocked himself cold; we've gorra take him straight round to the Stanley. The nurses there will know what to do.'

Jane's panic subsided as suddenly as it had arisen. 'Yes, of course, that's what we've gorra do,' she said thankfully. 'Gawd knows it's happened often enough wi' our kids. Sister Clemence says my mam might as

17

well tek over a bed permanent like, 'cos us kids have broke so many bones an' that.' She turned to Matilda, still stolidly scrubbing potatoes, having started on the task again as soon as she realised that the older girls had things in hand. 'Tilly, you'd best leave them spuds for the time being an' keep an eye on the littl'uns while Kathy and me's gone.'

Tilly turned away from the sink, sighing and drying her hands on the thin roller towel that hung on the pantry door. 'I'd near on finished anyhow,' she said resignedly. 'Only do you have to go the both of you? The kids don't mind me the way they mind you, Janey, an' Mam won't be back for hours yet.'

Kathy was still holding the unconscious Billy but she had no intention of arriving at the hospital without her friend's support. 'You'll just have to cope, Tilly,' she said firmly. 'After all, you were managing very nicely before we came in. Besides, it were an accident, you know it were, so it's not liable to happen again.' She turned threateningly towards Reggie, who had, she felt, started the fracas. 'Just you be a good little feller, Reggie O'Brien, or I'll tell your dad you've been a little bugger and he'll belt you till you can't sit down.'

This was an empty threat and all the kids knew it, since Mr O'Brien was a fond father. He was apt to return from work with a pocket full of fades for his youngsters, who fell on the bruised and unsaleable fruit with squeals of glee, and since he assumed that his wife disciplined the children and she assumed that he did, the O'Brien young, by and large, went uncorrected. Which is why they hit out at one another and brawl and never worry about consequences, Kathy thought now, as she and Jane headed for the door. Their teachers did not have a high opinion of

18

any of the O'Brien family, tarring them all with the same brush, but Kathy thought that Jane was remarkable and considerably undervalued. She looked after the younger children, frequently cooked meals, did the washing and even cleaned the house, though this was a hated chore and came last on Jane's list of priorities. In such a busy life, naturally, schoolwork was nothing more than a nuisance and Jane had always leaned rather heavily on Kathy, who was happy to help her friend whenever she could. Fortunately, Jane had an extremely retentive memory, so that a poem recited to her half a dozen times could be memorised as the girls went the rounds of the shops getting their mothers' messages, and rules of arithmetic could be learned by the same method.

Just now, however, Kathy had more important things on her mind than either housework or lessons. Billy was not a heavy burden, but Kathy was worried by the continued whiteness of his face and by a very odd little purring sound which he kept making. It was not a snore, precisely, and she was pretty sure Billy was not asleep, but she had a vague, uncomfortable feeling that such a sound issuing from a person who had been concussed was not a good sign. She and Jane had joined a first aid class almost a year ago. Their training had come in useful several times, particularly as Mrs O'Brien 'came over all queer' at the sight of blood, so any cut, graze or abrasion was now always dealt with by Jane, or by Kathy if she was there. Kathy winced over the bits of rag, never properly clean, with which Jane bandaged a wounded O'Brien child, comparing them unfavourably with proper lint and bandages. The Kellings had a neat biscuit tin, clearly labelled with a large red cross. It contained, amongst other things, an array of bandages, sticking plaster, lint and iodine, and was kept in the middle of the dresser, at eye level, where it was immediately obvious.

Kathy had once mentioned the pile of rags kept in the cupboard under the sink at the O'Briens' house to her mother, who had given her a very chilly look. 'Comparisons are odious,' she had said severely. 'It is a great deal easier to be neat and clean when you have only two children. When you have eight, you have all you can do to feed them, let alone to provide such things as bandages. You always hope you won't need them anyhow.'

At the time, Mr Kelling had been home, though he had not seemed to be taking much notice of the conversation, but he had lowered his newspaper and looked at his daughter over the top of it. 'A bandage is only a piece of rag when all's said and done,' he had commented mildly. 'And I reckon them O'Brien kids are pretty tough; their cuts mend all right, don't they?'

Kathy, laughing, had had to agree that this was so. 'In fact, our mam's only opened our tin twice so long as I can remember,' she said. 'Once when I skinned me knees and the palms of me hands, falling off a swing in the playground, and once when you scalded yourself, Dad, taking the kettle off the fire too quick so it splashed over.' She had grinned wickedly from one parent to the other. 'So why don't we just hand our first aid box to the O'Briens and have done with it? Isn't there a thing in the Bible which says, *Your need is greater than mine*?'

Mr Kelling had chuckled and disappeared behind his paper once more, but Mrs Kelling tutted disapprovingly. 'And how long do you think our first aid box would last?' she asked. 'Why, Reggie would be wearing the bandages for an Indian headdress and they'd likely spread the iodine on the cotton wool and feed it to that horrible mongrel of theirs. I've nothing against the O'Briens, as you well know; they do the best they can and it ain't as if Mr O'Brien drinks his money away like Mr Templeton does, because every penny he earns goes on feeding and clothing all those kids. But there's no denying there's a good deal of make do and mend in that household.'

Thinking back to that talk of the first aid box, Kathy thought bitterly that not the best bandages in the world could help when something really dreadful happened, like Billy's accident. Why, she had not considered for a moment running home with her little brother in her arms to look through the first aid box. She had known full well that he needed hospital treatment, and now that she had time to think she realised that it was all her fault. She should never have allowed Billy to scramble on the floor amongst the fighting O'Briens; she should have picked him up and kept him away from trouble. The truth was, she thought guiltily, hurrying along the road, that her mind had been too full of her new school and her smart school uniform to worry about her little brother, precious though he was to her.

At this point, the two girls entered the portals of the hospital where, according to Jane, her family spent such a lot of time. The truth of her claim was demonstrated almost at once when a sister came bustling up to them, saying as she approached: 'Oh, Jane, what's happened this time? Surely a little chap like that can't have been fighting with his brothers? Or is it a girl?'

'It's Billy Kelling, not one of us O'Briens,' Jane explained, looking a little self-conscious. 'He's Kathy's

21

baby brother; we were minding him for Mrs Kelling when – when our kids got into a bit of a rumpus on the floor and Billy got knocked over.'

'He hit his head on the fender and – and I think he's concussed,' Kathy said, rather timidly, and was relieved when the sister, who was a thin, bright-eyed woman in her early forties, glanced keenly at Billy and then at Kathy, and said: 'Sensible girl to bring him along straight away! I think you're correct, and that whack on the head has concussed him, which means he's in the right place because he's going to need hospital treatment, I'm afraid. Where are your parents, Kathy? Because I think someone should fetch them at once; we may need information only they can give.'

All Kathy's newfound confidence fled. 'Why – why d'you need me mam and dad?' she quavered. 'Our Billy isn't going to – going to *die*? Is he?'

The two girls were following the sister as she made her way across the hall and into a long corridor which Kathy remembered, from previous visits with Jane when an O'Brien was wounded, led to the children's ward. Now the sister halted her brisk pace for a moment, to smile soothingly down at them. 'No, no, you mustn't get in a state,' she said reprovingly. 'But we'll need forms signed so that we can take an X-ray of Billy's head and carry out some tests. So you two run along and fetch Mr and Mrs Kelling and before you know it, young Billy will be right as rain, sitting up in bed and demanding roast beef and two veg, and a glass of Guinness for his tea.'

Laughing at the absurd picture this conjured up, Kathy laid Billy on the examination couch, and then she and Jane made their way back through the hospital, considerably reassured by the sister's jokey comment. 'You know where me dad works, don't you, Janey?' Kathy said presently, as they emerged on to Stanley Road. 'He's in the Sidney Sawmills on Melrose Road. He's in the offices but if you just ask for Jack Kelling, someone will take you to him. Everyone knows Dad,' she finished.

'Oh . . . but wouldn't it be better if I went for your mam?' Jane said rather anxiously.

Kathy guessed that her friend was not too keen to carry such bad news to a man, who might react violently. Besides, Jane knew the shop where her mother worked very well indeed; also, it was nearer home. Kathy had meant to run all the way to her mother's shop and then to accompany her back to the Stanley, but she realised it was unfair to send Jane on the longer journey. Her friend still had responsibilities at home, whereas she, Kathy, had gone and landed her little responsibility in hospital. Accordingly, she said with as much cheerfulness as she could muster: 'Yes, you're right. It will be much better if you go and stir up me mam and I fetch Dad. I don't suppose the sister really meant she wanted them both, just one or t'other, but they'll both want to be with poor little Billy, so I'll go to the sawmills and tell Dad while you run to Mam's shop. Besides, Dad goes down to the docks sometimes, when a load of timber is expected, so if I can't get hold of him I'll go straight back to the Stanley. Tell Mam, will you?'

Jane promised her friend that she would do so and the two girls set off on their separate errands. It was not far to the sawmills and very soon Kathy reached the high wooden gates and turned through them. There was a shout from a small, dusty little man in a cloth cap and overalls, sitting in a hut by the gate. Kathy went over to him and explained that she was

Mr Kelling's daughter, come on an urgent errand, and asked whether he might show her the way to her father's office. The little man had a thin weaselly face with eyes so close that they appeared to jostle against his nose and he seemed, to Kathy, to be both bossy and self-important. 'An urgent errand, eh?' he said. 'Whass wrong? Someone sick?'

Even with her own worry, Kathy decided she did not like this man. He had a crafty look in his eyes and his thin, pink nose whiffled with curiosity. She could see he was avid for gossip and would probably prevent her from entering the premises if he could. 'My little brother's in hospital with concussion,' she said coldly. 'The ward sister said I was to fetch my father at once. So, if you wouldn't mind telling me where I can find him . . .'

The little man sniffed juicily. 'I can't let you wander about these premises, miss. It 'ud be more than my job's worth,' he said portentously. 'I'll have to go meself – if it's really important, that is – whilst you wait here in this hut. Did you say the kid was seriously ill? Like to die? Only I dussn't interrupt Mr Kelling if it ain't real urgent and me instructions is clear: no unauthorised persons to enter the yard, pertickly kids. Sawmills is dangerous places, you know.'

Kathy could have screamed. It was just her luck to alight on a self-important, bossy little man who was too big for his boots, but there was nothing she could do about it. She would just have to hope her father would appear soon. 'Yes, Billy's dangerously ill, and they want me dad to go straight to the Stanley so's he can sign a paper; they won't X-ray Billy's head without a signature,' she said recklessly. 'Please hurry, mister, it's a matter of life or death!'

'Oh, well, in that case . . .' the little man said, his eyes bright with ghoulish excitement. 'I'll have your dad back here before you can say knife . . . but just you stay in me shed, d'you hear me? Don't you set one foot in the yard or you'll likely get took to the police station.'

'I'll stay right here,' Kathy said virtuously. There was little point in leaving the hut since she had no idea in which part of the offices her father worked. Apart from anything else, there were tottering piles of timber, great mounds of sawdust and huge lorries which kept lumbering through the gate and across the yard, their engine noise hidden beneath the screech and whine of the machinery which, she guessed, must be turning out lengths of wood at an enormous rate.

She watched the little man as he crossed the open space, keeping close to the brick walls of the various buildings which surrounded it, and saw him disappear through a green painted wooden door. To give him credit, he must have delivered his message pretty quickly for it was scarcely more than half a minute before the green door flew open again and Kathy's father erupted into the yard. He was white-faced, his eyes staring, and he simply tore across the paving towards Kathy, his mouth opening, though she could not hear the words he shouted for the din of the machinery.

Then everything happened so quickly that, afterwards, Kathy had difficulty in describing the events. A large lorry, entering the premises, swerved to avoid her father's flying figure and crashed into a huge stack of timber. Another lorry, closely following the first and consequently unable to see Mr Kelling, also swerved to avoid the tail of the first lorry, the driver trying desperately to wrench the steering wheel round while at the same time applying his brakes. Kathy saw the lorry skidding wildly and momentarily lost sight of her father. Then she heard the shrilling of a whistle and what sounded like a shriek, cut off abruptly. All thoughts of the little man's warning left her head. She darted out of the hut and ran as fast as she could towards where the second lorry now stood steaming and broken with some sort of liquid pouring from beneath it, emitting a sharp chemical smell and staining the sawdust darkly.

'Dad!' Kathy screamed, as the noise of the machinery died away. 'Dad, where are you?' She was still running towards the lorry when a blue-overalled figure jumped out of the cab, lifted her up and began to run as fast as he could away from the two vehicles, saying breathlessly: 'We've gorra get out of here, kid, 'cos if I'm not much mistaken there's going to be—'

His words were cut short by an almighty *whump*, and though they were halfway across the yard by this time Kathy felt the searing heat of the explosion. Turning in her rescuer's arms, she saw livid orange flames begin to devour the two crashed lorries and the stacks of timber.

'My dad's in there!' Kathy screamed, struggling to get away from her rescuer. 'I must go back – my dad's in there I tell you!'

The man was beginning to explain that she would be shrivelled up like a dry leaf if she went anywhere near the blaze when they saw a huge hose being dragged out of a nearby building by several sturdy, overalled men. Within seconds, a vast arc of water was descending on the flames and within perhaps ten minutes of the conflagration starting the fire was out and only the blackened ruin of the lorries remained. Kathy waited hopefully for her father to appear from amongst the wreckage, but nothing moved.

Chapter Two

Kathy had been afraid that her mother would break down at the funeral, but in fact Sarah Kelling seemed to be numbed by the disaster which had overtaken them. She stood in the pew, holding Kathy's hand, white and silent, and it was she who had to comfort her daughter when the coffin was carried back up the nave and the sweet smell of the great mound of lilies wafted across to them, bringing home, as it seemed nothing else could, the fact that Jack Kelling was no longer a mortal man who could put an arm about his daughter, tell his wife to bear up, and remind them that his main aim in life was to take care of them. Now he was translated; the scent of the lilies was not something with which Kathy would ever have associated her sensible, down to earth father. If he had been able, Kathy thought that he would have brushed the lilies aside, saying that they were not for a simple man like him. He had loved roses and she and her mother had chosen, with tears, the beautiful wreath in the shape of a heart made entirely of red roses; the lilies had come from the Sidney Sawmills and because of the quantity, and the strength of their perfume, the scent and sight of the Kellings' roses had been completely overpowered.

Kathy could not help the tears gathering in her eyes and slipping silently down her cheeks but she was comforted by the firm grip of her mother's hand. Mrs Kelling had been devastated but had drawn on hidden reserves of strength to cope with her husband's death, Billy's hospitalisation and, of course, the various arrangements which both events had brought in their train.

St Aidan's church was crowded, for Mr Kelling, and indeed his wife and daughter, were well liked. Kathy had been touched to see that several of the nurses who were looking after Billy had taken the time to come into the church to show their last respects, and just about everyone from Daisy Street, and a good few from the other flower streets, were there as well.

Before the service had begun, Kathy and her mother had visited Billy in the Stanley hospital. The X-rays had shown that the child had a hairline fracture of the skull and, though the staff assured them that Billy was making progress, both mother and daughter found the sight of his little pale face and lethargic movements infinitely painful. 'He's just a shadow of the little boy he were,' Mrs Kelling had said, only that morning, as the two of them left the hospital ward. 'But it's early days yet and the staff seem really pleased with him. It made me smile when he said he'd like his teddy next time we came in. I think that's a real good sign, don't you?'

'Yes, I do. Oh, Mam, the number of times I've wished that I'd picked Billy up the moment I went into the O'Briens' kitchen! But he seemed so happy . . .'

'If I've told you once, I've told you a dozen times that you aren't to blame yourself,' Mrs Kelling had said robustly. 'I've had a hard enough job to convince Mrs Hughes that she weren't to blame for sending Billy to stay with the O'Briens. Why, I've left young Billy with them myself from time to time, and those two eldest girls, Jane and Tilly, are as responsible as you are yourself, queen. What's more, with the Hughes boy having his front tooth knocked out, it were better for Mrs Hughes to leave Billy with someone else rather than try to take him to the dentist as well.'

'I wonder who she left the others with.' Kathy had said, momentarily distracted; Mrs Hughes babysat for five or six youngsters, she knew. 'I wonder why she didn't leave Billy with them an' all?'

'Because she knew better,' Mrs Kelling said grimly. 'She left the others with the Templetons and she knows very well I wouldn't want our Billy in *that* house. So Mrs Hughes acted for the best, and accidents can happen anywhere, at any time, and don't you forget it, young lady.'

Kathy had told her mother how she had let the little man at the sawmills believe Billy to be worse than he was, simply to get to him to take the message to her father. She had expected her mother to reproach her but Mrs Kelling had given her a hug and said with all her usual decisiveness: 'I'd ha' done the same meself, so don't fret about that, queen. Though I'd never hear a word said against him, your da' should ha' known better than to run into the yard the way he did. So don't you go blamin' yourself for that either, hear me?'

Her mother's attitude had been so sensible that Kathy had managed to push her deep feelings of guilt to the back of her mind, though they surfaced in dreams. During the week that had elapsed between her father's death and his funeral, she had had dreadful dreams every night, though Mrs Kelling had assured her that these would stop completely once the funeral was over.

'Life ain't goin' to be easy for us after this, but the three of us must stick together an' work to remain a close-knit, happy family,' Mrs Kelling had told her daughter. 'Your father had a life insurance policy but it won't make up for the loss of his weekly wage. Still, I dare say we'll manage pretty well once we get into the way of it.'

The service ended and the coffin was carried out by two of Kathy's uncles and four men from the sawmills. The congregation followed it, people stopping to murmur condolences and to ask after little Billy, but very soon the Kellings climbed into one of the funeral cars, which Kathy's Uncle Cyril had arranged and paid for. The big car crept in the hearse's wake to Anfield Cemetery and Kathy steeled herself for the part of the day she knew she would find hardest to bear. As she and her mother led the way to the graveside, she glanced around for Jane, then remembered that the O'Briens would be in Daisy Street, setting out the funeral meal. She saw other friends from Daisy Street School, however, and smiled, wanly, at Maria and Rose, both of whom had been in her class. It made her remember, with a slight sense of shock, the girls she had met at the high school and she couldn't help wondering whether her first day, which she had enjoyed so much, would also be her last. She had won a scholarship but that did not cover clothing or equipment, nor could it possibly make up for the wage she would earn if she left school and took up full-time employment in a factory or an office, once she was old enough.

But now was no time for such conjecture. The priest was gathering the family about him, the coffin was being lowered into the deep hole which had been dug ready and he was speaking. 'Man that is born of woman hath but a short time to live, and is full of misery . . .'

Kathy thought of her father, of his gentle teasing, his interest in all her doings, the way he always had time to read Billy a story or help her with her homework. She felt the tears gather and let them fall, sliding slowly down her pale cheeks. She was suddenly glad that Billy was not here, that he would not know this tearing sense of loss. She glanced up at her mother and saw that she, too, was crying at last, as though the ice that had formed round her heart had melted to let the grief escape.

Kathy's fears that she might never return to the high school proved to be unfounded. On the very day after the funeral, her mother had told her briskly that she would return to her new school on the morrow. 'It were what your dad wanted,' she had said. 'Come to that, it's what I want an' all. You've done really well, queen, and a scholarship means we've only to find the money for books an' that. You're already kitted out for this year and, so long as you don't grow too tall, for next year as well. So don't you even think about going back to Daisy Street School because it won't happen. Understand?'

Kathy had said meekly that she understood, adding that she would still understand if circumstances changed and they found themselves unable to cope. This made her mother smile and give her a quick hug, though Kathy could tell by the look on her face that Mrs Kelling did not intend to let her lose this opportunity.

There had been a letter of condolence from Miss Beaver and another from Kathy's class teacher, but because none of the girls lived in the area Kathy did not set eyes on them again until her return to school. When she walked into the classroom, she did not

know quite wh[...]
herself treated[...]
Ellis repeated[...]
on to say th[...]
in the class[...]
work Kat[...]
behind [...]
handir[...]
old t[...]
in s[...]
ne[...]
ha[...]
anything[...]
and Isobella [...]
anything you don[...]
to explain it to you.' Sh[...]
lighting up her thin, rather lo[...]
the seriousness of her normal e[...]
hurt Isobella to have some things [...]
second time,' she added in a consp[...]
'Poor girl, I get the impression that she's[...]
somewhat.'

So Kathy's return to school was made easier fo[r]
than she had feared. At some time or other, almos[t]
every member of the class found a moment to
whisper that they were so sorry to hear of her father's
death, but since no one embarrassed her by dwelling
on it she was able to get through the day pretty well.
When the bell sounded to announce the girls were
free to leave, she realised that she had enjoyed her
day and that she liked almost all her classmates,
though Ruby and Isobella were the ones to whom she
felt closest.

Making her way home that afternoon, she thought
about Ruby. She was a plump, fair-haired girl with

nstantly curved into a
he notes with Kathy and
ould give her a hand any
at the end of the afternoon
e did not think much help
ou were at Daisy Street School,
d said as the two of them made
the cloakrooms. 'My Aunty Anne
he says the Daisy Street School give
excellent grounding in all the basic
smiled at Kathy. 'So were you happy
en at this school right from the start. It
d to come to a new place when you're as
teen, especially when it means leaving all
behind.'

very happy there, but it's not so bad for me
ight be for some,' Kathy said, taking her hat
lazer off their hooks. 'I live in Daisy Street, you
so when I get home there are all me old pals
ting to greet me. Janey O'Brien's been me bezzie
nce we were old enough to toddle, so when I—'

Someone brushed past her, reaching up for a coat
on the peg next to hers and speaking as she did so.
'Well, Cynthia, I was wrong and I admit it! I never
thought a certain person would come back at all, not
after what happened. But clearly my luck is out. Still,
perhaps it's just for the one term, you never know.'
The girl put on a deliberately broad scouse accent.
'*I've gorra bezzie, her name's Jane* . . . if Miss Beaver
could hear that, perhaps she'd listen to my father
when he tells her that the riffraff want to pull us down
to their level instead of coming up to ours.'

It was, of course, Marcia, and despite herself Kathy
felt a hot flush rise to her cheeks. She would have
liked to hit out, to say something really biting back,

but knew that her best course was to ignore the other girl, so struggling into her blazer she said conversationally to Ruby: 'We've a good deal of homework, haven't we? I shall do mine before visiting the hospital, because my brother's not well enough to come home yet.' She was looking at Cynthia as she spoke and was gratified to see the other girl glance away quickly as hot colour flooded her cheeks. Marcia, however, continued to talk about scholarships and scholarship girls, actually raising her voice as Ruby and Kathy walked out of the cloakroom so that there was no possibility of their not hearing her words.

'You did well to say nothing,' Ruby said approvingly as the two girls left the premises. 'Marcia Montgomery is a real cat, but her father is Chairman of the Board of Governors. He's wealthy and influential but clearly not very bright since he believes every word his horrible daughter tells him. You'll find that people are very anxious not to get into Marcia's bad books. No one likes her though, not even the teachers. They know she'll tell tales on them just as she does on us, and of course their jobs depend, to an extent, on Mr Montgomery's good opinion.' Ruby sighed deeply and pushed her felt hat to the back of her head. 'I wish she wasn't in our class – she shouldn't be, she's a year older than the rest of us – but I'm afraid we're stuck with her. She had a year off when her father was working in the United States for twelve months and when she came back she was so behind the rest of her class that they kept her down a year.'

'Oh, I *see*,' Kathy said, light dawning. 'No wonder she doesn't like scholarship girls. I suppose she thinks we're all laughing at her behind her back because she's older. And – and she's not terribly clever, is she, Ruby? She talks as if she is, but Isobella said she was bottom of the class in the English test last week.'

'That's true. But let's not waste our breath talking about Marcia,' Ruby said, glancing diffidently at Kathy. 'To tell you the truth, we all wondered whether you would be able to come back. Most of us guessed that you would try to do so, but – but losing your father must have made things difficult. I know you've got the scholarship, but my mam and dad are always grumbling about the cost of extras, so it will come hard on your mother, won't it? The teachers will do their best to help you over books and equipment, but next year, when you're fourteen, and able to work . . .'

'I'm going to stay on just as long as we can manage it – right up to matriculation, I hope,' Kathy said firmly. 'It was what my father wanted more than anything.'

Ruby nodded understandingly and turned to smile with evident pleasure at the other girl. 'That's grand news,' she said joyfully. 'I'll do everything I can to help you so if you're in a puzzle over work or need someone to hear French verbs, then just say the word.' The two girls were now on Netherfield Road and Ruby drew Kathy to a halt as they reached the corner of Roscommon Street. 'I go down here until I reach the Scottie. You live further out than me so I suppose you'll want to catch a tram. Which way do you usually go?'

'The same way as you, I think,' Kathy said. 'I don't get a tram; I can walk easily enough. Where do you live, then?'

'Burlington Street.'

'I'm on Daisy Street, off the Stanley Road,' Kathy

said, as the two girls began to walk once more. 'Do you have brothers and sisters, Ruby?'

Ruby replied that she was an only child, and for the rest of the walk to Burlington Street their talk ranged over a number of subjects. Just before they parted, Ruby suggested that Kathy might linger on the corner of Burlington Street next morning, on her way to school, so that they could walk the rest of the way together. Kathy felt a warm glow at this evidence of friendship and agreed eagerly that she would arrive at the rendezvous no later than eight o'clock. She waved Ruby goodbye, not waiting to see into which house she disappeared, and set off for home feeling far more cheerful than she might otherwise have done. She liked Isobella, but during the week which Kathy had missed, Isobella had grown friendly with another girl, and at first Kathy had thought, with a sinking heart, that she was going to find herself either making an uncomfortable third or having to put up with a rather solitary existence. Now, however, Ruby had made it clear that she wanted them to be friends. She and Kathy had spent their lunch hour reading through the notes of the schoolwork which Kathy had missed and had found themselves immediately in accord. She can never take Jane's place as my bezzie because we've known each other for ever, Jane and me, but I do believe Ruby will be my best school friend, Kathy told herself, as she opened the back door. She knew that things would not be easy, that she and her mother would have a struggle to make ends meet, but she was confident that they would do so. Once Billy is out of hospital and back home with us, we'll be able to make plans, she told herself, beginning to get the ingredients for a simple meal out of the pantry. I suppose I'll have to give up things like visits to the cinema and ice creams on a hot day but it won't kill me to do without. After all, Dad had a real struggle just to get himself a decent job and he and Mam have worked hard all their lives, but we were all really happy until the accident and I'm sure Mam and Billy and me will be happy again.

It was Christmas Eve and freezing cold. The lamplight shone down on frosty pavements and scurrying shoppers, for every housewife knew that there would be bargains to be had late on Christmas Eve. This year, Christmas Day fell on a Wednesday and since school had only broken up the previous Monday Kathy and Jane had been hard pressed to buy such small gifts as they could afford in the time at their command. The O'Briens had acquired an ancient and ramshackle pram into which Jane had piled Tommy and Teresa, and Kathy had been happy to sit Billy between the two small O'Briens, for though he was out of hospital he was still not used to walking far and she usually ended up carrying him.

Now, however, they both had a long list of messages, and were heading for St John's market where Mr O'Brien worked, since the stallholders there were friendly and apt to lower their prices for the children of one of their own. Kathy was fond of both Jane's parents, though she knew her mother thought that Mr O'Brien did not pull his weight within the home as her own husband had done. Jane's father was a tall, heavily built man with crisp blond hair and grey eyes. Kathy thought he must have been handsome once, but now he was running to fat. He was always willing to help a neighbour and was renowned for his easy-going nature, but he was inherently lazy and though he used his considerable strength to good effect whilst working at the market he spent most of his time at home snoozing in a chair by the fire in winter, and on the front steps in summer. He loved his children, but it would not have occurred to him to take them on outings or play games with them, although he often handed over a ha'penny for sweets or gave Jane and Tilly tuppence to go to the Saturday rush at the local cinema. Kathy knew that Mr O'Brien expected whoever had received the tuppence to let the rest of the family into the cinema through the fire door, thus saving him a great many pennies. Her own parents would never have dreamed of doing such a thing, saying it encouraged dishonesty in the young, but Kathy privately thought it was fair enough. Unless the older ones obliged, the others would never see heroes like Tom Mix, Charlie Chaplin or Laurel and Hardy.

'I reckon we ought to visit the butchers first,' Kathy said. 'I'm after a nice piece of pork. It isn't worth getting a bird just for Mam and me, because Billy don't eat enough to cover a sixpence. If there's a bacon joint going cheap I'll get that an' all, and Mam says to get bones for stock because she doesn't think folk'll be buying bones, not with Christmas so near.'

'Aye, you're right there, and pork's a deal cheaper than goose or chicken,' Jane said sagely.

Kathy knew that her friend must have realised, from her messages alone, how much harder life had become for the Kelling family in the past few months. Before her father's death, they had lived comfortably, always having a joint or a fowl at weekends, and often eating meat during the week as well. Kathy had felt sorry for the O'Briens with their perpetual diet of damaged vegetables and the cheapest cuts of meat the butcher could supply, but now it seemed the roles of the two families were reversed; it was the Kellings who bought end-of-the-day meat and fish, and that only as a special treat. Vegetable stews were nourishing, soups made with bone stock more so, and one filled in the chinks with thick slices of home-baked bread and a smear of margarine. Kathy was never hungry, though she often yearned for a particular food which no longer graced their table. Pickles were one small luxury which had disappeared, though mainly because her mother had no time now to skin and prepare onions and cabbage for pickling. 'When I've got meself sorted, I'll make pickles again, and cook cakes and puddings for the three of us,' she had promised her daughter only the previous week. 'But now I'm workin' full time in the café, it means I'm so tired it's all I can do to cook ordinary stuff. But you're a good girl, Kathy. I've never once heard a grumble from you.'

Kathy tried very hard not to grumble, but she did miss her school dinners. For what had once seemed a small sum, she had had a proper cooked meal followed by a pudding every day, enjoyed in the company of friends. Now, she was one of the small number of girls who brought in a packed lunch to eat in an empty classroom, the girls – all from different years – demolishing their food as quickly as they could in order to get into the playground before the dining room emptied. Kathy's lunch was almost always bread and jam and an apple, and she was often dissatisfied by this repast, largely because of the tantalising smells of cooking coming from the school kitchen but also because her lunches rarely varied. Her mother continually urged her to take cheese in her sandwiches or to buy herself an orange, but she was far too conscious of the speed with which her mother's wages disappeared to take advantage of the offer. Kathy had noticed her mother getting thinner and paler as the days passed and had told her, only that morning, that she really must begin to take better care of herself.

'Where would Billy and I be without you?' she had scolded, eyeing her mother's plate upon which lay only bread and margarine. 'Porridge isn't expensive, Mam, and you make Billy and me eat it each morning. I'm sure it would be better for you than bread and marge – it's hot for a start.'

Mrs Kelling had been hurrying round the kitchen, getting herself ready for work. She had changed her job at the corner shop for a better paid one as manageress of Dorothy's Tearooms on the Stanley Road but, because it was full-time and she worked from eight in the morning until eight at night, she was often hard pressed. She had smiled affectionately at Kathy's words and paused to take a drink from the mug of tea standing beside her plate. 'I know it's hot and nourishing, but I can't eat porridge as I rush around getting ready for work and I can eat bread and marge,' she said cheerfully. 'The truth is, Kathy luv, that I'm not used to such a long working day and that's why I'm losing a bit of weight. In the corner shop I sat around a lot, but when you're in catering you scarcely get the chance to stand still for a moment, lerralone sit down. Don't forget, I get two good hot meals a day at the café, only because I'm new and keen to make a good impression I jump to me feet every time a customer comes in instead of letting the waitresses deal with them. Once Christmas is over, and we're not so hectic, I'll take advantage of the good food and begin to get on top of the job.'

'I'm sure you will, Mam,' Kathy had said warmly.

'I'm real proud of you and I think you look lovely in the uniform, honest to God I do.'

Mrs Kelling had laughed again. 'I feel rare foolish in it,' she owned. 'A black wool dress and a frilly white pinny makes me think of the maids in one of them French farces, but I'm glad you like it, queen. And now I'd best be off or I won't have a uniform or a job either!'

The conversation had eased Kathy's worry about her mother's condition, particularly when Jane had pointed out that she, Kathy, was also a good deal paler and thinner than she had been before her father's death. 'You've had your whole life turned upside down and you've had Billy's illness to cope with,' she reminded her friend. 'It 'ud be a bleedin' miracle if you weren't paler and thinner. But you'll find your feet, you and your mam, because you're fighters, the pair of you. My mam says so and she should know.'

By now, they had reached the market and were threading their way through the crowds, heading for Mr Raison's stall. Kathy was glad it was Jane pushing the pram because, had it been she, they would have been constantly held up. Jane, however, simply barged her way through, seemingly indifferent to the toes she crushed and the behinds she bumped, though when the owners turned and swore at her she always apologised very prettily. And of course, Kathy reflected, everyone was in a really good mood. Both customers and stallholders were beaming and the air was full of good smells. Bunches of holly, ivy and mistletoe clustered thickly around every stall; the flower sellers were making up wreaths, brilliant with chrysanthemums and Christmas roses, and Kathy decided to buy a bunch of chrysanthemums to put on her father's grave, when they visited it after church next day.

Thinking of her father brought the familiar onrush of sadness, but the feeling was speedily dissipated by the spirit of Christmas which was almost tangible amongst the stallholders and their customers.

Reaching Mr Raison's stall, they joined the scrimmage around it, quickly getting to the front as Jane continued to wield the pram like a weapon. Mr Raison beamed at them, for both girls were regulars, buying what meat they could afford from him whenever they were sent on messages to the market. 'Whazzit to be today, young ladies?' he said jovially. 'I've gorra goose for you, Janey, 'cos your dad ordered it earlier, an' a fine big feller it is. It ain't dressed nor plucked because that costs extry, but your da' said as how you and your mam would take care of that.'

The goose was indeed a fine one and when Mr Raison leaned over and dumped it into the pram the children shouted with glee, believing at first that it was still alive and could be petted and cuddled. Even when they found it unresponsive to their caresses, they continued to cuddle it, stroking its smooth head and admiring its orange beak. Kathy, who knew a little bit about geese, reflected that they would not have been so sanguine had the creature really been alive, for she had frequently met flocks of geese being driven into the city for the Christmas market and knew how aggressive the birds could be.

Jane's purchases finished, Mr Raison turned to Kathy. His little brown eyes were kind and she guessed he must know how her circumstances had changed since the previous year, when she had come in on Christmas Eve for the turkey which her mam had ordered. 'And now it's your turn, Kathy,' he said.

'I've a smaller bird, a nice, fat chicken, already dressed for table. There's enough on it for three an' you know I'll make you a good price.'

Kathy's mouth watered but she said firmly: 'Not this year, Mr Raison. This year me mam wants a joint of pork – not too big – some bones for stock and a smallish bacon joint.'

'Right you are, queen,' Mr Raison said jovially. He turned to the joints laid out on the back shelf, picked one out, weighed it, announced the price and was wrapping it all in one swift movement. Next he chose a bacon joint and did the same with that and then he produced two large marrow bones, wrapped a sheet of the *Echo* round them and handed the whole lot over, saying: 'Since you've bought two joints, you can have the marrow bones for stock. Still gorra lot of messages, have you?'

'Yes, we've got all the fruit and veggies, and thanks very much for the bones,' Kathy said gratefully, handing over the money. 'I hope you have a grand Christmas, Mr Raison, and please give your wife my good wishes.'

As they turned away from the stall, Jane giggled and nudged her friend. 'Ain't you polite, though? It's manners like them makes me mam say I oughter follow your example. I reckon as Mr Raison sold you that pork cheaper because you're always so polite.'

'He sold it to me cheap because he's nice, and because he's sorry about me dad,' Kathy said at once. 'Besides, we've been good customers in the past an' I reckon we will be again, once we've settled to – to a different way of life. I don't think I've told you but Mam's thinking about taking a lodger. We've got three bedrooms, same as you, and we really only need two of them. Because of Mam's job, she might

44

not be able to provide an evening meal, but she thought if she got a lady lodger then she could cook for herself, evenings. The trouble is, most of the folk wanting lodgings is fellers and Mam wouldn't want a feller let loose in her kitchen.

'A lodger!' Jane said, stopping the pram so abruptly that several people cannoned into them. 'I dunno as I'd like a stranger livin' in *my* house. How do you feel, Kathy?'

'Well, I'd rather not, if the truth be known,' Kathy admitted. 'Especially as Mam's warned me that I'll be up and down the stairs carting hot water and that first thing in the morning, and I'll have to make a proper breakfast for the woman – if we get a woman, that is. Still, I suppose it's needs must, and anyway, it may never happen. Mam's new job pays better than we'd thought because of tips, you know, and so a lodger would be a last resort. Mam says we'll see how we go for a year and then make a decision. Oh, look, that stallholder's marking down her veggies; shall we go over, see if there's anything we want?'

It took the girls the best part of an hour to get all their messages but by the time they wheeled the pram triumphantly out on to Elliot Street, it was heavily laden to the extent that the three children had had to draw up their legs in order to make room. Kathy and Jane were now sharing the task of pushing the pram and this caused much hilarity when they reached Lime Street since one would push forward, looking to the right and the other, looking to the left, would pull back.

'We'll have to get our act together,' Jane panted, quite weak from giggling. 'When it's clear your way, you shout OK, and when it's clear mine, I'll do the same. That way, we may actually get to cross the road without tipping the pram over or wrenching our arms out of their sockets.'

Kathy would have complied, but at that moment a large policeman saw their dilemma. He stepped into the road and with an imperative gesture held up the traffic in both directions. As they passed him he said cheerily: 'That's a lorra messages you've got there, kids. I can see you're going to have a rare grand Christmas.' When they reached the further pavement he strolled along beside them, then touched his helmet, bade them the compliments of the season and went on his way.

'Fancy a scuffer holding up the traffic for us,' Jane marvelled. 'It were nice of him, though, and saved us a deal of worrying. I dare say we'd ha' been another ten minutes crossin' the road if he hadn't done that.'

'It's this here Christmas spirit everyone's so full of,' Kathy said wisely. 'Why can't people be like it always, Jane? Even horrible Marcia said she hoped we'd have a nice Christmas, and she wouldn't give me nothin', norreven a cold in me 'ead.'

'She must be a really nasty girl,' Jane observed, not for the first time. 'If I ever meet her, I'll give her a piece of me mind. Still an' all, I don't suppose—'

She was interrupted. A hand descended on the pram, heaving it to a halt, and a familiar voice said: 'Wharrever are you two doin' out so late? Ain't it time these littl'uns were tucked up in their beds?' It was Jimmy McCabe, flushed in the face and carrying a huge canvas bag so full of food that it was in danger of splitting in two. 'Tell you what, if I pushes the pram, can I stick me bag on it? It ain't that it's heavy – well, it is, but I don't care for that – I'm afraid it's goin' to split with the weight and send me messages topplin' into the road.'

Kathy would have unhesitatingly refused but Jane said at once that it would be fine. 'Kathy and me's managed so far, but it's awkward crossin' the road when there's two of you pushin' the pram and it's already awfully heavy,' she said. 'Are you sure you can manage it though, Jimmy? It's goin' up an' down kerbs and crossin' the tramlines which is so difficult. Tell you what, why don't you push for a bit and then Kathy an' me'll take over?'

Jimmy said that that would not be necessary and pushed in grim silence for all of five minutes. Kathy was thinking, with some satisfaction, that the pram with its many burdens was obviously a good deal heavier than Jimmy had suspected and that he had no breath to spare for idle chat, when he slowed the steady pace he had been keeping up and turned towards her. 'I were real sorry to hear about young Billy's accident and your dad's death,' he said gruffly. 'I've not seen you since, except in the distance, like, so I've not had a chance to – to tell you how I felt. Your dad were real kind to me. When my dad got an allotment, none of us McCabes knew how to set about growin' stuff but your dad took me to one side an' gave me a heap o' help and advice. I don't suppose I'll ever be able to grow things like he could, but I'm goin' to have a bleedin' good try.'

Kathy muttered that it was good of him to say so and felt the tears rush to her eyes. In all the unhappiness of the past few months she had completely forgotten her father's allotment. Now she was wondering whether it was still theirs, whether she and her mother ought to catch the tram and go there. When she was small, she had visited the place almost weekly, digging her own little plot and planting radishes, Mrs Sinkins pinks and even a tomato plant, which she had watched over anxiously for many weeks, enjoying the resultant fruits far more than usual because they came from her very own plant. She remembered Dad had got raspberry canes, two gooseberry bushes and a fine blackcurrant, and realised that she and her mother had never given a thought to that neat square of garden out in Seaforth, which her father had tended so assiduously. There would be things that needed doing, even though it was winter. She imagined that the winter cabbage and sprouts which her father had planted would have been harvested by someone else; she could not imagine anyone stealing the prickly gooseberry bushes and she knew the raspberry canes would have died down long since, but the blackcurrant must be a temptation for it was well established and, in the summer, provided an enormous quantity of fruit. Without pausing to consider how it would sound, she turned to Jimmy. 'I expect all the cabbages and sprouts have gone because we'd forgotten all about the place, but are the fruit bushes still there? And how about me dad's little shed where he kept his tools? There were a padlock on the door but I dare say that's been forced and all his lovely tools carried off by someone who fancied them.'

She was watching Jimmy's face as she spoke and saw his lips tighten and his eyes flash. 'They're a decent set of fellows up at the allotments,' he said. 'None of 'em would touch so much as a sprout what didn't belong to 'em, an' there's others, beside meself, what have cause to be grateful to your dad. I think you'll find the place just as he left it, 'cept I've turned the earth over for him because I know – he told me – that that's the right thing to do once the main crop of veggies are all dug up. But though I've been workin' his allotment, I dunnit with me own tools and I didn't take nothin'.'

Kathy, feeling thoroughly ashamed of herself and blushing hotly, mumbled that she was sure she hadn't meant to cause offence. Then, growing angry, because she knew she was in the wrong, she added that she'd not meant to accuse any of the allotment owners, since she knew they were all honest men. 'But there's soldiers from the barracks come over the fence sometimes, and kids from the back streets, too,' she said haughtily. '*That*'s who I meant.'

'Oh, sure you did,' Jimmy McCabe sneered. 'It's likely one o' them would break into the shed to steal garden tools when none of 'em have so much as an inch of garden of their own. An' the only person likely to steal your bleedin' blackcurrant bush is another gardener, as well you know.'

Everyone hates being put thoroughly at fault and Kathy's first thought was to lash out at Jimmy and somehow get her own back. 'You can sell garden tools in Paddy's market, and probably you could sell a fine blackcurrant bush an' all,' she said wildly. 'But there were no need to jump down my throat, Jimmy McCabe, because I didn't mean—'

Jimmy McCabe pulled the pram to a halt and turned, furiously, on Kathy. 'I told you your dad had been good to me; I'd no more break into his shed and steal his tools to sell in Paddy's market than I'd steal from me own mam. How dare you say such things, you spiteful little bitch.'

At this point, Jane decided to pour oil on troubled waters. 'Shurrup, the pair of you,' she shouted. 'Kathy didn't mean *you* when she said you can sell garden tools in Paddy's market, she meant *someone* could. 'Well, if you two ain't fire an' water – you just won't mix. Jimmy, shut your gob and don't open it again till I say.' She swung round on her friend. 'Kathy, just you tell Jimmy you're sorry you didn't make it clearer that you knew he weren't a thief. Come on, own up. You made a mistake and you're sorry for it.'

It was easy for Jimmy, Kathy thought resentfully as she stammered out a grudging apology. All he had to do was button his lip, whereas she had had to eat humble pie. Then she remembered how garrulous Jimmy was and smiled to herself. Maybe keeping quiet was as hard for him as saying she was sorry had been for her. Smiling a little, she turned to him and repeated her apology in a much pleasanter tone. After all, he was pushing her baby brother and all her messages in the big pram and they still had a good walk ahead of them. No point in stomping along in gloomy and resentful silence; it had all been very unfortunate and they should do their best to forget it and act as though nothing had happened.

Jimmy looked slightly surprised at this second apology but took it in the spirit in which it was meant. ''Sorlright, queen,' he said gruffly. 'Me mam always says I only have to open me mouth to put me foot in it, and I dare say she's right. Let's talk about something different, eh? Shall I ask you about school, or shall I tell you what it's like working in the brewery?'

Both girls laughed but little Teresa leaned forward, saying earnestly: 'Please, Jimmy, will you show us how you put your foot in your mouth? I seen babies do it all the time, but I never seen a grown-up. Does you do it wi' your boots on? If so, you'll have to be rare careful where you tread.'

This innocent question caused a great deal of

hilarity and considerably eased the rather tense atmosphere. Jimmy hopped along the pavement on one foot, trying to get his boot somewhere in the region of his mouth, whilst the three children squealed with amusement and Jane and Kathy took over the pram once more. Jimmy only let them push it for a short way, however, before taking it again, and conversation became general, Kathy describing the carol concert at which her friend Ruby had sung 'Once in Royal David's City' as a solo and she herself had read one of the lessons. Not to be outdone, Jane described the lovely end of term party and entertainment which had been given for the parents at Daisy Street School and Jimmy told them about the office party at the brewery which seemed to consist of downing a good deal of Guinness and kissing any girl the men were able to grab. Kathy thought it all sounded pretty horrid but was prevented from saying so when Jimmy, who had gone on to tell them how he meant to go to the pantomime after Christmas, suddenly pulled the pram to a halt as they drew level with Daisy Street and plunged a hand into his pocket. He began to fumble something out, saying as he did so: 'You know me, always puttin' me foot in it, talking big, making a fool o' meself . . . but I thought you might not think too badly of me . . . seein' as it's Christmas . . . I had a few pence over so I got you something pretty . . . it ain't much . . . I never bought anything for a girl before . . .' He glanced shyly across at Kathy as he spoke and unwrapped the newspaper from around a tiny object, then held it up so that both girls could see. It was a necklace made up of thin little letters in gilt, which read: *Will you be my sweetheart?*

It was all very well apologising, Kathy thought crossly, feeling a blush steal up her cheeks, but she had no intention of getting involved with Jimmy McCabe. She was beginning to say so, to explain that she did not accept presents from anyone when she was unable to return them, when Jimmy gave her such a look of incredulity that she stopped short. 'It ain't for you, puddin' head, it's for Jane,' he said baldly. 'Wharrever made you think I'd spend me money on you, Lickle Miss White Socks?'

Kathy opened her mouth to say the last thing on earth she wanted was a present from him, that she had only thought it was for her because he had looked at her when he unwrapped it, then shut her mouth with a snap. Jane, dear, kind, tactful Jane, had leaped into the breach once more. Taking the necklace from Jimmy's hand, she professed delight and actually leaned across and kissed his cheek, and though he pretended to scrub it off, telling her she was a soppy girl, Kathy could see that he was really pleased.

'I've gorra present for you as well, Jimmy, but I'll have to bring it round tomorrow morning,' Jane said. 'I didn't know we were goin' to meet you, otherwise I'd have brung it with me. It ain't nearly as nice as me necklace,' she added, looking at the nasty little gilt thing as though it were purest gold, Kathy thought resentfully, 'but then I ain't workin' yet.'

Jimmy mumbled that it was all right, he hadn't expected . . . but the children in the pram, attracted by the brightness of the thin little chain, were begging to hold it for a moment and by the time this had been sorted out the girls had steered the pram into Daisy Street and Jimmy, with a wave of the hand, had taken his bag and left them.

'Do you *really* have a present for Jimmy?' Kathy asked. 'Mam can't give me pocket money but I've managed to earn bits and bobs here and there, so I've got her a present and something for Billy, of course. I've even got something for you, Janey, though it's awful small, but a feller . . . well, that's different.'

Kathy saw a pink flush creep into Jane's cheeks. 'I'll find something,' she said airily. 'I might get me mam to let me make some fudge; Jimmy's mortal fond of fudge. I don't think he smokes yet, otherwise it would be Woodbines, but don't you worry, I'll think of something.' As Kathy went to lift Billy out of the pram, her friend shook her head. 'No you don't, queen. We'll unload Teresa and Tommy and our messages and then I'll come wi' you, so you don't have to lug everything.'

The two girls pushed the pram into the kitchen and unloaded, then made for Kathy's house. As they walked, Kathy said curiously: 'I always suspected Jimmy was sweet on you, but I didn't realise it had reached Christmas present stage. Do you really like him, Jane? I can't say I do – he's always made a point of being rude and nasty to me. Until today, that is.'

'Jimmy's OK,' Jane said defensively. 'I dunno how it is, queen, but you've always managed to rub him up the wrong way. He's a nice feller, honest to God he is.'

'I dare say he's nice enough but I think that necklace is a bit cheeky,' Kathy said thoughtfully. 'If you wear it, you're as good as saying you *will* be his sweetheart and you're only my age – isn't that a bit young to be anyone's sweetheart?'

They reached her house at this point and began to unload the messages on to the Kellings' kitchen table. Jane looked defiantly at her friend. 'I *shall* wear it,' she said. 'And it won't mean anything because I shan't stamp "yes" on me forehead. Now give over, do, Kathy. You've gorra real gold necklace and two silver ones, which your mam and dad bought you.' She fingered the gilt chain. 'This 'un is me one and only. Now let's forget it and empty the pram or we'll still be in a muddle when your mam gets home.'

Chapter Three
Norfolk, February 1936

Alec Hewitt was crossing the Five Acre when he saw a tiny movement in the verge ahead of him. It was a miracle he saw anything since the rain was driving into his face, lashed by a cold east wind which, he thought resentfully, must be coming straight from Siberia. In fact, had the creature remained still, it was unlikely that he would have seen it; it was the movement that gave it away. Stooping over it, Alec's first thought was that it was a young fox. Probably on its first hunting exploration, it had somehow slid into the ditch and all but drowned, but as soon as he hauled the small animal out of the water and began to pump air into its lungs he realised his mistake. It was a pup no more than eight or ten weeks old, with the long floppy ears and distinctive colouring of a red setter. Alec tucked the pup, now struggling feebly, inside his jacket and turned towards home once more.

The pup settled down immediately and Alec grinned to himself. His pa would think he was mad but his mother would greet the pup with all the enthusiasm of a warm and generous nature. She loved all animals, and at present their house was inhabited not only by the three Hewitts themselves, but also by a collie, a black Labrador and a barn owl with an injured wing.

Alec felt the puppy wriggling beneath his jacket as life returned to its limbs and remembered that Mr Drayton's red setter bitch had had a litter several weeks ago. Mr Drayton had been disgruntled since the bitch had proved to be gun shy, so he had been getting rid of the puppies as pets; this one must have escaped from the Draytons' yard before getting thoroughly lost. So, if Ma will let me keep it, I'm sure Mr Drayton isn't going to object, Alec thought.

He unlatched the gate between the Five Acre and the next field and began to push his way through the crop. It was sprout plants which grew as high as his waist and shed icy water on him as he passed along the rows. But, though Alec personally hated sprouts and particularly loathed picking them, they had been a lifesaver over the past couple of months. Times were harder in farming than the Hewitts had ever known them. Prices were ridiculously low and the sudden influx of cheap food from abroad had caused a great many farmers to leave the land. Some had even killed themselves, seeing the acres that had given a living to their family for generations suddenly worthless, the crops standing unharvested and the beasts scarcely fetching more than a few pounds when taken to market.

Sprouts, however, seemed to be not too highly regarded by farmers in other countries, and because the farm was not a large one the Hewitts were still managing to keep their heads above water, albeit with difficulty. Bob Hewitt was an old hand at making ends meet and had decided some time back, when prices had begun to drop, that their best course was to grow crops which could, if necessary, be sold locally. Barley and wheat might not sell on the general market, but they could feed his stock as well as contributing to the Hewitts' own food require-ments, and so far he had been proved right. It was a long way to travel to Norwich market but prices in the city were a little higher than those in Stalham or Great Yarmouth, so Mr Hewitt thought the journey worth making.

Inside his jacket, the puppy whined, sounding more like a cat than a dog. It was almost certainly freezing cold and hungry, though the warmth from Alec's body would dry it out, probably by the time he reached the farmhouse. Alec glanced automatically up at the sky to check on the time since he and his father liked to get their cows milked before dusk began to fall. The sky, however, grey and lowering, gave him no indication of the time of day, so he continued on his way, putting on a slight spurt as the farmhouse, in its bower of leafless trees, came into view.

As Alec swung open the mossy gate which led into the yard he could smell cooking and he headed for the kitchen, pushing the back door open with a suddenly impatient hand, eager to be out of the cold. His mother was baking. A rabbit, already skinned and jointed and surrounded by onions and potatoes, was arranged in the big black roasting tin and Mrs Hewitt was rolling out pastry. She looked up as her son came in. 'I'll lay you're soaked to the skin, Alec; best get out of that jacket and hang it over the clothes horse,' she said, and then, as her son obeyed, added sharply: 'What have you got there then?'

Since Cherry, the Labrador, had waddled across the kitchen as soon as Alec entered and was now on his hind legs, energetically snuffling at the front of Alec's pullover, this was an obvious question and Alec answered it readily. 'That's a red setter pup, Ma. I found it in a ditch, drowned I reckon, but that were alive so I've brung it back, hopin' as you'd let me keep it. I reckon that's one of old Drayton's. His bitch had a

57

litter a couple of months back, but he'd found out she was gun shy so he can't sell her pups as gun dogs.'

His mother laid down her rolling pin and came across to peer at the puppy. She was a tall, sparely made woman, with the dark red hair Alec had inherited, and pale skin which freckled and burned under the rays of the summer sun. She had large hazel eyes fringed with reddish-brown lashes and the only lines on her face were those made by laughter, for she was as merry as her husband was serious. Alec adored her and thought her beautiful, and now he was waiting for her verdict upon the fate of the puppy without, it must be confessed, worrying unduly. He had never known his ma to turn away from an animal in distress and could not imagine her doing so today.

'Let's have a look at you, little feller,' Mrs Hewitt murmured, taking the animal. It reached up and licked her chin with a long, pink tongue. 'I'm in the middle of baking, Alec, and if your dad's goin' to get his tea on time I'd best get on wi' it, but you can sit down by the fire and feed this scrap some warm bread and milk. Thass a bitch, by the way. What do you want to call her?'

'Oh, a bitch, is it? No wonder Cherry and Patch seemed so interested,' Alec said, chuckling.

Alec stood up and transferred the pup to the back of the shabby old chair in which he had been sitting. Then he turned to the two dogs standing watchfully by and said: 'Thass just a baby, you two, so you int to go worritin' it; understand? Leave, Cherry! Leave, Patch!' Alec knew that now they would respect the pup and would not steal its food when it was older and able to take care of itself. 'I want you to name her, Ma,' he said.

Betty Hewitt's hands stopped fashioning the pastry around the rabbit pie dish and she stared thoughtfully at the gamely legged pup with its long drooping ears and soulful eyes. 'I disremember ever knowing a red setter with an ounce of sense and I reckon this one won't be no different,' she said musingly. 'So I reckon we'll call her Loopy. I suppose thass too much to expect you ha' picked the sprouts your dad wants for market tomorrow?' she added, with more than a trace of sarcasm. 'An' I take it you've brought Bessie and Buttercup and the rest in for milking?'

Alec grinned guiltily and set down the dish of bread and milk in front of the new pup, who began to attack it at once. He had gone down to Horsey Gap, meaning to see if there was anywhere from which he might fish, but the strong east wind had made it impossible. Instead, he had walked along the shore, battling against the elements, enjoying the wildness of the wind until the rain had started. Then he had simply turned for home, meaning to pick a sackful of sprouts before fetching the cows in from the Five Acre. And what had he done? He had swathed his head and shoulders in the empty sprout sack and had been crossing the Five Acre when he spotted the puppy. From that moment on he had simply forgotten his responsibilities and had made his way home. Sighing deeply, he reached for his still wet jacket and the soaking sack. 'Sorry, Ma,' he said humbly. 'I went to the shore to see if I could chuck out a line, get a fish or two, but there were no chance. I thought I'd pick the sprouts first, then bring the cows in, only . . . only.'

'Only you were in a dream, same as always,' his mother said grimly. 'You're a good hard worker, Alec, I wouldn't deny that, but you don't always concentrate too good. Best get them sprouts right away, then bring the cows in. This evening we'll make some butter; Dad can take that to market with him tomorrow. He brought in half a dozen rabbits earlier and they're all dressed and ready and I've boxed up a few eggs, though the hens never lay good at this time of year. But it should be enough to pay the rent, especially if this damned rain lets up.'

'Right, Ma. I'll fetch the sprouts and then get the cows in an' I'll work like a perishin' slave to do it afore Dad comes for his tea,' Alec said remorsefully. The life of a tenant farmer was a hard one and he was well aware that his parents needed every bit of help he could give. Slogging out to the sprout field, he reminded himself of how he loved the land and everything to do with it. In summer, he revelled in the hard work, the heat of the hayfield, the constant, never ceasing round of daily tasks. Spring and autumn were bearable, and sometimes enjoyable, but he and his parents simply loathed the winter. Despite Mr Hewitt's care, a field of winter cabbage had rotted in the ground because of the constant onslaught of the rain and the Five Acre, normally an excellent meadow full of sweet grass, had become poached and marshy for the same reason. Clark and Gable, the two mighty shire horses who shared the work of the farm, were apt to hang around by the gate at the lower end of the meadow and the mud there was so deep that only last week Alec had all but lost a wellington boot in it. He had managed to dredge it up from the depths, full of mud and small stones, and his mother had cleaned it up for him so that he was able to wear it once more, but now he avoided the lower end of the Five Acre, not wanting to risk a similar occurrence in which he might be unable to retrieve the boot.

He reached the sprout field, eyeing the long rows unenthusiastically. As each plant was picked clean, he cut the stem down with the knife he always carried, so he knew where he should start. The trouble was that the sprouts came to marketable size at different times, which meant that all along a row which had been mostly cut down there would be odd plants still waiting to be harvested. He knew he should really start on them, get them out of the way, but in view of the violence of the weather he decided against it. It can't possibly rain all winter, he told himself, beginning to snap the sprouts off a particularly well-grown plant. The family never ate the actual sprouts themselves but used the bushy tips of the stalks instead, so Alec shoved the plant tops into the bottom of his sack as he worked.

By the time the sack was full, Alec's hands were so cold that, mercifully, he could no longer feel them, and without the shelter of the sack across head and shoulders his ears, nose and chin were in a similar condition. He was glad to lean the full sack against the nearest hedge whilst he went across the field and into the Five Acre to fetch the cows home. The Hewitts possessed six cows and used their landlord's bull to keep the cows in milk. Most of the milk was either sold locally, used by the Hewitts themselves, or turned into butter for market. Normally, Alec would have brought Patch out with him to fetch the cows from the top of the pasture, but he had not thought it fair to do so on this occasion because it would have meant Patch's hanging around in the rain whilst he, Alec, picked the sprouts. Still, cows are pretty eager to be milked as the day wears on and their udders fill up, so Alec threw open the gate and shouted and presently the cows, a motley bunch, came surging out of the field, brushing joyfully past him and heading for the yard. On the other side of the hedge, Alec could hear Clark and Gable slithering and snorting as their great hooves met the mud and became mired to the fetlock, but he did not intend to let the horses into the yard, though he would bring them a bale of hay later and chuck it into the meadow where the mud was not so bad. Until then, the great horses would just have to endure the rain and turn their backs to the wind as they always did in rough weather.

Alec retrieved the sack of sprouts and hurried back to the farmyard in the wake of the herd. His favourite cow was Fenny, a gentle thorn-coloured creature who had caught his fancy at Acle Market some three years previously, when he had been a mere lad of thirteen. He had pointed out her many charms to his father and since she was undersized and going cheap Bob Hewitt had taken a chance and bought the wide-eyed, wobbly-legged calf, warning his son that if she did not thrive and prove a good milker she would have to be sold on. Fortunately, despite her small size, Fenny had always produced a high yield of very rich milk, and so far her calves had all been heifers. Mr Hewitt told his son that he thought Fenny was probably almost pure-bred Jersey, which would account for the richness of her milk and her small size, and the family thought themselves lucky indeed to own her.

The cows did not need to be persuaded into the cowshed tonight; they jostled and pushed in the doorway, steam rising both from their hides and their nostrils, each animal making for her own stall and beginning without delay to pull down mouthfuls of hay from the rack before her. Alec's father came into the cowshed, his pipe clamped between his teeth, and grunted approval when he saw his son tethering the cows and then fetching milking stools and galvanised buckets from the end stall. 'You start that end, bor, an' I'll start this,' he said gruffly. 'Your ma want to make butter so keep Fenny's milk separate from the rest. We don't need a great deal 'cos there won't be many folks at market tomorrow if this here rain keep up. I reckon we'll make it in the kitchen, sittin' round the fire and a-warming our toeses.'

'Aye, right you are,' Alec said, taking his place by Fenny and burying his head in her warm flank. The rich creamy milk began to hiss into the bucket and Alec glanced sideways at his father, amused as always that the older man had continued to grip his pipe upside down. In wet weather he always did this to stop the bowl filling with rain, but he usually forgot to right it again when the rain stopped, though his wife and son often teased him about it.

The two men were experienced milkers and very soon they were pouring the still warm milk from their buckets into the cooler from where it ran into the churn, though Alec kept Fenny's milk to one side. In summer, they made the butter in the tiny tiled room just off the cowshed which did duty as a dairy, but in winter the churn was carried into the kitchen and the three members of the family took it in turns to work the handle until the milk gradually thickened into butter. Alec's mother would then add salt to taste and carry the lump of butter back into the dairy where she would divide it into half-pound slabs and mark it with a wooden paddle which had a relief of a cow on it. Then the butter would be neatly wrapped in greaseproof paper and kept on the cold slab until it was taken off to market.

The milking done, Alec and his father headed for

the pump in the yard. It was a familiar routine; turn and turn about, they stripped and washed or pumped the icy well water up from the ground, and when they were both clean and respectably clad once more they made for the back door, eager to be in the warm. There were still jobs to be done, of course: pigs and horses to be fed, to say nothing of the poultry, though that was Mrs Hewitt's task. The cows would have to be taken back to their pasture in the morning, the horses fed on bales of hay and some chopped mangolds, whilst the wild cats which thronged the barns would have a dish of milk and water put down for them and Cherry and Patch would wolf any scraps left over from the Hewitts' own meal.

Indoors, Mrs Hewitt was waiting for them. At this time of year, they never ate until darkness had fallen, but after milking Mrs Hewitt always provided mugs of tea and a good-sized slice of cake. Sometimes it was an apple cake, sometimes a fruit loaf, and occasionally, when eggs were plentiful, a jam-filled sponge as light as a cloud and so delicious that it rarely lasted longer than a day, but whatever Mrs Hewitt provided it was always good and set father and son up for the tasks which lay ahead.

Today, it was a large slab of ginger cake, sticky topped and smelling of spices. Alec was halfway through his portion when he remembered the puppy and glanced around. He soon spotted it curled up in an old box stuffed with hay and smiled at his mother. 'She looks right at home and I guess you've already fed her,' he said. 'I was going to offer her a bit of my cake but I reckon she need all the sleep she can get right now. When do you think I ought to go and tell Mr Drayton we've found one of his pups half drowned in a ditch? What if he want her back? Only she'd mebbe stray again; she need someone to watch over her, eh, Ma?'

Bob set his mug down on the table. 'He won't want it back,' he said authoritatively. 'His bitch had a big litter; this one'll be the runt. He's a hard man but he wouldn't let a pup starve, so he'll be glad if your ma will take this one on.' He glanced across at the slumbering pup. 'I dare say it'll be more trouble than most, for them red setters are all scared of their own shadows and daft as day-old chicks, but if you and your ma want the responsibility I s'pose I'll hatta go along wi' it.'

Although the winter had been a wet one, spring came early. The trees which surrounded the Hewitts' farmhouse were in full leaf by the end of April, and by May the grass was well grown and the Hewitts were looking forward to an excellent hay crop. Alec, trudging along the lane that led to the village, one warm May evening, was comfortably aware that the family were beginning to do more than just keep their heads above water. For as long as he could remember, his father's ultimate ambition had been to own the farm and the land upon which he worked so hard, but because of the Depression such a thing had not yet been possible. Only the previous day, however, Mr Hewitt had taken the pony and trap into Stalham and had come back with a satisfied look on his ruddy, weather-beaten face. Alec had met him in the lane and had turned back to open the gate. His father had driven into the yard and then gestured to Alec to accompany him while he took the pony from between the shafts and made all tidy.

The men worked together amicably, and once the pony was untacked and the trap manhandled into the cart shed Alec went to rub Feather, the pony, down, assuming that his father would leave him to do the simple task. Instead, Bob followed him into the stable. Alec would not have described his father as a silent man but as a man of few words, who seldom chatted or passed on gossip, so he guessed that it was important when his father remarked: 'While I was out this morning, I decided it was time I took the bull by the horns, so I went into the estate office and had a word with Mr Mathews, Mr Rumbold's agent. I explained as how I'd always wanted to own my own farm; I knew the estate wouldn't want to sell our place but I wondered whether there might be another farm nearer the edge of the estate which they'd consider selling. Mr Mathews, he laughed, but in a nice sort o' way, and said that Mr Rumbold wasn't thinkin' of selling anything, not after all the work he and his forebears had put in, drainin' the marshes and settin' up the Horsey windmill to pump the water into the mere. It was only what I expected, o' course, but I must ha' looked a trifle downcast because he suddenly said: "Have you ever thought of increasing your acreage, Mr Hewitt? Only old Mr Brown can't manage his place no more and his son, Billy, int interested in takin' on the farm when his dad goes. It's hard up agin your land and I'm pretty sure Mr Rumbold would be happy for you to increase your holding by taking on Mere Farm. There's a neat enough house, though it's a bit run down, and your lad will be wantin' his own home one of these days. I know the land int up to much," he say, "but that'd be reflected in the rent, o' course."'

'I say, Dad,' Alec breathed, knowing that his face was shining at the prospect of increasing the size of their holding. 'That'd be as good as owning our own place, wouldn't you say? Rumbold's always been a good landlord, not the sort to increase the rent just because a tenant increases the value of the land he's workin', and one of these days I'd like a place of me own. So what did you say?'

'We shook hands on it,' Mr Hewitt said proudly. 'Mr Mathews, he's a man of his word, and old Brown is leaving to go and live with his daughter in King's Lynn when he's done harvestin'. A'course, there's forms to be signed and agreements to be reached an' that, an' old Brown will want us to buy the dead stock as well as the livestock, but I reckon it won't fetch much and I don't grudge giving the old feller a bit o' pocket money for his retirement. Well? What d'you say?'

Alec knew that dead stock did not mean dead cows and pigs but was the term used for such things as carts, ploughs, harrows and so on, right down to a trowel for transplanting garden plants and the rakes and pitchforks used to turn the hay. He grinned at his father, glad that Bob Hewitt was a generous man and not likely to quibble over such things, for of course they were unlikely to need a good deal of the dead stock, though it could always be put by to be used when their own implements were worn or broken. 'I think you've done real well, Dad,' he said appreciatively. 'I allus look forward to harvest, but it'll be better than ever next year because we'll be doubling the size of the farm. Poor old Brown. It'll be a blow to him, surely? I remember you telling me once that he and his son Tom were grand neighbours and first rate farmers, but that was before Tom was killed in the war, of course.'

'Aye. Tom's death seemed to take all the stuffing out of his father – and he's Mr Brown to you, young man – especially when it became clear that Billy waren't interested in the land. Perhaps it were because he were always havin' Tom thrust down his throat, or perhaps it was because Billy's an idle young blighter, but I 'member Mr Brown sayin' he were downright glad when Billy took off and found himself a job as postman down Stalham way. He got more work out o' his farmhands than he ever got out of his own son and that's a bitter thing for a man to have to accept.'

Alec nodded and stepped back, giving Feather a friendly slap on the rump as he did so. 'I can't imagine why Billy didn't want to farm, but I reckon we're all different,' he said sagely. 'I can't wait to see Ma's face when she hears the news, Dad! She'll be that pleased for you because she knows how you wanted more land.'

By now, they were crossing the yard together and Bob Hewitt caught hold of his son's sleeve, pulling him to a halt. 'Don't you say nothin' to your ma,' he hissed urgently. 'I want to break it to her myself. So just act natural, as if nothin' had happened, and leave me to find the right moment.'

Alec glanced sideways at his father with a grin. He was not a large man, nor a handsome one, and sometimes it crossed Alec's mind to wonder why an exceedingly pretty woman like his mother had married a short, square, solid farm worker whose prospects at the time must have seemed poor indeed compared to her other suitors.

Betty Grainger, however, had clearly seen through Bob Hewitt's plain exterior to the human dynamo beneath. She had once told her son that Bob had literally swept her off her feet. They had met at a hop in the village hall when Betty, who came from a village the other side of Norfolk, had been spending part of her summer holidays with cousins who lived up the coast at Waxham. She had been fourteen at the time and Bob seventeen, but he had not let her youth put him off. He had made a dead set at her, whisking her out during the interval and buying her cherryade and digestive biscuits, since the hall was unlicensed and that was all that was available.

'Was he a good dancer, Ma?' Alec had asked, intrigued at the thought of his square and solid parent doing the light fantastic.

His mother had laughed, then blushed. 'I don't think he could dance at all,' she confessed. 'But he held me very, very tightly and whispered in my ear that I were the prettiest girl he'd ever set eyes on and when we went outside, he – he – well, he kissed me. I'd never been kissed before – 'cept on the cheek, of course – and – and he did *that* awful well. I thought he was the nicest feller I'd ever met and I haven't changed me mind, not in thirty years.'

The two men entered the kitchen and Alec smiled across at his mother, flush-faced and bright-eyed from the warmth of the stove. She was the daughter of an exceedingly successful farmer and had learned, at her mother's knee as it were, all the tricks of the trade which came in so useful now. Alec acknowledged that, without his mother's help, Honeywell Farm would not have been the success it was. Old Mrs Grainger, his maternal grandmother, had been a great one for the traditional 'perks' of the farmer's wife. In her large orchard in the west of the county, she had had half a dozen beehives, a company of geese whose large eggs could feed a family, a great many Rhode Island Reds and a kitchen garden which was the envy of the neighbourhood. She borrowed one of the farm workers to do the heavy digging but distrusted the men so far as planting, weeding and harvesting were concerned, and worked in her garden herself, aided by her daughters, Betty and Irene. Irene had deserted the land upon marrying a well-to-do shopkeeper in Stalham. Alec saw his Aunty Irene and Uncle Mark and his three girl cousins quite often, but especially at Christmas, when Aunty Irene exclaimed with pleasure over her Christmas gifts of Hewitt honey, Hewitt goose, plucked and drawn, and a great many apples, neatly wrapped in tissue and handed over in a large box. 'Enough to last you the winter,' Betty was apt to say with a comfortable smile, happily receiving the silk stockings for herself, the fine linen handkerchief for Bob and the grand white cotton shirts which Alec wore for best. Alec knew that neither sister envied the other but he sometimes thought there was a certain wistfulness in Aunty Irene's eyes when Betty and Bob talked of the farm and of the improvements they were making there. But this was no time to be thinking of Christmas, so Alec watched as his father crossed the room and rumpled his wife's dark red curls, then gave her a peck on the cheek before asking whether supper would be long.

'Ten minutes,' Betty Hewitt said briefly. 'Thass a warm evening so you can wash under the pump, the pair of you.' She handed her husband a bar of red soap and a thin, striped towel and the two men returned to the yard, grinning ruefully at each other. 'That's no manner o' use tellin' your ma that I've bin to market in the pony cart, like a gentleman, an' not dirtied my hands all day,' Bob Hewitt said, casting his cap and jacket on to the wooden bench by the pump and beginning to roll up the sleeves of his best blue shirt. 'If I were a bank manager, I reckon she'd have me strippin' orf an' scrubbin' myself afore she'd let me get at my grub. As for tellin' my news, there's no chance of that until we're set down at the table with the food in front of us.'

'I reckon you're right,' Alec agreed, vigorously wielding the pump handle. 'Mind, she don't know it were me what rubbed Feather down, and before that I were milkin', so I suppose she've got a point. Anyway, I like cleanin' down before we have our evenin' meal. It's a sign, like, that work's over for the day.'

Presently, the two men went indoors to find the table already laid and food steaming on three plates. There was cabbage, boiled beef and carrots and some of the new potatoes that Alec had dug earlier in the day. Patch, Cherry and Loopy were circling the table anxiously but none of them made any attempt to touch the food on the plates. For one thing, it was far too hot, and for another, bitter experience had taught them that if they misbehaved and tried to steal food which was not in their dishes they would go hungry later. Instead, they sat down at a discreet distance from the table, eyes bright with anticipation and tongues lolling. Soon enough, they knew, when the family had finished their meal, their turn would come.

With his mind still very much on the Browns and the acquisition of Mere Farm, Alec had to be very firm with himself not to refer to the matter until his father had broken the news. His mother glanced at her son's empty plate. 'Ready for some suet puddin'?'

Alec admitted that he was and, as soon as they had all been served, heard his father clear his throat portentously. 'I got a bit of news for you, Bet,' he said, fixing his eyes on his pudding plate. 'I went into the estate office this mornin' and had a chinwag with Mr Mathews, the agent, and the upshot of it was . . .'

Chapter Four

Summer 1936

On the last day of term, Kathy came home with a heavy satchel full of holiday tasks but a light heart. This would be her first really long holiday since she had started at the high school, and though she had agreed with her mother that she would have to do paid work of some sort, she still intended to make the most of her free time. A great many girls of her age managed to do work in some capacity or another because folk took holidays, and whilst the Woolworths' girls were off on their annual trip to the Isle of Man somebody had to do their work.

Jane meant to work too, since Tilly would take the responsibility for the younger kids, but, like Kathy, she intended to have some time to herself. She had suggested the previous day that she and Kathy should job hunt together; if they did that there was always a chance, albeit a slender one, that they might actually be employed by the same shop or office.

Kathy glanced hopefully up the road ahead of her. It had rained lightly, but persistently, all day, and then at three o'clock the clouds had parted as if by magic and the sun had appeared. Now it shone on the wet pavements and the puddles reflected the blue of the sky. It was a good omen, Kathy decided, for the weeks ahead. She had hoped that Jane might come and meet her since Daisy Street School had broken up a couple of days previously, but it looked as though her walk was to be a solitary one. Never mind, Kathy told herself, you've always liked thinking time and you won't have much once you're in a job, so make the most of it, girl. Think about the holiday you, Mam and Billy will have come August, because Mam was taking a whole week off and even though she doubted that they could afford to go away she meant to take them for days out.

Just as Kathy's mind was beginning to dwell deliciously on the prospect of a coach trip to Rhyl or a railway journey to Southport, she saw a familiar figure coming towards her, pushing the big, old-fashioned black pram. Immediately all thoughts of holidays were banished. Dear Jane. Trust her pal to remember her and come to meet her! Since she had the kids with her, she was probably also doing her mam's messages but that didn't worry Kathy in the least. Her mam had left her a list this morning and now she fished it out of her blazer pocket and studied it doubtfully. The trouble was, she had no money with which to buy the goods her mother needed; still, perhaps Jane might be willing to turn back to Daisy Street, and if not, then Kathy would just have to do her own messages later. After all, she must pick Billy up from Mrs Hughes on time for that lady had become a little difficult lately. When Kathy had called for Billy, Mrs Hughes had prowled around muttering, starting sentences and then failing to finish them, saying darkly that she really ought to have a word with Mrs Kelling when she had time. Kathy had imagined that Mrs Hughes wanted to put her baby-minding rates up since young Billy, at three, was quite a handful and ate proper meals, but as yet Mrs Hughes had not found the time to argue her case, so things went on as before.

When Jane pulled the pram up alongside, however,

Kathy saw that Billy was already aboard. He had jam round his mouth and a good deal of dirt smeared across his cheeks, but when she bent to give him a kiss he responded immediately by throwing both arms round her neck and demanding that he be given a piggy-back.

'No, no, little feller, you stay in the pram with Tommy,' Kathy said, gently disengaging herself. She turned to Jane. 'It were kind of you to fetch Billy for me, queen. Are you getting messages? I've gorra list but no money so if you don't mind I'd best nip back home. Mam's left the money on the mantelpiece in the old brown purse, so I won't be more'n five minutes. You can wait for me here, if you like.'

'No, I'll walk back wi' you,' Jane said companionably, turning the pram and falling into step with her friend. 'And I didn't go and fetch Billy. Mrs Hughes brought him round at dinnertime. She said she had give him his dinner but couldn't keep him no longer.'

'Oh? What's gone wrong *this* time?' Kathy said, remembering with foreboding the only other time that Mrs Hughes had dumped her charge on the O'Briens. 'Don't say one o' the other kids has gorris tooth knocked out!'

'No, it were nothing like that,' Jane said. 'I dunno as Billy – or any of the others – were in trouble. It's just ... oh dear. The fact is, Kathy, Mrs Hughes don't want to babysit for your Billy no more.'

'Wha-a-at?' Kathy said, genuinely astonished. She had thought Mrs Hughes's attitude had changed of late but had never, in her wildest nightmares, thought that the elderly woman would decide to stop child minding. 'Is she – is she retiring then? Oh, Gawd, Jane, whatever will we do? After what happened last time, I dare not ask you if your Tilly could give an eye to him while Mam and I are working. There are other child minders, but Billy don't know 'em. There's Mrs Frayme on Snowdrop Street; she child minds, I know, and she might take young Billy on.'

'Well, you could ask,' Jane said as they turned into Daisy Street. 'The thing is, queen, Mrs Hughes says – well, she says Billy worries her. She – she don't think he's completely over the accident yet. She says he's too much responsibility for a woman what's lookin' after half a dozen little 'uns. Needs too much attention,' she finished, rather lamely.

Kathy was about to reply hotly that Billy was no more trouble than any other little boy of three, but realised Jane was only repeating what she had been told. No doubt Mrs Hughes had her reasons, and whatever they were, she and her mam would have to tackle them together. But there was no need, at this stage, to involve Jane. Kathy was fond of Tilly and thought her sensible and responsible but knew Mrs Kelling would never agree to let Billy stay with the O'Briens, or not for long periods at any rate. Still, Mrs Hughes's ultimatum had come at a good time with the school holiday stretching ahead. Kathy could cope with Billy for a few days and it would surely take no more than that to find a suitable child minder.

She said as much to Jane as they went down the jigger and entered the Kellings' small back yard. Jane agreed, and presently Kathy abandoned her school satchel on the kitchen table, stuffed her mother's purse into her pocket and went out into the yard once more, shutting and locking the door behind her and replacing the key in its hiding place above the lintel. Billy and Tommy were indulging in an argument over a large piece of orange peel which they appeared to have discovered in the bottom of the pram, and

Jane was just telling them to leave it alone, or she would abandon them to Tilly and the other children, when Billy's head tipped back and his eyes rolled up until only the whites showed. His small body went stiff and he began to utter peculiar grunting sounds whilst foaming saliva ran down his chin in a glistening flood.

'Billy!' Kathy screamed. She tried to pull him into her arms but he was spasming and quivering so hard that she let him lie back in the pram once more, afraid that if she picked him up he might jerk free of her and land on the ground. 'Billy! What on earth's the matter with you? Come on, chuck, it's only a piece of orange peel. You come to Kathy and I'll give you that piggy-back, honest to God I will.'

She went to pick Billy up once more but Jane pulled her back. 'He's havin' some sort of fit,' she said quietly. 'Best put him on his side and hold him; I dare say he'll be right as rain in a minute.' She whipped Tommy out of the pram as she spoke and Kathy began to struggle to turn Billy on to his side, but this proved impossible since he was stiff as a board yet still jerking like a landed salmon.

'I think we ought to get help,' Kathy was saying as Billy's grunts became a shrill, unstoppable shriek. She was utterly terrified and saw that Jane, too, was frightened, though she was doing her best to hide it. 'Will Mrs Hughes know what to do? She's been lookin' after kids for years.'

'No! I don't think so,' Jane said, swinging the pram round and heading for Daisy Street. 'We ought to take him straight across to the Stanley. The nurses and doctors there will know how to treat him.'

Kathy agreed and the two girls, hearts thumping, rushed up Daisy Street, across Stanley Road and straight into the hospital. Tommy, tucked under his sister's arm, was crying steadily, the tears pouring down his cheeks whilst he kept up a constant wail of fear. Kathy had never been so pleased to enter the casualty department as she was at that moment and the sight of a neatly uniformed nurse coming towards them was better, she told herself, than Christmas morning. The nurse did not look at Kathy, however, but at Jane and Tommy. 'What's the little devil done this time, then?' she enquired cheerfully. 'Fallen out of the pram and bumped his head?'

Jane began to explain but the nurse took one glance into the pram and realised immediately which child was the patient. She scooped Billy up and trotted across the crowded hallway to where a nurse stood sentinel against a door marked *Dr Trelawney*. 'The little lad's having a fit, Collins,' she said briskly. 'I'm taking him to number one cubicle; could you send Dr Trelawney in at once, please?'

The two girls followed closely on her heels, Jane with Tommy still in her arms. Kathy's heart was thumping so loudly that she could scarcely hear her own voice as she prayed to God to let Billy be all right, to let it be just something which happened sometimes and could be easily cured. She watched closely as the nurse laid Billy on a tall, cold-looking bed, holding him still with both hands for, though he seemed calmer, he still jerked now and then. The doctor, entering the cubicle hurriedly, glanced at Billy and then at the two girls. 'What happened?' he asked. 'Did he have a fall? Has this happened before?'

He was looking at Jane but it was Kathy who answered. 'He were in hospital with a fractured skull almost a year ago,' she said briefly. 'We weren't doing anything; he and Tommy were quarrelling over a bit of orange peel and Billy suddenly flung himself back and rolled his eyes up and all spit ran down his chin. He made horrible noises – animal noises – and he jerked and twitched so much I couldn't hold him. Is – is he very ill? He's my little brother,' she added unnecessarily.

The doctor had been peering at Billy as she spoke but he glanced up at her and gave a small, sharp nod. 'Good girl. You're not one to lose your head,' he said approvingly. 'I think your brother may have had a slight epileptic fit but I need to examine him properly and that may take a little while. So you go off and wait in the hall, and when I know what's going on I'll come and tell you. And you're not to worry because this might well be the result of the old injury and may never happen again.'

The nurse shooed them out of the cubicle but it was twenty anxious minutes before the doctor reappeared and came straight over to them, giving what he no doubt considered to be a reassuring smile. 'I've sent the staff nurse to get young Billy's records so that we can admit him to the ward.'

'Why can't I take him home, mister – doctor, I mean? Only me mam is at work and I ought to be getting the tea and there's a great many messages to fetch . . .'

'I'm afraid he'll be here for a little while,' the doctor said kindly. 'We shall want to keep him under observation for a day or two. But at any rate, he's come round now and he's asking for Kathy – I suppose that's you? – so you can go up to the ward with him and see him into his bed and then you'd best go and tell your mother what's been happening.'

He turned away but Kathy caught at his sleeve. 'Is Billy going to die?' she asked bluntly. 'He were ever so ill last year, but when he left hospital the nurses and doctors seemed to think he'd be all right. And he has been . . . until now.'

The doctor turned back. 'A fractured skull is a tricky injury,' he said quietly. 'It was only a hairline fracture and Billy's young – the younger you are, the easier it is to recover from such an injury – but no one ever knows quite how cranial damage may affect the sufferer. The more we can watch Billy and check his reactions, the better.'

'I understand. Thank you, doctor,' Kathy said. She set off in the direction of the cubicle with Jane close beside her, Tommy now asleep in her arms. Kathy's stomach was hollow with apprehension. She felt as though she were reliving the dreadful time last year when Billy had first cracked his head open and was determined, no matter what the doctor might say, not to fetch her mother out of work unless it was absolutely necessary. When Kathy was overtired and worrying, her dreams often became nightmares so that she saw once more the scene in the timber yard as her father ran out of the building and under the lorry. Once more, the explosion tore the air apart, once more her own screams filled her head . . . no, she would not go to her mother unless it was absolutely essential to do so.

As soon as they reached the cubicle in which Billy was ensconced and saw him, a great many of Kathy's fears receded, for he was sitting up on the bed and, although looking bewildered and heavy eyed, he smiled widely as soon as he saw her and held up his arms. 'Gi' me a cuddle, Kathy,' he commanded. 'Why's I on this bed? I come out o' hospital, didn't I? Why's I back in here?' His eyes strayed to Jane and the sleeping Tommy. 'Is it the middle of the night? Tommy's asleep.'

Jane laughed and sat on the end of the bed and Kathy sat down next to her. 'Tommy's asleep because he got rather bored waiting for the doctor to make you well again,' Kathy said glibly. 'Don't you remember what happened, Billy? You and Tommy were squabbling over something in the pram and – and you must have given your poor old head a knock. But the doctor soon made you well again, didn't he?'

A small frown etched itself between Billy's soft brows. 'I don't 'member anything about a pram . . .' he was beginning when recollection clearly returned. He sat up straighter and scowled at his sleeping friend. 'It were *my* piece of orange peel,' he said wrathfully. 'I were hungry, our Kathy. I were goin' to scrunch it down 'cos it were ever so old and dry only bleedin' Tommy snatched it off me. Make him give it back!'

'If you swear, you won't get so much as a sniff of orange peel,' Kathy said reprovingly, but with a light heart. It was wonderful to hear her little brother sounding so completely normal and demanding his rights. She did not know what an epileptic fit was, though it sounded frightening, and determined to ask the sister just what such fits entailed as soon as she could, but in the meantime she would be able to reassure her mother that Billy was completely himself again and could come home once the doctors had observed him for a day or two.

The two girls remained with Billy for half an hour, and, in fact, only decided to leave because as soon as Tommy woke up Billy grew restive and wanted to get out of bed and rush around the ward with his pal. Fortunately, one of the nurses Billy had particularly liked during his previous stay in hospital came on to the ward just at that point. She walked over and sat on the bed, putting an arm round Billy's small shoulders. 'Well, if it isn't young Mr Trouble,' she said, winking at Kathy. 'Did you know we've got a new rocking horse in the playroom? And I've a tin of chocolate biscuits tucked away in my little kitchen which I give to boys and girls who drink up their bedtime milk. Now, young Billy, you're in a nasty old hospital nightgown and not looking nearly as smart as you'd like, because when the visitors arrive Sister likes you to look your best, doesn't she? If Kathy goes off now, we'll give her leave to come back a quarter of an hour before visiting starts, with a pair of your best pyjamas. You'd like that, wouldn't you?'

Billy had begun to whimper as soon as Kathy stood up but now he heaved a deep sigh and nodded rather tremulously. 'Will you stay with me, nurse?' he asked plaintively. 'Sister said I won't be here long if I'm a good boy. Can I go home when me mam comes to visit?'

The nurse plucked Billy carefully from his bed and carried him down the ward beside the two girls, but turned left into the play area, chatting busily to Billy as Kathy, Jane and Tommy slipped out of the swing doors and back on to the corridor. They hurried along since Kathy was mortally afraid of pursuit; whatever would she do if Billy chased after her? But they reached the hall without incident and Jane plonked Tommy back into the pram with a sigh of relief. 'Wharra great elephant you are,' she said, seizing the pram handle. 'I'm awful sorry about Billy, queen, but it's like I said, he's in the best place. The doctors and nurses all know him and I'm sure they'll make him better in no time. Now what should we do? Do you want to go straight round to Dorothy's Tearooms and tell your mam your Billy's in hospital or do you want to get the messages?'

'We'll get the messages first, then I'll go home and make the tea so's Mam can come in to a hot meal. After that, I suppose I'd better go to the tearooms,' Kathy said, after some thought. 'Mam doesn't usually get home until quite late and she mustn't miss visiting, but there's no point in worrying her before I have to. Which shop is first on your list?'

The day that Billy returned from hospital, Kathy and her mother sat up late, mulling over what they should do. As soon as Mrs Kelling had returned from visiting Billy on that first evening, she had gone straight round to Mrs Hughes. She had asked the older woman, bluntly, just why she was no longer willing to child mind Billy and after some initial hesitation Mrs Hughes had admitted that Billy had been having 'queer turns'. Though these had not lasted long and could not, she had said firmly, be described as fits, they had worried her. 'I've got six little ones in me house from eight in the morning until four in the afternoon and it worried me that someone might give young Billy a whack when I weren't lookin',' she confessed. 'I have me niece, Emmie, to give me a hand but, as you know, she's simple. Oh, she loves the kids – Billy's a real favourite wi' Emmie – but she ain't reliable when a kid comes over queer. So I thought it best to say I'd not have him no more.'

'Just what do you mean by "queer turns"?' Mrs Kelling had asked suspiciously. 'He never had queer turns at home, not that Kathy and I can recall.'

'Well, that's just it. He never threw himself about or screamed, he'd just sit starin' at the wall with his mouth open, dribbling down his front like a newborn babby for five or ten minutes. You could speak to him, try to give him something, pick him up even, but he wouldn't take no manner of notice. Then he'd give a sort of shudder and be right as rain, playin' and shoutin' with the other kids as though nothing had happened. Which,' she added judiciously, 'it hadn't, if you get my meaning.'

Mrs Kelling had known what she meant but still thought her neighbour had been dilatory in not informing her of such strange behaviour. However, it was no use blaming Mrs Hughes. The doctor had advised that it was best to keep Billy at home with his mother or sister.

'From what we know of Billy's condition, a fit can be sparked off by over-excitement, a quarrel or a fight with another child, or even frustration if he is denied something he badly wants,' Dr Trelawney had said. 'Fortunately, Mrs Kelling, your son is a healthy young animal with excellent recuperative powers. He may have no more than two or three fits a year and by the time he's five or six he could have got over them altogether. But until then, you must learn how to deal with those fits so that Billy does not do himself – or anyone else – harm. You say Kathy is sensible and responsible but, in my opinion, Billy will need a mother's care at least for the next twelve months.' He had smiled very kindly at Mrs Kelling. 'I know your circumstances and realise how difficult this may be. Is it possible for you to get work which could be done in the home?'

'I've been thinking about taking lodgers,' Mrs Kelling had said slowly. 'We've a decent sized house down Daisy Street with three good bedrooms. We could let two of them and Kathy, Billy and meself could share the third. I'm good wi' me needle but piecework is so poorly paid I'd rather try letting rooms first.'

When this conversation had been repeated to Kathy, she had agreed eagerly that a couple of lodgers would be a good deal better than seeing her mother toiling over piecework from the local garment factory, or addressing endless envelopes or taking in washing. Besides, none of those things paid well at all, and she guessed that if they went down that path she would have to give up her place at the high school. Despite her busy home life, she was nearly always top of her class and her teachers were predicting a bright future, maybe even a university place. She knew her mother would work her fingers to the bone rather than see Kathy take a third rate job in a shop or office and thought that losing the privacy of their home would be a small price to pay to avoid that.

'Fortunately, your father's little pension pays the rent each week, so if we can get a couple of nice lady lodgers who are in steady work, then we should all manage very nicely,' Mrs Kelling told her daughter. 'I'll be at home all day, looking after Billy, so there'll be no question of you having to make lodgers' meals, though I'll appreciate your help in keeping the rooms clean and the washing and so on done. If you agree, you can write out a notice in your best handwriting, and copy it out twice. We'll take one copy down to the *Echo* office and purrit in the paper. It'll cost a bob or two, but I reckon we'll get a better class of lodger that way. The other copy can go into Mr Snelling's shop on Stanley Road – it's right near the hospital and the nurses pop in and out all the time. A nurse for a lodger would be ideal because, though you and I are to go up to the hospital so that they can teach us what to do when Billy's took bad, a nurse would kind of know instinctively, wouldn't you think?'

Kathy was secretly doubtful. There were so many nurses and they worked on so many different wards. She also knew from talking to the staff on Billy's ward that nurses were not well paid and wondered if they could afford the sort of price her mother would have to charge for a room. Shift work would also mean that they would expect to have meals provided at odd hours, or so she imagined; far from being ideal lodgers, therefore, nurses might be very difficult.

She said as much to Jane when the two girls met next day. Kathy flourished the two cards which she had written out in her very best Gothic script, and explained how she and her mother meant to cope. Jane admired the notices and agreed to accompany Kathy both to the Snelling's shop and to the *Echo* office on Victoria Street, though she was doubtful that the Kellings would get a woman as a lodger. 'There's plenty of folk on the flower streets as has lodgers, and they's all men,' she told her friend. 'Railway workers mostly, but there's one or two dockers, I believe – or fellers who work in the dockyards,' she amended. 'There ain't much work for women round here. Still, you might be lucky.'

The advertisement and the postcard in Snelling's window did not elicit an immediate response but since Sarah Kelling knew her daughter was the best person – next to herself – to look after Billy, she had no worries about him whilst the school holidays lasted.

As she cleaned around the kitchen and prepared their evening meal, she kept a casual eye on Billy, who was sitting on the hearthrug in a patch of sunshine, carefully building a tower with the blocks that Jack had made for Kathy when she was small. Billy was concentrating hard, his tongue poking out of one side of his mouth and his hands steadying the bricks, as the tower grew higher. Sarah was pleased to notice that the small, grubby hands were steady as rocks and that the tower was rising at an astonishing pace.

Billy had returned from hospital somewhat subdued, but otherwise his normal, cheerful self. 'Boys will be boys and your Billy is a grand little chap,' Dr Trelawney had told her. 'In my opinion, Billy must have knocked his head whilst squabbling with Tommy over the orange peel and this brought on a slight epileptic fit. From what you tell me of his behaviour whilst at the child minder's, he had been suffering from what we call "petit mal", which is a very mild form of epilepsy and one which he is almost certain to outgrow.'

This conversation had heartened Sarah considerably. She was determined to keep Kathy at school for as long as she possibly could, partly because it was what she knew her dear Jack had wanted and partly because she admired Kathy's bright intelligence and quickness of comprehension.

It was unfortunate that the job at Dorothy's Tearooms might have to be sacrificed. She had been there for ten months and in that time had learned to like both customers and staff. She was proud of the fact that the tearooms, which had not been doing particularly well before she joined them, were now the highest earners in the group. Dorothy McNab owned six tearooms scattered across the city and was truly pleased with the way Mrs Kelling had increased profitability and efficiency at the Stanley Road café. As a result, Sarah had received a generous bonus at Christmas and a promise of an increase in salary when she had worked a full year.

Because she was so happy there, she had said nothing to her employer regarding her intention to leave work as soon as she found some other source of income. She could not help hoping that some miracle would occur which would enable her to keep her job, if only on a part-time basis, but in her heart she knew this was impossible; the tearooms needed a full-time manageress. On the other hand, there were the school holidays. Unless Billy's fits were more frequent – and more frightening – she was pretty sure that Kathy could cope with her little brother at such times, so she toyed with the idea of getting a short-term job then, preferably in catering of some sort. And of course, if Billy improved, as the medical staff hoped, he would begin school in a couple of years, which would mean she might work once more.

When the knock came on the door, Sarah guessed that it would be a friend calling for either Billy or Kathy. Her daughter was upstairs in her room, working on an essay which was part of her holiday task, so Sarah crossed to the back door and opened it, her brows already rising. 'Kathy's busy, but . . .' she began, then realised that the man who stood in the small yard was a total stranger. Hastily, Sarah tried to smooth her hair behind her ears and glanced, rather self-consciously, down at the stained calico apron she wore. It was Sunday evening and she had not expected a visitor on such a day. However, she did not wish the man to think he had caught her out. 'Good evening,' she said politely. 'I'm so sorry, I thought you were a friend calling for one of my children. How can I help you?' She spoke with care for she had learned, in Dorothy's Tearooms, that a pleasant and unaccented voice won respect from staff and customers alike, and was pleased to see the man remove his cap as he answered.

'Evenin'. I take it I'm addressing . . .' he glanced at the piece of paper he held '. . . Mrs Kelling? I came to the back door because I thought it likely you'd be in the kitchen round about now and I didn't want to put you out. I've come in answer to your advertisement . . . is the room still vacant?'

'I'm – I'm not sure,' Sarah said cautiously and untruthfully. She had stated plainly that she wanted a lady lodger and one glance at the stranger on her doorstep, dark haired, broad shouldered and with a long and drooping black moustache, was enough to show her that he was most certainly not a female. 'I have had a couple of young ladies to look at the room but they've not let me know for definite whether they will be taking it.' She paused, eyeing him reproachfully. 'I did say that I wanted a lady lodger, you know,' she finished.

The man grinned. She judged him to be between thirty-five and forty and she realised he was an attractive fellow, though the very blackness of his hair and moustache made him look grim until he smiled. 'I can't pretend to be a lady,' he said, still grinning. 'But I can assure you I'm pretty desperate. I've been living on Crocus Street, with a family you may know – the Osterleys – but Mr Osterley has got a job as stationmaster somewhere in Cheshire, so they're moving out and the folk who are moving in don't need a lodger – they've got eleven kids.' He let his glance range around the pleasant kitchen and his eyes became wistful. 'You've gorra nice home here,

Mrs Kelling, and the Osterleys will give me a good reference. I suppose you wouldn't consider . . .'

Sarah was about to say that a male lodger was out of the question when Billy's small voice cut across her thoughts. 'Oozat, Mammy?' he asked curiously. 'It ain't me daddy, is it?'

Sarah swung round. 'No, of course it isn't your daddy, chuck,' she said gently. She turned back to her visitor, still hesitating. He was so very tall, and – and – broad, and – black! He was clearly a Liverpudlian, but he could have been a Mexican bandit, or a Spanish pirate, if looks were all you had to go by. 'You'd better come in for a moment, Mr – Mr . . .'

'Sorry, Mrs Kelling,' the man said humbly. 'Me name's Bracknell, Sam Bracknell. I brung me references wi' me, just in case you could let me have the room while I'm searching for somewhere else. You see, the Osterleys didn't tell me till today and they're movin' out at the end of the week, so as I said, I'm pretty desperate.'

He came into the kitchen and took the chair Sarah offered, then produced several letters from his pocket. One was clearly from the Osterleys, for it was ill written and ill spelt – Sarah knew the family and had no very high opinion of them – but the others seemed to be more official. One was headed 'The Liverpool & General Assurance Company' and another, on equally official-looking paper, looked like a letter from the gas company. 'Here's me references,' Mr Bracknell said, pushing them across the table towards her. 'You can see I'm a pretty steady sort of chap. I were in the offices of the Liverpool Gas Company in Duke Street for seven years, only moving to the Liverpool & General because there weren't much chance of promotion with the gas. All the clerks were young, like meself, so I changed to insurance – they wanted an agent for Bootle and district – and I've took to it like a duck to water, as you'll see if you read me reference.'

'It seems wrong of me to read your references when I've already told you that I want a lady lodger,' Sarah said, half apologetically. 'You see, apart from Billy there, we're an all female household, have been ever since my husband was killed, almost a year ago.' Sarah would not have admitted as much to a stranger had she not known that the Osterleys would undoubtedly have passed the information on, even if Mr Bracknell was not already aware of her circumstances due to having lived in the neighbourhood for some while.

'I don't mind who reads me references, 'cos they're good ones,' Mr Bracknell said, with a touch of complacency. 'Each one of 'em says you're welcome to check up that I've not writ 'em meself on headed notepaper. Oh, an' there's one from me old landlady, though it's a bit tattered like. I've been with the Osterleys five years, you see, and to own the truth I didn't plan to move on, not so far as lodgings were concerned. I'm a steady feller, Mrs Kelling, and I've been saving up for years to gerra place of me own. So if you'd just read me references an' give me a chance . . .'

'All right, Mr Bracknell, but I really don't mean to take any gentlemen,' Sarah said, as firmly as she could. She read the letters quickly. Both the gas company and the assurance company clearly thought highly of the man seated opposite her, for both references were glowing. It appeared that Mr Bracknell was a great favourite with most of his clients and was welcomed into many local homes.

This made Sarah think of her own insurance agent, who was a jolly little sandy-haired man with pince-nez spectacles and a set of false teeth which clicked when he laughed. She reflected that she would have trusted Mr Pickering as readily as she would have trusted Jane or Mrs O'Brien, so surely, if Mr Bracknell came out of the same mould, she could trust him too? But he was younger, considerably better looking and much more dynamic. The thought of him living in the house made her think, incongruously, of the three little pigs and the wolf. Though I'm sure there's nothing pig-like about us Kellings, nor anything wolf-like about Mr Bracknell, she told herself, turning to the Osterleys' letter.

It wasn't a particularly long missive but was, she supposed, sufficiently informative. Mr Osterley said briefly that Mr Bracknell was a quiet gentleman of regular habits, often out in the evenings since a good deal of his work involved visiting residences when the master of the house was at home. He had paid his rent regularly, had kept his room tidy and took his midday meals in the assurance company canteen except at weekends, when he often visited friends.

Sarah picked up the last letter which, as Mr Bracknell had intimated, had been written some time ago, presumably at least five years earlier. The lady said briefly that Mr Bracknell had lodged with her for 'many years' and had always been an ideal lodger, paying up when his rent was due and never causing problems with other residents. She went on to explain that he was tidy and helpful, but Sarah just skimmed that bit, handing the letters back to Mr Bracknell with an apologetic smile.

'Thank you; I'm sure you'll have no difficulty in getting lodgings. I'll have a word with my daughter this evening, but I really do think that our decision only to have lady lodgers must stand,' she said gently. 'However, if my daughter disagrees . . .' She rose to her feet and walked across to the door, holding it open for Mr Bracknell to pass into the back yard.

He gave a regretful sigh but, halfway across the yard, turned back for a moment. 'If you would just have me for, say, a month . . .' he began, but Sarah merely repeated that she would speak to her daughter and let him know their decision at the Osterleys' in a couple of days. Then she closed the door firmly and turned back to continue her interrupted tasks.

When the meal was ready, Sarah called her daughter down and told her about Mr Bracknell as they ate salad and baked potatoes. She half expected Kathy to scold her for turning down a possible let but instead, Kathy nodded approvingly. 'If you don't want a feller, then you don't,' she said. 'An' if you'd agreed to let him come for a month, or three weeks even, just how would you get rid of him at the end of that time? We don't *know* him, Mam, but we do know the Osterleys. I think Jane and her mam would say that a good reference from them wasn't worth the paper it were written on. It isn't that they're bad or wicked, or that they'd lie,' she added hastily. 'But their standards aren't – aren't our standards, Mam, nor yet the O'Briens'. I know Mrs O'Brien is a bit slapdash and untidy and buys bought cakes an' that, an' never stays in one job for long, but she's a far better housekeeper than Mrs Osterley. I'm not surprised Mr Bracknell only seems to have had his breakfasts at the Osterleys' either, because from what I've heard tell, it's mainly bread and scrape and cabbage soup with them.'

Her mother laughed. 'Well, you've relieved my mind on one score. We're both agreed we've to go on searching for a lady lodger, so later on you can nip round to the Osterleys' and pop a letter through their door for me. I think I'd rather write formally to tell Mr Bracknell we're very sorry, but we haven't changed our minds, so there can be no misunderstanding. Now, I'm back in Dorothy's tomorrow morning, so I'm afraid you'll have to keep an eye on Billy, but until we get a lodger we're going to need my money.'

'Oh, that's all right. I shan't have Jane, of course, because – did I tell you? – she's starting a permanent job tomorrow. It's not much of a job; she's helping out with Mrs Mitchell's fruit and veg stall in St John's market. Mr O'Brien says Mrs Mitchell is getting too old to hump sacks of potatoes and cabbages around and her eyesight ain't so good either. A couple of weeks ago there was a row over her giving the wrong change. Mr O'Brien says she's a lovely old lady and wouldn't cheat anyone deliberate, but she can't see what's what, so she needs someone bright and sharp and not too expensive.'

'You'll miss her,' Sarah observed, mashing Billy's potato and adding tomato ketchup to make it more palatable; Billy was no lover of salad. 'I do hope we gerra lodger fairly soon though, love. The advert's been in the *Echo* twice now and norra nibble.'

'I'm a bit worried meself,' Kathy said slowly. 'Jane and I were chatting about the number of lodgers living in the flower streets, and Mam, they're all men. Mrs Higgins in Crocus Street has got a married couple but she's the only one. All the rest are fellers, honest to God they are. I know there must be women who earn a good wage and could afford lodgings – well, I suppose there are – but they don't seem to end

94

up lodging in this side of the city. An' you don't really want sharin', do you?'

'No I don't,' her mother said decidedly. 'You get two or three young girls crammed into one room, wanting to make their own food in your kitchen and paying very little more than a solitary lodger would. Older, more responsible women won't want to share and they're the sort I'm after. Oh, I'm sure we'll get someone soon; I'll ask up at the hospital, I think. You never know, we might be lucky.'

Chapter Five
September 1936

'Only another week and I'll be back in school,' Kathy said dolefully, above the din of St John's market in full swing. 'And in all the weeks we've had our advert in, we haven't had one application from a lady.'

Kathy was ostensibly buying potatoes, carrots and onions from Jane and catching up on news as she did so. Jane, weighing out the potatoes on the huge scales, smiled sympathetically. 'I did tell you,' she said. 'So what's your mam goin' to do? If you left school, that would solve the problem, only I know your mam's dead set against it.'

'Oh aye, she won't hear of it,' Kathy agreed. She did not envy Jane her job and was sure that she herself would get bored to tears, lugging sacks of vegetables and attending to customers, but she did envy her friend the small independence which even the tiniest wage had given to her. 'She's decided to lower her standards; she's changed the advertisement so it doesn't say lady lodger.'

Jane giggled. 'Me dad would say she was raisin' her standards,' she observed. 'Wharrabout that feller from the Osterleys? Eh, when I heard your mam had turned him down, I were that vexed! I know he's too old for me but he looks just like Errol Flynn – or do I mean Clark Gable? Anyway, he's the best looking feller I've seen for years; if my mam had turned him down for a lodger, I'd ha' been heartbroken.'

It was Kathy's turn to giggle. 'Yes, he is nice looking,' she agreed. She and Jane had hung about near the Osterleys' to catch a glimpse of the insurance agent and had been impressed by his flashing dark eyes and raven's wing hair. Nevertheless, Kathy had agreed with her mother that a lady lodger would be a good deal easier than the handsomest of men. Answering Jane's question, she said placidly: 'He were fixed up weeks ago. Well, I say that because the Osterleys left weeks ago and he never came back to our house to ask Mam to change her mind. But there's plenty of fellows wanting lodgings so I'm sure Mam will have to tell Dorothy's Tearooms that she's leaving any time now.' She saw Mrs Mitchell eyeing her and raised her voice. 'I'll have three pounds of carrots and a nice big swede, please.'

Jane turned and began to take handfuls of carrots from the sack behind her, piling them up on the scale and adding a two-pound weight to the one already in position. 'But if she's to give a month's notice, an' she said she would, and you're back in a week . . .'

'I know, she's left it awful late,' Kathy agreed. 'Even if she gets a lodger tomorrow, it won't help that much, because we'll have no one to leave Billy with. But I think Mam's hoping they'll let her take him in to work, just for a week or two, while she teaches the new manageress the job.'

'I bet they won't. The last thing you want in a nice tearoom is a kid crawlin' round and meddling with the tables,' Jane said shrewdly. 'An' then there's the fits . . . only he doesn't have them any more, does he?'

'Not the bad ones. He's only had one of them since the time you and I rushed him to the Stanley,' Kathy observed. 'He doesn't have the little tiny things . . . the petits mals . . . so often, either. But we still dare not leave him with anyone who doesn't understand; it's got to be Mam or meself.'

'Tilly would be ideal, but she'll be back in school, same as you,' Jane said regretfully. 'Why doesn't your mam give a week's notice? She's paid weekly, ain't she? An' my mam says if you're paid weekly, a week's notice is all you have to give. An' she should know,' she added with a twisted grin.

'I know, I know,' Kathy said as Jane clicked her fingers for the shopping bag to be passed over. She watched her friend tipping the carrots on to the onions and potatoes already within, then fished her money out of her purse. 'But me mam wants her job back when Billy starts school an' she's afraid that if she only gives a week's notice, they won't consider her for a management position again.'

'That'll be one and threepence. And they probably won't consider employing her again even if she gives three months' notice. They say there's a hundred people after every job these days an' your mam's job is a good one. It'll be snapped up an' whoever gets it will hang on to it like grim death. You tell her to give 'em a week. Why, if they promote one of the waitresses, or someone from another of the tearooms, they won't want much training.'

'You're probably right,' Kathy said, handing over the correct money. 'But Mam doesn't want to give her notice until we've gorra lodger 'cos of the money.' She glanced around the stall, then pointed to a display of small red apples. 'How many for a penny?'

Jane picked up four small apples and handed them to her friend, taking the penny in exchange. Billy, seated in a pushchair and below the level of the stall, gave a crow of delight as his sister handed over the fruit. 'Ta ever so, Janey,' he shouted. 'I likes red apples – an' I likes that big plum what you give me last week.'

Mrs Mitchell, finishing with her own customer, leaned across the stall to beam fatly down upon her smallest client. 'That were a Victoria plum an' they's over now till next year,' she observed. 'You're a good little feller, Billy Kelling, so you shall have a pear. A nice William.'

When Kathy arrived home, her mother was in the kitchen. She looked up and smiled as her daughter entered the room. Mrs Kelling bent and picked Billy out of his pushchair, swinging him on to her hip. She kissed his fair curls, asking: 'Have you had a good day with your sister, then? Well, I've got a surprise for the pair of you; I've bought a nice big slab of fruit cake from the café and a bottle of cherry Corona so's we can have a bit of a celebration.'

'Mam, wharron earth are you doing at home on a weekday?' Kathy said, ignoring her mother's remarks. 'You never get away this early, and why are we celebrating anyhow?'

'I've give in my notice at the café,' Sarah Kelling said. She sat Billy down in a chair pulled up to the kitchen table, cut him a piece of fruit cake and then poured the bright red fizzy drink into his Bakelite mug. 'You'll never guess what's happened, Kathy! I had two answers to me advert in this morning's post; both of 'em meant to come round to the house this morning since, I suppose, they thought I were always at home and would be able to see them then. You'd gone off before the post were delivered, so I rushed round to the café and told Anita – she's the most senior of the waitresses – to hold the fort for me. I were lucky though; Mrs McNab, the café owner, popped in to have a word and when I explained the situation she said to take the day off and if the gentlemen took the rooms and I wanted to leave at the end of the week, they would manage. She were really nice, Kathy; she said I'd pulled the place up and she'd give me a first class reference when Billy starts school if there weren't no place for me in Dorothy's Tearooms.'

'Mam! You're not trying to tell me you've got two lodgers already,' Kathy squeaked. 'I can't believe it, after all the time we've spent trying to get a lady!' She pulled up a chair and helped herself to a slice of fruitcake. 'Who are they – the lodgers, I mean? Are they old? Young? Did they like the rooms? Do they want full board or just breakfast? Oh, Mam, I know you love your job but I were gettin' so worried that there'd be no one to look after Billy! It'll be grand to have you home all day.'

Sarah Kelling laughed and shook her head reprovingly at her daughter. 'What a heap o' questions! Now where shall I start? Well, one of 'em's twenty-six – that's Mr Philpott. He works at the Huskisson Goods Station so Daisy Street is right convenient for him.'

'And the second feller?' Kathy said when her mother did not immediately volunteer the information. 'What's he like?'

Sarah shot her daughter a look, half laughing, half guilty. 'You know the second one,' she said. 'It's Sam Bracknell, the feller who came round from the Osterleys' that time. He got digs all right, but they were on the other side of the city and he said he's never been happy there. He had to catch two trams to get to his area and there weren't never no question of nipping back for a meal of an evening, or anything like that. He said he missed the friendliness of the flower streets and his new digs were a big old house, converted into single rooms for unattached gentlemen. There were fourteen of 'em and they shared one kitchen and one bathroom. I felt real sorry for him so he's coming at the weekend and we've agreed on a month's trial for all parties. That's Mr Philpott as well,' she ended.

'Well – I'm – blessed!' Kathy said slowly, gazing at her mother with awe. 'I thought you felt Mr Bracknell was too – too dashing and foreign looking. Me and Jane thought he were the handsomest feller we'd ever come across outside o' the cinema, but you said something about his being kind o' dangerous.'

'Did I say that?' Sarah Kelling said vaguely. 'Well, I shouldn't have jumped to conclusions. He *is* very handsome in a – a foreign sort of way, but just because a feller's handsome that doesn't mean he's unreliable. Anyway, it's only for a month. If we don't care for one another, then both parties will agree to leave and no hard feelings. It were Mr Bracknell's idea, actually,' she added. 'He drew up a sort of contract, just to set me mind at ease.' She fished in the pockets of her overall and pushed the piece of paper she had produced towards her daughter. 'Read it; it seems fair enough to me.'

Kathy took the paper and read it. As her mother had said, it was simple, yet the wording made it clear that there was to be a trial period of a month for the Kelling family and their two lodgers. At the end of that time, either party could terminate the agreement, giving a week's notice.

Having read the paper, Kathy laughed across at her mother, her eyes full of mischief. 'It's a grand idea, Mam, but hasn't it occurred to you that you aren't the only landlady who has felt a little anxious over having Mr Bracknell as a lodger?' She tapped the paper with her forefinger. 'This is all writ down legal like so I'll be bound he's done it before when changing lodgings. But even so, it's a sensible precaution. After you've lived in the same house as someone else for a month, it might be difficult to give them notice, might lead to ill feeling, but this way it's all part of the agreement.'

'I'm glad you think I've done the right thing,' Mrs Kelling said, pouring herself a cup of tea and stirring a spoonful of sugar into it. 'Mr Philpott and Mr Bracknell will both be arriving on Saturday afternoon so you'll be able to give them the once over before you start back to school next week. They've agreed to pay a week in advance and they're paying extra for laundry. Apparently, that's quite common these days. I told them I'd do a hot dinner on a Sunday at midday and an evening meal to be served promptly at half past six on weekdays. Saturdays and Sundays, we'll just do what you might call high tea, and I've told 'em both that I'll want to know by breakfast time each morning if they mean to be out and miss a meal. No point in wasting good food,' she added virtuously.

'Well, I think we've been really lucky,' Kathy remarked, pouring herself some red fizzy drink. 'I can't wait to see Jane's face when I tell her who is going to be lodging at our house, come the weekend!'

At the end of the month, it was already clear that the Kellings were lucky in their lodgers. Mr Philpott was a fair-haired, rather nervous young man, who always thanked the Kellings effusively for any small act of kindness, no matter how trivial. It was soon obvious that his previous digs had not been good ones and his appreciation of Mrs Kelling's cooking and the comfort of her home seemed almost beyond belief. One Sunday, he accompanied Kathy and Jane to the nearest park, where they meant to take the younger children to play on the swings. He told Kathy then that his parents had died when he was only five and he had been brought up by an aunt who grudged him each moment of her time and every mouthful of food he ate. When he started work, his first landlady had been very little better, taking it for granted that he would be content with small helpings of poor quality food and showing no interest in him as a person. Kathy, looking into his rather watery blue eyes, could not help thinking that Mr Philpott's own attitude might be partly responsible for the way he had been treated. He was so very apologetic, so keen to merge into the background and to make no trouble, that she supposed a mean and niggardly landlady would begin to take advantage of him as soon as she got to know him. He described his last lodgings, with a Mrs Bryant who lived in Dryden Street in Bootle, and Kathy's heart bled for him. Apparently, she had had quite a nice house but Mr Philpott had lived in half a partitioned attic room where he had frozen in winter and baked in summer. He was Mrs Bryant's only lodger – she had a large family – and was always served last at mealtimes, getting only the scraps of food which other members of the family had not taken. That he had stuck with Mrs Bryant for three long years showed, Kathy thought, that he really had no backbone; anyone else would have insisted on their rights since he had paid Mrs Bryant the same money that he was paying the Kellings. According to his own admission, Mr Philpott had accepted this treatment and had only written to Mrs Kelling in desperation because Mrs Bryant had decided she needed his room now that her children were growing up.

Jane, of course, had listened to this recital as well as Kathy and, when Mr Philpott left them, gave her friend a speaking glance, placed one forefinger on her left temple and waggled it in the well-known gesture meaning that she considered Mr Philpott to be only ten pence in the shilling. 'He's norra bad chap; quite nice looking if you don't mind watery eyes and a pink nose,' she observed, as soon as it was safe to talk, which meant when the children, with whoops of excitement, had set off for the swings. 'He's awful weedy, but I suppose that's due to never being fed properly. Well, if there's one thing your mam's first rate at, it's cooking and feedin' folk, so I dare say she'll put some flesh on his bones. If only he had a better opinion of himself! But there, if we'd been treated the way he's been treated, we'd begin to believe we weren't of much account.' She glanced at Kathy through her lashes. 'How different from the glamorous Mr Bracknell! He's got a very good opinion of himself, wouldn't you say?'

Kathy laughed. 'I know he's good looking but, to do him justice, I don't think he knows it, or at least he acts perfectly normally and even seems sorry for Mr Philpott,' she said. 'They are completely different, though. Mr Bracknell has heaps of friends and goes off at weekends on rambling expeditions into North Wales, or he catches a bus into the countryside and has a day out with his pals. He really isn't in the house much, though the pair of 'em turn up regular as clockwork at mealtimes. Mr Bracknell sometimes says: "Thank you very much, Mrs Kelling, that was delicious", but he doesn't spread it on too thick, if you see what I mean. The lodgers get the same breakfast every morning – porridge and bacon and egg, lucky blighters – but Mr Philpott always says what a good breakfast and thanks Mam before going off to work. You'd think he was frightened of being given notice, only the month's well up and there's no question of it. We get along like a house on fire and they're both good wi' Billy. They chat to him, mealtimes, and don't mind givin' an eye to him if Mam's busy with the meal and I'm finishing off me homework. I tell you, Jane, I dreaded having lodgers sharing the house, but it's turned out to be better than having Mam out at the café all day.'

'The money must help,' Jane acknowledged. The two of them were sitting on a green-painted wooden bench, watching the children playing on the swings, and now Jane delved into her shabby black handbag and produced a roll of mints, which she offered to her friend. 'Want one?' she enquired. 'I put a packet of digestive biscuits and a bottle o' water into the pram in case the kids got hungry before we got home. How's school, by the way? Did I tell you Mrs Mitchell is puttin' me money up? She thinks I'm capable of takin' over from her two days a week – it'll be Tuesdays an' Wednesdays – so I'll have a bit more money for meself because Mam won't take any more off of me.'

'No, you never said,' Kathy assured her friend. She sighed a trifle enviously. 'I'm still doing my Saturday job – working in the kitchens at Dorothy's Tearooms – but I give the money to me mam. After all, she gives me a really good carry-out each day and the things I need for school aren't cheap, so I can't complain, but it would be nice to have a few pennies to spend from time to time.'

'Why don't you ask Dorothy's if they would take you on evenings?' Jane suggested. 'They must need help in the kitchen just as much then as on Saturdays.'

Kathy shook her head. 'No, there's a woman comes in regular to wash up, clean down, clear away and the like but she doesn't do Saturdays. Anyway, I get such a lot of homework that by the time I've helped Mam with the evening meal and washed up afterwards it's finish off my schoolwork and then straight to bed. I told Mam I'd be willing to do a job after school, but she's dead against it. She says we can manage on what's coming in and I think she's right. After all, I do the messages, Jane, and I couldn't spend so much time finding where the bargains are if I were working as well.'

Jane agreed and presently, as the afternoon began to darken into dusk, the girls piled the little ones into the pram and set off for Daisy Street once more. They walked briskly for the autumn air was growing chilly and Kathy could not help thinking, rather wistfully, that it looked like being a long time before she would be able to gain a measure of independence by working for her own living. Recently, she and her mother had been invited up to the high school to discuss her future. Miss Beaver had waxed enthusiastic over Kathy's abilities and had assured Mrs Kelling that, if she would allow her to do so, Kathy was quite capable of gaining both her School Certificate and her Higher. 'And then, of course, there would be university entrance,' she said briskly, her small brown eyes bright with enthusiasm. 'It isn't often that we have a scholarship girl as gifted as Katherine, Mrs Kelling. With three years at university and a degree to her name, there are few heights she could not attain. Her future would be assured, if only she can remain at school.'

Kathy had longed to object, to say that it was not fair on her mother, or her little brother, but she had scarcely taken breath to speak before her mother cut in. 'I agree completely, Miss Beaver,' Mrs Kelling had said. 'Kathy is a very bright girl and deserves her chance.'

Miss Beaver had smiled indulgently. 'Katherine does very well,' she said. She had risen to her feet and walked round the desk, shaking Mrs Kelling's hand warmly. 'Thank you for your time, Mrs Kelling. You have relieved my mind. So many girls have potential but are unable to fulfil it because of family circumstances. I'm glad that Katherine will not be one of them. Good afternoon to you both.'

'Penny for your thoughts, Kathy?' Jane said suddenly, bringing Kathy back to the present with a jerk. Above their heads, the street lamps were beginning to glow, and the yellow light streaming from the shop windows as they passed made Kathy even more aware of how the year was slipping away. Soon it would be November; the curtains would be drawn early and Mrs Kelling would prepare stews and casseroles to line their stomachs after a hard day's work. She and Billy would get out their winter coats and mufflers and they would begin to look forward to Christmas. She remembered last Christmas, how sad and bereft they had been and how passionately she had missed their father. She would miss him still, perhaps she would always do so, but she knew that the presence of the lodgers would add a new dimension to Christmas. It would not be fair on either Mr Philpott or Mr Bracknell to mope around, shedding tears into the turkey. She and her mother would have to put aside memories of other Christmases and face the different life which her father's death had brought about.

'Kathy! Will you stop gazin' at nothin' and answer me,' Jane said, only half laughing. 'Honest to God, girl, wharra dreamer you are! I asked you what you were thinkin' about, remember?'

'Sorry, Jane,' Kathy said contritely. 'I were thinking about Christmas. Last year was awful, what wi' me dad's death and Billy's illness and everything. But this year should be better, don't you think? I mean, we can't show a long face to the lodgers. Mam always tries to be cheerful and bright and, of course, I follow suit.'

'But suppose they go home for Christmas?' Jane said. 'Lots of lodgers do, so I'm told. I know Mr Philpott were brought up by an aunt but that don't mean to say he might not go off for the holiday. Damn it all, Kathy, there must have been someone in his past life who were good to him! After all, he's twenty-six or twenty-seven, isn't he?'

Kathy gnawed her underlip. 'I suppose Mr Bracknell might go to relatives,' she said doubtfully. 'Or to friends for that matter. But I don't reckon Mr Philpott will go far from Daisy Street, and I'm not sorry. It'll be better for Mam and me to have company over Christmas.'

'I expect you're right,' Jane said, though a trifle doubtfully. It was clear that she could not visualise a Christmas which was not strictly a family affair. Jane's parents both came from large families and it was their custom, each year, to share out the Christmas holiday between them so that, in actual fact, Mrs O'Brien only cooked a Christmas dinner once in every four or five years since everyone took a turn at being host to the rest of the family. Kathy had frequently been asked to Christmas tea at whichever O'Brien household was host that year and had thoroughly enjoyed herself. Kitchens were cleared of everything but chairs and cushions and the entire family joined in guessing games, charades, Chinese whispers and the like. But she had always been glad to return to her own quiet fireside, to lean against Dad's knee while he read Billy a story or to mastermind the setting out of chestnuts on the fire bars, where they could be roasted to a turn and then hooked off and crunched down as soon as they were cool enough.

Walking beside Jane, who was now chattering about recent developments at Daisy Street School which Tilly had passed on to her, Kathy allowed her mind to return to their lodgers. They were such complete opposites: Mr Bracknell so very hail-fellow-well-met and clearly far more experienced in worldly matters than Mr Philpott, doubtless owing to the fact that he had been married once. He had only recently told Sarah Kelling the sad story of a young wife who had died in childbirth after just a year of marriage. Sarah had been touched by this sad story and had wondered why he had not remarried, though it seemed tactless to ask him to his face. Kathy, however, had asked Mr Bracknell outright why he did not have a lady friend and he had given her a quick, amused glance before replying: 'What makes you think I haven't, Miss Poke-Nose? I shall call you Keyhole Kate, after the girl in the comic, if you keep trying to discover me dark secrets.'

Kathy had been confused by this ambiguous reply and had decided to keep an eye on Mr Bracknell. He was so very good looking; any woman would be glad to receive his attention, she felt sure. Perhaps he really did have a lady friend – perhaps he even had half a dozen – but if so, he never brought anyone back to

Daisy Street and had never been spotted by either the Kellings or the O'Briens with a female companion.

Mr Philpott, Kathy was sure, had never had a lady friend in his entire life. He was so bashful and quiet, and came home every evening and either sat by the fire, reading a book, or went to his room. Of course he went out occasionally – he belonged to a railway-men's club and sometimes spent the evening there – but Kathy was certain that none of these outings were taken in the company of young ladies. If Mr Philpott was in the kitchen when Jane came round to visit, he would turn red as a beetroot and sit hunched over his book, eyes fixed on the page, though Kathy had been unable to help noticing that he did not continue to read but stared at the same page for twenty minutes. If the girls began to laugh and chat and he felt himself forgotten, he would remain in the room, but if they glanced towards him or tried to include him in the conversation, he would quickly mumble an excuse and leave them.

'Kathy Kelling, I don't think you've been listening to a word I've said,' Jane said accusingly, as they turned into Daisy Street. 'I were going to tell you about Jimmy McCabe but I'm sure I don't see why I should. You aren't a bit interested in all the thrilling news of life at Daisy Street School so I suppose you won't be interested in Jimmy either.'

Kathy cast her friend a reproachful glance. Jimmy McCabe seemed to take a positive pleasure in making snide remarks about Kathy's school, her uniform and even her ambitions. He told her, whenever he saw her, that she ought to be in a job, like every other girl of her age, not wasting her time gadding around in a fancy uniform. Kathy knew very well that Jane would probably have explained the situation to him, told him that she was remaining at school in order to get a much better paid job when she eventually left, but it made no difference to Jimmy. He enjoyed taunting her and making her mad as fire and wouldn't stop, she imagined, until she left school and took a job of some description. She doubted that he knew about her job at Dorothy's Tearooms and she was grateful to Jane for not informing him of it because he would certainly jeer at the idea of "Little Miss White Socks" up to her elbows in greasy water every Saturday.

'I'm not interested in Jimmy; so far as I'm concerned, he's just a pest of a boy who likes nothing better than riling me,' Kathy said frankly. 'I don't know how you can stand him, Jane, but I suppose he isn't as nasty to you as he is to me. What's he done, anyway?'

'He's gone and got himself a better job than an office boy in that typewriter repair shop,' Jane said proudly. 'He's a delivery boy for the butcher on Heyworth Street. He gets paid nearly twice as much and he's gorra delivery bike, provided by the firm – it's a big old-fashioned thing and heavy as lead, Jimmy says – but when he's old enough, Mr McCready means to teach him to drive the van 'cos the old feller what drives it now is seventy if he's a day. Then it'll be a real good job because he'll take the van down to the markets to pick out animals for slaughter and then he'll collect the carcasses from the slaughter house and bring them back to Heyworth Street.' She glanced rather shyly at her friend. 'He – he's asked me to go to the Broadway on the Stanley Road with him one evenin' this week, to see the new film they're showing, starring Katherine Hepburn and Cary Grant. What do you think of that?'

Kathy looked at Jane with a most unfamiliar

sinking feeling in her stomach. It wasn't just that she disliked Jimmy McCabe. She suddenly realised that what she most disliked was change, and Jane going out with Jimmy was a change indeed. In fact, it would change everything. She thought of her total reliance on Jane's companionship. The two of them had been as close as sisters – closer – for as long as she could remember. It had been a blow when Jane started work and she remained at school but how much worse it was to realise that she would no longer be able to take Jane's company for granted. Kathy had no interest in boys, or at least not in boys like Jimmy McCabe, but she realised that if Jane had a boyfriend and she herself had none, their closeness could no longer be taken for granted. Jane would have secrets from her, or if not secrets at least experiences which she would not want to share.

Kathy stared at her friend, seeing for the first time how much Jane had changed since she started work. Jane's figure had burgeoned; she had a bust and wore a brassiere. She even wore silk stockings sometimes, though not, of course, in summer. Kathy's eyes glanced down at her own flat chest, which simply refused to provide her with anything to put in a brassiere. She had often envied Jane her height, her blonde curls and her slender figure but she had not realised, until this very moment, that Jane had matured into a young woman whilst she, Kathy, was still a child. Jane's hair was fashionably cut, and Kathy knew that the slogan "Friday night is Amami night" held true for her friend, though for herself she still ducked her head in the bath and rubbed it with whatever soap her mother provided. Shampoo was expensive but Jane obviously considered it worth every penny. And now she's got herself a boyfriend, I suppose she'll not want to mess around with someone still in school, Kathy thought dismally. I've got Ruby as my friend, of course, and I like Eunice, the Saturday girl at Dorothy's Tearooms, but neither of them could possibly take Jane's place. Oh, whatever will I do without the O'Briens?

'Well?' Jane said impatiently. 'And you needn't look as though you'd lost a quid and found a copper. I'm only going to the cinema with him, for God's sake!'

Kathy pulled herself together. 'Oh, I know, I know, and if it's what you want, I'm really glad for you,' she gabbled. 'It's – it's just that you and me have always gone to the flicks together; done almost everything together, come to that. I'd not – not noticed how grown up you were, Janey, and it's made me see . . . well, that things are going to change. You'll have Jimmy to confide in and – and you won't want me any more.'

'Of course I will, you fool,' Jane said roundly as they turned into Daisy Street. 'You're me best pal, always have been, always will be. There's all sorts of things I could never talk about to Jimmy, no matter how much I liked him, but I can tell *you* anything. And anyway, you'll have a boyfriend of your own soon enough. We're the same age, after all. It's just that you're wrapped up in your schoolwork and – and it's kind o' left me at a loose end, sometimes. Don't you worry. We'll be goin' out in a foursome – you and your feller, me and Jimmy – before we're much older.'

Kathy agreed rather doubtfully, knowing that Jane was doing her best to lessen the blow she had dealt her friend, but the hollow feeling inside her stomach persisted, and when she got to bed at last she cried a

113

few tears into her pillow. She knew everyone grew up, she knew that things had to change, but she did not have to like it.

Christmas arrived amidst all the usual excitement. Neither Mr Philpott nor Mr Bracknell went off to visit friends, though her mother told Kathy that Mr Bracknell had assured her he had had plenty of invitations for the holiday and would accept one of them if Mrs Kelling wished it. Mrs Kelling, however, had told him that she would like him to stay and had been delighted when he had come in shortly before Christmas and told her that she need not worry about providing a bird for the great day.

'I've a client on the Scotland Road who gives me a ham and a goose on Christmas Eve, every year,' he told her. 'I get all sorts at Christmas – bags of nuts, oranges, a pineapple and more boxes of chocolates and bottles of Guinness than you'd believe. I'll bring 'em all in as they're handed out to me, which should mean we'll have a grand Christmas and won't have to worry about the expense.'

'I suppose you have to buy presents as some sort of return for the Christmas boxes you're given,' Mrs Kelling had observed, the first time Mr Bracknell came into the kitchen and dumped a large bag, full of groceries, on the kitchen table. 'Can I make a contribution to what you have to spend? Only I had saved up to buy Christmas fare and you're welcome . . .'

'The firm sees to that,' Mr Bracknell said cheerfully. 'I get a supply of very handsome diaries and address books and a great many coloured pencils and colouring books for the children, so it won't be necessary for me to spend my own money, save in a few cases.'

Mrs Kelling told her daughter, however, that they would have to buy Mr Bracknell something really nice as a return for his generosity. He was a pipe smoker so they decided on a curly briar with a silver band around the mouthpiece and a smart leather pouch full of his favourite tobacco to go with it. In order not to appear to have favourites, the Kellings bought Mr Philpott a smart leather wallet, since his own was so worn and threadbare that you could almost see the money through it. Kathy had been inclined to think this unfair to Mr Bracknell, but was glad of her mother's foresight when, on Christmas morning, Mr Philpott came down to breakfast carrying three attractively wrapped parcels. Mrs Kelling's gift was a beautifully crocheted tablecloth of cream-coloured lace, whilst Kathy and Billy were given scarlet woollen caps, scarves and gloves. Mrs Kelling was delighted with the tablecloth and insisted on spreading it over the table at once and presently, after Mr Philpott and Mr Bracknell had exclaimed with pleasure over their own gifts, she served up the roast goose and they all sat round the table, enjoying their food and in very good charity with one another.

After the meal, the men sat on either side of the hearth in the front parlour and snoozed whilst Kathy and her mother did the washing up and cleared the kitchen table so that it would be ready for tea. As they were finishing off, Mr Philpott came through and said that he and Mr Bracknell had decided to go for a walk since they had to take some exercise in order to make room for the tea their landlady was preparing. The two men set off together into the cold afternoon, and in due course Mrs Kelling got Billy's pushchair out from its nook under the stairs and said she thought it would do them good to follow their lodgers' example. 'I dare say you won't want a whole day to pass without seeing Jane,' she said as she wrapped Billy's brand new scarf around his small throat. 'They won't be at home, mind – it's Jane's Aunt Edith's turn this year – but a walk up to Alfonso Road will be quite pleasant and if we go by the Kirkdale Rec then Billy can have a play on the swings.'

Billy gave a crow of delight at the thought and very soon the three of them were making their way along Fountains Road, enjoying the briskness of the cold air after the warm and rather stuffy kitchen. They stopped for a quarter of an hour so that Billy might swing and clamber up the slide, but it was no afternoon for standing around and Kathy and her mother were glad enough to pop Billy back into the pushchair and set off once more, sure of a welcome in Edith O'Brien's happy if overcrowded home.

Jane was delighted to see her friends and anxious to show off her presents; a handful of ribbons and hair slides had come from aunts and uncles and brothers and sisters whilst her parents had contributed a smart chiffon scarf to go with her best dress and a pair of the precious silk stockings which Jane loved to wear. Kathy noticed a little silver necklace from which dangled the letter J, and asked whence it came, though she knew very well what the answer would be. 'It's from Jimmy,' Jane said, a becoming blush turning her cheeks pink and making her eyes shine. 'But look what Aunt Edie bought for all of us to share! It's that new game, Monopoly, and it's ever such fun. We've already had one game – do you want to have a go, Kathy?'

'I'd love to play, but I don't know what time Mam told the lodgers to come back for tea,' Kathy explained, looking longingly at the board. Girls at school had talked about the fascinating new craze which was beginning to sweep Britain as, earlier in the year, it had swept the United States of America. 'They've gone for a walk to work up an appetite for tea – Mr Philpott and Mr Bracknell, I mean. We'll have to be back before them, because we never said we were going out as well.'

'Ask your mam,' Jane advised. 'It isn't a hard game; you can learn how to play as you go along. A whole game takes ages, of course, but we could start one up and then, when you have to leave, Tilly or one of the cousins could take over your place.'

Kathy's mother, exchanging banter with Aunt Edie and Mrs O'Brien, told Kathy that it was quite all right for her to remain in Alfonso Road for a while. 'I told the lodgers we'd be serving high tea at six, but there's no need for you to come home so early,' she assured her daughter. 'There's almost no preparation because I boiled the ham yesterday and all the rest's cold. So you stay here and enjoy yourself.' She turned to Mrs O'Brien. 'Kathy works real hard to see that the lodgers get their meals on time.'

Kathy was as pleased by the praise as she was by the prospect of playing this grand new game with her pals, but nevertheless determined to leave just before six. There would be nothing to do towards tea, perhaps, but she knew her mother liked to have her around so that she could see that Billy ate his food and didn't simply play. Her mam also liked her to keep an eye on the lodgers because Mr Philpott was so shy that he would never take a second helping unless pressed to do so. It was only lately that he had begun to request that the bread and butter be passed, so Kathy had formed the habit of anticipating his wishes, seeing that everything he needed was within reach and handing such things as the sauce bottle or the cruet without waiting to be asked.

As luck would have it, Jimmy McCabe came through the front door at a quarter to six. As soon as he spotted the game of Monopoly in progress, he went over to Jane, rested one hand lightly on her shoulder, and began to advise her how to play, taking not the slightest notice of Kathy.

There were groans of protest from the other players at this uncalled for interference but Kathy, though she sighed as she stood up, offered to let him take her place and held out the rather thin collection of banknotes that still remained to her and the cards containing the details of the properties she had bought. 'Look, Jimmy, it's time I were heading home anyhow, and since it's clear you're determined to have your say you might as well do it properly and take my place,' she said resignedly. 'I've got to get home now, otherwise I'll miss me tea.' She turned to her hostess, who was sitting on the couch playing gin rummy with three of the other adults. 'Thanks ever so much for having me, Aunt Edie . . . I mean Mrs O'Brien,' she said politely. 'I reckon that Monopoly is the best present you could have given me pals and I expect we'll play it often because it's a grand game. It makes you feel really rich!'

The O'Briens were a hospitable crowd and urged her to remain and have her tea with them, but Kathy was firm. Jimmy, who was sorting out money and the properties which Kathy had handed him, looked up and spoke to her for the first time. 'You plannin' to go alone?' he said gruffly. 'Best not; I suppose me and Jane ought to walk you home.'

It was said grudgingly and Kathy answered in the same spirit. 'Thank you *so* much, but I wouldn't dream of troubling you,' she said frostily. 'I'm quite capable of walking half a mile without putting anyone out and I can see you're longing to start spending my money and taking the rent on my properties.'

Jimmy mumbled something but Kathy was already heading towards the door and soon found herself trudging along Alfonso Road, glancing curiously at the brightly lit windows as she passed. Most of the rooms into which she peered were decorated with paper chains, holly and mistletoe and Kathy thought it was like passing half a dozen stage sets, for the people inside, playing games, wearing paper hats, pulling crackers, were totally unconscious of the watcher outside in the cold.

It really was cold too, and of course full dark, though it was a clear night and high above the rooftops the stars twinkled frostily down, reminding Kathy of that other Christmas Day, when the three wise men had converged on the stable in which the Baby lay, enthroned in his manger. She crossed Rumney Road West, then hesitated. The obvious way home from here was to go along North Dingle, but for the first time it occurred to her that because there were no houses flanking the road on either side – it ran between the recreation ground on one side and the school on the other, passing right through the Kirkdale until it met Orwell Road – it would mean a rather dark and lonely walk. However, she decided she would prefer it to going via Melrose Road, which would have meant passing the sawmills. She could never see the yard without remembering her father's death, so, squaring her shoulders, she set off along the North Dingle.

She had passed the school and was level with the

bowling greens when she thought she heard a slight sound behind her. At this point, mature trees overhung the road, so when she looked back she could see nothing. By now, she was approaching the stretch where the road actually ran through the tannery, whose buildings loomed huge and black only a few yards ahead of her, and for some unaccountable reason there was a long gap between lamps. The smell from the tannery was strong on the air but a glance towards the buildings convinced Kathy that the place was not working. Once more she glanced back but could see nothing, and telling herself not to be an idiot she pressed on. Rounding the bend, she saw the lights on Orwell Road with considerable relief. Without realising it, she had quickened her pace, but now she slowed, chiding herself for being over-imaginative. It was Christmas Day, after all; why should anyone be lurking with evil intent down such an ill-lit and unfrequented road?

Kathy hurried on, but now she thought she could hear something right behind her. Before she could so much as turn her head, a hand had gripped her arm, then slid down as though to try to take her fingers, whilst a man's voice spoke in her ear, his tone scarcely above a whisper. 'Don't be afraid. I don't mean to hurt you. I – I like you so much! Oh, stay still. I swear you'll be awright if you just stay still! I been watchin' you wi' that other girl, the yaller-headed one . . . an' . . . an' I do so want . . . you're so pretty. You've got lovely hair . . . lovely an' smooth an' shiny . . .'

Kathy drew in her breath for a desperate scream and the man heard her quick inhalation and his other hand covered her mouth. 'I said don't move, an' that means don't scream! All I want, I swear it, is just to talk to you! I tell you you're safe as houses. It's just . . . it's just . . .'

Kathy gave a desperate wriggle and the man laughed breathlessly. 'I'm a deal stronger than you, you pretty thing,' he said. 'I just want a kiss and mebbe a bit of a cuddle . . . it's Christmas, after all! Come on, give us a kiss!'

It occurred to Kathy at this point that the man must definitely be drunk. If he had seen her with Jane, and still thought her pretty, he must be clear out of his mind, but if he had drunk too deeply . . . She stopped wriggling and stood quite still for a moment, and as the hand across her mouth relaxed she spoke quickly, before he could gag her again. 'You scared me – it's awful dark – but if a kiss is all you want . . .'

'Oh, it is, I swear it! If you'll only put your arms up round me neck, so I can cuddle you properly . . .'

Kathy pretended to relax, actually leaned towards the dark figure . . . and then she ducked quickly and began to run. In the distance she could see a street lamp gleaming; once she reached the main road she was sure he would not pursue her.

As luck would have it, however, she did not even need to gain the main road for even as she set out in that direction she heard the sound of several voices drawing nearer and saw the outline of heads bobbing against the lamplight. There was a good deal of laughter, and then the clearer sound of voices, voices which presently began to sing 'God rest ye merry, gentlemen' in a very jolly, if inebriated way. Behind her, there came the sound of someone abruptly skidding to a halt, and then a voice said: 'I didn't mean no harm; don't set the scuffers on me, missy,' and then – oh joy – the sound of her attacker's footsteps fading as he ran off in the opposite direction.

Kathy straightened her coat and looked around her for her hat, then decided that it would have to remain where it was until the following day; she did not intend to stay in this narrow, dark lane searching for it! Instead, she set out towards the men, saying as she did so: 'Excuse me, but would you mind walking back to the main road with me? Only some feller . . . I dare say he's harmless, but he gave me ever such a fright . . .'

The men paused, staring into the darkness, then one of them exclaimed sharply, and came over to her. Kathy realised she must have been all but invisible in the dark and moved into the circle of light from the torches they carried. 'He's probably harmless . . .' she began again, and was suddenly aware of how very shaken she was and how very frightened she had been. She gave a gulp and her words trailed off into silence as the men gathered about her. Reaction was setting in and she began to tremble, though she told herself pretty sharply to pull herself together and simply be glad that the group of men had come along just at the right time.

'What feller?' one of the men said quickly. 'Did he try it on, queen? Which way did he go? Did you gerra look at his phiz? By God, wharra way to carry on, and it's Christmas, an' all. Here, fellers, this gal's been attacked! Which way did he go did you say, queen?'

'He ran off towards Rumney Road,' she said. 'He – he kept sayin' all he wanted was a kiss, but he grabbed hold of me . . . I was scared . . . Oh dear, I think . . . I think . . .'

Her stomach gave a convulsive lurch and poor Kathy was sick at the feet of her rescuers.

*

The men had all been drinking but their kindness and concern could not have been doubted. They sympathised with Kathy over her fright, and four or five of them set out to look for her attacker. They had no luck, but they brought back her pretty little hat. Then they took her all the way home, though two of their number peeled off, announcing firmly that they were going straight to the police station and would bring the scuffers round to Daisy Street so that her attacker could be traced. This was the last thing Kathy wanted, but when she explained what had happened to Mrs Kelling and the lodgers, they agreed that this was the proper course. When the scuffers arrived, they asked for a description of her attacker but Kathy was able to tell them very little, save that the man was taller than she, had been dressed all in black, or some other dark colour, and had had some sort of covering – a balaclava perhaps – which completely hid his face and neck.

'Well, missy, we'll do our best to catch the feller but I dare say he's miles away by now,' the large police sergeant told Kathy. 'I don't want to worry you, queen, but you did a foolish thing, going out alone in the dark down the North Dingle. The lighting's awful poor and it's just the sort o' place a feller would lurk if he were up to no good. Didn't you have no pal who could have walked home with you?'

'Someone did offer,' Kathy admitted grudgingly. 'He's me best friend's feller, though, and he doesn't like me very much. If I'd have said yes and let him come with me, he'd have spent the whole walk being rude about me.'

'Well, I should have thought a bit of teasing might have been preferable to strangulation,' the policeman said bluntly. 'Oh, I know you said all he wanted was a kiss and a cuddle, but that's what they all say; you've had a narrer escape, young lady. There's been a feller what's attacked a couple o' girls in the past month. He's not killed anyone yet, but he's not had many of the kisses he's asked for, either, an' fellers like that can easily get desperate an' end up hurtin' someone real bad. So in future, queen, you make certain sure you go walkin' at night with someone you know and trust, right?'

Kathy agreed, with a shudder, that she would be more careful in future, but despite the fright the man had given her she was determined to forget the incident as soon as she possibly could. She had been incredibly foolish to enter that dark lane alone but it had taught her a lesson. In future, I will think before I act, she told herself firmly, but I won't let it spoil my holiday for me and I won't be too proud to accept someone's company another time, either.

Chapter Six

Summer 1937

It was a hot and sunny day and Kathy had done well in the end of term examinations. She had been looking forward to the holiday which stretched ahead, thinking that she would be able to find a job and actually earn some money, but, yesterday, her mother had returned to Dorothy's Tearooms to work over the summer holidays, moving from one restaurant to another to cover for people away on their annual breaks.

Mrs Kelling had been delighted at the offer of work – and well paid work, too – for eight weeks over the summer, but though she had promised to give Kathy money for clothes her daughter was still extremely disappointed. Because Jane was in work full time now, Kathy had grown closer to Ruby, and the two girls had meant to go job hunting together. There were always a few summer jobs going at the big stores in the city centre, or even at somewhere like New Brighton. The journey to and from the seaside resort would involve a bus ride and then the ferry crossing. It would have been exciting, an adventure! Looking after Billy from dawn till dusk was neither, though it could be a worrying experience, for Billy was still subject to fits, so to Kathy's disappointment over the loss of a possible job was added the task of being a permanent child minder when she had hoped for some independence.

What was more, Kathy's school uniform had

reached the stage when not even the most careful darning and patching could disguise the fact that it was in danger of falling apart. It was also very much too small for her, the dark green tunic – paled by many washes – so short as to be almost indecent and the once cream blouse, greying round collars and cuffs, strained at its buttons to such an extent that Kathy had sewn little loops on the edge of the material to prolong its life as much as possible. Her green school cardigan would never again be done up and the sleeves had grown matted the way wool does after repeated tubbing, so that she usually pushed her sleeves up to hide the fact that they were both felted and far too short. One of the teachers constantly ordered her to pull her sleeves down unless she was training as a washerwoman, and although the others were, in the main, a little kinder, Kathy knew that her fellow pupils – and not only Marcia and Cynthia – were beginning to make remarks behind her back. Someone had asked her why she could not let down her hem because when she bent over her bloomers showed, and though the remark had not been meant spitefully but more as a joke it had unfortunate consequences. Later that same day, Isobella, the other scholarship girl, who was a good deal taller than Kathy, had offered to pass on her own last year's tunic since her mother had recently bought a new one. Kathy knew she should have accepted gratefully but, unfortunately, her pride had spoken first. 'Thank you, Isobella, but I'm not yet in need of charity,' she had said coolly. 'I'll get a new one in the autumn term because we'll be in summer dresses quite soon now.'

Isobella had turned away, flushing hotly, and since then relations between the two girls had been very strained, though Kathy had done her best to make amends by being particularly friendly whenever their paths crossed.

Jane, of course, sympathised deeply with Kathy's plight but could offer no easy solution. All through the year, Kathy and her mother had to survive on the money from the lodgers; the salary which Sarah would be bringing in from Dorothy's Tearooms would see them clothed and fed, but would not run to the sorts of prices paid in a shop such as Browns on Clayton Square.

'Why don't you go for something from the market? It might not be exactly the same as the things they made you buy when you started school, but surely folk wouldn't notice?' Jane had suggested. 'I dunno as I've ever seen a tunic in that particular shade of green, but what about dyeing one? You see grey ones all the time in Paddy's market. An' them little badges what's sewn on the right breast and on the pocket of the blazer . . . well, couldn't you cut them off your old ones?

Kathy looked doubtful. 'I'm willing to try anything, but first of all I've got to earn some money. I've got by without wearing my blazer all through the summer and we don't wear them in the winter, so that's something I don't have to face till next May.' So, naturally, she had been positively longing to earn some money.

'I doesn't need a coat, Kathy; it's a hot day, you know it is. I won't wear a coat nor that 'orrible 'at either.' Kathy was in the kitchen getting ready to go shopping and Billy's voice was perilously close to a whine. Kathy saw, with some dismay, that his cheeks were reddening and his lower lip was sticking out, a sure sign of troubled waters ahead. She sighed but continued to push his arms into the light cotton jacket. Billy was beginning to rebel against being 'bossed about', as he put it, by his elder sister and had decided, a couple of days previously, that his mam was the only one whom he would obey without question. This meant an argument every time Kathy told him to do something and she was already heartily sick of it. She knew that if Billy had been an O'Brien, he would have received a slap across the legs, but their mother did not approve of smacking and Kathy had to go along with her. Apart from anything else, she dreaded starting one of Billy's fits and knew she would never forgive herself if she made her little brother ill. So instead of telling him sharply to do as he was told, she began to reason with him, firmly inserting him into the jacket as she did so.

'Now come along, Billy, don't act daft, you're a big boy now. You know Mam would be upset if I took you to the shops without your jacket and cap. I know it's hot, but there's a nice breeze, and if you're a good boy I'll buy you some sweeties from Ma Kettle's.'

Billy muttered something beneath his breath and permitted his sister to button his jacket and put on his cap at a rakish angle, but when she lugged the pushchair out from its home beneath the stairs he uttered a wail of protest, seizing the handle and pushing it roughly back into its previous position, announcing roundly that he would not ride in the pushchair like a bleedin' baby but would walk along with her like the big boy she kept telling him he was.

Kathy thought about arguing, then changed her mind. She knew that in ordinary circumstances she would have taken it for granted that Billy would walk with her, for he was a sturdy lad and quite capable of doing so. Because of the possibility that he might have a fit, however, she preferred to take the push-chair, knowing that if he should collapse she could pop him into the chair and run to get help. For a moment, she considered going round to the O'Briens' and suggesting that they did their messages together. Mrs O'Brien had had another baby the previous March, so their old pram was still used regularly, but she decided that this was not such a good idea after all. She might be unable to persuade Billy to sit in the big pram, and when he got with the O'Brien children he speedily became over-excited and noisy, which was not, she thought, good for him. No, better to stick to her original plan and do half of her messages, then meet Ruby as arranged, so that they could do the other half together.

'All right, Billy, we won't take the pushchair, but if you get tired I'm not carrying you because you're far too heavy for me,' she warned him. 'And you'll have to do your share of carrying the messages because Mam wants a heap o' stuff and I don't want to have to go out twice in one day.'

'Why don't we go with the O'Briens?' Billy whined as Kathy handed him a large canvas bag and picked up another for herself. 'Then we could put the shopping in the pram with that 'orrible new baby of theirs.'

'It's horrible, not 'orrible . . . and anyway, it's a lovely little baby,' Kathy said hastily, all too aware that Billy frequently repeated her remarks out of context and at the worst possible moment. 'Besides, I'm meeting Ruby outside Beasler's at half past ten, and I don't mean to be late.'

'Tell you what, Kath,' Billy said, as his sister began to pull him towards the door, 'we could take the pushchair all folded up like until we reach the shops and then we could pile the full bags into it. I've only got lickle arms,' he added piteously. 'And when I carries heavy bags, they aches like anythin'. Jerry Waters says his mam makes him carry bags so heavy that by the time he's growed his knuckles will be brushing the floor. I don't want arms like a gorilla, does I, Kath?'

Kathy giggled at the thought of Billy with knuckles that scraped the pavement but decided that it was time Billy learned a lesson. 'No, Billy, if you don't want a ride in the pushchair, then we aren't taking it,' she said firmly. And then, seeing his wobbling lip and the tears filling his eyes, she added hastily: 'It's all right, silly. I'll carry the two big canvas bags and you can carry something light. Could you manage a bag of sticky buns and a few apples, do you think?'

Relieved that he was not to be used like a pack-horse, Billy agreed sunnily that sticky buns and apples would cause him no problems and the two of them set out, Billy chattering like a sparrow and dancing along beside her. He even consented to hold her hand, though this was something which he considered babyish and would not have done had they been with the O'Briens. Once the canvas bags began to fill up it was impossible to hold hands, but since Billy stuck close to her side it did not seem to matter. Very soon they reached the baker's shop and stood, Billy with his nose pressed to the glass, and examined the delicious contents of the window. Having weighed up the respective delights of sticky buns, iced buns or those knobbly but delicious objects known as rock cakes, they decided on the sticky buns because they would get more for their money, and went into the shop. Mrs Beasler came forward to serve them and, with her usual generosity, gave both children a small square of sponge cake. They left the shop eating busily and almost bumped into Ruby, who was hurrying along the pavement, her round face flushed and her plait of fair hair bouncing on her shoulder. As soon as she saw Kathy and Billy, the anxiety left her face and she beamed at them, slowing to a walk. 'I thought I were going to be late,' she said breathlessly. 'Me mam was so slow writing out her list, I thought I'd never get away. Have you just been into Beasler's? Only I've got to go in there for six iced buns, a large tin and three almond tarts.'

'We've been there already; we're on our way to the Charlotte Street market now,' Kathy said, consulting her list. 'But we can spare five minutes while you get your stuff. We can have a look in Kettle's while we're waiting, because I promised Billy some sweets if he was good.'

'An' I have been good, haven't I, Kath?' Billy said anxiously as the two of them walked towards the sweetshop. 'Can I have an ounce of aniseed balls or a sherbet dip? Can I have both? If I can, I'll be good on the way home as well as on the way to the shops.'

Kathy laughed but agreed and presently the three of them met up again, Billy enthusiastically dipping away at his sherbet with the small hollow liquorice pipe provided. Ruby and Kathy always had a lot to talk about but today, because it was holiday time, their thoughts were turning away from school subjects, for a change.

'When are we going to start job hunting?' Ruby asked eagerly as they set out along the pavement. 'My mam says I can keep all the money I earn.'

Kathy sighed. She had not seen Ruby since her mother had gone back to work at the tearooms and dreaded telling her friend that a good many of her plans would have to be shelved. But it would not have been fair to keep Ruby in the dark a moment longer than necessary, so she took a deep breath and began on her story. 'I'm afraid none of what we'd planned is going to happen, because as soon as the school holidays started Mam nipped into Dorothy's Tearooms . . .'

When the story was told, Ruby gave a squeak of dismay. 'Oh, Kathy, it would have been such fun to work together,' she lamented. 'Don't say one of the lodgers has left! I thought you said your mam was managing really well, what with their money and the extra she made by cooking "specials" for Dorothy's. I know she'll go back to work when Billy starts at proper school, but you said that wouldn't be till next Easter. I really *did* think that we would have this summer holiday together.'

'So did I,' Kathy admitted mournfully. 'The trouble is, Ruby, that Mam can earn so much more than I can. Even if I got a good job, they'd pay me as little as possible because fifteen isn't very old and they know there's hundreds of kids longing for a job of some sort. Mam says she'll pay me pocket money for looking after Billy, but it won't be the sort of money you can save out of, if you know what I mean.'

Ruby, who had been getting her Saturday penny as a matter of course ever since she started school nodded glumly. 'So you've not lost either of the lodgers?' she enquired after a moment. 'Oh dear, now I shall have to job hunt all by meself. Tell you what, though, I'll try for a part-time job, either mornings or afternoons, or perhaps just two or three days a week. Then you and me can share looking after Billy when I'm not working. What do you say to that?'

'Oh, Ruby, you are kind,' Kathy said, agreeing that

this would be a good deal better than having to cope alone all week. The talk then turned back to the lodgers, for Ruby had met both men and was deeply interested in the saga which Kathy presently proceeded to unfold, though she kept her voice low for fear of Billy's overhearing and repeating her words. 'Well, as I told you weeks back, Mr Bracknell seems to be rather more interested in me mam than I like. He's asked her to the cinema several times – she actually went once – and though he's out most evenings, I'm pretty sure he brings bits and bobs in for her. There's a tiny bottle of perfume – Californian Poppy it's called – on her dressing table, and I know Mam wouldn't waste our money on anything so frivolous. He's become extremely helpful, too. He clears the plates away when we've finished our food, and sometimes he dries up for Mam while she washes the crocks. I know I've told you all this before, but I've not told you what I discovered last week; I heard Mr Bracknell asking Mam if she'd like to go out for the day on Sunday. He said they might go to New Brighton and have their dinner out. Honestly, Ruby, can you *believe* it? I mean, he's *old* and Mam's *old*!'

'She's not that old,' Ruby objected. 'Gosh, fancy your mam having a real gentleman friend, eh? I know she went to the pictures with Mr Bracknell once, because you told me so, but she's not been again, has she?'

'Not so far as I know,' Kathy said guardedly. 'But then I'm not there, am I, half the time. But no, I think she'd have to tell me if she went out at night, so that there was someone in to look after Billy if he woke. But, you know, after Billy and I have gone to bed, both the lodgers and me Mam sit together in the kitchen and if Mr Philpott goes up early, which I'm sure he often does because he's such a wet week, then that leaves me mam alone with the Mexican bandit, and I don't approve at all. I don't want me mam marrying again or any of that nonsense.'

'Why ever not?' Ruby said. She sounded amused and Kathy shot her a rather resentful glance. It was all very well for Ruby to talk, secure in the possession of two parents who loved one another. But she had no wish to argue with her friend, so changed the subject, nodding in the direction of Billy.

'Do you have a lot of messages, Ruby? And don't forget, little pitchers . . .'

'Little pitchers have long ears, little pitchers have long ears,' Billy warbled happily. 'I's a little pitcher, ain't I, Kath?'

'Yes you are,' Kathy said severely, but with a quivering lip. 'When we've done our messages, I'd like to nip into Paddy's market, if you don't mind, Ruby. Jane said to keep an eye on the clothing stalls because sooner or later someone's bound to have a green cardigan for sale – one of the school ones, perhaps. Mam offered to knit me one and I know some girls do wear home-knitted cardigans, but I don't think she'll be able to do it before term starts now that she's working. And you never know – all the outgrown tunics from the older girls must go somewhere.'

'I expect they cut them up for dusters,' Ruby said prosaically. 'I like Paddy's market, it's full of interesting stuff, but why don't you get Jane to pop in on her way to and from work to keep a look out for you?'

'The thing is, Jane doesn't have the time. Remember, she's one of a big family and her mam and dad both work – most of the time, anyway. I'm sure she'd do her best to check up if I asked her, but it wouldn't be fair.'

Ruby agreed that this was so, and presently the three of them turned into Paddy's market. They began to make their way between the fascinating stalls and Kathy was just eyeing a cardigan when she heard, from behind her, a voice she knew.

'Isn't it a weird sort of place, though? My mama would have a fit if she knew I'd come slumming down here, but I thought it would be a real laugh and I know you like a laugh, Claude.'

Kathy would have swung round to take a better look at the speaker but Ruby grabbed her by the arm. 'It's that bleedin' Marcia. She's gone and got herself a feller,' she hissed. 'Don't look round or she'll see us and you know what she's like. She'll say something cutting and you'll be upset for the rest of the day. Keep your head down and go on looking at that perishin' cardigan until they've passed by.'

Kathy obeyed, aware of how easily she could be upset by Marcia, and all might have been well but for Billy. He had been moving along the front of the stall, poking about amongst the various garments, and suddenly he tugged one out from underneath, announcing in a clear and penetrating voice: 'Look at this, our Kath. It's one of them posh blazer things what you said you needed. I bet it'll fit you a treat. Ain't I a clever lad then, eh?'

For a moment, Kathy stood where she was, literally frozen with horror. Of all the people in the world, Marcia was the very last person she wanted to see her buying second-hand school uniform. But it was too late; the much-hated voice said, with a cat's purr in the words: 'Well, well, well, if it isn't little Kathy Kelling! I should have known you'd be in here, trying to get a bargain. Now that *does* look a nice blazer; if you were to patch the elbows, it would be a good deal better than the one you've been wearing this past year.'

Kathy swung round to face her tormentor and was about to reply hotly when Marcia's companion broke in. 'I take it you're about to introduce me to one of your schoolmates, Marcia,' he said affably. 'Is she in your class?' He held out a hand towards Kathy, giving her a bright smile as he did so. 'I'm Claude Peveril, Marcia's cousin, and you're Kathy Kelling, I presume, from what Marcia said, in her jokey way. Is this your little brother? And now you must introduce me to your friend.'

Blushing fierily, but grateful for his intervention, Kathy shook his hand, admitted that Billy was her brother and introduced him to Ruby. She was delighted to see Marcia biting her lip and beginning to scowl and thought that Claude, despite being Marcia's cousin, was a nice person. She knew, of course, that Marcia's remark had not been meant in a jokey way but it was easier to pretend that it had not been intentionally wounding. Accordingly, she admitted that she was interested in purchasing the blazer, since new ones were so expensive and would have returned to her study of the stall had not Marcia spoken again. 'Kathy is a scholarship girl, Claude,' she said pointedly. 'They're always scrimping and saving to keep themselves decent so I'm not surprised to find her here, raking over the rags on this stall, especially as I believe she's got a loony brother.'

The shock was so great that Kathy acted before she had thought. She dropped the canvas bags she was carrying and grabbed Marcia by the front of her summer jacket, pulling her down so that their faces were on a level. 'You spiteful bitch!' she shouted. 'Take that back or I'll wipe the grin off your nasty face!'

'I'm sure she was only . . .' Claude was beginning, when Marcia said, loudly and defiantly, 'She's just a gutter brat; she doesn't know any better. Let's get out of here, Claude, before I forget I'm a lady.'

It was too much. Kathy punched Marcia as hard as she could, hitting her squarely on the nose with a satisfying thump. Marcia screamed piercingly and tottered back, both hands to her face, and Claude said: 'I say, old girl, you rather asked for that.' He turned to Kathy. 'Mind you, you should never descend to violence, young lady, no matter what the provocation. Now come along, both of you shake hands and apologise.' He seized Kathy by the wrist and pulled Marcia's hands down from her face, revealing tear-drenched eyes and scarlet cheeks, but nothing more. The blow on the nose had not been hard enough, Kathy thought vengefully. 'Now come along, young ladies, I said to shake hands and I meant it. We can't have high school girls indulging in a brawl in a public place.' He smiled across the combatants' heads at Ruby. 'Don't you agree, Ruby?'

Ruby had bent to pick up Billy and was comforting him, for the violence of Kathy's reaction had clearly frightened him badly. 'You're right, mister,' she said, grinning at Kathy. 'Best shake hands and make up, the two of you.'

Kathy reluctantly held out her hand and was annoyed that she had done so when Marcia touched her fleetingly, as though Kathy's hand would contaminate her. 'I'm only doing it for you, Claude,' she said in a muffled voice. 'And remember who it was who used violence, because I would never hit anyone, no matter what the provocation.'

'Marcia, if you were ever thrown into a snake pit, you'd argue with the snakes,' Claude said humorously. 'Now, do you want to see the rest of the stalls or don't you? It's a grand place. I'd like to take a look around, but if you'd rather leave . . .'

'We're going now, anyway,' Kathy said hastily. 'Come along, Ruby, Billy, we've spent more time doing our messages than we should. Let's go home and I'll make us dinners.'

'But what about the blazer . . .' Ruby began, but Kathy shook a reproving head. She had no money for blazers or cardigans and though she had meant to enquire the price, it no longer seemed important. What was important was putting as much space as possible between herself and the hated Marcia. She liked Claude Peveril, thought him a real gentleman, and as she hurried Ruby and Billy away she wondered why he bothered with Marcia, cousin or no. He was a tall, handsome young man, probably all of eighteen years old, with thick, light brown hair and dancing hazel eyes. She thought him far too good looking for Marcia, with her long swan's neck, sloping shoulders and arrogant expression. I expect he was forced to take her out by her snooty school governor father or her snobbish mother, Kathy told herself, as the three of them emerged on to Scotland Road. She had seen Mr and Mrs Montgomery at a school function and had not been impressed. They were both enormously tall, as was their daughter, and both looked as though there was an unpleasant smell somewhere in their vicinity. Ruby and Kathy had had a good giggle and had then dismissed the Montgomerys from their minds.

But as they made their way home, Kathy told herself there was no point in dwelling on the incident.

138

Marcia had been hateful but she knew nothing of Billy's fits – no one at school did, apart from Ruby – and was merely being her unpleasant self.

When they reached Ruby's turning, her friend said that she had better just nip home for a moment with her messages, rather than carry them all the way to Daisy Street and back. Billy and Kathy accompanied her and Kathy looked enviously round her friend's neat, nicely furnished kitchen as Ruby began to put away the shopping she had bought. Mr Myers was a skilled carpenter and had made beautiful racks, shelves and cupboards out of clean, polished wood. The walls were hung with attractive pictures and all the implements such as saucepans, ladles and colanders hung in a neat row beside the cooking stove. The Welsh dresser was an old one which had once belonged to Mr Myers's grandmother, Ruby had told her. Its shelves were laden, not with the usual assortment of elderly, unmatched crockery, but with fine china bowls and dishes, making the kitchen look grand, Kathy thought. There was cheerful red linoleum on the floor and several rugs lay scattered across its surface; not the rag rugs which Sarah Kelling made out of any odd pieces of material, when she had the time, but rugs made of thick, soft wool in beautiful patterns – roses, a country cottage, some poppies and delphiniums, so bright and colourful that they could have been real. Two wages coming in, a bit of inherited money and only one child made things a lot easier, Kathy supposed, as the three of them left the house, Ruby carefully locking the door behind them.

'Kathy?' Billy was tugging at her sleeve, his face turned up to hers. 'Kathy, what's loony?'

Kathy sighed. 'It's just a rude word which kids fling

at each other,' she said dismissively. 'It's like you calling Teresa or your pal Jacky a fool or a mutton-head. You don't want to take any notice of that.'

'That's right, Billy,' Ruby said at once. 'You see, Marcia's a really nasty girl, jealous of your sister and wanting to make trouble. She knew if she called Kathy a loony it wouldn't mean anything, so she called you one instead, knowing it would upset Kathy. Don't give it another thought, old feller.'

'But if it don't mean nothin', then why did Kathy smack her on the nose?' Billy asked after a moment's thought. 'I've never seen our Kathy hit anyone, even when she's blazin' angry. She never smacks me, not even when I'm being really bad.'

'No, but she loves you. I *told* you, Billy, that your sister hates Marcia and Marcia hates your sister, so you see, it were like a match to gunpowder. Sooner or later, there's bound to be a great big bang.'

To Kathy's great relief, Billy chuckled appreciatively at this remark and began to talk about being a soldier when he grew up. When they arrived home, Kathy led her friend into the Kelling kitchen and Ruby began to unload the messages with Billy's help while Kathy made some workmanlike cheese sandwiches and brewed a pot of weak tea.

'I s'pose you'll be wanting to go job hunting this afternoon,' she said rather wistfully as they finished their meal. 'I'm going to have to talk to Mam about finding myself some school uniform – not new stuff, just second-hand. I know she'll give me the money as soon as she can.'

'I don't see why it has to be second-hand,' Ruby objected. 'I remember my mam saying once that there's a dressmaker in Crocus Street who can do miracles when she puts her mind to it. Who's to say she couldn't copy my tunic if your mam bought the material and that?'

Kathy stared at her friend wide eyed. 'Why didn't I think of that?' she marvelled. 'You're right; your mam must mean Miss Tucker. She doesn't work full time making dresses any more, but does alterations for the big shops. Mam's quite friendly with her, and when she wants something altered she and Miss Tucker put their heads together and Mam gives Miss T a big batch of soda bread or a rich fruitcake or a nice meat pie and Miss Tucker does the alteration in return.'

'I thought of it 'cos I'm bleedin' brilliant,' Ruby said, smirking. 'There's a shop on the Scottie what sells material – particularly end of roll – quite cheap. You're only a little thing so I dare say a couple of yards would be all you'd need, and if your mam really can knit you a cardigan, surely she could do a bit each night after work? After all, you'll be getting the messages, cooking the meals, clearing away and seeing to the lodgers while Mrs Kelling works, so I'm sure she wouldn't grudge giving up an hour or so each evening to knit for you.'

'I reckon you're right,' Kathy said, still round eyed at her friend's cleverness. 'Oh, Ruby, maybe not working isn't going to be quite so bad after all.'

It was hot in the harvest field. Now that the Hewitts had taken over Mere Farm there was a good deal more work to be done, but since Mr Hewitt had kept the Browns' three farmhands, Joel, Ned and Bert, to work alongside himself, his son and their own farmhands, it was perfectly possible to get the harvest in before the weather broke, if one worked from dawn to dusk, as they were doing now.

Of course, the neighbours came and helped, as the

Hewitts, in their turn, helped others. Mr Mathews saw that the baler and thresher went the rounds of the farms on the estate and the men followed it. This year, they had been fortunate, when you considered how summer had started. Torrential rain had marred the coronation of George VI, and later in May, Norfolk at any rate, had suffered from terrible storms which had seemed likely to do standing crops no good. But the crops had recovered and now the August sun poured down on the corn, barley and rye as field after field was harvested and the workers toiled in the burning heat.

They were working on the Ten Acre and had reached the stage where the binder had cut its wide swaths across most of the field, only leaving a small circle of standing corn in the centre. The men were waiting around with hefty sticks, eager for their own particular harvest – the terrified exodus of rabbits, stoats, mice and the like from the last small patch of standing corn. Alec hated this part but did not wish to be considered squeamish so simply continued with his own work, keeping his eyes averted from the sudden flurry of activity as the great horses pulled the binder too close for comfort and small creatures began to emerge and to run for their lives.

It was at this point that his mother and several neighbours' wives entered the field, carrying the harvest tea. Alec wondered whether his mother had deliberately created a diversion, for when she shouted to the men to take the heavy cans of tea most of them turned towards her for a moment, a moment in which a good many rabbits made it to the safety of the wide grass verge and the deep, tree-hung ditch which separated the field from the lane.

Nevertheless, most of the men bagged at least one

rabbit and Alec, knowing how essential it was that the farm workers got at least some meat in their diet, told himself firmly that rabbits were a pest, taking more than their fair share of the corn. However, he was secretly glad that a good few of them were now safely hidden in burrows or ditches where the men could not follow them.

'Come along, Alec. We've brought everything we'll need, so if you'll give a hand to unpack the baskets . . .' His mother beamed at him and Alec was sure he had been right; she had deliberately chosen to bring down the tea at that particular moment in order to save some of the rabbits. If he put it to her, she would tell him it was just a coincidence and then add that men were such fools; if they killed all the rabbits then how would they go on next year without so much as a sniff of rabbit pie? But Alec did not want a discussion about rabbits so he began to help his mother to unpack the baskets, laying out the tin plates and mugs on the thin, much used white and yellow tablecloth. He watched, with keen interest, as Annie and Sylvia Bates, the daughters of another tenant farmer whose land bordered theirs, began, in a very professional manner, to slice the great meat and potato pie which his mother made year after year. She considered it far more filling and a good deal tastier than the sandwiches which some other farmers' wives provided, and Alec knew that the men agreed with her and always looked forward to the Hewitts' harvest tea.

No utensils were necessary; one ate with one's fingers, and that included the large pickled onions and the jars of pickled cabbage which stood in the centre of the tablecloth, along with a huge fruit cake, its top crusted with brown sugar, every crumb of which would be devoured before his mother returned to the farmhouse.

There were other edibles, of course: cold boiled potatoes, individual apple pies and gallons and gallons of hot, sweet tea; and Alec knew, from experience, that the only thing his mother ever carried back to the farmhouse were baskets piled with empty plates and mugs. The harvesters would gorge themselves and then return to their work, the better for having had a meal and a rest. Alec had indulged in a great many harvest teas provided by other farmers' wives and knew, complacently, that no one else could hold a candle to Betty Hewitt. The fact was, his mother loved cooking and enjoyed feeding people, considering herself a hostess who was paying for the men's labour by feeding them well; other wives might not agree but fortunately, Alec thought, the spirit of competition amongst women when it came to harvest teas was strong. They would all do their utmost to follow his mother's example – as they tried to follow Bob Hewitt's, since he insisted on doing his best to keep abreast of all modern farming methods – and the result was that, despite their exposed position, the farms on the estate flourished.

The Hewitts had been farming the Browns' land for over nine months but this, of course, was their first harvest and Bob was pleased with it. As he always did, Bob had kept a close eye on the crop, testing its ripeness by the age-old method of taking an ear of corn, rubbing the grains between finger and thumb, and then popping them into his mouth. He told his son he could judge when the grain would be ready for cutting by this method, and Alec believed him.

Alec knew that his father was pleasantly surprised by how well the grain had grown on fields which old man Brown had scarcely bothered to fertilise for many a long year, but then he and the men had worked hard, spreading the great heap of manure in the corner of the Browns' stack yard over all the Mere Farm fields the previous autumn, working right up to Christmas. Indeed, they would have continued muck-spreading into the New Year had not the ground been too frost-hardened to make such a task practicable. They had cut their own fields first and were now working on the new acreage, and everyone agreed that there was very little difference between former and latter.

'Want another slice o' pie, Alec? There's plenty, and you know your ma won't think o' takin' any home. She want to see the baskets empty, same as always.'

Alec glanced up at Sylvia, nodding and smiling. She was a pretty girl with a braid of long pale gold hair and a tan which equalled his own, for her father had only produced daughters and she and her sisters worked the land with as much enthusiasm – and nearly as much strength – as any farmer's son.

'Thanks, Sylvia.' He took a big bite out of the pie, chewed, swallowed, then addressed the girl again. 'What do you think of the new land, then? We kept all Brown's fellers on, but even so it's been a hard graft to get the whole place into production. Next year, Dad wants to double the size of the milking herd and get more sheep; he thinks sheep would do as well on the marshes as cattle do, but I'm not so sure myself. Your dad goes in for fatteners, don't he? I wonder if bullocks might be a better bet than dairy cows. Most of the farmers round here seem to prefer bullocks.' He grinned at Sylvia, who grinned back. 'Perhaps that's why Dad wants to double the dairy herd, though. He likes to be first in the field, so to speak.'

'He do well at it,' Sylvia observed. 'The rest of us follow his example, you must ha' seen that for yourself, boy Alec! Tell me, what happened to that setter pup your ma was keeping in the kitchen last time I visited?'

'Oh, you mean Loopy,' Alec said, chuckling. 'The trouble with her is that she's got feathers instead of brains in her head. We can let the other dogs out, knowing that they'll behave themselves, but Loopy runs riot unless there's someone with her. She does all the things farm dogs should never do: chases chickens, runs under the pony's belly, gets mired up to her stomach in the salt marshes. In fact, she's a pest, but we love her anyway.'

'Well, if your ma can put up with behaviour like that, she's got a deal of patience,' Sylvia observed. She drained the tea in her tin mug, then got to her feet. 'You're a lucky feller, Alec. Your ma's the best cook I know and your dad's goin' to be one of the biggest farmers in these parts, so you'll do OK.'

Alec, following suit and standing up, chuckled. 'My dad may own the biggest farm but at five foot five he'll never be the biggest farmer,' he said. 'Only three more fields to go and Farmer Reed's fields to tackle and we'll have finished harvesting for the year, so let's get goin'.'

Chapter Seven
November 1937

When the lorry had delivered a great many bundles of what looked like twigs wrapped in straw and sacking, Alec had been unable to believe that this was the new orchard his parents had planned. They did not look worth the bank loan which Mr Hewitt had had to raise in order to pay for them. They meant to go in for fruit in a big way – apples, plums, pears, cherries and the like – and this, of course, would mean a good deal of work for everyone, for his mother had declared, stoutly, that she was as capable of planting a tree as any man, would probably prove better at it since increasing the size of their orchard had been her idea.

Ever since the time they had doubled their holding, Betty Hewitt had been active in how they used the extra land. She had put a whole field down to gooseberries, and red, white and black currants, and though the cropping had been fairly light the previous summer the bushes were showing great promise, their branches a good deal sturdier than they had been twelve months before.

'I know everyone's grumbling about cheap imports hitting our markets and lowering our prices,' Betty had said as they harvested the currants, 'but soft fruit doesn't take kindly to much pushing and shoving around. There'll be a good sale for these locally – in Stalham and Acle, Norwich even – when they begin to fruit in earnest. And we needn't go through the big suppliers – we can cut out the middle man and sell straight to the greengrocers themselves.'

Some of the first crop, therefore, had gone to shops in Stalham and Acle and the rest had been bottled and now stood in shining rows on the top shelves of Betty Hewitt's enormous walk-in larder. Bob, who was mortal fond of gooseberry pie, had been happy to see the jars of green and gold fruit outnumbering even the currants, though his wife had been a little disappointed that they had not sold quite as readily as her other produce.

The fruit trees had arrived the previous week, since the grower thought mid-November the best possible time for planting. By an annoying coincidence, the ten new dairy cattle which Bob had bought to augment their herd had arrived at the very same time. Since the weather was cold and clearly about to get colder, Bob, worried for the comfort of his new stock, had commandeered his son to help with the building of an extension to the cowshed, which meant the orchard planting had had to wait. The two of them had worked from dawn till dusk, helped by the farm-hands, and when the job was finished and the new cows safely housed, had turned with some dismay to the hard, frost-crackled field which was to be the site of the new orchards. Alec had pointed out that they could scarcely dig holes for the trees in such fearful weather, but when he woke the next morning rain was falling in a steady torrent from lowering grey clouds and there was a mildness in the air which augured well for the planting. Accordingly, the family and two of the farmhands assembled in the yard as soon as it was light enough to see what they were doing. The men draped sacks around their heads and shoulders and Alec followed suit, but his father wore the oilskins which he had inherited from a fisherman uncle, and Betty wore her elderly mackintosh and a thick, though faded, headscarf. Thus clad, the five of them began to cart the young trees out into the field and to place them at intervals along the furrows which had been ploughed earlier in the year. Then Bob began to dig holes at six-foot intervals, into which Bert dropped a good dollop of muck from the pile close by the gate. Joel came behind him scattering soil so that the roots of the young trees would not plunge straight into the richness of the manure. Behind Joel, Betty carefully sank each tree into place whilst Alec brought up the rear, filling in the holes and firming down the soil. Loopy, who always accompanied Alec whenever she could, tried to snatch at the branches of the little trees and was sharply reprimanded. After that, she trailed, sulkily, in her master's wake, getting wetter and wetter and muddier and muddier, but refusing to abandon him, even for the comforts of the farmhouse or the warmth of the straw-filled barn.

For the first hour, the work proceeded with a will, but in the pouring rain they were all soon soaked to the skin, even Bob admitting that the water had somehow managed to get in around the collar of his oilskin so that he was wet from neck to waist. Despite the fact that it was warmer than it had been, Alec soon noticed that his hands were blue with cold and, though he rubbed them vigorously as he stamped down the soil around the little trees, feeling would not return. After what seemed like an eternity of hard, back-breaking work, he looked anxiously through the driving rain at his mother. Her job was not a particularly exacting one for she did not use a spade but merely had to hold the trees in position whilst he filled in and firmed down, but he was sure she was even colder than he, lacking the warming activity of digging and stamping.

Betty interpreted his glance and smiled reassuringly. 'Thass cold, int it, bor Alec?' she said, imitating the broad Norfolk accent of the farmhands. She often told Alec how she and her sister, Irene, had been forbidden to talk Norfolk in the house and had consequently grown up with two languages – broad Norfolk when they were with other children or the farmhands and the King's English at home. Alec, almost without realising it, had done exactly the same, for though Bob was Norfolk born and bred, his marriage had caused him to tone down the broadness of his speech.

'Yes, it's terrible cold,' Alec said now, in answer to his mother's question. 'But isn't it about time you had a break, Ma? That's not so bad for the rest of us because we're using our muscles and that makes the blood flow quicker and warms us up. But you are only steadying the trees and spreading the roots. You must be frozen stiff.'

His mother was about to reply when Bob came back along the row. 'We'll take a break now,' he said, pulling a large turnip watch out of his breeches pocket with some difficulty, and examining its face. 'We're done three hours' hard graft and I told young Mrs Wright to bring a basket wi' flasks of tea and a foo scones down to the lean-to. I seen her just now so though we're not halfway yet I think thass time for a break.' He turned to survey the great, puddled field. 'I reckon we're done a good third,' he said thoughtfully. 'That int a bad morning's work but we'll do another hour before we have a real break for our dinners.'

The five of them went thankfully into the small lean-to and Joel's wife greeted them cheerfully. When he had bought Mere Farm, Bob had helped the farmhands to convert the house into three respectable dwellings, moving the workers out of the run-down and dilapidated little tied cottages they had inhabited into the comfortable, roomy farmhouse. All the men were married and their wives had been delighted with their change of circumstance. Annie Wright, the only one with young children, came up to Honeywell Farm three or four times a week to help Betty with the cleaning. The extra money came in useful and despite a considerable difference in age, for Annie Wright was not yet thirty and Betty was in her forties, the two women had become good friends. Now, Annie tutted disapprovingly as she handed a tin mug of hot tea to her employer. 'You're soaked to the skin, Miz Hewitt; you're doin' a man's job, and a hard job at that,' she scolded. 'I seen you a-bendin' down to spread out the roots and then standing stock still holdin' the little tree steady while young Alec here firmed that down. You aren't no chicken, Miz H, and the fellers could manage very well without you. Why, Fred's finished milkin' and cleanin' down the cowshed and doin' his jobs around the yard. Why not send him up to take your place? Then you could help me make the dinner once you've dried out a bit.'

It was a sensible suggestion and kindly meant but Alec was not surprised when his mother shook her head firmly. 'It was a kind thought, but a bit of rain won't hurt me. I'm not made of sugar,' Betty observed. 'Going in for fruit and doubling the size of the orchard was my idea, and anyway, by dinner time we'll have done half.' She glanced up at the sky, blinking as the rain ran into her eyes. 'Besides, the rain looks likely to stop soon,' she added, and Alec had to laugh at the complete lack of conviction in her tone. You did not need to be a weather prophet to see that the rain had set in for the day.

Annie shook her head but did not argue further, handing round the scones and filling tin mugs from the flasks in her basket. Alec shared his food with Loopy, feeling truly sorry for the dog but knowing it was useless to order her back to the farmhouse until he went home himself. Presently, warmed and fortified, if not dried, by the break, the five workers returned to the field, with Loopy trotting dismally behind, and began their task once more.

That night, when the family had finished work for the day and eaten their supper, they gathered round the fire which Annie had lit in the parlour, thankful for the softness of the chairs and their warm, dry clothing. Alec was aware that he was more tired than he had ever been before. The work in the new orchard had been back breaking and, despite their best efforts, they had been unable to finish before daylight faded. Alec had expected his father to call the workers off when it grew dusk, but instead Bob had sent Joel and Bert to fetch hurricane lamps. Betty had been summarily dismissed, Bob telling her that she'd done a grand day's work already but now her job was to 'feed the troops', and the four of them would manage the work that was left without troubling her.

Alec had glanced towards his mother, half expecting to hear a refusal, but Betty had nodded exhaustedly, her face grey with fatigue and her clothing black with rain, and had begun to walk slowly back in the direction of the house. Alec, Bob and the two farm workers had finally finished planting the trees at nine o'clock. Having to work by the light of the hurricane lamps had slowed them up but they were glad they had persevered when, at half past eight or thereabouts, the clouds had rolled back to reveal a full moon and a sprinkling of stars. 'A clear sky; that mean a frost,' Bob observed, digging more furiously than ever. 'Thass a good job we're all but finished, 'cos once the frost gets a grip on this wet old soil we shan't be plantin' anything, not even cabbages.'

Alec, groaning as the work speeded up, remembered planting a field with cabbages earlier in the year. At the time, because of the constant stooping and straightening, he had thought cabbage planting the worst job in the world. Now he knew better. Planting an orchard beat it by a good head. However, one set an orchard once in a lifetime, whereas cabbage planting was an annual event.

Now, sitting by the fireside, with his stomach comfortably full and the glow of achievement making him feel relaxed, Alec remembered something strange that had happened earlier in the day. It had been when they had temporarily abandoned the work for their dinners. He had been holding the weathered old gate open for his mother and the men to walk through and had swung it closed, glancing rather bitterly at the puddled field as he did so. His mother was beside him and she, too, had turned to look at the scene of their uncompleted labour. She had gasped as she did so and Alec had half turned towards her, and in that moment had known why she had gasped. When one turned one's head quickly, an optical illusion occurred. One saw the field as a sheet of water, almost a lake, and the little fruit trees looked like the tops of larger trees, just showing above the flood.

It was over in a flash. The eye blinked and the picture was once more a puddled field and scores of immature fruit trees standing forlornly in the rain. Alec had turned to his mother, grinning with relief. 'Did you think what I thought?' he asked her. 'Just for a minute, it looked like an orchard in a lake. That gave me quite a turn.'

His mother nodded and caught hold of his arm. 'Daft what you can see when you're tired,' she observed, giving a little shiver as they turned their steps towards the house. 'I remember the floods of 1912 when Norwich was under water for days and houses collapsed. There were terrible stories – a lot of folk got drowned – and even in country places we were flooded out. At this end of the county, it's usually the sea which comes in aways and does damage, but in 1912 it was torrential, unbelievable rain and tempests which went on for two or three days. Then the rivers burst their banks and it was every man for himself. We were luckier than most, being on high ground, but my father took Irene and myself into the city and we saw with our own eyes how folk were suffering. They say it'll never happen again, the houses are made stronger and drainage is better, and I just hope they're right.'

Sitting warmly by the fire, it was difficult to imagine the chaos of those long ago storms and Alec was just letting his mind drift comfortably off into a sort of half-sleep when his mother got to her feet and went over to the old bureau against the wall. She drew from its depths a large book of cuttings, frowned over the contents for a moment, then handed it to her son, already open. 'Alec and myself were talking about the 1912 floods earlier,' she told Bob, who was dreamily sucking on an empty pipe. 'I was telling him how devastated Norwich was so I thought he might like to look at these old newspaper cuttings.'

Bob grunted. 'Sometimes thass best forgotten,' he observed. He grinned at his son. 'It were a long time ago but us as saw it won't ever forget.'

Alec looked curiously at the pictures and thought that his parents had been right. The flood had been devastating and the pictures proved it. Ruined houses, a railway track looping over a yawning gap, machinery lying useless with the water washing over it, furniture floating on the flood. It was impossible to recognise Magdalene Street, which he knew well, impossible to believe that the street in the picture could ever become the street he knew.

On the opposite side of the hearth, Bob stretched and sighed. 'Time for bed, old gal,' he said, getting to his feet and holding out his hands to help Betty to hers. 'We might as well get our rest since the rain's stopped so there'll be no excuse to lie abed tomorrow morning, despite working so late tonight.' He turned to his son. 'And by the same token, boy Alec, you'd better get up them stairs. As I recall, you and Joel are on milking tomorrow and I want them churns ready for the lorry at the end of the lane no later than half past seven.'

'Fair enough, Dad,' Alec said, getting to his feet and following his parents up the stairs. 'When do you reckon we'll get the first fruit off of the trees we planted today? They aren't very big so I dare say it'll be a year or two.'

'The bigger the tree the more you pay for them, and the bank weren't willing to part with money for older trees as well as for the dairy cattle,' Bob observed, going heavily up the stairs, the long black shadow thrown by his bedroom candle bobbing ahead of

Alec's own light. 'But I reckon there'll be a bit of blossom come the spring and probably two or three fruit per tree will come of it.'

Ahead of him, Betty peered back at her son. 'It's better not to let 'em fruit for the first year, because it wastes their strength,' she said. 'And that's a job I think I'll keep to myself. It's easy work, walking slowly along between the rows, picking off the young fruit before it begins to swell.'

'Oh,' Alec said, rather taken aback. Yet when he thought about it, he could see the sense in his mother's words. If you wanted a prize sweet pea, for instance, you picked off all the tendrils and side buds as the plant grew, and it was the same with tomatoes. His mother had not yet been able to afford the greenhouse for which she longed, but she had a good many cold frames and started her tomato plants from seed each year. As they grew and flourished, she transplanted them to a sunny spot against the wall, and from that moment on the side shoots were picked out daily until she felt that each plant would produce fine swags of tomatoes which could grow large and fat, rather than letting it produce a great many smaller, inferior fruit. It stood to reason that the same rule would apply to apples, plums, pears and the like. But his mother was still peering down at him, plainly expecting a reaction, so he said rather lamely: 'Yes, of course. Only . . . only you let the goosegogs and currants fruit this year so I thought it might be the same for the apples and that.'

'That was different; the bushes are more mature. But if you fancy an apple or two, there'll be plenty in the old orchard,' Betty said consolingly. 'For myself, I dare say I'll dream of fruit trees for a night or two, and they'll be more like nightmares if they're dreams of planting! Goodnight, now, young Alec.'

Betty had done her best not to show how truly dreadful she felt now that she had rested for a while, but she ached in every limb and was so stiff that it had cost her a considerable effort to climb the stairs without a groan of pain at every step. Now that Alec had gone to his own room she might have let go a little, confided in Bob, but she could not bring herself to admit how crushingly painful the day had been, nor how very ill she felt. It was not just the pains in arms, legs and back which plagued her, but an unaccustomed hotness in her head and a low, growling ache in the pit of her stomach which made her doubt that she would be able to get a good night's sleep. And she knew that only a good night's sleep could begin to bring back her ease of both body and mind, so she sat down at her dressing table and began to brush out her hair, doing so with great care for it had suddenly occurred to her that she might incautiously raise an arm and find herself unable to lower it again.

Bob, undressing with all his usual lack of ceremony and having a somewhat sketchy wash in the bowl of water which always stood on their washstand, came over and took her by the shoulders, giving them a tiny shake. 'You feel like death, old gal,' he said, concern and affection in his lowered voice. 'You're bin and gone and overdone it, thass what you're done. But will you admit it?' He shook his head sadly over her obstinacy, but she could see the gleam of reluctant admiration in his eyes. 'Well, I'll tell you suffin' for nothin'. Come tomorrow morning the aches will begin to ease and by supper time you'll hev forgot all about it.' He put a gentle hand on her forehead and wagged a finger at her through the mirror. 'Thass wouldn't surprise me if you're got a little fever, being out in all that wet. Ah well, a day in bed works wonders.'

Betty got to her feet and began to undress, shaking her head chidingly at her husband as she did so. 'I'm not staying in bed for an extra hour, let alone a whole day,' she said robustly. 'All right, so I overdid it – I'm not as young as I was, I'm the first to admit it – but I've worked through worse. And now let's get to bed, because I reckon you're as tired as ever I am – more, probably, since you worked almost five hours longer.'

'Aye, it's been a long day,' Bob agreed, climbing into bed. As he always did, he waited until she joined him and then leaned over and gave her a hug. 'Goodnight, my woman. Sweet dreams.'

'Goodnight, Bob,' Betty murmured, and smiled to herself as her husband's rhythmic snores began to sound almost before the words were out of her mouth.

Kathy, enveloped in her mother's large calico apron, was making a steak pie for the lodgers' evening meal, for the November days were short and grew chilly towards dusk and the men, Kathy knew, were always glad of a hot meal. Her mother had stayed on at Dorothy's Tearooms now that Billy was in school, and Kathy had taken over a good few of her tasks. She generally cooked at least a part of the evening meal and, of course, she kept an eye on Billy, though he seemed much stronger than he had been. Jane's sister Tilly, now a sensible thirteen-year-old, met him out of school and kept him with her until Kathy was able to take over, and despite their fears Billy seemed to enjoy school and had had no fits since he started.

Kathy had returned to school in September with a uniform which fitted her. After a couple of rather suspenseful days, during which she and Marcia had pointedly ignored one another, she realised two things. The first was that Marcia would not easily forget the punch on the nose which Kathy had delivered, and would, in future, avoid her whenever possible; certainly, it was unlikely that she would insult the younger girl to her face whatever she might say behind her back. Second, it seemed that no one had noticed anything wrong or unusual about Kathy's school uniform. Her mother had knitted the green cardigan and made a very good job of it and Mrs Bullivant, a cheerful fat old shawly, who had a second-hand stall in Paddy's market, had turned up a set of buttons which were the very same ones used on bought cardigans from Brown's department store. Miss Tucker, the dressmaker in Crocus Street, had been happy to make a tunic exactly like Kathy's old one, only a good deal larger. It had a deep hem on it and there were darts in the bodice that could be let out as Kathy grew. Her Aunt Lily always sent her two pairs of beautifully knitted black stockings as a Christmas gift and three pairs of socks for the summer, and the shoes had been purchased second-hand from Paddy's market, as had two cream-coloured blouses.

Kathy had waited rather apprehensively for sneering comments from her schoolfellows, but there had been none. Indeed, Isobella had told her she looked really smart and Kathy had been doubly grateful, for the remark had put them back on the friendly footing which her sharpness the previous summer had almost destroyed.

'Kathy, can I have a butty? I'm turble hungry and

it'll be ages before supper.' Billy was sitting at the other end of the kitchen table. A bigger boy who lived further up Daisy Street had given him an old Meccano set and Sam Bracknell had begun cleaning up the various pieces and repainting them. As he finished each piece, he gave it to Billy, showing him how to connect it to the others with small nuts and bolts. Kathy had thought the set far too old for Billy and had been astonished and delighted when she was proved wrong. Billy's small fingers were quick and accurate on the nuts and bolts and he could already make a recognisable crane and a box-shaped object which he assured Kathy was the "bed" of the truck which he would make when he had enough pieces.

'Kathy? I'm starvin'. All the other kids gets a butty or a cake or some biscuits when they gets back from school.'

'So do you, young man,' Kathy said severely, dusting her hands together and abandoning her baking reluctantly. 'I know full well that Tilly gives you something to eat as soon as you reach the O'Briens' place. Still, I dare say another jam butty won't hurt you.' She went over to the pantry and got the loaf and the jar of mixed fruit jam. She cut a substantial slice, spread it and handed it to her little brother. Billy was just sinking his teeth into the bread when the back door opened and Mr Philpott came into the room with the slightly apologetic air which had always annoyed Kathy, though her mother told her she was being silly. 'Sorry if I'm inconveniencin' you,' he mumbled. 'I was on early this mornin' so I gorroff early as well; mind if I sit by the fire and – and watch you workin'? Me bedroom's chilly at this time of day and . . . and . . .' His voice trailed off.

Kathy knew he was shy and as she agreed to his

suggestion she thought, for the first time, that he was far more at ease with her mother than with her. Perhaps it was because she had less patience with his timidity, which she thought ridiculous in a man of his years, but, whatever the reason, he always stuttered and stammered when he found her alone – alone apart from Billy, that was.

Mr Philpott took off his coat and cap and hung them on the back of the kitchen door. Then he went and sat in one of the fireside chairs, moving it round so that he could watch her work. Kathy rolled out the suet crust she was making and placed it carefully over the top of the pie dish. Her mother had already cooked the meat and onions until they were tender; now she would paint the pastry with some milk to make it shine, pop it in the pre-heated oven and start to peel the potatoes and prepare the cabbage her mother had bought.

'You makin' a pie for our supper, Miss Kathy?' The remark was so unexpected that Kathy jumped, then muttered an acknowledgement. Silly fool, what on earth did he think she was doing, making a dress? But her mother had impressed upon her the need to treat the lodgers with great respect and anyway, being sarcastic to Mr Philpott would have been like taking candy from a baby. He would blush and stammer and probably not open his mouth again for weeks and Sarah Kelling would guess that her daughter had snubbed him and would not be best pleased. Sarah had noticed lately that Mr Philpott was making what she called "an honest effort" to become more at ease with the family, and since she assured her daughter that this would lead to an even pleasanter atmosphere in the house it would upset her if Mr Philpott was, in his turn, upset.

Kathy finished making the pie and carried it across to the oven, saying as she did so: 'It's a steak pie, Mr Philpott. Mam pre-cooked the steak and onions before she went off to work so all I had to do was to make a suet crust, but I'm making a treacle sponge for pudding and that will be all me own work.'

She glanced across at Mr Philpott as she spoke and saw that he was looking pleased. Her conscience smote her; it was such a little thing to do, to be nice to a shy and awkward man. She really must make the effort; it would please her mother.

'I – I think it's remarkable the way you and your mam manage,' Mr Philpott muttered. 'Your mam is bringing you up to be a real good little housewife.'

Kathy straightened, feeling her cheeks grow hot. The last thing she wanted to be was a good little housewife! She was going to make something of her life. She was going to college, would be the first person in her family to get a degree, would become a teacher or perhaps go into business of some sort. She had no real interest in boys and did not mean to marry, or at any rate, not until she was very old, perhaps thirty or forty. But Mr Philpott clearly thought of her as someone who made beds, cleaned floors, polished windows and cooked substantial meals. Well, let him think it. He was nothing to her, but their lives would be easier if she kept her mouth shut, so she just smiled as pleasantly as she could, thanked him prettily for what she realised he thought was a compliment and went across to the sink to begin peeling potatoes.

She finished the potatoes, plopped the last one into the saucepan and turned away from the sink. To her relief, Mr Philpott had drawn a large sheet of paper from his pocket and was studying it closely. He held a pencil in one hand and every now and again tried to make a note on the paper, which Kathy recognised as a timetable, without very much success. He really is pathetic, Kathy told herself, crossing to the sideboard and getting down one of her mother's cookery books. She handed it to Mr Philpott. 'Use this to press on, Mr Philpott. You'll find it a good deal easier to see the pencil marks if you've got something firm behind the paper.' She looked curiously at the timetable. 'I didn't know you brought work home? Or is this a journey you mean to make yourself?'

It was an innocent enough question but it seemed to throw Mr Philpott into considerable confusion. He went pink and began to mumble, then spoke out a little more strongly. 'Oh, it's – it's a sort of exercise, Miss Kathy. My boss has suggested we work out routes and write them down in a notebook, so's we can give the public advice straight off, without having to look up the timetables. I get asked a lorra questions about trains goin' to London, Manchester and Leeds, so I'm just memorisin' what I'll say to the customers on the busiest routes.'

'How interesting,' Kathy said, trying to sound as if she really believed her own words. Actually, she thought it almost as boring as Mr Philpott himself, but I suppose that's the sort of dead end job a dead end man ends up in, she thought, carrying the saucepan full of potatoes across to the fire. 'You're going to be busy if you have to learn all the major routes by heart, Mr Philpott. How long do you think it will take you?'

She glanced at the lodger as she spoke and saw he was looking gratified. 'It may take rather a long time, Miss Kathy,' he said eagerly. 'But I truly believe it will be worth my while. There's – there's the possibility of a promotion coming up and – and there's just a chance I might be considered. I'm a steady sort of chap, reliable an' that, even if I ain't as pushy as some of the younger fellers. So – so . . .'

'I'm going to be a train driver when I grow up,' Billy announced. 'I'm going to drive the great big 'spress trains what goes to London an' – an' Scotland and that. And I'm goin' to make engines, an' drive fast cars and be the richest man in the whole of Kirkdale!'

Kathy laughed and turned to the sideboard to get out a clean tablecloth, warning Billy that he must move his Meccano and play on the floor until after supper, but Mr Philpott answered Billy as seriously as though he had been another grown-up and not just a boastful small boy. 'That's right, Billy, you aim high,' he advised. 'I used to think I'd like to drive the big engines, but somehow I've never got round to doin' nothing about it. There's exams an' that, you see, an' I weren't never good at exams.'

'I'm ever so good at 'zams,' Billy said boastfully, without having the slightest idea of what the word meant, Kathy knew. He rather spoiled the effect by adding, slightly more truthfully: 'Well, I will be good at 'zams when I can read.'

Mr Philpott laughed and Kathy realised it was the very first time she had ever heard him do so. She turned to look at him, opening her mouth to make a comment and then closing it again. Damn the man, his awkwardness made her awkward, too, and besides, she could scarcely tell him that he never laughed; it was as bad as accusing someone of having no sense of humour, a particularly deadly insult to a Liverpudlian, because most of them made a joke of everything and enjoyed laughing at themselves almost as much as they enjoyed laughing at other people. Instead, she said: 'And if you attended to me and to our mam, Billy, you'd be reading already. Still, just you clear that mess off the table and then you can help me lay it up for the evening meal.'

Sometimes Billy moaned and muttered when he was asked to help, but it seemed today he was in a good humour. He grinned at Kathy and turned to grin at their lodger as well. 'It's lucky you ain't one of our fambly, Mr Philpott,' he said. 'Else she'd make you put coal on the fire an' fetch the knives an' forks out o' the dresser drawer.' Kathy pretended to smack him and he gave a squeak. 'Awright, awright, I'm workin' like you said,' he announced. 'You can get started on the sponge pud – is it to be lemon, or ginger, or just that lovely sticky stuff?'

'That's right, the sticky one,' Kathy confirmed, taking a tin of golden syrup out of the pantry and standing it near the fire so that it would run nicely. 'I'm using the golden syrup your Uncle Andy helps to make.' She turned to Mr Philpott. 'That's Andy Bishop. He used to work with me dad at the sawmills but twelve months ago he took on a job at Tate's so now Mam always says we're eating Uncle Andy's work when we have golden syrup.'

She had hoped to win another laugh from Mr Philpott but he merely nodded, and the next time she glanced in his direction he was making notes on his timetable once more. Kathy, beating eggs, sugar and margarine together with a whisk and adding flour, spoonful by spoonful, was not discouraged by the lodger's return to his work. She thought it a sign that he was now more at ease with her, as she placed her pudding in the oven on the shelf below that which held the steak pie. Closing the oven door, she was aware of a warm feeling of achievement. Perhaps it might not be such a bad thing to become a housewife in the fullness of time, she thought. When she had got her degree and was securely established in some sort of grand job, then it might be quite fun to cook delicious meals for an admiring family.

Half an hour later, the Kellings and their lodgers were seated round the kitchen table, enjoying their meal. Mr Bracknell was in tearing good spirits. A policy had matured for one of his clients and when he had taken the cheque round to their house they had given him an early Christmas present of a bottle of whisky and a box of chocolates. 'And I'm to go back nearer Christmas because Mrs O'Mara's brother works on a farm outside Blackpool and always sends them a fine turkey in time for Christmas Day. But this year they've already had the promise of one from cousins who are going to spend Christmas with them. So there won't be no need for you to buy a bird, Mrs Kelling,' Mr Bracknell said exultantly. 'Do you realise in another month it'll be Christmas?'

This naturally excited Billy, who began to gabble of the presents he intended to ask Santa Claus to bring him, and even Kathy found herself wondering just what she would receive this year. Sarah Kelling was earning good money at Dorothy's Tearooms, and in the days leading up to Christmas customers always tipped with far more generosity than usual. Both the lodgers had announced their intention of remaining in Daisy Street over the Christmas holiday and Kathy thought that it would be nice to have a big party at home, similar to the one Jane's Aunt Edith had had the previous year. They could invite Aunty Irene, any O'Briens who were not otherwise engaged and perhaps a few friends who lived further afield. Kathy decided to suggest it to her mother when they were alone. Why, they might invite some of the staff from Dorothy's Tearooms.

Kathy was still dreaming about the possibility of a party when her mother began to dish up the sponge pudding. It had risen beautifully to the top of the pudding basin and when her mother placed a jug of custard in the middle of the table and told the lodgers to help themselves, Kathy reaped the reward for her hard work in the congratulations that followed.

'Aye, our Kathy's doing all right,' Mrs Kelling said when the last of the pudding had been eaten and they were beginning to clear the table. 'And now if you'll put the kettle over the fire, Kathy, we'll all have a nice cup of tea.'

The Hewitt family were seated around their kitchen table, having just enjoyed one of the best Christmas dinners ever. Beneath the table, Loopy's head still rested on Alec's knee, for he had slipped her several pieces of turkey and she was always hopeful that there would be more to come. The other dogs lay on the hearthrug, patiently waiting for whatever came their way, but Loopy was Alec's darling, and knew it. Now Alec, glancing at his parents, thought he had never seen them more happy and relaxed. In farming, it is always dangerous to assume that things will go right; there are so many factors – the weather, the health of your beasts, the likelihood of pests and disease – which can suddenly turn a good year into a bad one; but Christmas had arrived and things really seemed to be settling down. In the new orchard, the little trees stood firm, the buds on their branches already beginning to swell. Betty Hewitt's beehives had settled down for the winter and at intervals either

Betty or Alec took down their ration of sugar water which enabled them to survive when there were no flowers from which to obtain nectar. The hens were a mixed bunch now, with Rhode Island Reds and White Leghorns mixing freely in the stack yard. Betty had bought the White Leghorns for the sake of their big brown eggs and was hopeful that, since they were young birds, they would come into lay in January, thus providing eggs at a time when the other hens would be taking it easy. Winter egg production was always poor but it seldom stopped altogether and next year, if Betty's plans worked out, they might actually have eggs to sell in the market as well as sufficient for family use.

'Well, my woman, that were the best Christmas dinner you've ever made and you've made some good 'uns in your time,' Bob said, reaching for the bowl of nuts in the centre of the table. He selected two walnuts and cracked them in the palm of one hand, doing it so neatly that the kernels remained whole, sitting in his palm looking like two miniature heads, Alec thought. 'Mind if I light up my pipe while you get on with the washing up?'

Betty laughed. She was looking her best, Alec thought. Her short, crisply curling red hair was decorated with a tiny bunch of mistletoe; she was wearing a new dress of dark green wool, Bob's Christmas gift, and her cheeks were flushed from the good food and the warmth of the kitchen. 'You oughta offer to wash up for me, Bob Hewitt,' she said chidingly. 'Still an' all, you'd likely make a mess of it and leave half my pans covered in grease, so you and Alec can go into the parlour while I clear away.' She indicated the laden table and the wooden draining board covered with dirty pots and pans. 'It looks a lot but I've a good kettle full of boiling water so it won't take me more'n half an hour.'

Alec grinned affectionately at his mother. 'Then you'll sit down for a few minutes, to listen to the King's speech, fall asleep in the middle and wake up with a jump when they play the National Anthem. Then you'll look at the clock and get to your feet, saying it's time we got the tea started. So don't argue, Ma, I'm going to dry the dishes for you and put them away.'

'You and your dad were up doing the milking at the crack of dawn,' Betty said weakly, going over to the sink, 'and as soon as the King's speech is over the pair of you will be off to do the evening round, so I can manage here, really I can.'

'I dare say you could, but you aren't going to,' Alec said gaily, picking up the nearest tea towel. 'Besides, the evening milking won't be as bad as the morning. Ned and Joel were both quite willing to give a hand, so there will be four of us at it, and not just Dad and myself.' His mother began to pour the contents of the big black kettle into the sink, and to add cold from the bucket beneath. 'Come to that, you've the poultry to feed and the eggs to collect . . . and then there's the pigs. I reckon the left-overs will have them all scrambling to get their snouts in the trough first.'

'You usually feed the pigs,' his mother said mildly. 'Not that I mind doing it when you and your dad are busy. They're so eager . . . I rather like feeding them, particularly the sows and their piglets.'

Alec smiled at her. They had three sows now, two of whom were in pig, and half a dozen fatteners, and he could understand completely why his mother enjoyed feeding them. Pigs, he thought, definitely had a sense of humour as well as enormous appetites.

His mother had named the sows Dolly, Dimple and Dora, and that was all right; they were almost pets and answered to their names, rearing up on end to look over their pigsty walls or trotting to the doors of their large, wire-nettinged runs whenever they heard someone approach. Whilst the sows continued to produce piglets they would stay on the farm, but at the end of the day the fatteners were being reared for meat, and it did not do to name or make too much fuss of them. Alec was farmer enough to take the autumn pig killing in his stride, and enjoyed the joints of pork, ham and bacon when they were on his plate, but he suspected that would not have been the case had they named the young pigs, and knew his mother shared this feeling. Even when the time came to kill off old and non-productive hens she always kept well away from the stack yard and refused to pluck or draw the birds, telling Bob frankly that either he or the farmhands must do it.

'They come when I rattle the bowl with their meal in, or when I just call,' she had explained once to Alec. 'I know it's silly, but . . . oh, I can't explain.'

She did not have to do so; her son understood, even though he kept such feelings of his own in check. Farmers must have a regard for their animals, but it did not do to get sentimental. One had to eat.

Now, Alec began to put a handful of cutlery in the dresser drawer, then turned to speak to his mother once more. 'As I said, Ned and Joel are coming up to help with the milking, so I'll feed all the pigs this evening, if you can do the poultry. Now wasn't I right to stay and give you a hand? We've done, and in record time, too!'

As soon as the washing up had been put away mother and son went through into the parlour, to find

Bob asleep in front of the roaring fire and a sonorous voice on the wireless announcing that the King was about to address the nation.

'I wonder how he feels?' Betty said idly as she sat down in one of the old but comfortable fireside chairs. 'A couple of years ago he was just the King's younger brother, the Duke of York. This is his first address to the nation since his coronation, of course . . . it must seem very strange.'

'Stranger for his wife, because she married him not even dreaming that his big brother would be idiot enough to hand over the crown,' Alec said. 'As for those two pretty little kids . . . well, I suppose I shouldn't call them that, because they're princesses, all right. One of 'em – Elizabeth, isn't it? – might be Queen of England one day, if the Duchess . . . I mean the Queen . . . doesn't have a son.'

'Ye-es. But she'll surely have other children, wouldn't you think? I mean ruling the country isn't easy. It's a job for a man, I always say. Why, only the other day . . . oh, hush, he's starting!'

Chapter Eight

February 1938

It was a wet day, and not the first wet day of the month by any means. Kathy and Ruby, slogging along the road towards school, knew that once again there would be no chance of playing out during the break. Now that they were older, break-time was usually spent walking round the school grounds, talking earnestly. They also knitted squares which would be made into blankets and sent to Africa, though Kathy wondered, privately, what Africans would want with woollen blankets in the fetid jungle heat.

But now, heat was the last thing on Kathy's mind. She was thoroughly cold, despite over-sized gum-boots and a pair of thick socks over her woollen stockings. She had had porridge for breakfast – Sarah always made both children eat porridge on cold mornings – but even so, Kathy was already thinking longingly of her school dinner; as far as she was concerned, saying goodbye to her packed lunches had been one of the best things about the lodgers' arrival. Now that they were in the fifth form, and considered all but adults, they had their dinner late, taking part in the second sitting and having to control their hunger for an extra forty minutes. Kathy was growing taller but she was still very thin and often remarked to Ruby that though the rest of her body was no longer a junior, her stomach was still in the fourth form and expected to be fed promptly at quarter past twelve.

Ruby splashed through a puddle and swore softly beneath her breath. 'I wish I'd had the sense to wear gumboots,' she said gloomily. 'But I'm always in a hurry first thing in the morning, I don't know why. It isn't as if I get up late because I get up as soon as me mam calls me, but somehow, by the time I've washed and dressed and got meself down to the kitchen, the hands of the clock have fairly whizzed round and before I know it Mam's bunging me into me coat and shovin' me out through the door and I'm having to run.'

'And there's me standing on the corner waiting for you and wondering why I do it,' Kathy said, grinning at her friend from under the dripping brim of her school hat. 'Oh, Ruby, don't you hate the winter? The dark mornings, the ice on the water in the jug, your mam getting to work with the bellows to liven up the fire so that everything gets covered in ash, your little brother whining because he's cold . . .'

'I wish I had a little brother to whine at me,' Ruby said enviously. 'Me mam's always telling me I'm dead lucky to be an only child but I think you're a lot luckier. Me dad is one of a big family so I've heaps and heaps of cousins and most of them live either on Burly or in one of the nearby streets. But it isn't the same as having someone sharing your house.'

Kathy gave a muffled giggle as they turned on to St George's Hill. The rain was running down the pavement as though it were a river and she pulled a face as she saw it splashing over her friend's stout walking shoes. 'I wouldn't change Billy for the world; he's a grand little feller and I love him,' she said. 'But there's times when even the best of little brothers can drive you mad and put your mam in a bad temper. He's bored, you see, because it's so wet and he can't play out. Now, Mam's given me five bob and a list of messages. I'm to do them on me way home from school, so this evening can we go home along Netherfield instead of cutting across the little streets? Only I need to visit the markets, Mr Beasler's confectionery, the hardware store and several others, and it 'ud be more fun if we did it together. Your mam won't mind if you're a bit late for once, will she?'

'She won't know,' Ruby said cheerfully, sloshing onward. 'Today is one of her working days – she does shift work at the bottling plant from time to time – so provided I'm home before seven o'clock, it'll be all right.'

'We shan't be *that* long,' Kathy pointed out as they turned into the school grounds. 'When we've got all the messages, we can nip into the tearooms. Mrs McNab's ever so generous; she gives me a free dinner when I work there Saturdays, and if I pop in during the week there's usually a cup of tea and a bit of bread and jam coming my way.'

'That 'ud be grand,' Ruby said, rubbing her rain-drenched face. She took off her felt hat and actually wrung it out on the cloakroom floor, doing it a good deal of harm in the process.

'That's no way to treat your hat . . .' Kathy was beginning when Miss Nelson strode into the cloak-room.

'So you got here, girls,' she said cheerfully, 'though judging by the state of you, you must have had to swim! And I'm beginning to think I should call myself Noah, and the high school the Ark! Now come along; the central heating seems to be working for once so if you hang your wet things across the radiators, maybe they'll be dry by going home time.'

*

The northerly gale had raged all day Friday and though Alec had gone to bed late, having agreed to do all the evening feeding and shutting up of the stock, he was awoken in the early hours of Saturday morning when the wind gave the house such a buffet that he thought for a moment the roof would surely go. However, after a few moments, he concluded that the house had probably withstood worse gales in its time and buried his face in the pillow. He was on early milking next day and did not mean to lose his sleep just for a bit of wind.

But something odd was happening. There was a roaring, louder even than the roar of the gale, and if he listened hard, he thought he could just make out the murmur of his parents' voices. They must have been woken, as he had, and were probably discussing whether to go out and check the stock and the barns in case there was pandemonium in the stack yard.

Alec sat up on one elbow and peered towards the window but could make out nothing through the total darkness. He knew it was not time to get up because his alarm clock had not sounded but he decided, ruefully, that there was no point in lying here wondering what the gale was doing. It was better to get up and take a look. If a roof was in danger of blowing off then he and his father must take whatever steps they could to save it. The stock in the fields – beef cattle and the dairy herd for the most part – should be safe enough but if the hen coop took off or the pigsties blew down, then obviously their occupants were in considerable danger. Better safe than sorry, his father always said, checking and rechecking both his beasts and his property, and Alec agreed with the sentiment.

He was almost fully dressed when his bedroom

door burst open. Bob Hewitt stood in the aperture, his eyes wild and his hair blown up into a comical crest. He snapped: 'She's gorn. There's water comin' across Binnacle's Piece faster'n a hoss can gallop. Don't worry about your coat; the wind'll likely tear if off of your back. Foller me!'

He whipped round and began to clatter down the stairs. Alec grabbed his boots and followed. When they reached the kitchen, Betty was standing there, staring through the window into the stack yard. She was wearing a headscarf, a winter coat and boots and the face she turned to her son was white as a sheet. 'I tried to open the back door but that's impossible against the strength of the water,' she said in a high-pitched voice. 'We'd best get up them stairs again, Bob, 'cos when the water breaks the door down we'll be caught like rats in a trap.'

Beside her, Loopy whined, fixing her great dark eyes on Alec's face. She was shivering, shifting from foot to foot. Her unease was plain and now she moved over to Alec and leaned against his knee.

Alec caressed the dog's silky head. He couldn't believe this was happening. Water in their stack yard? What did his mother mean? It had rained a little, on and off, for the past week and then the gale had come, rattling the windows, shaking the trees and, he had thought, drying out the land. He turned worried eyes to his father, the question in them plain to the older man. 'What is it, Dad? What's happened? Have the tempest done a lot of damage – is that what you mean?'

His father strode to the back door and began to try to push it open, then stopped as a flood of dirty brown water came surging in. 'Your mother's right,' he said hoarsely. 'We'll ha' to try to get out through the parlour window. When I said she's gorn, I meant the sea had breached the marram bank, old feller. I'd gone out to check on the beasts in Binnacle's Piece and I actually saw the wave what done it. It were high as a house – higher – and it came crashing down on the bank as though it were no more than a foo reeds. Then it come surgin' across the fields, black and wicked and topped with foam, and I had to run like a bloody rabbit or I'd ha' been carried away.'

'The sea? You mean the sea's come inland, like it did before they built the pumps and the dykes?' Alec asked him incredulously. 'But they said that wouldn't happen no more, Dad.' His father gave a derisive snort of laughter and hurried through into the parlour. It was hard work getting the window open against the gale and, of course, it let the wind into the room where it shrieked like an evil spirit, plucked the pictures from the walls and cast them on to the floor, and slammed the parlour door so resoundingly that Alec feared it might have been broken from its hinges. 'Careful, Dad,' he shouted, his voice sounding thin and reedy against the roar of the tempest. 'If you let the wind in, it'll mebbe wreck the place. Where's your cap?'

'Gawd know, for I don't,' Bob said, heaving himself on to the window sill. 'It blew orf or fell orf, I ain't sure which.' He dropped into the water outside, which was already up to his knees, and beckoned Alec impatiently to follow him. 'I'll shut the window as soon as we're both out; tell your ma to get up to the bedrooms and stay there,' he shouted.

Alec turned to obey but his mother was nodding; clearly she had heard Bob's instructions and intended to follow them. It would have been madness not to do so with the water outside the house already knee high.

Alec dropped into the flood and felt its freezing grip, gasping with outrage at the suddenness of it. There was a splash and Loopy joined them, paddling in the floodwater; she seemed happier out here and stopped whining, suddenly finding her feet. Alec and his father closed the window – not without difficulty – and Alec watched his mother cross the parlour, open the door and go through it, shutting it carefully behind her.

'Will she be all right, Dad?' Alec shouted as the two of them, with the dog beside them, began to make their way towards the stables. Alec saw that the stable door had been ripped from its place and saw the big shire horses, Clark and Gable, already over their hocks in water. 'Wouldn't it have been best to get Ma out of the house and on to higher ground? The church and the parsonage are on a bit of a hill; we could have taken her there.'

Bob was battling his way into the stable to release the horses, the dogs and the pony, Feather, who pulled the trap. Both Clark and Gable were normally placid but now they were rolling their eyes wildly. Bob opened the low doors of their stalls and drove the great beasts, and the pony, into the stack yard. 'How would we get Betty to safety without a boat?' he asked, wading across towards the pigsties. 'Best open all the doors, lad, and give the animals a chance, at least. I'll do the pigs while you do the poultry.'

'Ma could ride up to the vicarage on Clark or Gable; horses can swim pretty good. I remember reading at school that men going into battle made their horses swim across rivers,' Alec said.

His father shook his head doubtfully. 'But this is the sea, and it's getting deeper every minute,' he said, raising his voice to combat the howl of the gale. 'Look towards Binnacle's Piece if you doubt me.'

Alec did not doubt his father's words but looked towards the great meadow anyway, and saw . . . the North Sea, black as the night itself, save where the waves were white tipped with hurrying foam. It came towards them, relentlessly advancing, engulfing meadows, trees and hedges as though they had never been.

As the water bore down on them, Loopy suddenly seemed to go crazy. She charged into the flood, barking wildly, and began to swim purposefully back towards the farmhouse. Alec grabbed at her but Bob shouted at him to leave the dog alone. 'She's gorn back to your ma,' he bawled, above the howling of the tempest. 'We'd best follow her example. C'mon!'

For the first time, Alec felt truly frightened. What in heaven's name should they do? He doubted if even the stoutest horse could swim against the force of such a sea yet he could think of no other way of getting his mother to safety. 'I know what you're saying, Dad, but the farmhouse isn't a safe place any more. Come to that, how are we going to reach high ground?'

His father hissed in his breath between his teeth, glancing comprehensively around him, then he nodded and seized Clark by his mane, heaving himself up on to the horse's broad back. 'You're in the right of it, young feller,' he said. 'We'll fetch your ma down and find high ground while we still can. Then we'd best get a working party together, see if there's anything we can do to mend the breach. High tide will come and the sea will take everything if we don't attempt to stop it. Come on!'

*

The days that followed were the most frightening Alec had ever experienced and he knew they would stay in his mind for ever. They managed to get Betty out of the farmhouse and the three of them, together with Patch, Cherry and the horses, made their way to safety. There was no sign of Loopy.

The farm that took them in stood on higher ground with woods at its back – not that Alec or his father stayed there long. They left Betty with kindly Mrs Agar, the farmer's wife, and, having explained that the marram bank had collapsed, began to gather a working party. With what turned out to be undue optimism, they assumed that when the tide began to ebb they ought to be able to repair the breach, and very soon men and materials from as far away as Norwich were gathering along the shore, trying to build up the bank with anything they could lay their hands on. There were slabs of concrete, bollards, railway sleepers, even trees, but nothing could hold back the sea when it was whipped into a frenzy by the terrible northwesterly gales.

Two days after the original breach, Bob told Alec privately that he thought they would fail. 'The moon's at the full tonight and the spring tide will be at its highest; unless the wind drops, I reckon the water will burst through again and go further this time. Your ma will be safe enough at the Agars' but I doubt whether anything else in the village will be standing by morning.'

Alec thought his father was exaggerating, but that night the wind rose to hellish proportions. The sea roared inland once more and this time nothing could stop it. The men who had been working on the breach quailed before its fury and were lucky to escape with their lives. Alec and Bob slept uneasily in their borrowed beds that night, when they finally got back to them in the early hours of Tuesday morning. Alec was first to wake and opened his eyes to the grey light of dawn. For a moment he lay there, puzzled by the unusual hardness of the bed and the fact that the window was in the wrong position, but then it all came back to him and he sat up, glancing around him. Mrs Agar had taken in any villager who needed shelter and Bob, Betty and himself were bedded down on the kitchen floor. His mother and father had a mattress and blankets but Alec himself was simply wrapped in a car rug, with a sofa cushion for his head. Sitting up, he rubbed his elbows ruefully. Last night the kitchen floor and sofa cushion had seemed soft as any feather bed for he was weary to the bone, but this morning both felt pretty damned hard. He glanced towards his parents, still slumbering peacefully, and then got cautiously to his feet. He folded the rug neatly and went over to the window. Outside, the dawn light shone upon what looked like a huge inland sea. From his present position, he could not see a single roof, not even the tips of trees.

Alec frowned. From where he stood he was pretty sure that he should have been able to see, in the far distance, the roofs of the farmhouse, the out-buildings and the tops of the trees which surrounded them. He leaned closer to the window, letting his gaze travel slowly from left to right, but could still see nothing, no familiar landmarks, only water in every direction.

On the mattress behind him, his father stirred and sat up, knuckling his eyes. Alec went over to him. 'The gale has died down, Dad,' he said in a whisper, 'but something strange seems to have happened. I can't believe the water is as high as the elms and oaks and beeches around the farm, but I can't see a sign of them. Come and take a look.'

His father got cautiously out from under the blankets – like Alec, he was still fully dressed – and went to stand beside him at the window. Presently, he turned away with a sigh. 'I int familiar with the lie of the land from here but I'm sure the water int as high as them trees,' he said heavily, at last. 'I can't say as I've ever stood in the Agars' kitchen afore, lookin' towards Honeywell Farm, but I reckon it's hid by their outbuildings. It'll be more to the left, if you see what I mean. But there's no good ever come of meetin' trouble halfway. We'd best get down there and tek a look.'

They would have left at once only Betty stirred and sat up, saying in a sleep-drugged voice: 'Is it morning? What day is it? The wind's dropped, thanks be to God; I woke in the night and saw the moon and the clouds scudding across it and realised I couldn't hear the howling of the wind.' She began to get out of bed. 'Now don't you two go chargin' off until you've got something inside you. I'll blow up the fire and pull the kettle over the flame, then there'll be hot tea ready for the Agars when they get up and you can start off with something to line your stomachs.'

The two men exchanged glances and Alec began to demur, to say they must not waste time, but his mother ignored him, and very soon they were drinking hot tea and eating bread and jam as quickly as they could.

'Oh, I know you're in a hurry,' Betty said, smiling indulgently at them both. 'But there won't be much you can do until the water goes down. Then there'll be work enough for an army, I dare say.'

Bob mumbled that she was probably right and he

and Alec escaped into the yard, leaving Betty making porridge in a huge black cauldron and advising them to return before it was all eaten by the other refugees from the storm.

'Well, now to see what damage has been done,' Bob said grimly, as they set off in the direction of their home. 'Your ma will have lost them beehives, though, more's the pity. She's been doin' so well with 'em, too. Still, we can buy in new stock, though it'll be a blow if the hives have gone.'

As they got to the end of the lane, the water met them, ankle deep at first, then knee deep, then up to their thighs. 'We'd best take to the fields,' Bob advised his son. 'They're a bit higher than the lane and the water won't be so deep.'

They struggled through the hedge and stood for a moment, surveying the bleak and terrible scene. It was just water. The tops of the hedges were beginning to show, but of other landmarks there was no sign. Alec glanced to his left, to where there should have been the protective stand of trees which had surrounded the farm. He grabbed his father's arm and pointed. 'Half our trees have gone,' he said bluntly. 'The big oak is down and must ha' brought a couple of the elms with it. Oh, my God, look at the house!'

It was impossible to believe, at first, that they had lost everything. The house where Alec had been born and brought up was little better than a ruin. Most of the roof had gone and the windows stared, glassless, across the wreck of the stack yard to the tumbledown remains of the farm buildings.

Alec gasped and pointed. The roof of one of the pigsties was more or less intact and sitting on it, looking remarkably sheepish, was Patch. Close to him squatted Betty's little cat, Tansy, amidst half a dozen bedraggled hens. 'Look at that,' Alec marvelled. 'Thank God old Patch is safe – and Tansy, of course. But I doubt anything in the barns or the sties could have survived.' Bob nodded grimly.

When they made their way, in stricken silence, down to the meadows where the stock had been grazing, they found only bloated corpses and, in the lee of a hedge, quantities of freshwater fish that had been killed by the sudden influx of salt water. Alec saw one of his mother's six hives, but it had been smashed to matchwood and would never house bees again. He discovered Dolly, the oldest and most productive of the Wessex sows, dead in her pen, with the tiny forms of her newborn piglets dead around her, and realised that, despite the open gate, she would not have deserted her helpless babies to venture out into that terrible storm.

All around them, disaster lay thick. The new orchard had gone – he had expected nothing less – but so had the old. The young apple, pear and plum trees had been torn out of the ground by the fury of the waves, and where the water had receded furthest a thick layer of stinking mud covered everything, forbidding growth.

That evening, the Hewitts assembled in the Agars' big kitchen with another farming family who were in an equally sorry plight. No one knew what to do or what to say. They had lost everything and that, it seemed, included hope. Starting again might have been possible had their homes not been wrecked. Rebuilding was essential, but how could they hope to do that? They had nowhere to lay their heads while such work went on, for the Agar family could not be expected to house them indefinitely. Mr Agar murmured that there would surely be government aid to help them rebuild their homes, their lives, and already a public subscription had been opened for the flood victims . . . but such words meant little to men who had seen their life's work wrecked in three days and nights of appalling storms.

Alec thought he had never seen his father so totally defeated. Like all farmers, they had known bad years when nothing seemed to go right for them, but Bob had always jutted his jaw, tilted his cap forward over his nose and advised his family to 'get on with it', and they had always obeyed him. They had built up the farm into one of the best in the area and now, Alec knew, they must set to and build it up again.

Things were not quite as bad as they had first appeared, however. Almost half the milking herd had sought higher ground and were still safe, although on someone else's property, and though the farm and outbuildings were in a terrible state they could be rebuilt given time. Alec said as much and saw, to his relief, some of that determination and grit which were part of his father's character begin to gleam from the older man's eyes.

'Aye, you're right, boy,' Bob said after a moment's thought. 'Most of us what've been hardest hit are Mr Rumbold's tenants. He's a good man, and when it comes down to it you could say the buildings are his'n and not our'n. Mebbe he'll see fit to house us somewhere – anywhere – until the farm is rebuilt and fit for occupation again.'

The other tenant farmer, Harry Mills, spoke for the first time and Alec saw how his father's sudden rush of hope had affected the other man. 'I reckon you're right, Bob, and he'll see we don't suffer unduly,' he said. 'I've got a sister what lives with her husband in Martham; they've only got a small house but I know she'll take us in until we can find something else. There int going to be no work on the land, not for months mebbe, so I reckon if we all turn to and help one another we can rebuild our houses after a fashion and mebbe move back into them before next winter.'

Mrs Mills and their two grown sons had listened silently as he spoke, but now Bernard, the eldest, put his oar in. 'Sam and me will get work somewhere,' he said gruffly. 'Then we can send money home. No point in housin' us and feedin' us when there's no work for us to do. We're both strong fellers and can earn good money, I reckon.'

Alec looked at Bernard with dawning respect. The older man was right. He, too, could earn good money away from the farm and there was little point in hanging about here when the money he made could be used to give his parents some degree of independence. He nudged his mother. 'I'll do the same as Bernard,' he whispered. 'I dunno what I'll do but whatever it is I'll send money home. It'll be a deal more useful than hanging round here, eating my head off with no farm to work.'

He half expected his parents to disagree, to urge him to stay, but they were both nodding; his mother took his hand and carried it to her cheek. 'You've always been a good lad, Alec,' she said in a low voice. 'We shall hate to see you go, but – but the money will be *so* useful. I don't know if your father's remembered, but we've a sizeable bank loan . . . all those fruit trees and the dairy herd . . . so any money that we can scrape together will probably go on that. In fact, if I'm able, I'll take on a bit of work myself. We're on better terms with your grandparents than we were – I'm sure they'd give me work on the farm if I couldn't get anything anywhere else.'

Alec stared at her, scarcely believing his ears. When Betty had first married Bob, her parents had been furious, making no secret of the fact that they thought him a poor bargain for their girl. Until Alec was ten, the two families had exchanged Christmas and birthday cards but had not met since the wedding, but as Bob Hewitt gradually increased the size of his holding, and improved Honeywell Farm, old Mr Grainger had been big enough to acknowledge that he had been mistaken about his son-in-law. He had suggested a visit, had brought his wife and his two youngest daughters round to Horsey, and had admitted he was impressed by what Bob was doing and how he was managing his land. Later, when Bob had been considering taking on the Browns' farm, old Mr Grainger had been enthusiastic, had actually offered to lend him money should he need it for the project. Bob, however, had been determined to take nothing from his in-laws and had gone to the bank for a loan instead. Would he now allow his wife to return to her father's farm and work there whilst he himself laboured to bring life and prosperity back to his acres once more? Bob Hewitt was a proud man but this, Alec realised, was no time for pride. When a man was drowning in heavy seas, he would grasp any hand that offered. If old Mr Grainger said he would lend them money Bob would have no choice but to accept it, for Alec was realist enough to see that any money he himself earned would be but a drop in the ocean when compared to the bank loan his father had taken out.

'Well, chaps, I'm glad to see you've already decided to fight your corner, and I don't need to tell you that the wife and myself will do anything we can to help,' Mr Agar said jovially. 'The first thing to do is to arrange a meeting with Mr Mathews; I can do that for you, or you can go up to the office yourselves; he might see you on the spot. And the next thing to do is to decide where you'll be living for the next few weeks, for though you're very welcome to remain here my kitchen floor makes a hard bed and I know you ladies' – his eyes encompassed Betty, Mrs Mills and the wives of two of the farmhands who had taken shelter with him after their cottages had been devastated – 'like to have your own things around you and your own fireside to sit by.'

'We'll go over to Stalham this afternoon,' Betty said. Alec was smiling to himself at Mr Agar's unconscious faux pas, for none of his guests were likely to have their own things around them or their own fireside to sit by for many a long week. 'My sister Irene is a good sort and she'll take us in, no problem. D'you suppose my bike – and Bob's old machine – will be usable when the water goes down, because we'll have to feed the cows and do the milking morning and night, same as always. I've ridden over to visit Irene often enough; it's a reasonable distance for cycling. And once we can get at the trap, we can drive Feather back and to if someone in Stalham will stable her for us,' she concluded.

'I'm sure that won't be a problem,' Alec said reassuringly.

Betty smiled. 'Then we'll be staying at Irene's tonight, though words can't express how grateful I am for your kindness, Mrs Agar.'

'You'd ha' done the same for me,' their hostess said equably. 'But if you're off to Stalham, Mr Agar will give you a lift in the old Ford, because you don't want to be caught out at dusk. What'll the rest of you be doing?'

'We'll be off to Norwich,' Bernard said. He glanced across at Alec. 'Coming with us, young Hewitt? We can walk to Martham and catch a bus.' He cocked an eyebrow. 'Got any money, bor?'

'No, but I'm sure someone will lend us enough to pay our fares into Norwich, because I'll certainly go with you,' Alec said. 'Do you two have any money?'

'We're none of us got nothin' but the clo'es we stand up in and they ain't much cop,' the younger Mills brother said truthfully. 'But I reckon that ain't a bad thing to go job huntin', wi' salt lines all over your clothin' and no chink in your pockets. Happen folk'll give us a job easier because we're flood victims.'

Everyone grinned and Mrs Agar told them to stand out of the way while the women laid the table for a meal before they went. 'I made a big rabbit stew and there's a load of spuds to have with it,' she said. 'Did you have a potato clamp, Mr Hewitt? And what about mangolds an' the like? That's odd how the sea do behave; sometimes it'll take every last tree standin' up and pass over a good big potato clamp without doing no damage.'

Bob shrugged helplessly. 'We had 'em all right, but we won't know what we've got left until the sea drains off,' he pointed out. 'If the clamps are still there, we'll be eatin' potatoes and nothin' else for months. I reckon there won't be a rabbit left alive, either, except on higher ground, so we best make the most of your stew, Miz Agar,' he added as a mouth-watering smell began to fill the large kitchen.

'Oh, I reckon the rabbits and other wild things would have took fright and fled before the water came through the gap,' Mr Agar said breezily. 'I see plenty of dead stock in the fields but no wildlife; even the birds took flight and kept well clear, though I did see a dead swan over the marshes.'

'I wonder what happened to rest of my hens? I dare say they'll come home a few at a time as the water goes down, since after all they can fly. The ducks and geese should be all right since they can swim,' Betty said, as they sat down to enjoy their meal. Alec kept his mouth shut and did not remind his mother of the force of the gale. Wild birds which were used to wild conditions – and to using their wings – might have flown inland but he thought, personally, that a heavy-bodied hen would have had her work cut out to remain upright, let alone fly.

'The snag's goin' to be where they've gone to and whether someone else has took 'em in,' Bob remarked, after a moment.

'Oh well, never trouble trouble till trouble troubles you,' Mrs Agar said. 'Anyone for more stew? There's still plenty in the pot.'

In the end, Alec and the Mills boys went with Mr Agar and Betty and Bob, all crammed into the old Ford truck. They stopped at Stalham, where Alec's Aunt Irene was happy to take the Hewitt family in, and then Mr Agar insisted on driving the three boys into the city. He also gave them some money for their fares home and wished them luck before driving off, leaving them standing on Gentlemen's Walk, opposite the market. He had advised them to go first to the city hall to explain their situation and see whether any sort of help for flood victims was yet in place. However, the boys felt that this would be rather tame and decided they would see whether they could get work first.

'We'd best split up,' the elder Mills lad said first. ''Twouldn't do for the three of us to descend on an employer all at once.' He glanced up at the golden figures of the clock on the city hall tower. 'Let's meet back here in an hour, say, and if none of us int done no good, we'll go the city hall then.'

They duly met up as arranged and were soon laughing over the strangeness of fate, for each had come independently upon the Forces' recruiting office. The elder Mills had joined the Navy, the younger one the army, and Alec himself had signed on for the Royal Air Force and had been told he would get a letter some time in the next few days, telling him where to report for his initial training.

That evening, he returned to Stalham. Surrounded by the family in Aunt Irene's pleasant living room – Aunt Irene herself, Uncle Mark and Alec's three girl cousins, as well as the Hewitts – Alec explained, rather diffidently, that he had joined the Royal Air Force. He waited for expressions of incredulity or even annoyance from his parents, but he need not have worried. He did not know whether to be excited or apprehensive about the new course his life was taking; the great advantage, of course, was that he would not only be paid quite a respectable wage, but also be fed and clothed at His Majesty's expense. He explained this carefully to his parents.

Bob nodded sagely. 'You know my views, boy Alec. There's bound to be a war, and when it starts young fellers like yourself won't have no choice. You'll be shovelled into the Forces like grain into a sack; you won't have no choice of what you do or where you go. Gettin' ahead the way you have, that's the sensible thing to do.'

'Ma?' Alec asked anxiously. 'What do you think?'

Betty gave the question her mature consideration and then smiled at her son. 'I agree with your dad. You've done the right thing,' she said decidedly. 'Which trade did you put down for? I hope you don't intend to go flyin' planes, because farmin' people are best with their feet on the ground, but you've always been good with engines. Look at that old motorbike you put together in the barn when you were younger and had a bit more time. Any chance of you workin' with engines, do you suppose?'

'I'd dearly love to fly,' Alec said, unable to keep the longing out of his voice. 'But it's like everything else, you have to start at the bottom of the ladder and work up. Actually, it's more what they need than what you want yourself. The sergeant in the recruiting office advised me to go for aero engine mechanics, so that's what I've put on my form. But there's no knowing what I'll end up doing,' he added conscientiously.

'Well, I won't deny, we'll miss you dreadfully,' Betty said. 'But the truth is, Alec, my dear, that until the farm is rebuilt you're better off away from here. Your cousins have all moved into one bedroom so that Bob and I can have the third room and we've made you up a bed on the floor in Uncle Mark's study, but if you're off with the air force it'll make things easier.

Aunty Irene and Uncle Mark cried out that they would manage very well, that Alec was not to feel unwelcome, that something could always be arranged, but Alec could see they were relieved. He guessed that it would be difficult enough to have his three girl cousins all crammed into one bedroom and his parents occupying the remaining room, without having Uncle Mark's study taken over as well. What was more, he realised that without his work on the land to keep him busy he would very soon grow bored. The Clampett house was pleasant and set in a large garden but there was nothing to *do* there. Uncle Mark was a prosperous shopkeeper, a man of means you might say, and would not thank his nephew if he tried to interfere in the smooth running of his home.

The three girl cousins were still at school – the eldest was only twelve – and rode to their classes each morning on shiny bicycles. Alec imagined that rather than returning to her parents' farm his mother would probably get work of some sort in Stalham itself, whilst Bob would obviously go back to Honeywell – along with Joel, Ned and the other farmhands – to start the work of cleaning up the terrible mess and finding out how much, if anything, was left to them. Alec had never known a flood like this one in his eighteen years, but both Bob and Betty had seen Norwich in 1912 when the city had suffered the worst floods in living memory, and remembered the devastation that had been caused by the stinking mud which was revealed as the flood gradually subsided. Anything that had been covered in mud and water for several days was affected; cars would not work, bicycles were rusted and clogged up, wooden floorboards had rotted and shrunk and such things as rugs, chairs and tables and sofas were effectively ruined. And that, Alec recalled now, had not been seawater but merely the result of a torrential downpour – half a year's rain in a few days. Of course, he would do his best to help his father in the work of salvage, but he knew very well that the money he would earn was what the family needed. He had no doubt of Mr Rumbold's good will, knew that their landlord would do his best by his tenants, but he also knew that this would take time. Mr

Rumbold had a huge estate, a good deal of it further from the coast and on rather higher ground, so he would not suddenly find himself penniless. But farming was going through a really bad depression anyway. Cheap foreign imports were ruining men who had known their markets and relied upon supply and demand. Prices had fallen dramatically and probably even Mr Rumbold would be feeling the pinch.

As though he had read his son's thoughts, Bob cleared his throat and spoke. 'Mr Mathews sent a messenger to all Mr Rumbold's tenants what's been affected by the flooding,' he told his son rather gruffly. 'There's a meeting up at the Hall tomorrow morning at eleven for all Mr Rumbold's tenants and that includes the farmhands and families. He's offered transport, so a lorry will be picking up between nine and ten. I said we'd be much obliged and to keep room for the three of us aboard the lorry; I know you're joining the air force but I think you ought to come along. The farm's your future, and in wartime every bit of food we can grow will sell, you may be sure of that.' He chuckled grimly. 'I never thought I'd look to a war to mend farming fortunes, but that's what'll happen, you mark my words.'

That night, in his makeshift bed on the study floor, Alec thought about what his father had said. In common with most young men, he had not really taken talk of war seriously. After all, had they not fought the 'war to end all wars' scarcely twenty years before? But now he considered it and he realised there was a strong possibility that his father was right on both counts. The way that Hitler was behaving, it looked as though there was only one way of stopping him and that meant war, for talk, in Alec's opinion, seldom had much lasting effect. If a boy asked you not to play with his football, you would agree to let it alone and after five minutes you'd be in there again, kicking away. But if the same boy gave you a punch on the mouth so that you were spitting teeth into the playground, you'd steer clear of him – and his football – for years, if necessary.

And if a war did come, then he guessed that shipping would be a deal too busy fighting to consider bringing in cheap imports of grain, meat and other such commodities. New Zealand lamb would stay in New Zealand, and the little flock his father had been gradually building up would be eagerly sought after . . . or would have been. He remembered with a jolt that, in fact, they were no longer farmers. Others might reap the benefits that a war would bring, but the Hewitts and the other farmers in Horsey would not. Their stock floated, swollen and stinking, in the still flooded countryside, their orchards had been uprooted, their crops devastated, their homes destroyed. It was easy to say they would make them good, but it would take time and no one could tell what the next few months would bring.

Alec turned on his side and buried his face in his pillow; he must get to sleep so that he would be sharp and alert at the meeting next day. But presently he remembered Loopy and despite telling himself not to be a fool, that she might yet turn up, a salty tear slid down his cheek before he slept.

It was halfway through March, with a fresh and boisterous wind drying out the land, when Alec's papers arrived. He was told to report at Cardington on Wednesday, the 23rd of the month, and a railway pass and a postal order – which he was told represented one day's pay – were enclosed, so that the journey to his new life would cost him nothing. Despite knowing how his parents must feel, Alec had difficulty in concealing his jubilation, for with no farm to work on the month which had elapsed since the flood had been almost unbearable. Of course, there had been clearing up in plenty and Alec had played his part with the rest. As had been predicted, the mud was their worst enemy, and seeing things he had loved and taken for granted ruined had been hard. His mother's beehives had disappeared save for the one that was smashed to matchwood, but they had managed to salvage a good many farm implements such as the plough, the harrow, the seed drill and the like. Betty went along to the farm every day to help with the milking and collect the tools which the men handed in as soon as they were clean enough. Then she worked diligently away with wire wool and an old file and the oil can until they were usable once more.

The saddest thing, the thing which sent Alec off by himself for half a day, was the finding of Loopy's body. He had been cleaning a ditch which ran down to the mere and saw an obstacle ahead which looked like a bundle of hedging with hay matted amongst its twigs. It was blocking the channel, and when he dug his fork in to move it he realised that it was a good deal heavier than it should have been. He heaved and struggled and got it out of the bank and then saw, through the thicket of twigs, the flopping red ears and slender muzzle which he had known and loved so well. He knew he had given a strangled cry and had begun tearing the sticks away as though there was some hope and had then seen, with sick horror, that the dog's body was actually impaled on his fork.

He had turned away and thrown up his breakfast, kneeling beside the ditch with tears running down his face. It was no use scolding himself, telling himself that Loopy was, after all, only a dog and not even a sensible or useful one at that. She had been beautiful and loving, her foolishness amusing and never annoying, her affection warming. He could not help it; he wept.

Alec had attended the meeting on the day following their removal to Stalham and had been heartened, as had all those present, by the promise of help both from their landlord and from the flood fund. They would receive an allowance for food, clothing and similar expenses and Mr Rumbold had not been idle; he had engaged a team of bricklayers to start the rebuilding as soon as it was safe to do so and had told them that all his farms had been insured against the dangers of fire, flood and other catastrophes, for though the premiums for such cover had seemed heavy when he first took them out, they had fallen to more respectable levels as he installed more pumps and a windmill to keep the low-lying land as dry as possible. He reminded them that it had been over forty years since the sea had last inflicted such damage and created vast areas of salt marsh, and hoped that it would be many more before such a thing happened again.

'But we shall make sure, this time, that the authorities do not simply talk about sea defences but actually build them,' he told his tenants. 'Why, this time, some of the best farming land in this area has been ruined and some of the finest beasts are now dead.' He raised his voice. 'This must not happen again!' he thundered and everyone present wholeheartedly agreed with him.

But so far, things were still moving very slowly. Builders came, examined the land and said it was still too wet to sink foundations or to use the existing ones to build upon. Between them, Bob and Alec and the farmhands rebuilt the stables and the pigsties but there was no question, as yet, of restocking. The horses were repatriated to their stable block, as was the dairy herd, and were fed hay, mangolds and supplements, which were brought round to the farms in a wagon three or four times a week. However, it soon became obvious that the beasts could not be put out to graze and, regretfully, Alec and Bob took them inland to a farm whose fields had not been affected by the flood. The new grass was not yet coming on but would do so over the course of the next few weeks and the farmer, appreciating their plight, said he would graze the horses free until the storm damage was all repaired and grass grew on their meadows.

Alec and Bob opened up the potato clamp. The first layer of potatoes was smelling and turning bad already, but when they delved deeper they found good, sound vegetables. Every day they carried a basketful back to Betty, who cooked them over an oil stove and served them, well peppered and salted, with any meat or other vegetables which she had managed to buy. Then the farmhands and the family gathered round the large wooden table – salt stained but otherwise much as it had been before the flood – and ate their midday meal before returning to work once more.

On the day Alec's papers arrived, they worked as usual, but during their dinner break Bob told the farmhands gruffly that they would soon be a worker short. 'Young Alec's had his papers for the air force, but the truth is, fellers, that we're gettin' through the clearing up and soon enough there won't be a lot we can do except wait. I've no doubt that Mr Rumbold mean well and intend to do all he can to get Honeywell Farm straightened out, but there's bound to be a period where there's nothing to do and no money to pay wages. I've asked around and you'll get work in the neighbourhood – some farms will even give you accommodation for a short while – but I'm afraid it's going to mean families splitting up or moving right away.'

There was a short silence and then Bert Brister spoke. 'Are you givin' us the sack, Mr Hewitt?' he asked bluntly. 'None of us will blame you if 'tis so, but we've gotta know. Thass bin a hard time for ev'ryone, but we're all in it together, high and low, and the parish money don't cover everything, not by a long chalk it don't.'

Bob grinned at the old man. He knew, none better, how sturdily independent was the Norfolk countryman and appreciated how his men had hated taking what they thought of as 'charity', but he also knew there was no help for it. They had to live and to live they must eat and that meant accepting the relief money with what grace they could. 'Trust you to come right out with it, Bert,' he said resignedly. 'Of course I int sacking anyone, least of all fellers who've stuck by me and done me proud over the years. But you know I'm on relief, same as you are, an' that don't allow for no payin' of wages. What I *am* doing is trying to get you some sort of employment, just temporary like, while we wait for the land to recover. Mr Rumbold will rebuild your cottages just as soon as he can and they say folks in the big cities have been handing in all sorts – tables, beds, chairs, rugs – anything they think might help folk what've been

199

flooded out. But of course this'll all take time, and while we wait we might as well earn whatever money we can.' He turned and grinned at his son. 'Young Alec here'll be pretty independent, and Mrs Hewitt and meself . . .' he hesitated a minute and ploughed on '. . . are accepting her father's kind invitation to live on his farm and give a hand when needed. He's give me a couple of meadows so's I can start rearin' a few calves and my old woman says she'll buy day-old chicks – good ones, you know. Mr Agar has agreed to look after the herd in return for the milk until we're back agin, so by the time Honeywell's ready for occupation we'll have something, at least, to start with.'

The farmhands murmured amongst themselves for a moment and then Joel spoke for all of them. 'We're rare grateful, boss,' he said, twisting his cap round and round in both hands. 'And we'll take any job what's offered and be glad of it. There int much use hangin' about here, 'cos we'd soon starve and we don't want to outstay our welcome wi' the folk what've taken us in. If you'll give us the details we'll take ourselves off as soon as we possibly can. And we'll be back as soon as we possibly can an' all,' he finished, with a rueful grin.

The men's cheerful acceptance of what must have been a blow to them touched Alec and he knew it touched his father too, saw him turn away to hide his emotion. But then he turned back, shook hands with each of his men in turn and handed them a scruffy sheet of paper on which he had set out the names and addresses of those employers who had agreed to accept them whilst Honeywell Farm was unworkable. 'We won't forget you an' I hope you won't forget us, so keep in touch,' he said gruffly. 'And remember, there'll be a place for you at Honeywell as soon as I'm on me feet again.'

'We shan't forget, boss,' Joel said, once more speaking for all of them. 'You're bin a good boss to us and my old woman won't ever forget the way Miz Hewitt comforted her when she lost her first littl'un, nor how your missus could always find up a foo treats for the kids come Christmas. I int much of a hand at letter writing but my Annie, she's a real scholard. She'll drop you a line whenever she's a moment to spare.'

That evening as they were making their way back to Stalham, Alec asked his father how long he thought it would be before Honeywell would be fit for occupation once more. He did not mention the astonishing fact that his parents meant to move in with his grandparents. He thought it must have been the hardest blow Bob had ever suffered, almost like admitting defeat, and guessed that his father would not want to talk about it. The prospect of moving back into Honeywell Farm, however, was one which could only cheer and Bob seized on it joyfully. 'The builders say, if they get good weather, it'll be habitable again by autumn,' he told his son. 'An' Joel int the only one whose letters will be watched for. I expect your ma told you to write every day; well, I int that daft, I know you'll be busy, but a weekly letter would give us suffin' to watch out for. I int much of a letter writer meself but your ma will write an' I'll mebbe add a line or two.' He gripped his son's shoulder as they turned into the short drive which led up to Irene's house. 'Don't forget now, boy, send the letters to your granddad Grainger's place, 'cos we're movin' in there the day after you leave.'

'I'll do that,' Alec promised. 'But what'll happen to

Patch and Cherry, Dad? They're miserable at the Agars', good though they are to have them. They're not young dogs and they're longing to get back to you. I know you go up and visit them every so often, but it's not the same. Patch is a one-man dog, and you're that man.'

They had reached the back door of Aunt Irene's house and Bob turned to his son, his eyes lighting up. 'Your granddad says they can come with us,' he said joyfully. 'He's even offered to lend us the pony and trap, so our next job will be to get that cleaned up.' He chuckled. 'It'll be a deal easier on your ma and myself to ride in the trap instead of on these dratted bicycles.'

Chapter Nine
May 1939

Kathy and Ruby were heading for home, though at a very leisurely pace. As they walked, they were taking it in turns to hear each other's French verbs. It was May, and in less than a month they would be embarking upon examinations. Last year they had both gained their School Certificate with flying colours and now they were in the Lower Sixth and coming up to the end of year tests. They had another year to go before they took their finals, of course, but these exams would decide what subjects they took in their Higher and were consequently important. Both girls had agreed that modern languages were likely to be needed since they were sure – as was everyone else – that sooner or later a full-scale war would break out on the Continent, a war in which Britain would almost certainly become involved. Already there were unmistakable signs; the school had arranged for the Lower and Upper Sixths to go on a study week in France, but as soon as school started after the Easter break this had been cancelled. It had been too dangerous, their headmistress had decided, and in a way it had been a relief to Kathy since it meant she did not have to admit that the Kellings could not possibly afford such luxuries as trips to the Continent.

Sarah Kelling was worried about money and shared her worries with Kathy, though she was still insisting that her daughter remain at school and then go on to university. But Billy's fits had not disappeared as the doctors had hoped and expected, though they were infrequent and very mild. The teachers at school, however, would only accept Billy as a pupil if his mother was near at hand in case of an emergency, so she had not felt able to take on full time work again. They still had both lodgers, but Sarah had told Kathy only the previous day that in the event of war she believed both men would join the armed forces. Sarah was on good terms with both their lodgers and still went out from time to time with Mr Bracknell, but he had already made it plain to her that he meant to join up as soon as war was declared. 'They'll probably put me in the perishin' pay corps,' he had said gloomily. 'But I've always been good wi' me hands and I used to drive a delivery van, a big one, so I reckon when war comes I'll apply for a driving job.' He had grinned at Sarah's obvious dismay. 'It's all right, queen, I'll see you get me allotment . . . there's nobody else it can go to . . . so you won't be that badly off, and when I get leaves I'll come here and pay the full whack, o' course.'

Sarah had pretended that this would be fine, that the withdrawal of Mr Bracknell's weekly rent would not affect her, but he had seen that she was worried and had given her a quick hug. 'If things had been different, I meant to axe you if – if you and I might name a date,' he had said, reddening slightly and pulling at his moustache. 'But as things are, Sarah, it wouldn't be fair to neither of us. I might get sent abroad – I reckon they'll want troops on the Continent any time now – or I might get killed and widder you twice over. Besides, you might meet someone else when I'm not on the spot, so I think it's best that we don't commit ourselves to nothing.'

Sarah had told him bracingly that she and the kids would be just fine and that whenever he came on leave he would find a great welcome waiting for him, and he had appeared satisfied with her assurance and had mentioned the matter no more. But when Mr Philpott had blushingly admitted that he, too, meant to join the Forces when war was declared, Sarah told her daughter that she had felt a shiver down her spine. She still could not return to the tearooms – and in the event of war they might not want her – and guessed that folk would not be searching for lodgings at a time of national crisis. 'I've always been determined that you shall have your chance and go to university,' she told Kathy almost tearfully. 'But I just don't see how we're going to manage, chuck. What's more, the last time I had an interview with your headmistress, she told me that even if you got a scholarship, it would still cost quite a bit for you to take a degree. At the time, with the two lodgers and wi' me hoping Billy would improve, I reckoned I could manage, but as things stand . . .'

Kathy had assured her mother that she quite understood and would leave school tomorrow if it would help, but Sarah Kelling had shaken her head. 'I won't have you missing out on your good education,' she had said firmly. 'Something may turn up, though I can't imagine what, which would mean we were in the money again. So just you work as hard as you can and get the Higher School Certificate under your belt. After all, if you do have to work, the more qualifications you have the better. I know we're all suffering a bit because I'm not working, but I have to keep a nice house and a good larder for me lodgers. If only Billy does outgrow the fits, then life will be so much easier. Mr Bracknell pays a decent rent – the same as Mr Philpott – and he often brings home little extras. Oh, I'm managing pretty well really, with the money from your Saturday job an' all, but there's never a penny to spare and I know you're growing out of your school uniform again – how you do grow! But if war does come . . .'

She left the sentence unfinished but Kathy had known what she meant. If war did come, life would change for all of them, though she was not yet sure what course such a change would take. The Spanish Civil War had been raging for three years and shocking stories had filtered through to Britain, brought back by the many young men who had joined the rebels in their efforts to overpower Franco's cruel and wicked forces in order to give themselves some hope for the future. The German air force – the Luftwaffe – constantly bombed Madrid, causing horrendous damage in that great city, though despite the facts Franco still obstinately repeated that he would never allow the capital to be razed to the ground nor threaten the lives of innocent *madrileños*. Photographs of the damage appeared in British newspapers and the stories of those who managed to escape had sickened and disgusted everyone who heard them. Kathy knew that the British were building up their own air force as fast as they could, for Chamberlain's 'peace for our time' was looking less and less likely as Hitler's troops rampaged across Europe and his air force 'blitzkrieged' the Spanish Republicans.

But these were depressing thoughts and Kathy was not sorry when Ruby dug her in the ribs and demanded to know what she was mooning about. 'Are you still disappointed because they cancelled the trip to France?' she demanded. 'I know you said you didn't think you'd be able to go because your mam couldn't produce five pounds just like that, so why worry? Or are you worried because they said it was too dangerous?'

'Oh, I didn't really care about the French trip being cancelled because, as you say, I couldn't have gone anyway,' Kathy admitted. 'It's our lodgers that's worrying me. I really thought that Mr Bracknell were fond of my mam, but fond or not, he's going to join up as soon as war's declared and Mam says Mr Philpott is goin' to do the same. It'll – it'll make things even more difficult without their rent coming in, though Mam says we'll be able to economise on food and laundry and such.'

'They're always tellin' us we can economise on food, but I don't see it myself,' Ruby remarked, swinging her satchel energetically as she walked. 'Though the papers say that farmers are in despair over foreign imports, it doesn't seem to make food any cheaper, so far as I can see. When me mam sends me for the messages, I seem to get less for me money, not more.'

'I quite agree. Why, Dorothy's Tearooms have put their cream tea up to one and fourpence and though Mam thought it would put folk off they still fork out, though some of 'em grumble something awful,' Kathy said. 'The only thing that does worry me is me French accent. I got through the French oral at School Cert level by the skin of me teeth, and Mademoiselle keeps naggin' on about pronunciation, though I'm sure I do my best to speak exactly like she does.'

'I'm resigned to failing my mocks in French oral next month, but if I pass the written, then Mademoiselle says I can resit the oral in the autumn,' Ruby remarked as they passed a greengrocer's. She jerked Kathy's sleeve. 'Look, they've got damaged oranges for a ha'penny . . . real big ones! Shall we buy one and divide it between us? Only French verbs make me throat awful dry.'

The two girls had parted and Kathy was walking along the Stanley Road, sucking the last remnants of fruit left on her half of the orange. If she had been nearer school, she would not have dared to do such a thing, but here, on home ground, she seldom saw anyone from the high school and felt safe enough from detection and the inevitable order mark which would result from being caught eating anything in the street, let alone an orange.

Suddenly, a hand smote her in the middle of her shoulders, making her gasp and choke. She tried to turn to retaliate but someone tipped her straw hat forward over her eyes, nearly removing both ears as the elastic caught them, and plunged her, quite literally, into the dark. Kathy dropped her orange and snatched the hat off her head, then turned angrily towards her tormentor. 'Jimmy bloody McCabe! I might have guessed it would be you,' she said bitterly. 'Why can't you let me alone? I've never done you any harm, though I'd like to.'

Jimmy McCabe had grown tall and quite good looking but that didn't make him any more likeable, so far as Kathy was concerned. She thought Jane was a complete idiot to be taken in by him, though she did realise that he behaved very differently towards her friend. The trouble was, he despised high school girls and thought them all terrible snobs, though she had no idea why. She tried to be pleasant to him when they met, never told Jane what she really thought of him and appreciated that he had a hard life. His parents were feckless and selfish, made him responsible for his younger brothers and sisters without a second thought, and, until recently, had taken every penny he earned. Now, however, Jane assured her friend that Jimmy was beginning to fight back. The previous winter he had told Mrs McCabe roundly that unless she wanted to see him move out she would accept half his wages and be thankful. He meant to save up so that he and his girl – that was Jane – could marry one of these days and he also meant to take Jane about a bit instead of 'going Dutch' as the saying went.

Mrs McCabe had seen all Jimmy's lovely money disappearing into the wide blue yonder if she failed to agree to his terms, so now Jimmy did have money of his own and had begun to dress quite smartly. He had changed his job and now worked in a factory making wireless parts, and he had a second job as a projectionist in one of the local cinemas. He had not told his parents about his evening work, so he was able to keep all the money he earned from that and Kathy imagined that he spent most of it on clothes, and probably on little treats for Jane.

So if she admired him and was nice to him, why was he so horrible to her? She said as much as she rescued her orange peel – there was no orange left in it now – from the gutter, tucked her hair behind her ears and looked enquiringly up at him.

Rather to her surprise, Jimmy gave the matter serious thought. He frowned down at her, an arrested look in his dark blue eyes. At last he said slowly: 'Now you've asked me, queen, I can't say as I know why, unless it's force of habit. But you're right, you haven't been horrible to me for months. Years, maybe. So what'll we do about it? We've got two choices so far as I can see. You can start bein' horrible to me again or I can start bein' nice to you; which would you prefer, queen?'

He was laughing at her but Kathy found she no longer minded. There was warmth and even understanding in his face now, and a smile was quirking the corners of his mouth. She found herself smiling back and answering gaily, making it plain what her preference would be although she judged it safest to put it into words. 'Well, since your girl is my best friend, I guess it'll be a good deal easier if you're nice to me, even if it goes against the grain! But what are you doing out at this time in the afternoon, Jimmy? Don't say you're sagging off work, the way you used to sag off school?'

She thought for a moment she might have overstepped the mark, because at one time Jimmy had been in constant trouble for truanting. It had not been his fault – his mother had simply left him in charge of the younger ones – but Kathy knew it had been a sore point and could have bitten her tongue out as the words escaped her lips. However, Jimmy grinned, clearly taking her remark in the jokey spirit she had intended. 'I asked me boss for an afternoon off, and because I'm such an ideal employee there weren't no arguments,' he said grandly. 'Jane knows what I wanted to do, but she don't approve. She'll be rare angry when she finds I've been and gone and dunnit anyway.' He grinned again, looking half pleased and half shamefaced, and so like a small boy caught nicking apples from the fruit stall that Kathy had to laugh.

'Just what have you done then?' she enquired. 'And why should Jane be annoyed? She's an even-tempered girl, not the sort to ring a peal round your ears over a disagreement.' He hesitated and Kathy wagged a reproving finger at him. 'We're going to be nice to one another, remember? Spill the beans, McCabe, or I'll land you one.'

Jimmy laughed and heaved a deep sigh. 'I've been and gone and joined the Royal Air Force, and it don't pay nearly so well as me job at the factory,' he told her. 'But it's about time I gorraway from me family and tried a bit of independent living. Besides, everyone knows there's going to be a war – they've been diggin' trenches in Hyde Park, so they tell me, and conscription is going to start any day, I'm sure, so I'd have to go anyway, mebbe in a few weeks. But the fellers say that if you join early, before you're made to I mean, you'll have a better choice of trades. I'd like to be a driver . . . no, I really want to fly . . . but anyroad, for better for worse I've done the deed, signed on the dotted line, took the King's shilling, or whatever you want to call it. In two weeks' time I'll be in uniform an' all the girls will be chasin' me, but I reckon Jane will be ahead of the pack, wharrever she may have said.'

'Oh, Jimmy, no wonder Jane was upset,' Kathy said, her eyes rounding. 'Why, you might get sent anywhere . . . abroad even. You certainly won't stay in Liverpool.'

'Yes, I know, that's the worst thing really,' Jimmy admitted, suddenly looking more serious. 'But look at me, Kathy. I'm stuck in a bleedin' groove at the factory. I work six evenings a week at the Commodore cinema. I have me work cut out to make sure any money I save don't get nicked by – by some 'un who's got no right to it, and though Jane's a grand girl and her family are ever so good to me I want to be the one who's good to her, if you get my meaning. When I join the air force, they'll give me a real smart uniform, they'll feed me – they clothe you from the skin up, you know; underclothes, socks, shoes, the lot – they'll give me rail passes and the like so's I can travel free and they'll teach me a proper trade so when I come out I won't have to go back to makin' wireless parts but can do something I'll be proud of.'

'What?' Kathy asked baldly. 'What do you *want* to do, Jimmy? I thought, from what Jane told me, you were getting on grand at the factory and doing pretty well as a projectionist an' all. What'll the air force teach you that you couldn't learn right here in Liverpool?'

The two had fallen into step beside one another and were rapidly approaching Daisy Street. Jimmy came to a halt, his eyes bright with excitement. 'First, they'll teach me to drive and it won't cost a penny,' he told her. 'Then they'll teach me all about engines because if you're going to drive a vehicle, they reckon you've gorra know how the engine works. Then they'll let me take exams so's I can get on – I were always top of me class at Daisy Street, despite missing so many lessons – but best of all, I hope they'll teach me to fly. When this war's over, I reckon fellers who can fly will get the top jobs. Why, I might even stay in the air force and become a – a squadron leader, or even an Air Vice-Marshal!'

Kathy giggled. She knew very little about ranks in the Royal Air Force but had a suspicion that that of Air Vice-Marshal would be more than a little above Jimmy's touch, even if he proved a competent driver and mechanic. 'Well, if you tell Jane you're aiming that high, I'm sure she'll be delighted,' she said encouragingly. 'Just you tell her that conscription would mean you'd get called up anyway in a few months, and maybe she'll forgive you. But thanks for telling me, Jimmy; I'll do my best to make Jane see you've done the right thing. I don't suppose you know, but Mr Bracknell and Mr Philpott – they are our lodgers – both mean to join up as soon as they're able.'

She thought that this would impress Jimmy, but instead he sniffed disparagingly. 'But they're old fellers; none of the Forces are goin' to want them. Why, the one with the walrus moustache must be all of forty, and the other couldn't pop a paper bag without having a fainting fit. I can't see the air force takin' either of 'em.' He laughed suddenly. 'Mind you, if the one with the moustache held his arms out to the side and made his moustache whiz round and round, they might think he were a Spitfire and offer him a job as an aeroplane!'

Kathy tutted disapprovingly, though she could not help smiling. The thought of Mr Bracknell, moustache whirling like a propeller, was an amusing one. However, Jimmy was wrong to think their lodgers too old for military service. 'Mr Bracknell's thirty-six, or so he says, and Mr Philpott is no more'n twenty-seven or twenty-eight,' she told him. 'What's more, Mr Bracknell used to drive heavy lorries and I think he's sounded out someone in the army who told him they need experienced drivers desperately.'

'Oh, the army,' Jimmy said, dismissing the "brown jobs" with a flick of the fingers. 'I dunno about them, they're probably desperate for anyone they can get. But the air force, they're different. Everyone wants to join the air force.'

'I thought everyone wanted to join the Navy, it being the Senior Service,' Kathy said severely, but with a twitching lip; Jimmy had signed up for the air force barely an hour ago and already it seemed his partisanship knew no bounds. 'I suppose it's because we're a port, but all the lads down Daisy Street are talking about joining the Navy as soon as they're old enough.'

'Oh well, it takes all sorts,' Jimmy said vaguely. 'But I don't fancy bein' shut up in the steel hull of a ship while the enemy shoot them torpedo things at us.' He glanced at Kathy out of the corner of his eye. 'Tell the truth, I don't much like bein' shut up in small places. You wouldn't catch me travelling in a lift when I can run up the stairs, an' I've only gorra think about them submarines to break out in a cold sweat. No, I'll leave the Navy for them as likes swimming.'

'But I thought you said you wanted to fly an aeroplane. They've got little tiny cockpits,' Kathy pointed out. 'Or were you thinking of flying bombers? They're a lot bigger, I believe.'

'I'd rather fly fighters. But you aren't closed in, the way you would be in a ship or a submarine,' Jimmy said. 'You can slide the perspex roof back, you know – that's how the pilots get in and out – so I reckon you wouldn't feel enclosed. But I don't s'pose there's much chance of bein' taught to fly, really. I expect I'll be ground crew, no matter how hard I work.'

They reached the corner of Daisy Street and Kathy slowed, beginning to say cheerio, wishing him luck, but Jimmy interrupted her. 'I'm comin' your way, queen,' he said gruffly. 'I've gorra face up to tellin' Jane sooner or later and I reckon it 'ud better be sooner. She'll get used to the idea, see if she doesn't.'

'I'm sure she will; and besides, it may never happen – the war, I mean,' Kathy said, in what she hoped was a heartening tone. 'Cheerio for now, Jimmy.'

'Tarra for now, chuck, and thanks for your company,' he said.

Continuing on her way down the street, Kathy reflected that Jimmy had never been so nice to her before and decided that she rather liked it. He had been horrible to her when they were both kids but she suspected that she had been pretty horrible to him, too. I believe I was jealous, she thought now, rather shocked at the realisation. The thing is, Jane and me have been friends all our lives and it was a bit of a shock when she started turning to Jimmy for companionship. It was wrong of me to be jealous, because I had Ruby and all the other girls at my new school, but once Jane had left the Daisy and started work she really had no one of her own age to go around with. Almost everyone in the market is old and, of course, I couldn't be with her in the way I once was because of homework and school activities and that. If it hadn't been for Jimmy, she'd have been terribly lonely.

Reaching her back door, she found it was locked so took the key off the lintel and let herself in. She entered the kitchen and found a note on the table asking her to start the supper since Mam had taken Billy over to the Stanley for a check-up. As soon as she saw the words, Kathy remembered that Billy had an appointment with a new consultant at the hospital, who had considerable experience of head injuries such as Billy had suffered. The staff at the Stanley were hopeful that the new doctor might be able to start some different treatment which would help Billy to overcome his fits completely. For a year now, her little brother had been aware that he was in some way different from his classmates, and though he still did not know what happened when he had a fit and seemed to assume that he fell unexpectedly asleep, he no longer took such moments in his stride. He worried that he might 'nod off' at some important time and had actually confided in Kathy that he meant to stop himself 'nodding off' when he was a bit older, though he was unable as yet to explain how he could do such a thing.

Kathy and her mother were full of hope that the treatment the new doctor might recommend would help Billy. She settled down to the task of preparing vegetables, scrubbing potatoes and flash-frying the pieces of scrag end which Sarah had left ready. When someone rattled the back door, she looked up with a smile, expecting her mother and Billy, and was almost disappointed when Jane bounced into the room. Her friend was flushed and bright-eyed but Kathy saw at a glance it was temper, and not pleasure, which had brought the roses to her cheeks. Jane slammed the back door behind her and, to Kathy's astonishment, shot the bolt across before sinking on to one of the wheel-backed chairs and addressing her friend in a hissing whisper.

'The bugger! Oh, I'm so angry I could hit him! When he told me I just ran out of the house, didn't bother with me coat, didn't tell anyone where I were goin'. I left him standing in the middle of our kitchen with his gob open and his eyes like saucers. Just like a bleedin' man to think he can break your heart and trample on your feelings and you'll never say a word, just tell him what a clever feller he's been. Well, he knows different now and if he comes knockin' on your back door we'll pretend you're out, shallus? Only I don't want to see 'im or talk to 'im until I've cooled off a bit.'

Kathy, standing at the stove and stirring the pieces

of scrag end, stared round eyed at her friend. She had never seen Jane so angry and realised, with a little shock of surprise, that she had never seen her look lovelier either. Jane's mass of golden curls, which she usually wore pulled back into a bun, were tumbled round her face and her big blue eyes, sparkling with anger, looked larger than ever. Her creamy complexion was greatly enhanced by her angry flush and she had bitten her lower lip until it glowed scarlet. However, now was scarcely the time to congratulate Jane on her looks; instead, Kathy said placatingly: 'What on earth's the matter, queen? Surely you're not getting into a tizzy just because Jimmy's joined the air force? After all, he'll have a choice of trades now, whereas if he waited for war to break—'

'He *told* you?' Jane squeaked. The colour in her cheeks brightened to scarlet. 'He told *you*? But – but how could he possibly have told you? He only signed on an hour or so ago and he said he'd come straight to me.' She ground her teeth; Kathy distinctly heard her and could scarcely stop herself from smiling. She had never expected to see the mild and sweet-tempered Jane in such a rage and suddenly realised that she did not fancy the rage being turned on her. She had best explain quickly how she and Jimmy had met by the merest chance before Jane stormed out as she had stormed in, intent upon facing Jimmy with this new perfidy.

'Calm down, queen,' she said, therefore. 'I were walking back from school and your Jimmy caught me up. He started being nasty to me – he tipped me hat over me eyes, the way he always does – and I asked him why he was so rude. He seemed a bit took aback and said he supposed it was force of habit and then I asked him why he wasn't at work and he told me he'd signed on with the air force. He was on his way to see you so we walked up the Stanley together; that's all there was to it.'

'Oh,' Jane said rather lamely. She was clearly taken aback by the explanation but unwilling, as yet, to surrender her grievance. 'Well, he shouldn't have told you, even though you're me best pal. He – he should have talked about other things instead of showin' off and boasting about joining the cream of the Forces, or wharrever it is he's been saying this past month. I'm sick of the sound of the Royal Air Force, I don't *want* to be told how marvellous his life is going to be.' She sniffed and Kathy saw a tear trembling on her friend's long, curly eyelashes. 'He expects me to be pleased, *pleased* – that he's going away from me, leavin' me stuck here with me family, workin' every hour God sends at the market and then goin' home and workin' at housework and cookin' and cleanin' until I bleedin' well drop.' She sniffed again and knuckled her eyes with the backs of her hands. 'I were really lookin' forward to marryin' Jimmy and havin' me own littl' home somewhere nice and quiet, out in the suburbs,' she wailed, her voice wobbling. 'And now I'm worse off than before because I won't even have Jimmy to take me about or buy me chocs when we go to the cinema. It'll just be work, work, work.'

'Yes, of course, you'll miss him horribly,' Kathy said tactfully, putting into her friend's mouth the words she should have said, Kathy felt. 'And it is hard on you to be left behind but, as Jimmy said, if he hadn't volunteered he would have been conscripted as soon as the war actually started. This way he'll have a choice.'

'Yes, yes, I know, I've heard it all before,' Jane said

dismally, but her colour was beginning to fade. 'I know all the arguments because Jimmy's been bombarding me with them for weeks, but I still think it was a mean thing for him to do, to go and leave me before he had to.' She produced a large and very ragged handkerchief and blew her nose violently, then stuffed the handkerchief back into her pocket, saying in a choked voice: 'I really love him ever so much, Kathy, and that's the trouble. I want what's best for him, I want him to be happy, and I don't really think that joining up is what he wants. He thinks it's all going to be glamorous and wonderful; he can't see beyond the lovely smart uniform – blue was always his colour – to what might happen when war really does start. You're ever such a long way up in an aeroplane and if you get shot down . . . oh, Kathy, I can't *bear* it! Suppose he's killed? People do get killed in wars; remember Claude and Neville Ellis? They went off to fight Franco and – and never came back. And in the last lot, ever so many fellers copped it – me Uncle Fred, Mam's cousin Cuthbert . . .'

By this time, Kathy had abandoned her scrag end, pulling it away from the heat before she did so, and had both arms tightly round Jane. 'Poor old girl, poor old Janey,' she crooned. She was so used to Jane's being the taller of the two that it came as quite a shock to realise they were now the same height, but it certainly made comforting Jane easier. 'Look, it's useless reproaching poor Jimmy, because what he's done can't be undone. He's joined the RAF, signed all the papers, and he'll be going off to training camp before you know it. So if you love him like you say, you've got to tell him so and pretend like mad that you know he's done the right thing. You've got to back him up when he tells his mam and dad what he's done and you've got to be proud of him, tell all his pals how brave he is and agree with him when he says it's a grand life in the Royal Air Force, even if you secretly believe he'll be fed up and disillusioned in a month. Because if you go on moping and whining, it'll be a downright pleasure to get away from you and he won't miss you one bit! Now what do you say to that?'

As it was meant to, this made Jane give a watery laugh and presently, when someone tried the back door, she did no more than murmur a protest when Kathy went over, slid back the bolt and flung the door wide. A wild-eyed Jimmy erupted into the room, beginning to speak as he did so, but his words were muffled as Jane shot across the kitchen into his arms and began to kiss him, muttering that she was so sorry, that it was because she loved him and would miss him so much that she had been nasty earlier, that he was to forgive her at once please, because she could not bear him to be angry with her.

Jimmy, clearly considerably taken aback, cuddled and fussed and winked at Kathy over his love's tousled golden head. Then he steered her, with an arm still about her shoulders, out of the back door. He called to Kathy over his shoulder that they would probably see her later, but Kathy, closing the door thankfully behind them, thought that this was unlikely. Lovers' quarrels might be long and painful, but she imagined the making up would take even longer and be eminently satisfactory. She did not expect to see either Jimmy or Jane again that evening but settled down to the task of preparing a meal with a contented mind. She was sorry that Jimmy was going away, for Jane's sake, of course she was, but for herself it was a different matter. Jane would be eager for Kathy's company and Kathy looked forward to renewing their old intimacy once more.

She was thinking how pleasant it would be to go about with Jane again when another interruption occurred. The back door shot open and Billy ran into the room with Sarah close on his heels. Both were beaming. 'I seen the new doctor, Kathy,' Billy shouted joyfully as soon as he saw her. 'He's ever so young and ever so nice and he thinks he can help me stop my little sleeps so I'm going to the hospital three times a week after school and they're going to put a thing on my head – it don't hurt, he done it today and it didn't hurt – an' I'll soon be better. What do you think of that, eh?'

'It's wonderful, Billy,' Kathy said and saw that her mother had tears of relief in her eyes.

PART II

Chapter Ten

February 1941

'Kathy! Hey, Kathy, wait for me!'

It was a cold, dark February afternoon. Because of the blackout there were no streetlights to show Kathy who had shouted, but she knew her friend's voice so well that it was no surprise when Jane pounded up beside her. Both girls were now working in a large factory making parts for guns and had just finished the day shift. Kathy's dreams of a place at university and then a degree had come to nothing, because war had been declared back in '39 and everything had changed, almost overnight it seemed.

Mr Bracknell and Mr Philpott had joined the army and Navy respectively, and though Mr Bracknell had kept his promise to see that part of his wages were sent home to his landlady every month, Sarah Kelling had not argued when her daughter had not returned to the high school for her final year but had got herself a job. First of all, she had gone to the Empire works in Park Street, Bootle, working as a packer, but when Jane told her that she was going up to the munitions factory in Long Lane, she had decided to go there as well. Everyone knew that such places paid high wages – as much as £3 a week – and such a sum would relieve Kathy's mother of a good few of her worries.

But now, almost eighteen months later, she was beginning to be irked by the boredom of her work, and also, if she was honest, the attitude of the factory girls. They talked of nothing but clothes, make-up and young men, and when Kathy admitted that she was studying in the evenings so that, when the war was over, she might perhaps get some higher education, they had made it clear they considered her a prig, not one of themselves. Jane was different, of course, but it was hard to work amongst people who despised you and did not attempt to hide it.

But there were advantages, too. The money was good; she and Jane took home double what they had earned at the jam factory, but there they had been able to walk to and from their place of employment, whereas now they caught first a tram and then a bus to reach their destination. They then worked a twelve-hour shift, standing at their bench and concentrating on what they were doing, for men's lives might depend on their work. Whenever she was tempted to chat to her neighbour or to glance around the room, Kathy remembered that somewhere a soldier might one day pull the trigger only to find his gun jamming when he needed it most. If he died it would be her fault and Kathy was determined to have no one's death on her conscience if she could possibly help it.

Others, she knew, were not so fussy, and this was another reason for not wanting to be on particularly friendly terms with her fellow workers. A good few of them, she acknowledged secretly, were grand but there were others whose selfishness extended even to their work. Of course the supervisors who patrolled the vast echoing factory floor soon jumped on anyone who did not keep her nose to the grindstone, so though Kathy was beginning to dread the long, darkening days at her bench she did not intend to abandon the best paid job she had ever had.

Not that money was as short as it had been in the early days of the war. The new doctor's treatment had worked wonders for Billy; he had not had a fit for fifteen months and Sarah Kelling had gone back to work with the hospital's full approval. She had returned to Dorothy's Tearooms and despite the complications caused by rationing was managing their largest café and bringing home as much money as she could have earned in a munitions factory.

Billy, meanwhile, returned to the O'Briens' home after school and at holiday times, where Jane's grandma, who had moved in with them at the start of hostilities, looked after him, as she looked after the young O'Briens. Tilly had left school and was a machinist in a factory that made uniforms for the Forces, but old Mrs O'Brien was strict and sensible and of course, being so much older, could control her charges even better than Tilly had. Sarah and Kathy were happy to leave Billy with her, therefore, and arranged that whichever of them arrived home first would pick him up.

'Why didn't you wait for me, queen?' Jane said now, as soon as she had breath enough to speak. 'You're not usually in such a bleedin' hurry and I particularly wanted to talk to you. You know that feller we met at the Grafton, the one who said me hair was like sunlight on the sand? Well, he wrote me a letter; he wants to meet up again. I – I'm not sure whether I should 'cos he wants me to go to the flicks and you know what some fellers are like when they're buying you six penn'orth of dark. Now if you were to come along of us . . .'

'Jane, how can you?' Kathy said reproachfully. 'When Jimmy was on leave last spring I scarcely saw you, and ever since, you've been telling me how you're as good as engaged. If that's so, you can't possibly mean to go to the flicks with anyone else, particularly a six-foot Scottish seaman with red hair and a broken nose.'

Jane gave a delighted gurgle of laughter. 'I didn't mean *him*, you fool,' she said, still giggling. 'I meant the air force type with the little moustache and the twinkling blue eyes. As for being unfaithful to Jimmy, you know I wouldn't! Only – only I do love the flicks and it would be nice to go out and have someone else pay for a change. But I wouldn't go alone with him, only if you'll come too . . . what's happened to that feller who dated you? Paul, wasn't it?'

'As if you didn't know,' Kathy scoffed. 'Paul is on convoy duty between here and the States, or at least I think he is. If he gets leave then he'll come round to Daisy Street – if it's a forty-eight, that is. But if it's a long one he'll go home to Barnstaple – that's the town in Devon where he lives. So the chances of him being around are pretty slight.'

'Well, couldn't you come by yourself? Or you could bring Billy, or your mam,' Jane said with a hint of desperation in her tone. 'He's ever so nice, honest to God he is, Kathy.'

'I'm sure he's charming,' Kathy said sarcastically. 'However, I don't mean to play gooseberry just so that you don't get kissed in the dark. Besides, if you tell him about Jimmy . . .'

'If I tell him about Jimmy then he won't take me to the cinema,' Jane said flatly. She sighed, then gave her friend's arm a squeeze. 'You're right, of course. I do love Jimmy and I don't really want to complicate my life by going out with anyone else. But the truth is, Kathy, that I'm bored, and some of the girls. . . well, they can be spiteful, and when someone's gorra down on me I wonder whether I wouldn't be better off workin' in a shop, or – or back at the jam factory. I know we get paid good money but there's hardly anything to spend it on; I've been cleaning me teeth with soap – yuck – for the past week because there doesn't seem to be a scrap of toothpaste left in the whole of Liverpool and I'm browned off.'

'I know. Friday night is Amami night just doesn't apply any more,' Kathy said, returning the squeeze. 'I've not seen a bottle of shampoo for – oh, for ages. My hair isn't all curly and lovely like yours but I can tell you it isn't improved by being washed in carbolic.'

Jane laughed. 'We shouldn't grumble, not really,' she said. 'There's decent girls at work – Jenny, Freda, Annie Browntoes. And though the work's bleedin' boring, it isn't all that hard. Tell you what, queen, let's take ourselves to the flicks this evening, just the two of us. And at the weekend, we'll go to the Grafton and dance with all the handsome, homesick young fellers and tell 'em we're happily married to six-foot dockers. Hey, there's our bus!'

'Thank God there's a queue,' Kathy panted as the two of them tore along the pavement in the direction of the bus stop. It was difficult to see the destination board, though it was lit up with the greyish-blue light from the interior, but both girls recognised passengers from their factory and knew it was the right vehicle. They made it by the skin of their teeth and, as they were last aboard, stood on the platform clutching the stair rail and holding out their season tickets for the conductor to scrutinise. 'Tell you what, Janey, I bet you sixpence that there's a letter for you when we get back to Daisy Street. Your Jimmy's a first-rate correspondent. He must write two or three letters a week. So that'll cheer you up, won't it?'

'It'll cheer me up if he's getting some leave,' Jane admitted. 'A letter is always grand because it's the next best thing to being with him, but I do so long to see him, grab hold of him and give him a great big hug. Do you realise, Kathy, that it's nearly six months since I saw him last? It's too long, and it's not as though I can have some time off and go and visit him, because they keep moving him about and anyway the trains are dreadful, aren't they? And . . . and I'd be a bit afraid of trying to cross England all by meself. I wanted to join the WAAF when war started and be truly independent, but now I'm glad I didn't do it because they might have sent me even further away from Jimmy. Why, he's in Lincolnshire or Norfolk or some other outlandish place and they could have sent me to Scotland or – or Cornwall! But at least I'd have been doing something worthwhile, which is more than we're doing now! Oh, I know that the Forces need guns but anyone can work on an assembly line. Being in the WAAF could have been really useful; I wish I'd had the courage to join up right at the start, and it would have been more fun, too. I hate twelve-hour shifts, especially in winter when we get to work in the dark and reach home in the dark as well; it's as though we only have half-lives, like moles or rabbits or something.'

'Yes, I know what you mean. I wanted to join up when war broke out as well, even though I haven't got a boyfriend in the Forces, like you have,' Kathy assured her friend. 'But it wouldn't have been fair on Mam, because of Billy. She needs the money I earn, of course, but if I'd joined the WAAF I could have sent all my money home, just about. I mean, they clothe you and feed you and so on. So it wasn't the money so much as having someone else to share the responsibility, like. And now . . . oh, I don't know, I suppose I'm in a rut and it's easier to stay in it than scramble out.'

'We're both in a rut,' Jane said gloomily. 'Hey up, here's our stop!' The two of them tried to leave the bus and were considerably jostled by passengers trying to board. Jane became indignant. 'Mind my toes, you dozy bugger, or I'll loosen your teeth for you,' she said wrathfully to a young man who was trying to jump on as they alighted. 'Honestly, men! You'd think they were the only people on the perishin' planet!'

Kathy laughed as the two of them hurried off in the direction of the nearest tram stop that would take them to the Stanley Road. 'Well, there's nothing like telling a feller what you think of him,' she observed. 'Fancy you calling a total stranger a dozy bugger, Jane! Still, if he'd been a gentleman, he'd have waited for us to get off before trying to cram his way aboard.' She glanced down at her friend's feet in their cheap utility shoes. 'Did he get you? There's mud on your instep.'

'Yes he did, and I only hope he hasn't laddered me bleedin' stockings,' Jane said, slowing to examine her foot as they reached the tail end of a rather long tram queue. 'Good job they're only lisle; if they'd been me best silk pair, I'd ha' given him a knuckle sarnie, honest to God I would.'

Kathy shook her head reprovingly, thinking that her friend must be even unhappier at the factory than she was herself, for Jane was naturally sweet tempered and easy going and had never, to her knowledge, offered violence to a total stranger before.

'Life isn't *so* bad when you consider it carefully. I mean, think of the Londoners; they've been blitzed and bombed and absolutely crushed, and they aren't the only ones. We're lucky to be pretty well out of range of the Luftwaffe – that's what Mr Bracknell said the last time he came home on leave, anyway.'

'It's nice that he thinks of it as his home,' Jane said thoughtfully. 'Do you know, I were *sure* he were going to ask your mam to marry him . . . only he never has, has he?'

'I don't know,' Kathy said honestly. 'He likes her ever so much, you've only got to see the way he looks at her, but Mam's never said.'

'Does she like him, though?' Jane asked. 'I were never sure how she felt.'

'She likes him, I'm sure she does. But whether liking is enough, I don't know. Remember, Jane, you're the one with experience in the liking and loving field, not me. I'm nearly nineteen, and I've never had a serious boyfriend. And I probably shan't, either,' Kathy added honestly. 'Not while this bleedin' war is on, anyway.'

Jane was starting to reply when a tram came charging out of the darkness and drew to a halt beside them. 'This one'll do,' Jane said, peering up at the destination board. Kathy was clad in a thick coat and scarf with a woolly hat pulled down over her eyes but the cold was biting and she was truly glad to get aboard the tram. They were draughty, rattling vehicles at the best of times, but because this one was so full she guessed that they would soon warm up among the folk crammed up like sardines in the tin-like interior.

It was difficult to hear each other speak above the din but they managed to agree that they would go to the late showing at the Grosvenor Picture Theatre that evening, having first eaten whatever meals their respective mothers had provided. 'But we'll have to hurry,' Kathy warned her friend, 'because I do hate going in halfway through the big feature. Oh, I am looking forward to it; it'll be my first outing for absolutely ages. Damn these twelve-hour shifts!'

Alec sat in the crew room with a blue notepad before him. It was a mild and cloudy day in early April and he was writing to his mother, though if he had said as much to the young men who surrounded him there would have been jeers of disbelief. But it was perfectly true; Alec wrote home once a week when circumstances permitted and though he had been out with several of the pretty Waafs who worked on the station he thought, ruefully, that he had seldom had time to form any sort of lasting relationship. Certainly he had never felt sufficiently fond of a girl to want to start a correspondence – letter writing had never been his forte – so he wrote short letters regularly to his mother and occasionally to his grandparents.

Receiving letters was different, of course. He loved getting his mother's rambling epistles, full of stories of the charms of the rebuilt farmhouse and occasional grumbles or jokes about the number of land girls who had been foisted upon them. Because their farmhands had all been called up the Min of Ag had billeted six girls on the Hewitts and they were as good as men, Bob thought. Betty said that at least it saved them from evacuees, though she had added rather wistfully that she would not have minded taking in children. It was the parents of the evacuated young, she had heard, who caused so much trouble and dissension in rural circles.

Alec had not been home very often because, it seemed, the life of a member of the Royal Air Force was to be moved from pillar to post. He had been on half a dozen stations since the early, pre-war days, had taken – and passed – a great many examinations and had attended many courses, and finally had ended up as he had wanted to do, as aircrew – a navigator in a Blenheim bomber. When he had been posted to Watton he had been delighted, thinking that it was much nearer home than his other stations had been. However, it had not been so easy to get away because ever since the Battle of Britain, aircrews had been pretty constantly on call, and when he was able to snatch a forty-eight the journey was tedious and often meant a long walk at one end or the other. Because of the war, everything the farm produced was wanted and needed and the Hewitts were in a fair way to making Honeywell Farm even more successful than it had been before the flood. Bob, Betty and the land girls toiled remorselessly and when Alec did get home he followed suit, often returning to the station completely worn out. The rebuilt farmhouse, though sparsely furnished, was as good as it had ever been and Betty worked hard to make it a comfortable home.

Now Alec was writing to his parents to tell them that there was about to be another change in his life, for aircrews were wanted for the heavier bombers, and his whole crew were about to convert on to Wellingtons. This would mean a three-month course at Church Broughton, outside Derby, and after that there might be other courses. Certainly it would mean that their three-man crew would have to take on two extra bods – Wimpeys carried a five-man crew – and then they would be posted to a more permanent station.

Alec was happy enough as navigator, particularly as his best friend, Jimmy McCabe, was the gunner of the crew and the pilot, Frank Collins, was an easy-going, friendly sort of chap, twenty-six years old and an experienced flier. He had been piloting planes for a couple of years before the war and Alec knew they were lucky to have him. Alec was wise enough to realise that he would probably have become friendly with whoever had made up the crew, but he and Jimmy, though different in just about every way, had got on from day one. In the air, they had to look out for one another, to share the same heightened awareness that made them a successful team and brought them back from sorties safely. On land, it became equally important to stand shoulder to shoulder, whether in a bar, in the city or in the mess, or even in the cookhouse.

'Oh, Alec, not writin' to your bleedin' girlfriend *again*.' A hand smote Alec between the shoulder blades, making him gasp and cough. 'How about a trip into the city? There's a gharry leaving in half an hour and it's not raining for once even though it's cloudy.' Alec glanced up; it was Jimmy.

'Sorry, old man, wrong again. I'm writing to my parents; as for girlfriends, chance 'ud be a fine thing. But now that you mention it, I wouldn't mind a trip into the city; there's a film showing at the Haymarket which I'd really like to see. It's a comedy, *The Ghost Train*, and it's had terrific reviews. How do you fancy six penn'orth of dark?'

'Oh, is that the one starring Arthur Askey and Richard Murdoch?' Jimmy asked. 'Yes, I'd love to see it. Some of the fellers went earlier in the week, and they say it's grand. Besides, once we get to Church Broughton it may not be so easy to get in to the flicks.

Where did you say it were near? Derby? All I know about Derby is that there's a racecourse there. Or is it just in the song?'

Alec cast his eyes up to heaven and laid down his pen. 'I don't know any more about Derby than you do . . . but if we get a move on and get the gharry we could be in time to catch the early evening performance for a change and come out before the pubs shut. We could have a couple of jars and a sandwich or perhaps a meat pie at the Lamb, that pub almost opposite the Haymarket.'

Jimmy plunged a hand into his pocket and produced his loose change. 'Yeah, I reckon I could run to a beer and a cheese sarnie,' he said, having counted his money. 'Of course, we don't get paid like officers, but I can still afford the odd night out and I dare say you're the same. Shall we go, then?'

'OK; I'll just finish off this letter,' Alec said, scribbling busily.

Within a very few minutes he was folding the paper and stuffing it in the envelope. He had run out of stamps but would buy some more in the city. He stood up. 'Come on then,' he said. 'Let's go!'

The gharry carried them into Norwich uneventfully enough, though the driver told them laconically as they climbed aboard that the city had been bombed a couple of days before. 'They got the railway lines again and Caernarvon Road was hit, which mean water and gas mains and telephone lines are down,' he told them. 'Still, you fellers will be headin' for the centre, I reckon, so that won't affect you.' Alec agreed and when the gharry stopped on Castle Meadow, as all the gharries did, a crowd of men got down and soon dispersed, leaving Alec and Jimmy to cut through Davey Place on to the Walk. Presently they were comfortably ensconced in the cinema, roaring with laughter over the antics of the two stars and an excellent supporting cast. It quite took Alec's mind off the war, the strangeness of travelling up to Derbyshire and the occasional doubts which attacked him. He was used to the small Blenheim bomber, and the crew, but he was sure that Frank was right; if they were to survive they needed a bigger aircraft with better armaments, more speed, even more manoeuvrability. The three of them had studied all the available information on the Wellington bomber and had decided to go for it, and had then waited, with some apprehension, to hear whether they had been successful in their application. Now it seemed they had, and would, once more, be moving on. But the antics of Arthur Askey and Richard Murdoch gave them a breathing space, time out so to speak, before they confronted the next stage in their war.

The two young men came out of the cinema when dusk was falling and made straight for the Lamb. As they entered the pub, Alec glanced up at the sky and commented that there was unlikely to be a raid that night because of the low cloud. A local man, leaning against the bar, overheard him and ambled towards them. 'You fellers don't know nothin',' he said mockingly. 'We're had the bloody raid earlier in th'afternoon. They hit Thorpe Station this time and made a right mess of it. There's a couple of fellers killed, I heard. So there's no sayin' that they won't be over agin tonight.'

'They won't,' Alec muttered to Jimmy as the man swayed unsteadily back towards the bar. 'A daylight raid is OK when the cloud is low and visibility poor, but weather like that make night flying impossible. The trouble is, Norwich is the first sizeable place the

Luftwaffe reach after they've crossed the sea so they drop their bombs and incendiaries and that, and probably go home and tell their masters they've flattened London.'

'But they really are flattening London,' Jimmy reminded him. He shuddered. 'I know Norwich has been hit but we're lucky we weren't posted to the south coast because they're getting a pastin' an' all. Norras bad as London, but they must hear enemy aircraft goin' over most nights and, of course, if they haven't got their target they'll jettison the bombs somewhere on their way back, so they aren't carrying them when they cross the Channel.'

'Aye, the further north you are, the safer, I reckon,' Alec said. 'A good thing you're from Liverpool and not Southampton, old feller. They say Southampton and Portsmouth have been practically wiped out. The Jerries were after Harland & Wolff and the shipyards an' that, but of course, when your home's just a pile o' rubble and your kids are killed, that's no comfort to know the bombs weren't meant to drop on you but on some factory or other.'

'True,' Jimmy said. 'Whose shout is it? If it's yours, I'll have a pint and one of them meat and potato pies, but if it's mine I'll have half and a cheese sandwich.'

'We'll go Dutch, as usual,' Alec said, punching his friend's shoulder. 'Oh, damn, I meant to post my letter but I forgot to buy a stamp. Never mind, I'll send it from the station tomorrow.'

'It's about time I wrote home,' Jimmy said rather remorsefully as they bagged a corner table and settled on to the long, leatherette seat. 'My girl – that's Jane – has gorra good job an' she's having a gay old time, what with the place being full of sailors and lots of soldiers as well, I gather. They embark 'em from

Liverpool when they're sending 'em to foreign parts, 'cos it's safer than Southampton or Portsmouth. But she's true as fire, my Jane, and she lives for me letters, she's telled me so many a time. Yep, when we get back to the station tonight, I'll go to our hut and sit down and write her a good, long letter.'

On 2 May, Kathy called for Jane at their usual early hour. When Jane came to the door, already with her coat and headscarf on, she was hollow-eyed from lack of sleep, for the previous night the city had suffered a heavy bombing raid and no one had got much rest.

'Jane, I'm so glad you're all right! We looked for you in the shelter but I suppose you must have gone to another one. Wasn't it dreadful? I thought my eardrums would burst when that big one went off – I dunno what time it was, about half an hour after we got to the shelter, I think – and Billy was shaking like a little leaf. Mam and I were scared it would make him ill again, but it didn't, thank God. The women were great: they started a sing-song . . . one woman passed round a bag of sweets – she'd made them herself, lovely slabs of toffee – and another lent blankets to anyone who was cold. If it hadn't been for the fearful noise, it would have been quite an adventure.'

'It weren't the noise so much as the shakin',' Jane said, as the two girls began to walk up Daisy Street. 'The windows rattled – I thought they'd come in – and the teapot and the cups bounced on the table. It were horrible, worse even than the raids last Christmas. Dad was fire watchin' and Mam decided it were too much of an effort to trek out to the shelter, what with Gran being crippled with arthritis – she takes an hour to get going mornin's – so we all stayed put. We didn't realise it were goin' to get as bad as it did and by the time we did realise, it were too dangerous to go on to the streets. Dad were that furious when he came home at dawn and found we'd not used the shelter. He made Mam and Gran promise on their lives that they wouldn't be so foolish again. Only – only I kept thinking you can be killed in a shelter just as dead as you can in a house, if you see what I mean. Remember all those people who were killed in Anfield when their shelter received a direct hit? The *Echo* said there weren't one survivor,' she concluded with a shudder.

'Yes, I remember,' Kathy said, 'but I think the reason they make us go to the shelter is because a dug-out is pretty deep and the roof is concrete and iron, quite a lot stronger than tiles. What's more, in a house you can be crushed by a ceiling falling in or a dresser toppling over, but shelters don't have such refinements.'

'Ye-es, but I hate the smell in those places,' Jane said as they reached the tram stop. 'Dad said there were terrible fires raging last night. He said the fire brigade couldn't begin to cope. It were mostly in the city centre, mind, but he reckons there's been a deal o' damage done.' Her face brightened. 'I wonder if the factory were hit? If so, they'll send us home, I suppose.'

'If it's been hit, then the night shift will have bought it,' Kathy said grimly. 'And if there's no factory there's no work, and if there's no work there's no money. Honestly, Jane, your mouth doesn't seem to be connected with your brain this morning.'

'I know, and I'm sorry. I'm not usually this stupid,' Jane said apologetically. 'I think I must still be asleep, for all I don't look it. My cousin Nellie is on nights at the moment and I'm rare fond of our Nellie. Why, I wouldn't want anyone hurt, not even Miss Bridges.'

Miss Bridges was the most hated supervisor in the whole factory. A thin, bitter woman of fifty or so, she ruled the girls with a rod of iron, would not allow them to speak so much as a word when she was on duty and forbade them to leave their benches even to go to the toilet. Jane and Kathy invented ridiculous – and probably slanderous – stories about Miss Bridges's imaginary past. But nothing entirely took away the dread which overcame them when they walked on to the factory floor and found her in charge of their section.

Kathy laughed again and squeezed Jane's arm, beginning to say she knew her friend would not harm a fly and that the remark about the factory had been spoken without thought. But at this moment the tram drew to a halt beside them and both girls climbed aboard. Kathy, looking around her, realised that she and Jane were not the only ones to have suffered a sleepless night. Everyone, even the conductress, was pale and heavy eyed and as the tram rattled along Stanley Road Jane commented that the queues of workers waiting to come aboard were shorter than usual.

'I do hope all the people who usually catch the tram haven't been killed,' she said apprehensively but Kathy, cheered by the fact that so far the streets and buildings looked much as usual, told her tartly that it was likelier to be folks sleeping in late and using the air raid as an excuse.

Presently, the girls descended from the tram and caught their bus, arriving at the factory in plenty of time to clock on. There, they heard tales of what had been happening in other parts of the city and realised that they had been lucky only to lose sleep. 'But it were a big raid. Someone said fifty or more bombers attacked the city last night,' Jane said, as the two girls sat in the canteen eating sawdust pie and leftover lettuce, which was their name for the dish which the canteen staff had christened pork pie and salad. 'I don't s'pose anything like that is likely to happen again.'

On Saturday, neither Kathy nor Jane was working so they slept late and then met to do their messages. Kathy told her friend that the doctor at the Stanley Hospital had suggested the Kellings might like to evacuate Billy from the city. 'You're even nearer the docks than we are,' he had observed when Sarah had taken Billy into his consulting room on Friday morning. 'It's the docks they're after, you know, and the shipping, of course. If they can cripple our Navy then half their work is done. Don't you think, Mrs Kelling, that it might be as well to take young Billy here into the country for a spell? No one knows how long these raids may go on, now that they know they can get this far north.'

Mrs Kelling and Kathy had discussed, very seriously, whether this would be wise, but Sarah was still nervous, thinking that if Billy did have a bad fit she would prefer to be within reach of the Stanley. 'It's all very well for the doctor to talk about being safer in the country,' she had said. 'But how do I know Billy won't be worse away from home? And what about you, queen? There's your work . . . come to that, there's my work. We've got to earn . . . oh, I don't know, I'm sure, but for the moment we're stayin' put.'

It was a bright and pleasant morning and Kathy

and Jane did most of their messages locally. Mr O'Brien had told them that the fruit and vegetable market in Cazneau Street had been damaged and he doubted whether it would be open for business until the corporation had had a chance to clear up the mess. They had a busy day but as it grew darker Kathy was conscious of a horrible tightening in her stomach. Later, as night drew on, she began to feel increasingly uneasy, especially when she looked up and saw that the sky was clear, save for a scattering of ragged cloud which never obscured the moon for more than a moment.

She and Jane parted company and Kathy went home to help her mother to prepare the evening meal. Dorothy's Tearooms had been hit by blast and, though the main structure of the building was undamaged, the windows had blown in. After they had cleared up the mess, the staff had all been sent home, so Mrs Kelling was already in the kitchen working, whilst Billy sat at the table, building a Meccano tower and singing beneath his breath.

Sarah turned round and smiled at her daughter, but Kathy went straight into the subject most on her mind. 'Mam, Jane and I met a girl we were at school with and she was telling us that they're evacuating' – she spelled the word out carefully so that Billy would not understand – 'mothers with children under ten. It isn't what you might call a regular evacuation,' she added hastily, seeing her mother begin to frown and shake her head. 'It's only for night times. Apparently, they've got reception centres in places like St Helens and Crosby. They'll take you out there around nine or ten and return you to your own homes next morning. What do you think? It would be a sort of trial run to see how you-know-who takes to being away from home.'

Billy looked up. 'I'm you-know-who,' he remarked. 'What's evac – evac – whatever you said? Only I aren't goin' to another school and I aren't goin' away from me mam, either.'

'Sharp as a perishin' needle,' Sarah said cheerfully. 'No sense in trying to pull the wool over that young busybody's eyes! What do you say, Billy? Would you like to spend a night in the country, with me and Kathy, too, so if there are any more bangs and flashes you won't have to hear them?'

Billy's eyes grew round. 'Would it be like a – a – sort o' holiday?' he asked, his face lighting up. 'There's fellers at school what've had holidays. They goes to the sea, so they does, and has a great time. I wouldn't mind that – I'd like it.'

This put a very different complexion on things so Sarah decided that they would give it a go. She packed a bag with their night things, two bottles of cold tea and some jam sandwiches wrapped in greaseproof paper, and they set off for the playground at Daisy Street School, where Kathy had been told that vehicles would pick up families with young children who didn't want to face another bombardment.

Billy knew a great many of the children waiting there and very soon they began to play Relievio, using one end of the playground as 'home'. But though they waited for more than an hour, no vehicles arrived and no one in authority either and Kathy, looking apprehensively up at the clear sky, told her mother that she thought they ought to make for the nearest shelter instead.

'Something's gone wrong – it always does,' she said gloomily. 'But you never know, the Jerries may give us a break, let us have a night off, so to speak. I guess we all sleep much better in our own beds, but on the other hand, if we get down the shelter early, we'll be able to pick our places and might even sleep through the night if nothing happens.'

Sarah agreed that going to the shelter was the wisest thing, and presently they were joined by the O'Briens and various other neighbours. Kathy had the feeling that everyone was in the same boat and they were all prepared to help one another in any way they could. They must have been in the shelter for at least an hour when the alert sounded. By the time the terrible reverberating rhythm of enemy aircraft was heard overhead and the first appalling crashes of falling bombs came to their ears, Billy and the other children were beginning to whimper and cling to their mothers. Sarah picked Billy out of the bunk and sat him on her knee and the three of them swigged cold tea from the bottle and tried to eat jam sandwiches, although no one had much appetite. A heavy blanket hung at the door of the shelter and Kathy and Jane were unable to resist nipping out once or twice to take a look at what was happening. They came back white-faced and appalled.

'There's fires wherever you look; the whole city's burning,' Kathy muttered to her mother as Billy seemed likely to go off to sleep from sheer exhaustion. 'There won't be anything left tomorrow, and they've not even started on the docks yet, by the look of it. Mam, you and Billy *must* get out of it! Nothing could be worse for him than this.' And indeed, by three in the morning, when the terrible noise outside had not abated by one iota, Kathy was proved right. Billy began to have a fit of terrifying proportions, rolling his eyes back in his head, whimpering and frothing at the mouth.

'We've got to get him to hospital,' Sarah gasped, lifting Billy in her arms. 'Give me a hand, Kathy. He's a big boy now and I'll never get him all the way to the Stanley without your help.' The two of them, holding Billy between them, somehow got themselves out of the shelter. Outside, it was like a scene from hell. As Kathy had reported earlier, fires were blazing everywhere and the shrill whistle of descending bombs, followed by the *crump* of their impact, seemed ceaseless. Kathy was sure it was madness to try to reach the hospital in such conditions, but the noise was too appalling for any remarks to be heard, so they rushed the unconscious Billy into the hospital, only to find the staff far too busy to give them the attention they needed. There were casualties everywhere; children with heads gashed open by flying shrapnel, women nursing what looked like broken limbs, and figures on stretchers, some ominously still. Sarah took one quick, comprehensive look around her and turned back to look for the entrance once more. 'No point in staying here. They've got their hands full,' she said briefly. 'By the time he's seen, he'll be out of it – he's beginning to stir already. I were wrong to bring him but it's really taught me a lesson. We'll leave the city tomorrer. I'll find a job somewhere; I don't care what I do; but I won't stay here to see Billy lose his chance of outgrowing these fits.'

'Shall we go back to the shelter, Mam?' Kathy asked as they left the hospital. 'Or shall we go home? Surely it'll stop soon.'

Outside, their faces were lit by the flickering fires and it seemed no more foolish to go back to their own home than it had seemed to try to reach the hospital. Sarah, however, shook her head. 'We'll go back to the shelter,' she said firmly. 'It's nearer and young Billy won't know a thing's happened if he comes round where he passed out, so to speak.'

For the rest of the night, they stayed in the shelter, too weary to leave even when they heard the sweet notes of the all clear sound. But, eventually, they began to believe that the raiders really had gone and straggled up into the daylight of an unseasonably cold but bright May morning. Billy had come round, apparently unaware that he had been ill, and the O'Briens and the Kellings separated and went to their own homes almost in silence, too shattered and shocked by the night's events to want to talk. Indoors once more, Kathy made the breakfast porridge while Sarah wrapped Billy in blankets and tucked him up on the sofa, with a pillow behind his head. 'It's Sunday, so there's no work to go. Besides, I've got arrangements to make,' she said firmly. 'We're all going to need to catch up on a night's sleep so as soon as young Billy's finished his porridge he can cuddle down on the sofa and get a few hours in.' She turned to her daughter. 'You keep an eye on him, queen.'

Kathy agreed to do so, but in actual fact she did not keep an eye on anyone. She sat down in one of the shabby old armchairs with a bag of potatoes on her lap, meaning to scrape them for the pan, and fell deeply and immediately asleep, not waking until her mother returned, very much later in the day. Since Billy had also slept, it did not matter, but Kathy felt deeply ashamed and kept trying to apologise until Sarah put an arm round her and gave her an affectionate shake. 'You're only human, Kathy me love,' she said robustly. 'We're all dead beat an' I'm sure the moment I sit down I'll nod off meself. But oh, Kathy, the sights I've seen! I walked right across the city to reach Mrs McNab – there were no trams running and precious few buses – and the devastation is terrible. I feel real worried about Mr O'Brien, because the market in Cazneau Street just – just ain't there and it's still black and smouldering. Paddy's market was the same – the Scottie has taken the brunt of it, if you ask me – and no end of the shops are just rubble.'

'I wonder how the factory is?' Kathy said, round eyed. 'Oh, Mam, if the factory's been hit, what'll we do? Only you did say that the tearooms might not be open for weeks, and that was before last night's little lot.'

'I dunno what we're goin' to do, except that Mrs McNab was a real brick and repeated the offer she made me when the tearooms was hit. I didn't tell you because I didn't want to take it up, but Mrs McNab – she's Miss really, you know, because she's never been married – has a sister in the same line of business, what lives in Rhyl. She's closed her little tearoom and moved into the country, being mortal afraid of an attack by sea. But she told Mrs McNab that if she wanted to open up the place and use the flat – and the tearoom, of course – for the duration, then she was welcome to do so. Mrs McNab says it's a good little business and if I don't mind the work of the café then we're welcome to it. Mrs McNab won't leave Liverpool herself, but she's happy for me an' Billy to go.' She turned anxious eyes on her daughter. 'What d'you think, Kathy? Things here is in a rare terrible state and I dare say we won't find a bus or a train to take us to the North Wales coast on a Sunday, but I reckon we can get there tomorrow. Will you come?'

'I think it's wonderful of Mrs McNab,' Kathy said at once. 'It's a grand opportunity and you'd be mad to turn it down. I'd love to come with you just to take a look at the place, but I can't do it, Mam. I know I've said a lot of rude things about the factory, but we are producing munitions for the war effort. I can't just turn my back on it and not go in tomorrow – well, you wouldn't want me to, would you?'

'No, I suppose you're right,' Sarah said grudgingly. 'But when Billy and I leave, what'll you do? You can't stay in this house all by yourself, queen!'

'I guess I could move in with the O'Briens, share Jane's bed,' Kathy said, after a moment's thought. 'You're quite right, Mam, I wouldn't want to stay in the house alone. But Mrs O'Brien's ever so kind in her way and Gran is awful good. She gets the meals, you know, now that Mrs O'Brien is working full time, and keeps an eye on the kids and so on. I'm sure they'd let me stay with them until – until I've worked something out.'

In normal circumstances, Kathy knew her mother would have been immediately suspicious, would have asked just exactly what her daughter meant by 'working something out', but she was far too involved in her own plans. Indeed, had she asked, Kathy would not have been able to tell her precisely what she meant. It had irked her for some time that she had such a long and complicated journey to reach the factory and she thought, once her mother and Billy had left, she might try to get herself lodgings in one of the many small streets surrounding the factory. However, there was still the possibility that her workplace might have been bombed . . . in which case, I shall join one of the services, Kathy told herself resolutely now, beginning to fetch food from the pantry to make a meal. I should have done it long ago but I felt if I did I would be abandoning Billy and Mam to their fate. I can't say I thought that the Jerries would ever bomb Liverpool the way they have, but I did think that Mam needed my support. But all that's a thing of the past; now she's the one who's leaving, and a good job too. I'm sure she'll find an excellent hospital in Rhyl and I'm equally sure that she will make a real go of the tearoom. What's more, it'll be so much better for Billy. There's sea air and quietness, because I don't suppose that trippers will be going there the way they did before the war. Yes, the more I think of it, the more sure I am that Mam's doing the right thing.

'You're very quiet, Kath,' Sarah remarked presently, bending to wake Billy so that he might share their meal. 'Come along, old chap. I've got some exciting news for you – and there's a sultana fruit cake for tea!'

'Sorry, Mam,' Kathy said contritely. 'It's just that there's so much to think about. Do you mind if I nip out to the O'Briens' after? I'll only be gone half an hour.'

Sarah said that was fine and, after the meal, settled down in the armchair to have a nap while Billy spread out his troops of lead soldiers on the tabletop and began to arrange them in battle formation. Kathy could not help smiling at the speed with which her mother fell asleep. Then she hurried along to the O'Briens', where a considerable shock awaited her. Jane answered her knock, her face very pale. 'Dad's in hospital,' she said in a small, shocked voice. 'He were fire watching at the fruit and veg market when it were hit. He's lucky to be alive but he's broke his arm and several ribs. Poor Mr McCabe was halfway down the stairs and he were crushed by falling masonry. He's in the bed next to our dad and Mrs McCabe has sent for Jimmy because they think – they think mebbe he's goin' to die.'

'Oh, Jane, how dreadful! I'm so sorry,' Kathy said. 'Your poor dad – and poor Mr McCabe too. I remember you said he were awful kind to you when you and Jimmy first took up with each other. I really am *so* sorry.'

'You'd best come in,' Jane said, belatedly remembering that one did not keep one's best friend standing on the doorstep. She conjured up a wan smile. 'At least they're both in the Stanley, so it won't be difficult to visit them. And though it's for a horrible reason, it'll be grand to have Jimmy home again.'

Alec and Jimmy heard about the raid on Liverpool as they sat in the cookhouse on Sunday morning, eating their dinner.

'Sounds bad,' Jimmy said, through a mouthful of overcooked potato. 'Hope my mam's all right, and the rest of the family. Hope Jane's all right, come to that. The trouble with the news is they're so scared some Jerry spy might be listening that they only give you the bare bones. Well, pal? Have you decided whether to go home for this seventy-two-hour leave of ours? Only I know it's difficult for you because it's an awkward cross-country journey, an' then there are the land girls that your mam's housin'.'

'Yes, I think I'll go home; the kitchen floor isn't a lot harder than my bed . . .' Alec was beginning, when a warrant officer stopped beside their table, a yellow telegram in one hand.

'It's for you, McCabe. Hope it's not bad news,' the man said brusquely, and moved away as Jimmy tore the envelope open. He scanned the small sheet, then shoved it into Alec's hand.

'Well, that's made up me mind for me,' he said

huskily. 'I meant to go home anyroad, but now I've got no choice. If our dad's so bad Mam has to send a telegram . . .' He pulled a face and Alec saw that his lip was trembling and remembered how close a family the McCabes had always seemed. 'I – I suppose you wouldn't consider coming with me, old feller? Only if me dad's real bad, I may have to stay for a while and – and it would be easier if you was with me.'

'Of course I'll come, only won't your mam feel that she wants the family around her and not strangers?' Alec asked uneasily. It sounded as though the bombing raid on Liverpool the previous night had been pretty bad, though he realised that a man could be severely injured in any sort of attack, and he imagined that the last thing Mrs McCabe would want would be an uninvited guest. Jimmy, however, waved his fears aside. 'There's plenty of folk wi' spare rooms in Crocus Street . . . and in Daisy Street for that matter, where me young lady lives,' he said grandly. 'Besides, you've never been to Liverpool, have you? It's a grand city wi' lots o' cinemas, theatres, markets, big stores . . . why, you'll be out o' the house mostly, having a gay old time.'

As it happened, it was easy for Jimmy and Alec to confirm their leave and get their rail passes. On a course such as this it was really the pilot who needed most retraining, since a navigator and a gunner would do very much the same job in whichever aircraft they happened to be flying. So, when Jimmy showed the telegram to his CO, he was immediately told to get his rail pass and leave early the following day, and his request that his friend might accompany him was granted without any argument.

Accordingly, the two of them set off at an incredibly early hour next day and were stepping down off the bus which had brought them as near to the centre of Liverpool as it could by early afternoon. Lime Street station had been put out of action three days before by the bombing raids.

What they saw there shocked Alec almost as much as it shocked Jimmy, to whom the scene had once been as familiar as the back of his own hand. It was a city in ruins, with a thick pall of smoke still hanging over it. To be sure, the bulk of St George's Hall, up there on its plateau, was unharmed, but Lime Street station looked as though it would be out of commission for some time and there were ruined buildings everywhere, some of them still smouldering. They had to clamber over heaps of bricks and rubble in order to reach the only taxi rank in sight.

'Where's you headin', fellers?' the taxi driver asked them as they piled their kit bags and themselves on to the cracked leather seat. 'Because there's roads mashed to bits all over the place, sewers spewin' up, telephone lines down, rubble stoppin' a car or a bike from passin' . . . I dunno as I can promise to get you anywhere in under an hour.'

'Crocus Street; it's a couple o' streets past the Stanley Hospital, on the opposite side o' the road,' Jimmy began, only to be told brusquely, though not unkindly, that the driver knew the flower streets as well as he knew the rest of Kirkdale.

'But it'll be a roundabout route,' he warned. 'The Scottie's took a beatin'. Paddy's market bought it, as you fellers say, and one o' the cinemas . . . but I'll get you home, don't you worrit yourselves.'

'What else has been hit?' Jimmy asked apprehensively, as the taxi began to make its way through the shattered streets. 'Surely the Stanley Hospital is still standin'? Me dad's in there . . . we're goin' there as soon as I've dropped me stuff off at home.'

'The Stanley's awright so far as I know,' the driver assured them. 'I'm from Bootle meself, so I come in to work that way and the hospital were there this mornin'. The Royal and the Millfield infirmaries have both been hit, though, and have you heard about the *Malakand*? She were an ammo ship in Huskisson Dock until this morning – she's a load of scrap metal now. Destroyed everything around her when she blew,' he added with mournful relish. 'It's to be hoped they won't come again but there's no bleedin' reason why they should stay away, because our air force seemed to be busy somewhere else for all the protectin' they did. An' if they do come again tonight there's no sayin' what'll be left by this time tomorrer.'

'I don't know about the air force in these parts, but I'm damned sure we're doing a pretty good job in the south and east of the country, though the fighters are pretty thin on the ground since the Battle of Britain,' Alec said. 'Didn't you see *any* of our chaps? But I dare say you didn't see much at all since you were probably down in the shelter.'

'In a shelter? Let me tell you, you cocky young bastard, that I'm an air raid warden, nights.' He turned towards the young men and Alec saw that his face was grey and his eyes bloodshot from lack of sleep. 'I've not slept for three nights, and I only get a couple of hours of a mornin' before turnin' into work. *If* there were fighters up last night, for instance, they didn't come over my part of the city. Why, the only plane to crash – it were a Heinkel – was brought down by a barrage balloon. Mind you, last night's raid weren't as bad as the one on Sat'day night, but it was still bloody frightening and more damage were done.'

'Sorry,' Alec mumbled. 'I shouldn't have said that. I didn't mean to give offence. But we've been bombing Germany, taking off from Norfolk in a Blenheim bomber, an' I can tell you we're very grateful to the chaps who fly Hurricanes and Spitfires when we see them come screamin' down on the Jerry aircraft. They wouldn't hold back, I'm tellin' you.'

'Well, I'm sorry too, then,' the driver said handsomely. 'I'm sure you're right and there was a good reason why our planes didn't try to stop them Jerries bombin' us. Truth to tell, I don't think anyone ever thought the Luftwaffe would come this far north. O' course, the ack-ack blazed away, but the Jerries never came low enough to get within range, or so they tell me. Still, no use cryin' over spilt milk; p'raps they've done enough damage and will leave us alone for a bit.'

At this point, Jimmy leaned forward, grasping Alec's arm and pointing. 'Look!' he said hoarsely. 'There's a bleedin' building there still afire – wharrever's happenin'? Where's the fire brigade, then? Dammit, there's another, smoulderin' away. If they don't put 'em out before dark falls, enemy bombers will have a perfect target, blackout or no blackout.'

The taxi driver agreed that this was so but said, defensively, that the fire service was doing its best, helped by the fire departments from towns as far away as Manchester. 'The trouble is, when the fire seems to be out the fellers move on, but they've only damped it down like and underneath it's still burning,' he explained. 'And there's so many fires, and they're everywhere. The ARP – that's my little lot

– do their best but we don't have the equipment, see? They give us bass brooms an' tell us to extinguish fires with 'em.' He snorted disgustedly. 'That shows what them fellers up in London knows about the sort of fire which happens when an incendiary gets dropped.'

They turned into Crocus Street at this point and drew up before the McCabe house. Alec stopped to pay the driver and by the time he joined Jimmy at the front door it was already beginning to open. A small and very dirty child stood in the aperture for a moment, staring up at them and plainly seeing the uniforms alone. Then she focused on Jimmy's face and flung herself forward, wrapping her skinny arms tightly round his waist and butting him with her head. 'Jimmy, Jimmy, Jimmy!' she wailed. 'Oh, I'm so glad you're home! Our daddy's dead.'

Chapter Eleven

Jimmy put his arm round the child and went into the house with Alec close on his heels, feeling absolutely awful. This was a house of mourning and he wished himself anywhere but here. They walked down a short passageway and into the kitchen, which was crowded with young McCabes. A woman he took to be Mrs McCabe was sitting at the kitchen table with her head resting on her sprawled arms. She was crying rhythmically in great tearing sobs and the children around her were crying too. Alec saw brimming eyes on each side of him and felt his own grow wet. Jimmy was crying, wiping his face with the heels of his hands as though he, too, were still just a little boy at heart. Perhaps we all are, Alec thought humbly, knowing that he would have reacted much as Jimmy was doing had it been his own father who had died.

'Jimmy. Oh, my dear, I'm so dreadfully sorry. I came round just as soon as I heard the news to see if there was anything I could do.' The speaker was a tall, slender girl with a mass of golden, curly hair and large blue eyes. Even at such a moment, Alec saw that she had the longest eyelashes he had ever seen, a small straight nose and skin like milk. He imagined that this must be Jimmy's sister, Annie, and thought her a real little smasher. He was just wondering why Jimmy had never told him that his sister was beautiful when Jimmy crossed the room in a couple of strides and took the girl in his arms.

'Jane, my darling, it's like you to come round to help us,' he said huskily. 'But why are you home at this time? Shouldn't you be at work?'

'We're on earlies this week,' Jane said. 'Who's your friend?'

'Oh, I forgot. This is me pal, Alec, Alec Hewitt,' Jimmy said.

Jane detached herself from Jimmy's arms and smiled across at Alec. 'Nice to meet you, Mr Hewitt,' she said formally, and moved across the kitchen whilst Jimmy bent over his mother and hugged her, telling her soothingly that she mustn't make herself ill with weeping.

'Da' wouldn't want you makin' yourself bad, grievin' for him,' he said coaxingly. 'Poor Mam, you've always worked hard but now you're goin' to have to work harder than ever. There's a lot to talk about, but we can't do that until you're a bit calmer. When – when did Da' die?'

Mrs McCabe had sat up straight as her son spoke and now mopped at her tear-blubbered face with a large handkerchief her son handed her. 'We've only just heard,' she muttered. 'There were a knock at the door – oh, ten minutes ago – and it were a young lady from the hospital. She told us he were gone and said to come up to the ward when we were ready. Oh, Jimmy, I dunno what I'll do wi'out your dad!'

'There's time enough to decide what to do when we've visited the hospital,' Jimmy said quietly. 'Oh, look, Jane's made you a nice cup o' tea. Just you drink that down and eat somethin' – a slice of bread and jam perhaps – and then we'll get the kids fed and settled down before we go over to the Stanley. Where's Annie? I suppose Joe and Rupe are off out somewhere.'

Mrs McCabe sighed and reached out a hand for the enamel mug. She blew gustily on the tea, then took a long swallow before answering. 'Annie's workin' – didn't I tell you? She's a nippy at Lyon's restaurant and doin' pretty well for herself. Joe's workin' at Laird's and young Rupe went out early this mornin' to collect shrapnel and any bits and pieces – bullet cases and the like – he can pick up. All the kids do it,' she added defensively, though neither Jimmy or Alec had said a word.

'It's all right, Mam,' Jimmy said soothingly. 'I just wanted to check up on all the kids. Lucy answered the door to us and the others are all in here.' He turned to Jane, who was serving up some sort of soup from a large, blackened saucepan into a variety of ill-assorted crockery. 'That smells good! Gorrany spare for a couple of hungry aircrew?'

Jane turned away from the stove and gave both young men the benefit of her brilliant smile. 'It's blind scouse 'cos I couldn't lay me hands on any meat, but me dad brings plenty of veg home from work. And there's heaps, help yourselves.'

Soon the entire family, including Alec and Jane, was sitting down to plates of the blind scouse. Jane had added a good number of potatoes to each helping and Alec was heartened to see how the food cheered everyone up. Even Mrs McCabe stopped crying, and presently she and Jimmy left the house to visit the hospital and sort out what must be done, leaving Jane and Alec to clear away, wash the crocks and keep an eye on the younger McCabes. Alec could not sort them out, but he counted six of them, all tatty-headed, ill-clothed and rather dirty. Jane suggested that they should wash the children and put them into clean clothes, but this idea was vetoed by the McCabe young who insisted that they had no clean clothes and that Mam would probably give them a good strip down wash later.

Jane shrugged but told Alec in an undertone that if the kids refused to clean up there wasn't much she could do about it. 'Mrs McCabe has too many kids to be able to take proper care of them,' she said softly. 'And Mr McCabe . . . well, I'm really sorry that he's died, of course I am, but – but he weren't a great deal of help to his wife and family. He were hardly ever at home and Mrs McCabe told my mam often and often that he drank more of his wages than he handed over. Don't say nothing to Jimmy, but for the past six months he's had a lady friend and he spent all his gelt on her, I believe. So, financially, Mrs McCabe might even be better off; I suppose she'll get a widow's pension and she won't have to hide her wages away like she used to.'

'Oh, does she work then?' Alec asked, placing a pile of dried cutlery on the dresser. 'I didn't know Jimmy's mam worked.'

'In Liverpool, everyone works; them as don't work, don't eat,' Jane said promptly. 'Mind you, before the war, most women were paid peanuts, no matter what they did. But it's different now. Mrs McCabe works in a factory, making munitions – I think it's bombs and that – out at Aintree. She's well paid, like we all are now.'

Alec nodded. He realised that the life led by the ordinary people of Liverpool was very different from that of those, however poor, living in a rural community. The only work in his part of the world was for farm labourers, and their wives might clean at the 'big house' or help in the harvest fields when they could. Though there were no proper paid jobs for women, the solution to their financial problems lay in their own hands. They filled their gardens with vegetables, fruit bushes and the like, and usually kept a few fowl. There was a pig in the sty at the end of the garden, fed from the scraps which the family did not eat, and the pig's manure was spread on the ground to enrich the soil for next year's crops. Countrywomen made their own bread because there was no alternative, just as they baked their own pies and cakes. Alec had noticed two bought loaves of baker's bread standing on the dresser in the McCabe kitchen, and a jar of mixed fruit jam with a Hartley's label on it. Country people were often very poor; a bad season could mean real hardship for everyone, but there were always the woods and the hedge-rows, where fruit and nuts could be gathered free. And there were rabbits and pigeons which could be either shot or trapped to grace a farm labourer's table. Yes, Alec concluded, it must be hard for the women of Liverpool to make ends meet, particularly if they had too many children and feckless husbands.

By this time, he and Jane had finished the work in the kitchen and Jane had just made a pot of tea and suggested that they should sit down and enjoy it. 'Jimmy and his mam won't be back from the hospital for a while yet,' she was beginning, when someone banged on the back door and it shot open. A slender young woman with long, light-brown hair came into the room, talking as she entered.

'Excuse me barging in, Jane, but I've just got back from the hospital and Mrs McCabe said you were here, so I thought—' She broke off, clearly seeing Alec for the first time, and Alec noted, with amusement, the swiftness with which the colour rose in her cheeks. 'Oh, I'm awfully sorry, I didn't realise . . . Mrs McCabe never said . . . I just wanted to tell Jane . . .'

'Kathy! No, I don't suppose Mrs McCabe would have said that Jimmy brought his pal home with him – you know about Mr McCabe, of course?'

The girl called Kathy nodded her head vigorously. 'Yes. As soon as I saw Jimmy, I guessed something was up. It's dreadful, isn't it? I felt so sorry for Mrs McCabe because when it came to it, she didn't want to go on the ward. I stayed with her while Jimmy went ahead to talk to the nurses. And then he came back for her, put his arm round her waist and led her away.' She looked around the kitchen, empty now save for themselves. 'Where are the kids?'

'I told 'em to go out to play,' Jane said. 'We fed 'em first, of course, and then Mr Hewitt here helped me to clear and wash up. Oh, I haven't introduced you! Kathy, this is Mr Hewitt, Jimmy's best pal. Mr Hewitt, this here's *my* best pal, Miss Kathy Kelling.'

The two shook hands and Alec said firmly: 'I'm Alec to my friends, Miss O'Brien, and I hope you won't object if I call you Jane, because Jimmy always does.' He turned to Kathy, smiling. It had just occurred to him that, if he and Jimmy were to go around the city whilst they were here, a foursome would be a good deal pleasanter than playing gooseberry. 'What do you say, Miss Kelling? Shall we dispense with formality and call each other Kathy and Alec?'

Both girls agreed, Jane with easy assurance and Kathy with another blush, and whilst Jane poured an extra cup of tea and chatted to her friend, Alec eyed both girls covertly. He decided that Kathy would pass for an attractive girl in any company other than Jane's, but next to Jane's brilliant colouring and astonishing good looks Kathy would be almost unnoticed.

The three of them settled themselves around the fire with their cups of tea and Jane turned to her friend. 'Why did you come in here in such a rush, queen?' she enquired. 'You looked as though you had news to impart, only then you saw Alec here and it went out of your head.'

Alec watched as Kathy clearly gathered her thoughts. 'Well, Mam and Billy went down to Rhyl this morning to have a look at the flat I told you about, the one over the teashop. We'd arranged she'd ring Mrs McNab so I popped in and actually managed to speak to her too. She says the flat's grand and partly furnished, so she and Billy are going to stay there – it's daft to come back into danger, even for one night, when you don't have to. Mam wanted to come back to Daisy Street to collect things, but I said I'd pack up all the stuff she wanted and take it down tomorrow. I – I had hoped you'd come down with me, only I don't suppose . . .'

'Of course I'll come,' Jane said at once, 'that is unless the McCabes need me, and I don't suppose they will. They're a big family, and everyone will get permission to stay away from work at such a time. And Jimmy says he'll get a week's compassionate as soon as he rings his CO to let him know what's happened.' She turned her brilliant blue gaze on Alec. 'What about you, Mr . . . I mean Alec? Will you be able to stay? If so, perhaps you'd like to come down to Rhyl with us, rather than hangin' around here while Jimmy and Mrs McCabe make funeral arrangements and so on.'

'I'd like to do that very much,' Alec said at once. 'I've never been to . . . Rhyl, was it? Is it far from here? Can we go by train or bus, or could we walk?'

Both girls laughed heartily at this and Alec, who knew very well where Rhyl was, was happy for them to do so. But they told him that once they'd crossed the water, a train would probably be easiest, adding that the journey down and back would take them all day, so he had best be quite sure that he was not wanted back at Church Broughton before he committed himself.

Alec laughed. 'I don't mind doing jankers for a week if it means having the company of two such delightful young ladies for a whole day,' he said gallantly. 'But I'd best clear it with Jimmy and the CO first, I suppose.' He turned to Kathy. 'What will you do tonight, Kathy? I gather from what you've said that you've only one brother, and he's gone with your mother to Rhyl. Does that mean you're going to sleep in an empty house?'

'Well, I may end up sleeping in the shelter anyway, along with half of Daisy Street, if there's another raid; if not, though, I was hoping that Jane would move in with me, just for a night or two,' Kathy said. 'It would be company, you see, because even going to the shelter is better if there are two of you.'

Alec liked her voice; it was low and musical and held almost no trace of a Liverpool accent. He wondered at the differences between two girls of roughly the same age, living in the same area for most of their lives. Kathy's speech was almost unaccented, whereas one could never fail to realise that Jane was from Liverpool. He knew he could scarcely comment upon it but decided to ask Jimmy as soon as circumstances permitted.

'Of course I'll move in wi' you. There's dozens of us O'Briens, so Mam can spare me,' Jane said at once. She turned towards Alec, giving him a smile in which sweetness and coquetry were nicely mingled. 'Unless Alec here would prefer to share your nice neat home, rather than muckin' in with a dozen McCabes,' she said teasingly.

'Jane, how can you?' Kathy squeaked, colour flooding her face once more. It made her eyes look very bright and Alec noted, for the first time, that her hair was not just brown, but contained other shades of chestnut, auburn and gold. Surprised, he looked at her again and saw she had large hazel eyes fringed with dusky lashes, beautifully clear skin, not cream and roses like Jane's, but sun-kissed, and her mouth, when she smiled, had an upward tilt which was very appealing. But now she was scarlet with embarrassment and telling Jane off in no uncertain way. 'You've embarrassed me and poor Alec must think us very odd people up here in Liverpool, so just you say you're sorry.' She turned back to Alec as Jane, laughing, said that it was only a joke and Alec was not to mind her. 'Where do you come from, Alec? I don't think it's London, because Mrs Bellis, one of our neighbours, comes from there and her voice is – is sort of sharper than yours.'

'I'm from Norfolk,' Alec said at once. He grinned at the two girls. '*Norfolk born and Norfolk bred, strong in the arm and thick in the head*, that's an old country saying. My mother always uses it when Dad or I annoy her by not immediately taking on board what she's saying. Not that she's one to talk, because she's Norfolk born and Norfolk bred, just as much as Dad and me.'

'Norfolk! I don't think I've ever met anyone from that side of the country, but aren't there lots of airfields there? It's East Anglia, isn't it? And I seem to remember it's very flat and sort of sticks out into the North Sea,' Kathy said, after a moment's thought. 'I wasn't bad at geography at school but we didn't do a lot on Great Britain, it was mainly abroad. Capital cities and big rivers and stuff like that, and who produced what, of course. China was rice and silk, I seem to remember, and India was tea and – and . . .'

'. . . and elephants,' Jane said triumphantly. 'Or was it ivory? I weren't no good at anything much when I were at school. But what's the odds in the end? Me and Kathy work side by side at the same bench, making parts for machine guns. We get paid the same, we get bawled out by the supervisor when she's in a bad mood, and we eat in the same canteen, yet Kathy here won a scholarship to the high school and is ever so clever, whereas I stayed at Daisy Street till I were fourteen and then gorra job on a fruit and veg stall in the market. An' I only got that 'cos me dad worked there,' she finished.

Kathy gave a snort. 'Jane was just as clever as I was but she's the eldest of a big family and her parents didn't think education was much good for a girl,' she told Alec. 'And anyhow, they've been proved right. I meant to go to university but, as Jane says, we're both factory hands now.'

'Do you like factory work?' Alec asked curiously. 'It must be pretty boring, I'd have thought.'

Kathy stared at him. 'Yes, it is,' she said slowly. 'In fact, if it hadn't been for my mam and little brother I wouldn't have stuck it for so long. But now that they've left Daisy Street . . . there's no reason why I shouldn't do the same.' She jumped to her feet, crossed the kitchen and pulled Jane away from the sink so that they were facing one another. 'Jane, now's our chance!' she said excitedly. 'Mam and Billy don't need me now. *I'm* going to sign on for the WAAF – care to join me?'

Alec had known air raids before. He had been in Norwich when it was bombed, had been on airfields when the Luftwaffe had come in low, guns spitting, and had dropped bombs on the runways and even on the huts. But he had never been in a raid such as the one Liverpool suffered in the early hours of Tuesday morning. He had bedded down on the McCabes' kitchen sofa, well wrapped in blankets, and had slept at once, exhausted by what had been a very long day. He supposed that he must have heard the sirens, warning that an attack was about to start, but if so they had not completely woken him, for it was Jimmy, shaking him roughly, who brought him struggling up out of a sleep that seemed fathoms deep to find himself sitting up in the dark kitchen, whilst all around him children murmured and collected the things they would need in the shelter.

'Sorry to wake you, old feller, but I'm gettin' Mam and the kids down to the shelter before the Jerries get goin',' Jimmy said. His mother, plainly used to evacuating her family on a nightly basis, was handing out blankets and packing a basket with a loaf of bread, a pot of jam and a flask which, Alec assumed, contained tea. 'I'm not goin' to stay in the shelter meself. I'm goin' along to the Stanley Hospital or one of the air raid wardens' posts to see what I can do. If those bastards drop more incendiaries, then we're in real trouble, and it's me *home*, old feller! I can't sit in a shelter while me home burns.'

'I'll come with you,' Alec said at once, climbing rather stiffly off the couch and folding his borrowed blankets into a neat pile. 'What about the girls, though, Jimmy? Should we go round to the Kellings' house, persuade them to go to the shelter? They're only young and they've been awake every night since the blitz started. It would be awful if they slept through it and – and got themselves badly hurt or – or killed.'

Jimmy, hustling his younger brothers and sisters towards the door, raised a quizzical eyebrow. 'D'you think our Liverpool judies is made of sugar, old mate?' he asked. 'Believe me, you're wrong. Jane will have woken at the first sound of the siren and be halfway along to her own home before you can say knife, and Kathy won't be far behind. Mrs O'Brien's a lovely woman but she's always been a bit of a butterfly, if you understand me. Mr O'Brien and Jane are the steady ones in that family, and Mr O'Brien's still in hospital, so it'll be Jane what supervises and bullies them all into the shelter, just you see if it ain't.'

And presently, Alec saw that his friend was right. Ahead of them in the darkened street, lit only by the moonlight, he could just make out the slender figures of the two girls, shepherding a rabble of kids ahead of them towards the shelter. In the distance, only just on the edge of hearing, he could make out the thud and thrum of the heavy bombers. He recognised the engine notes of Dorniers, Heinkels and Junkers and reflected, bitterly, that this seemed to presage an enormous raid, as big or bigger than the one which had been reported on the national news the previous weekend.

By the time he and Jimmy were settling Mrs McCabe and her family into the shelter, the planes were directly overhead, a carpet of fearsome sounds but, so far, without the whistle and thud which announced the arrival of high explosive bombs. Alec put his mouth close to Jimmy's ear and remarked, optimistically, that since nothing had been dropped yet it might merely be that these planes were on their way to bomb someone else. After all, having found that they could reach Liverpool with ease and return safely, the Luftwaffe must also realise it was on the west coast of Britain that His Majesty's Government had the most shipping, docks and warehousing.

Jimmy agreed that Alec might well be right but his voice lacked conviction and soon, when the two young men came out on to the street once more, it became glaringly clear that whilst a large number of enemy aircraft had indeed passed overhead without inflicting any more damage on the city, those that followed were by no means friendly. Incendiaries lit up the night sky and very soon more buildings were in flames, though mostly it seemed that the target tonight was south and central Liverpool.

When they presented themselves at the nearest wardens' post they were hailed with considerable relief and given a section of streets nearby to patrol. 'Kick the incendiaries into the middle of the road, where they can do little harm,' the chief warden advised them. 'We're supposed to carry a bucket of sand to extinguish them, but it weighs you down and besides, we've run out. If you see anyone above ground get them off the streets and into the shelters wherever possible, and if you see a really big fire starting go to the nearest telephone and dial 999 for the fire brigade. They'll come if they can . . . and if you come across a newly bombed building try and rope it off so kids can't run inside and get hit by masonry which is ready to fall.'

'Right,' Alec said, a little bewildered by these rapid instructions. 'Anything else we should know?'

'Don't think so,' the man said. 'Just use your common sense – the one thing folk don't do in an air raid, unfortunately. They run back indoors to fetch a photo of Aunt Lizzie, or to rescue a cat which has probably been out all night anyway, and then they're surprised when they get themselves killed.'

'What about dogs?' Alec said as the two of them turned away from the post and set off towards the streets they were to patrol. 'The noise alone is enough to send any dog mad wi' fear, I reckon.'

'We'll use our common sense and try to persuade them to go down to the shelters,' Jimmy said with a grin. 'God almighty, that was a near one!'

The all clear did not go until past three in the morning, by which time Alec and Jimmy would have been glad to return to their beds, but unfortunately they were in the vicinity when a warehouse containing lard and margarine was hit and set on fire. It was near enough to the docks to endanger shipping and everyone who could be spared immediately began to try to at least contain the conflagration, so it was not until five in the morning that Jimmy and Alec were able to fall, exhausted, into their beds.

When, scarcely two hours afterwards, Alec felt his shoulder being shaken, he groaned aloud and tried to bury his face in his pillow, saying groggily: 'Go 'way. That can't possibly be morning yet.'

'Gerrup, you lazy great Norfolk dumpling,' Jimmy said cheerfully. 'Don't you remember? You said you'd go down to Rhyl with Kathy and Jane and they're waitin' for you. Mam and me will be busy all day with funeral arrangements and Annie's asked for time off so she can look after the kids. Oh, come *on*,

Alec, or you'll find yourself dressin' wi' half a dozen McCabes lookin' on.'

That made Alec scramble upright and cast off his blankets. He had met Annie the previous evening and, though he would not have dreamed of saying so to Jimmy, he had thought her far too sexually aware for her years. He had been uneasily conscious that she lost no opportunity to press up against him and constantly suggested that he might like to see the city in her company the following day.

However, he need not have bothered. He was up, dressed and out of the house before any of the other McCabes were out of bed. Jimmy seemed unaware of his sister's forward behaviour, though he did say, uneasily, that 'it were about time the lazy lummock gorrout of her pit and came down to give a hand wi' breakfast'.

Since breakfast consisted of tea and bread and jam – they had run out of porridge oats the day before – it was a meal which Jimmy and Alec were quite capable of making for themselves, but presently there was a tap on the door and Jane's head appeared in the aperture.

'Mornin' both,' she said cheerfully. She stepped into the room, glanced around and then went across to Jimmy, giving him a quick hug and a kiss on the side of his face, though Jimmy immediately tried to kiss her properly and was repulsed. 'Stow it, Jimmy! This ain't the time or the place for canoodlin'. You're home for a week, remember, but today we've simply got to get Kathy's mam settled in. I've already told them in the factory that we're not coming in for a day or two.' She turned towards Jimmy's companion. 'Are you ready, Alec? It's high time we were off. We've packed up all the things Kathy's mam wanted

271

and divided 'em into three bundles, one each. Yours is the heaviest! Have you had breakfast?'

'Yes thanks,' Alec said, somewhat thickly, through his last mouthful of bread and jam. He turned rather awkwardly to Jimmy. 'You're sure it's all right if I go, old feller? Only it seems awfully mean to leave you here alone to do all the – the arranging and that.'

'Yeah, it'll be better. I'd feel awful guilty takin' you with me, an' worse leavin' you to Annie's tender mercies. She seems to have turned into a maneater while I were away.'

Kathy had followed Jane into the kitchen and the remark made her giggle. 'I think the nippies have to be able to deal with their male customers and that means they're always quick with an answer,' she said. 'Are you sure you don't mind comin' down to Rhyl, Alec? It would be such a help.'

For answer, Alec headed for the back door. 'Where's my bundle?' he asked. 'Lead me to it, fair damsels!'

The three of them went out into the street. It was a clear morning, though still somewhat chilly, and suddenly Alec was seized with an attack of reasonless optimism – they were going to the seaside! And they were also going, he felt sure, to have a grand day out.

It was late when Alec returned to the McCabe house and he did so reluctantly, since the girls had refused his invitation to accompany him. 'Jane and I will make ourselves a hot drink and a snack and then try to get some sleep before the sirens sound,' Kathy had said, smiling at him. 'Thank you ever so much for your help, Alec; I don't know how we would have managed without you. And didn't our Billy take a shine to you? He's determined to join the air force as soon as he's old enough, which makes a change from train drivers or ship's captains!'

'He's a nice kid,' Alec had said. 'See you tomorrow, then.'

'See you in the air raid shelter, you mean,' Jane had said. She twinkled up at him, a grin lurking. 'We've come to accept that we'll be stuck down that bleedin' shelter for the best part of every night, you see.'

Alec's heart gave a lurch. She was, without doubt, the loveliest creature he had ever seen and he envied Jimmy his good fortune. Fancy going to the same school as a little smasher like Jane – fancy being the one to squire her to dances and cinema shows, theatres and amusement parks. And it wasn't just that she was so adorably pretty, she had a lovely bubbly personality as well. He liked her quiet little friend but not, he realised ruefully now, as he let himself into the McCabe kitchen, the way he liked Jane.

'Alec! How did you get on, old feller? You're awful late but we guessed you would be. Want some supper? Our mam bought one of them pie things – sausage meat ain't it? – and there's still some spuds left. I can pour some gravy over it, heat it through and you can get it down you before the sirens start shriekin'.'

'Thanks, that 'ud be grand,' Alec said. 'And we got on grand an' all. We took the stuff up to Mrs Kelling's flat – that's a nice place, right on the main street – and then we went down to the beach and had a paddle. Most of it's wired off, of course, but there's a strip you can use which goes right down to the sea.' He remembered Jane, flushed with excitement, lifting up the full skirt of her blue gingham dress and running

273

into the sea, as pleased to splash into the salt water as any child would have been. He had run after her, and when Kathy was helping Billy to gather shells he had grabbed Jane whilst her hands were busy holding up her skirts, lifted her off her feet and let her slide back into the water again, kissing her full on the mouth. He had half expected a slap round the chops or at least a murmur of protest, but when he released her she did not look angry. She looked, he concluded now, as though she had enjoyed the kiss and had half expected more.

By the time they had left the beach, Alec believed that he was fathoms deep in love with Jane and despite his friendship with Jimmy he meant to win her, if he possibly could. He knew she liked him but did not know how she behaved with other young men. He guessed that she was innocent, only ever having had one boyfriend in her whole life, and decided that she had simply fallen into a relationship with Jimmy, accepting him as her boyfriend, without ever having asked herself whether she really loved him or whether it was simply that they had known one another for ever.

'Penny for your thoughts, old man? You're sittin' there with your gob open, starin' into space as though you'd seen a perishin' vision. Whazzup?'

At the sound of his friend's voice Alec, guiltily, dragged his mind away from Jane and back to the present. 'Sorry. I were just thinking that I wouldn't mind living in Rhyl myself, when the war's over,' he said untruthfully. He looked around the kitchen. 'Where is everybody?'

'They've gone to the shelter. They thought they'd get settled in the bunks before the raid starts tonight,' Jimmy said. He had been stirring a pan on the stove and now he tipped the contents on to a plate and slapped it down in front of his friend. 'There y'are, a dog's dinner made wi' me own fair hands. Get it down you, then we can try for some kip.'

Alec looked down at the mashed up mixture of sausage meat pie, gravy and potatoes and pretended to shudder. 'That looks as though you've cooked the dog rather than his dinner,' he said, beginning to shovel the food into his mouth. 'Mmm, but you aren't a bad cook, old Jimmy. This here's real tasty.'

Kathy and Jane returned to the Kellings' home to find it cold and empty. Kathy looked around her, at the kitchen which had always seemed so warm and welcoming when Mam was here. Seeing it thus confirmed her intention to join the WAAF. She and Jane were both working girls and they would be coming home to a cold, unwelcoming house every night of the week. Moving into digs nearer the factory did not really appeal to her and she said so as she got out the loaf and a box of Oxo cubes.

Jane agreed with her that there was no point in remaining in Liverpool. 'Because if I do – stay here I mean – I'll be hauled back every two minutes to take over from me mam,' she said frankly. 'And Tilly is every bit as good at it as I was. No, I'm determined to join one of the services – the WAAF if they'll have me – and *really* help the war effort.'

The kettle boiled and Kathy made two large mugs of Oxo and cut two thick slices off the loaf. It was her mother's homemade bread and she thought, wistfully, that she would be unlikely to taste anything as good in the WAAF. Settling down opposite Jane at the kitchen table, she began to sip her drink. 'I saw you helping with the war effort in Rhyl earlier in the day,' she said slyly. 'Just what did you think you were doing, kissing Mr Hewitt?'

It was said half laughingly but Kathy saw that it brought a flush to Jane's cheeks. 'Me? It weren't me, it were him,' Jane said at once. 'I think it were just the sea and the sun and me being near at hand . . . it were just a bit of fun.'

'Try telling Jimmy that,' Kathy said, still only half serious. She had known Jane for so long, and for years now it had been generally accepted that Jimmy was her boyfriend, would one day be her husband. She had grown quite fond of him herself, thought him good fun and even nice looking, though she reminded herself now that he was nowhere near as nice looking as Alec. Still, she couldn't believe that Jane would ever look twice at any man other than Jimmy, which was a good thing, since from the first moment she, Kathy, had seen Alec she had known she was going to like him very much indeed. And it was not just his looks either, she told herself. He was kind, thoughtful, sensible. He had been marvellous with Billy, patient and funny, yet when Sarah had said he must have younger brothers of his own he had said no, he was an only child. What was more, Kathy remembered, he had behaved beautifully towards her mother, telling her about his own home and parents, helping to move furniture around when necessary and congratulating her on the excellence of the meal she had provided.

He was pretty nice to me, as well, Kathy thought now. Talking to me on the journey home, asking about school, my work at the factory, what my likes and dislikes are. And he told me a lot about the WAAF and what trades are available to someone with my sort of education. He's nice to everyone, I should say. Jimmy's lucky to have such a pal.

'I'm not going to tell Jimmy anything, an' nor are you,' Jane said, breaking into Kathy's thoughts and suddenly sounding almost aggressive. 'Jimmy an' me know each other and understand each other, but if he thought I'd been playin' fast an' loose with his best pal ... well, don't you dare say a word, Kathy Kelling, or you an' me will fall out.'

Kathy was astonished. Jane had never spoken to her in such a manner before, and for the first time she began to wonder whether Jane really did like Alec. Oh, not in a friendly sort of way, but in a kissy and cuddly sort of way. She stood her mug down on the table and stared across at her friend. Jane's blue eyes met hers defiantly but she thought she saw a trace of shame in their depths. 'Jane, how could you? As if I'd dream of upsetting your Jimmy by telling tales! I know it was only a bit of fun really, but I thought at the time it was a good thing Billy's living in Rhyl and not in Daisy Street, because you know how tactless kids are. The first thing he would have done the next time he saw Jimmy was tell him you'd kissed his pal, and then the fat would have been in the fire.'

'Like in that warehouse full of fat and margarine that went up last night, during the raid,' Jane said dreamily. All the aggression had left her face and a gentle smile curved her lips. 'I know it were only a bit of fun, but – but Alec's awful good looking, don't you think? I do like his hair – what colour would you call it, queen? It ain't red, norrit ain't brown. It's something between the two, and his eyes are the same colour. I've never knowed anyone with eyes and hair the same colour, have you? And his teeth are ever so white and even. I didn't think teeth mattered, but they do, you know. Jimmy's teeth are a bit crooked and a bit sort of yellowish, wouldn't you say?'

'No, I would not,' Kathy said roundly. Her friend was talking in a way which worried her – surely Jane wasn't going to cast her warm and loving relationship with Jimmy aside because she'd met a young man with beautiful white teeth? 'Jimmy's teeth look fine to me. Anyway, you don't fall in love with someone because they're handsome!'

'I haven't fallen in love with anyone – except Jimmy of course – and I certainly don't mean to make a fool of meself over Jimmy's best friend,' Jane said, putting down her own drink and reaching for a slice of bread. 'Remember, Kathy, those two fellers are aircrew in the same plane. If they were bad pals it would wreck the whole team. Jimmy's told me, often and often, how important it is that they genuinely like one another. Now, what shall we do when we've finished our food? Go up to bed here, or go down to the shelter?'

Kathy decided that she would rather try to get a good night's sleep in her own home and presently the two of them made their way upstairs in a rather constrained silence. Kathy glanced sideways at her friend as they entered the main bedroom, for they meant to share the double bed rather than the two singles in the room Kathy had shared with Billy. She and Jane had never, in all their long friendship, seriously fallen out before and it was silly that they should quarrel over a young man who would leave Liverpool in a couple of days and probably never return. Alec was very good looking; he had a good figure, being wide shouldered and narrow waisted, and Kathy admitted to herself that she had hoped he might want to keep in touch with her, but of course the hope had crumbled to dust when she had seen him kissing Jane. Kathy was a realist; she had taken her friend's golden good looks for granted since the first day they had met, so it was absurd to feel slighted by Alec's complete lack of interest in herself. She knew she should expect nothing else, because boys had been ignoring her for years, always smitten by Jane's looks into not noticing Kathy.

But as she snuggled down in the big bed, Kathy admitted that this time it was different. She had never met a man whose opinion truly mattered to her until now. But she really wanted Alec to think well of her, wanted him to suggest that they might go out together, meant to ask him, before he left for Church Broughton once more, whether she might write to him. That way, she hoped they could remain in touch without his guessing how she felt. Because I won't give up without a fight, she found herself thinking. Jane's beautiful and I'm not, but Jane isn't free, and I am. I won't, I *won't* just give up meekly and let Jane take the only man I've ever met who means anything to me.

And on that thought, she fell asleep.

Chapter Twelve

Alec and Jimmy had enjoyed a restful night since they were so tired that they slept straight through the alarms and excursions that happened in the early hours of Wednesday morning. What was more, when they did awake, Mrs McCabe was already up, having fed the children and packed them off to school. 'I doubt there'll be any lessons but at least it'll keep 'em off the streets, and the streets is dangerous wi' buildings still smouldering and masonry tumbling whenever a heavy vehicle goes past. I'll have to do me messages later,' she added. 'Unless you fellers fancy a bit o' shopping?'

Jimmy said, rather discontentedly, that he supposed they would have to do her shopping and Alec, who had wondered why on earth Mrs McCabe should want them to take messages for her, realised that this was yet another piece of scouse talk, and grinned to himself. The first time Jimmy had offered to mug him to a beer, he had thought he had misheard, but Jimmy had explained, patiently, that this was scouse and meant that he would pay for the beer.

'Oh, I *see*,' Alec had said as light dawned. 'I reckon we'd say we'd treat you. That's a right queer language you speak, old feller.'

Jimmy had replied with spirit that at least he didn't refer to a young girl as a mawther, nor call a snail a dodman. 'And nor I don't have a mardle wi' me mates, when I mean I'm having a crack,' he said, causing Alec to give a hoot of laughter; clearly Jimmy was not aware that in most parts of the country a crack did not mean a gossip.

'I'm a-going to write you a list, because there's a deal o' stuff we'll need for the wake,' Mrs McCabe said now. 'It'll be on Friday, after the funeral. We'll have it here and all the neighbours will give a hand; you know how it is.' She turned to Alec. 'I dunno whether you'll still be here but I fancy you will. Me cousin Bertha's boy is in the army; she's a widder so they've sent him home to give a hand. Her house is awright but there's several been bombed in her terrace and the government are sayin' we need all the help we can get. So I reckon they'll let you stay.'

'I'll ring again once I've had me breakfast,' Jimmy said, causing Mrs McCabe to clap a hand to her mouth.

'Honest to God, Jimmy, I think I'm goin' round the bend, so I do. Kathy popped in earlier and said would you go round to her house for breakfast. She said her mam had give her a bag of eggs and a lovely loaf of homemade bread, so she's goin' to scramble 'em – the eggs not the bread – and thought you deserved a share for helpin' her yesterday.'

Jimmy's face brightened. It was clear that any chance to see Jane was a welcome one, and Alec himself hoped that sharing breakfast might mean that the four of them would spend the rest of the day together. After all, Mrs McCabe had made it plain that the neighbours would all rally round to help with the funeral tea and that would surely include Kathy and Jane? True, they did not live in Crocus Street, but Jimmy was always saying that the flower streets stuck together. What was more, Kathy and Jane would need to get shopping for themselves since it seemed they would remain in Kathy's house now for a while, at least.

Alec was very soon proved right. They went round to the Kellings' home to find Jane sitting at the table, writing a shopping list to Kathy's dictation whilst Kathy herself broke eggs into a white china basin, whipped them with a fork and added salt and pepper. Both girls momentarily suspended their tasks as the young men entered the kitchen and Kathy pointed to a pile of bread slices and asked Jimmy to shovel them under the grill whilst she scrambled the eggs. 'I've had to use a bit of dried milk because no one's delivering fresh at the moment,' she said, carefully pouring her mixture into a saucepan. 'Alec, can you mash the tea? These eggs won't take a minute, so if you make the tea and pour it, we'll be having our breakfast in no time.'

The meal was a good one, for Mrs Kelling had been generous and had given Kathy at least a dozen eggs. As soon as it was over, the girls got their coats and headscarves, picked up their shopping baskets, checked that they had money and coupons, and set out for the shops, the boys beside them. They had agreed to pool their shopping efforts, though for such essentials as butter, sugar and bacon they all had to go to the small grocer's shop on Stanley Road with which they were registered. After that, they split up, each taking a copy of the list and agreeing to buy whatever they could from it. If more than one of them should purchase plenty of potatoes, or an extra loaf of bread, it would not matter nearly as much as being unable to buy such an item.

Alec knew, of course, that food was rationed, but he was considerably surprised at how little was actually available for sale. Many shops had been destroyed but even the ones that remained seemed to have empty shelves, and Alec thought wistfully of home. His mother grew enough onions, potatoes and the like to feed the farm labourers as well as the Hewitts, and although they had to cater for the land girls as well as themselves there was still food to spare. Every possible niche in the farmhouse was filled with apples from the one remaining tree in the old orchard which had survived the flood, and bottles of fruit which his mother had picked from the young bushes they had planted in the autumn of '39. Lately, she had mentioned in her letters that they were having to mount guard over the garden and always brought the dairy herd in at night, though once it would have been easier to leave them to graze in the meadows. He had not thought it particularly important at the time but now, searching the shops without success for onions, cooking apples, a couple of pounds of rice, any dried fruit which could be used in a cake, and some golden syrup, he realised how incredibly difficult was the life of a housewife in a big town. She would spend far longer searching for ingredients than in preparing a meal and he found himself thankful that his parents lived in the country, even if they did have to guard their vegetable plot against thieves. He knew there was a black market in almost everything that was on ration or scarce and hoped that the spivs, who were willing to steal as well as to sell for exorbitant prices, would not gain access to his parents' acres.

Jimmy had rung their CO and he had told them they might both stay in Liverpool until the weekend and travel back on Sunday, if it was possible to do so. Jimmy had pointed out that the railways used Sundays to service engines and check track, but added that they would hitch-hike if that was the only way they could return to Church Broughton by Sunday evening. This seemed to satisfy their CO, who merely said he would like them back on the course by Monday at noon, if it was at all possible. 'You have a duty to support your mother and the rest of the family until they are over the worst, but young Hewitt does not. However, with the bombing so heavy, you are both probably more useful there than here. Just do your best, McCabe, and keep me informed.'

So now, trudging through the Liverpool streets in search of something as prosaic as an onion, Alec had the time to look about him. He had watched Jane and Kathy, armed with ration books, disappear into a grocery shop, and then examined his list. It would be a feather in his cap if he got even half the things Jane had written down, but though Stanley Road had been a thoroughfare, lined with shops and cafés, it was easy to see that they suffered from perennial shortages. Most of the smaller shops had empty packets or pictures of the goods they usually stocked in their windows, and though folk went in and out they did not seem to emerge with bulging shopping bags. Still, you had to admire the way the shopkeepers continued to trade, with broken glass littering the pavements, bombed out buildings still smouldering, and nothing very much to buy or sell. He also admired those he passed in the street. They had cheerful faces and a smile for everyone, despite what they had endured in the blitz. Folk in shops were friendly, and also inquisitive, because they could tell the moment Alec opened his mouth that he was not local. They mentioned the raids, seeming to take it for granted that now the Jerries had got their measure they would be back, but they did not appear to have any particular fear of what might come. I suppose everyone thinks that he or she is somehow special and won't get in the way of a bomb or a bullet, Alec told himself, joining the queue outside a fruit and veg shop, whose window held only turnips. Kathy had said that the theatres and picture houses had remained open throughout and he supposed that since most cinema showings finished by half past ten or so, and the worst of the raids occurred after midnight, this was not as silly as it had first seemed. Folk had to keep their spirits up and what better way was there than to transport themselves to the imaginary world of Hollywood – though he thought that the Pathé News, which was always shown between the main and the second feature, would bring them down to earth rather abruptly.

'Alec, Alec!' Kathy arrived beside him, breathless but cheerful. 'How are you doing? It's awful hard, but we've managed to get most of our stuff.' She peered inquisitively ahead. 'What are you queuing for? Have they got some fruit?'

'I dunno,' Alec admitted, feeling extremely foolish. 'I saw a queue and joined it, just in case they'd got something good. I mean all these women wouldn't queue just for turnips, would they?'

Kathy laughed. 'That's the real wartime spirit; you've caught it, Alec! Next thing we know, you'll be wearing a turban on your head and a wraparound apron and asking the woman next door how to make an egg and bacon pie when you've got no eggs and no bacon! Hang on, though, Mrs Bullivant is in the queue ahead; I'll nip up and ask her what they've got.' She was back in seconds, her eyes rounded, her face sparkling with mischief, and Alec thought, once again, that she was really rather fetching . . . that is if it hadn't been for Jane . . .

'It's oranges,' she hissed as she rejoined him. 'Two different sorts, Mrs Bullivant says. The nasty bitter ones you make marmalade with and the lovely big juicy ones you eat in your hand. I think we ought to wait, don't you?'

'Yes, I suppose we ought,' Alec said, as the queue shuffled forward a foot or two. 'Where's Jane and Jimmy though? And how much did you get of the stuff that's on the list? I got most things but not the golden syrup . . . and do you think I could find cooking apples? No one actually laughed, but that was because they felt sorry for me! And as for onions . . . well, if I'd known they were like gold dust, I'd have nicked a few from the stores on the station. I'm sure they wouldn't have missed an onion or two.'

'Oh, onions never seem to be in the shops. I wasn't that keen on them before the war, but now I dream about being given a heap of fried onions, all crispy and golden brown, and being allowed to eat and eat. Then there's bread and honey. I used to love bread and honey when I was a kid, but now it's disappeared, like the onions.'

'Aye, and like tablets of soap, razor blades, toothpaste and – and oranges,' Alec said, grinning. 'Someone said that things were either rationed or unobtainable. It's easier for us in the services, because our shopping gets done for us, and if the food's boring – which it usually is – at least it's served up regularly so that all we have to do is eat it. Never mind. It looks as though we might get something here, at least.'

The queue seemed to edge forward with incredible slowness but when they reached the head of it they were glad that they had waited. The fat, brown-coated greengrocer sold them two oranges, though he was forced to tell them, regretfully, that the Seville oranges, used in the manufacture of marmalade, had run out. 'But I do have a lemon still left,' he said in a conspiratorial whisper, producing a fruit so wizened that it fell like a stone into the bag. 'You can have that for nowt and use the extra sugar that you're allowed for marmalade to make a nice big jug of lemonade. Tell your mam it's with me compliments an' I hopes as how she and Billy are both doin' fine.' He eyed Alec curiously. 'You've got yourself a young feller, I see! Hope you enjoy your oranges.'

Alec saw Kathy flush scarlet at the remark but made no comment himself. When they regained the road, however, Kathy said shyly: 'Sorry about that, Alec, but I've known Mr Dickinson all my life, and you know how it is, some folk leap to conclusions. But I was wondering . . . well, if you're not too busy, if you'd like it . . .'

She broke down in confusion and Alec put an arm round her shoulders to give her a squeeze. 'Whatever's the matter, old girl?' he said gently. 'I can't imagine myself taking offence at anything you could say. Where's your self-confidence, Kathy? Do I look as if I eat little girls for breakfast?'

'No, of course not,' Kathy said with an embarrassed laugh. 'It's just that it seemed such a cheek . . . but I'll ask you anyway! I don't have brothers, apart from Billy, so I don't know anyone in the services. Oh, I know Jimmy and fellers who were in my class at the Daisy Street school, but they've all got families and girlfriends and so on. I – I just wondered . . .'

Alec was wondering, apprehensively, whether she was about to proposition him, when Kathy took a deep breath and started again. 'Would you like me to write to you?' she said, all in a rush. 'You needn't write back if you didn't want to, only I'd like it most awfully if you did. You see, it would mean we'd keep in touch, know how each other's lives were going on. What – what d'you think Alec?'

'I think that's a grand idea, and of course I'll write back,' Alec said heartily. It was a grand idea, too, because it meant that, if the two girls stayed together, he would know what was happening to Jane as well. He knew that Kathy and Jane had been friends all their lives, knew that they hoped to join the WAAF and knew that, even if they were sent to totally different parts of the country, they would still keep in touch. He looked down at Kathy as he spoke and caught her looking up at him with eyes full of an emotion which he had no wish to identify. Oh, Lord, the bloody girl's falling for me, he thought, dismayed. He had not meant it to happen, had merely treated her as he had treated other young women, but somewhere along the line – perhaps because she was so inexperienced – she had decided to fall for him. But next moment, she had looked down, letting her long sweep of bright brown hair fall, concealingly, across her face, and when she looked back up at him again there was only friendship in her large hazel eyes.

'Good!' she said joyfully. 'I felt ever so out of it, not having anyone to write letters to, apart from my mother's lodgers, and they're really more like a couple of uncles than friends. Well, now that's settled, we'd best go back to Daisy Street and join the others. Thanks ever so much for saying you'll write; you are so kind.'

When they entered the Kelling kitchen they found Jane preparing a scrap meal which Jimmy declared was plenty, breakfast having filled them up. 'We won't need nothin' more till supper time,' he assured her. 'I s'pose you two are going to be busy all afternoon, bakin' and makin' jellies an' that for Friday? Can we help or would you rather we made ourselves scarce?'

'We'd rather you helped,' Jane said promptly. 'Many hands make light work, you know, and I thought if we got through in time we might give ourselves a night off and go to the flicks. There's a good film showing at the Metropole, and if there's a raid it's almost next door to the Co-op, and there's a huge shelter there. What d'you say, fellers?'

The fellows thought it was a grand idea and offered to buy the girls a meal either before or after the show. When their bread and jam was eaten, they began to make fruit jellies – Jane had wheedled some sheets of gelatine out of a friendly grocer – pies and other edibles which would be placed in the pantry to await the funeral tea on Friday. The task kept them occupied for the whole afternoon and all of them were looking forward to a meal which they had not cooked, though Jimmy warned them that he would probably disgrace himself by falling asleep in the cinema.

'Never mind,' Jane said gaily. 'Unless the film is very exciting, we'll probably all fall asleep, because Kathy and I went to the shelter last night, and it were awful noisy. Oh, won't it be grand to see a film – it's been ages, or it feels like ages, since we've been out on the spree.'

The girls had worked hard at cooking and preparing food all afternoon, and when Jane announced that she meant to go home and put on her best dress and decent winter coat Kathy was quite glad to have a chance to clean herself up and consult her wardrobe. In the end, she decided on a navy blue flannel suit of her mother's. Mam won't mind, seeing as it's a special occasion, she told herself, reaching the suit down from her mother's cupboard and admiring the brooch on the lapel. It was a golden bird and looked really nice against the dark blue, but in the end she took it off and put it carefully in her mother's dressing table drawer. Better not wear it. Suppose she lost it? The brooch had been a present from her father; she would never forgive herself if it was not in her mother's little jewel case to welcome her when she got home.

So Kathy put on the navy blue suit with a pale pink blouse beneath it, then covered her borrowed finery with her old navy blue mackintosh and perched a pink beret on her smoothly brushed hair. She thought about a ribbon – to tie her hair back in a tail or to wind round her head in order to pin her hair round it, a popular fashion – but decided in the end to let it stay as it was. She wanted to look her best, as Jane did, but thought, ruefully, that simplicity was sometimes the best thing if your hair was not either a wonderful golden blonde or naturally curly. Jane's hair, needless to say, was both . . . lucky Jane!

Kathy ran down the stairs and glanced up at the clock over the mantel. She had plenty of time so perhaps it would be as well to spend some of it in putting the food she had prepared into the tins Jane had borrowed from various neighbours – if it was cool, that was. She tested a couple of cakes and several trays with baking spread out upon them, and was just beginning to transfer some of it to the tins when a knock sounded at the back door.

Kathy frowned. Odd! If it was Jane – or any other member of the O'Brien family – they would have knocked, then barged in. Another glance at the clock told her that it was rather late for anyone such as the insurance man, or a coal deliverer. Sighing, she went across and opened the back door.

A limp-looking figure stood in the yard, leaning wearily against the linen post. The light was behind him, and it was a moment or two before Kathy recognised her caller. 'Mr Philpott!' she exclaimed sharply. 'Oh, goodness, I didn't know you were coming home this week, and I don't think Mam knew, either. Oh, I'm sorry, do come in and sit down. You look exhausted!'

It was true. Mr Philpott was pale and travel stained and Kathy remembered, as she hurried over to the stove to pour hot water on to the tea leaves already in the pot, that her mother had told her they would not be seeing much of Mr Philpott since the homeport of his latest ship, the *Clwydian*, was Southampton.

She said as much, in an apologetic tone, and Mr Philpott reached eagerly for the mug of tea and took a long drink before replying. 'Aye, your mam were right. But the poor old *Clwydian* were torpedoed two days out from New York on convoy duty. Some of us – the lucky ones – were picked up by a frigate, the *Godetia*, whose homeport is Liverpool, so they brought us back here. We were told to go to the sailors' home and await further instructions, but I explained that I – I lived in Daisy Street and they said I'd best come home. They'll send a telegram when they've sorted out where they want us next.'

'I see,' Kathy said uneasily. It occurred to her now that her mother should have let the lodgers know that she and Billy had moved down to Rhyl. After all,

Sarah had not known that Jane had moved in with her. She, Kathy, might easily have been placed in a difficult position had she been alone in the house when Mr Philpott had returned. Not that folk would be that censorious in wartime, she supposed. After all, poor Mr P. had come home after having his ship sunk under him to wait until he was sent to another vessel. He could scarcely be blamed if he found her, Kathy, alone in the house! And besides, the chances were that the only person to sleep in the house that night would be the lodger, for she imagined that she and Jane would be sleeping – or at least spending most of the hours of darkness – in the shelter once more.

'Is – is everything all right, Miss Kathy? . . . With – with the rest of the street, I mean. I heard about the *Hood* . . . young Reggie Dwyer was aboard her at one time. Did he . . . was he . . .?'

'He died,' Kathy said gently. 'Old Mr Dwyer was very bitter, planned to do all sorts to the first Jerry he could lay his hands on, he told everyone. Then, last Saturday, he never came home – he was fire-watching and they found his body, or some of it, a good way from where he should have been. A mate of his said they saw a landmine floating down on its green parachute and the old feller seemed to go mad. He said it were a Jerry invasion. He – he kept an old First World War bayonet tucked inside his boot and his pal said he set off at a gallop towards the 'chute, shouting that he'd soon settle the Hun's hash. The mine exploded on impact . . . blew him to bits. They only knew it were him by the bayonet tucked inside the boot.'

'Dear God, that's terrible,' Mr Philpott muttered. 'But where's your mam . . . and where's Billy? I disremember ever comin' into this kitchen without seein' the Meccano set out on the table, or Billy's lead soldiers . . . or are they out visitin'?'

'Mam's taken Billy down to Rhyl, on the coast, to be out of the raids,' Kathy said, taking the fireside chair opposite Mr Philpott. 'I'm sure she meant to let you and Mr Bracknell know just as soon as she could, but you know what communications are like in wartime, especially to foreign parts. And of course, she knew your homeport was Southampton so she wouldn't expect you to come back here. But it doesn't really make any odds, because . . . well, have you heard how Liverpool's been blitzed this past week? I've been sleeping in the shelter most nights, with Jane and all the others, so probably you'd best follow our example. You might get a couple of hours' kip before the warning goes,' she added. 'But then you have to go to the shelter, or at least we're told it's sensible, and I suppose it is.'

She was watching Mr Philpott as she spoke and saw the deep shudder which shook his thin frame. He had always been thin, she remembered, but surely not quite as skeletal as he seemed now? And surely not as nervous, either? But he was speaking, his voice scarcely audible, so she leaned nearer.

'I'm not goin' in no shelter,' he was saying. 'I don't like bein' closed in, don't like the feelin' that there's tons and tons o' water waitin' to burst in on me. I'd feel just the same if it were earth all round me, an' a great slab o' concrete an' steel above. No, I'll take me chance in the house, if you don't mind, Kathy. I'm sure it's as safe here as anywhere.'

'You're probably right,' Kathy said. 'Oh, but whatever am I thinking of? Here, I've just done some baking . . . have a couple o' sausage rolls and some bread and margarine. I'm so sorry it isn't a proper meal, but Jane and me's going out tonight with a – a couple of pals. It'll be late by the time we come back, so we may go straight to the shelter under the Co-op . . . if there's a raid, that is, and there's been one every night for what feels like a lifetime!' She put the food down in front of him, glancing uneasily up at the clock on the mantel as she did so. 'I'll have to go, Mr Philpott. I'm so sorry, on your first evening home, but I said I'd go round to the O'Briens' house by half five, and it's past that already.'

'It don't matter; you're young, you should go out when you get the chance,' Mr Philpott said vaguely. He picked up a sausage roll and took a bite, then chewed it solemnly, watching her as he did so, his eyes black and haunted looking. 'I never thought you an' Billy an' your mam might leave Daisy Street, though I've seen it often enough in Southampton. I suppose they ain't trekkin', are they? That means goin' away each night and comin' home each mornin',' he added, as he saw Kathy's puzzled look.

'No. They'll stay away for the duration, I reckon,' Kathy said at once. 'But it's all right; I'm going away myself in a while. I'm joining the WAAF . . . but it won't be for a bit yet.'

'The WAAF?' Mr Philpott considered it for a moment, then nodded slowly. 'Yes, I suppose girls feel they want to do their bit . . . what'll happen to the house, then?'

'Oh, we'll go on paying our rent,' Kathy assured him, though in fact she had not even thought about the fate of the house. 'Mam and Billy will come back as soon as it's safe to do so. But I suppose it won't be much use to you – or to Mr Bracknell for that matter –

so it might be best if – if you did go to the sailors'
home next time you're in port.'

'I'll probably be back in Southampton next time,'
Mr Philpott said rather gloomily. He sighed, then
took another pull at his tea. 'It's a pity you're goin'
out, but I never were a very lucky feller. It's just that
. . . well, I've dreamed of comin' back, seein' Daisy
Street again, and – and yourself, of course.' He stared
at her, his eyes suddenly very bright. 'But you'll come
back here after your – your outin'? All I want, I swear
it, is just to talk to you. If – if you came back we could
sit by the fire and I could tell you . . . oh, all about the
Navy, and me job, and . . .'

It seemed little enough to ask and Kathy, remembering some of the dreadful stories she had heard
from seamen about the horrors of war in small ships,
was opening her mouth to say that of course she
would come back to the house when there was a bang
on the door. It flew open and Jane, Jimmy and Alec
tumbled into the room. 'Kathy, wharron earth are you
doin'?' Jane asked. 'We said half five at my place but
it's near on six, so we thought we'd best come and
fetch you otherwise we'll miss the big picture.' Her
eyes fell on Mr Philpott and she looked somewhat
taken aback. 'Oh, it's you, Mr Philpott! I'm awful
sorry, I didn't see you sittin' there, only we're off to
the cinema. There's a Cary Grant film showing . . .
come *along*, Kathy, or we'll bleedin' miss the start and
I hate goin' in halfway through a performance with
everyone cursin' you as you push past them.'

Kathy jumped to her feet, realising as she did so
that she was glad of the excuse not to have to make a
definite promise that she would return to the house.
After all, there was no need for her to do any such
thing; Mr Philpott would probably be in Liverpool for

several days. 'Help yourself to anything you fancy, Mr Philpott,' Kathy said recklessly. She supposed she could always do a bit more baking if Mr Philpott took her literally and gobbled up half the preparations for the funeral tea. 'I'll see you later then.' The others were hustling her out of the door but she suddenly remembered that she had said nothing about Mr McCabe's death and turned back. She hurried across the kitchen and bent over Mr Philpott. 'I didn't have time to tell you what all the baking was about, Mr Philpott. Jimmy McCabe's dad was killed in one of the raids; his funeral's on Friday.'

Mr Philpott opened his mouth to speak but Kathy shook her head at him and hurried back across the room, joining the others in the yard with a distinct sense of relief. There was something about Mr Philpott which niggled away at the back of her mind, though she could not remember exactly what it was.

Outside, they made for the street and were soon chattering about a number of things, though Kathy took the opportunity to explain to Alec who Mr Philpott was and how he came to be sitting in their kitchen. They had divided into two couples to walk along Stanley Road and presently, seeing Jane and Jimmy entwined ahead of them, Alec put a casual arm round Kathy's shoulders. He grinned down at her, saying: 'We're going to have a grand evening, the four of us, and if you ask me there won't be a raid tonight. Bomber pilots don't care for cloud because they can't see what they're bombing, and if they drop below it they're within range of the ack-ack and they can fly into tall buildings and barrage balloons and so on. Now where should we go to eat when the performance is over?'

*

It was a good film, made perfect for Kathy because after ten minutes or so Alec had taken her hand. I'm nearly nineteen and this is the first time I've ever let a boy hold my hand in the flicks, she told herself, half guiltily. I've always been so determined to have a career, to be a person in my own right, that I've never given even a thought to courting or marriage. And yet, ever since I first saw Alec, I've felt quite differently about him from the way I've felt about any other bloke I've ever met. And when he touches my hand, or looks down at me and smiles, my tummy sort of squeezes up and I go hot and cold and – and I just want to be close to him. I might ask Jane if this is love, but somehow I don't think I shall. It's – it's a very private feeling, not the sort of thing you talk about, not even to your mam, or your best friend.

When they emerged from the cinema, the cloud cover overhead was beginning to break up so that occasional silvery shafts of moonlight fell upon the blacked-out city. During the performance, they had once or twice heard the thrum of the heavy bombers passing overhead, but though there may have been the odd bomb or incendiary dropped the alert had not sounded. Because of Kathy's tardiness they had decided not to have a full meal before the showing of the film. After it, however, they meant to eat, so they went along to a restaurant on Stanley Road, which did a main course and a pudding for one and tenpence a head. They were chattering away, the two men telling the girls what they knew of life in the WAAF and making them laugh with stories of some of the exploits they had heard of, when the alert sounded.

'Oh, Christopher, there go Moanin' Minnie, and that's the end of our meal,' Alec remarked.

Kathy glanced around the restaurant and saw that the staff were ushering people out of the door. Presumably, there were no cellars here, and since the place consisted largely of huge glass windows it was clearly unwise to try to remain.

'Eat up, girls,' Jimmy ordered, shovelling food into his mouth as fast as he could. 'We'd best get you two into a shelter and then Alec and meself will go along to the nearest wardens' post. Ah, here comes the waitress to collect our money, but we've not had our puddin' yet. How much will they knock off for an uneaten puddin' do you suppose?'

'Nothin', you cheeky young devil,' the elderly waitress said, overhearing, snatching the almost empty dinner plate from under Jimmy's nose as she spoke. 'You may not have ate the puddin' but we's had to cook it, so pay up, please; then we can all gerrout of here afore them nasty Germings start a-bombin' of us again.'

Jimmy and Alec began to argue vociferously, but it was no use. They paid up rather grudgingly, Jimmy remarking that he'd be back for his puddin' as soon as the All Clear sounded. As they left, Kathy saw that the friendly clouds had completely disappeared and the full moon was shining down upon the city yet again, illuminating everything far more efficiently than the searchlights were lighting up the darkness above. She tugged at Alec's arm. 'We might as well be on the stage,' she said in a hushed voice. 'They'll be able to pick out the places they want to bomb as easy as anything. Oh, why don't the clouds come back and hide us?'

'Yes, it's a bomber's moon,' Alec agreed and Kathy realised, for the first time, that both young men must have looked on a moonlit night such as this with approval when they were in their Blenheim and heading for a target over Germany. How odd it must seem to them now to be the attacked instead of the attackers! The roles had been reversed indeed and she thought, fleetingly, how dreadful it would be if they were killed by the bombers even now beginning to appear across the Mersey.

Jimmy looked behind him to make sure they were following. His arm was once more round Jane's waist and his face very close to her friend's mass of golden curls, though in the moonlight these shone pale as silver. 'We'll make for the shelter under the Co-op that you were talking about earlier,' he said to Kathy. 'You'll be snug enough down there.'

But when they reached the shelter, Kathy suddenly made up her mind that she would not go below, for it was easy to see that the shelter was already crammed to capacity and, what was more, something of Mr Philpott's dislike of enclosed spaces seemed suddenly to infect her. At the foot of the steps, she turned briskly round and hurried up them again, dragging Alec with her. 'I'm not going down there, not tonight,' she said decisively. 'It's going to be a bad night, with the moon at the full and so many aircraft overhead. I'll stay with you two, and do whatever I can to help.' She looked up into Alec's face, trying to smile. 'Women are as good as men any day of the week; Jane and me's going to be Waafs, so we might as well start fighting the war right now!'

It was a dreadful night, particularly bad for north Liverpool and the docks. Jane had quite agreed with Kathy that they should not go to the shelter, so the two girls worked side by side, doing everything that was asked of them. Their tasks varied enormously, from carrying around jugs of hot tea to workers desperately engaged in fire-fighting, to roping off bomb-damaged buildings and helping to move rubble where they could hear the voices of those buried beneath it. By the time day dawned and the All Clear had sounded, they were beginning to see the extent of the damage. The roads were white with splintered and shattered glass; in some streets, blast had seen to it that not a single window had stayed in situ. Fires smouldered or roared, according to how recently the incendiaries had fallen, and the roads were impassable. Tramlines had been severed and stuck up at unusual angles, as threatening as snakes to vehicular traffic. Water mains spouted, telephone lines were down, electricity cables fizzed, spat and went dead and chaos reigned.

Kathy and Jane, their best clothes ruined and their skin blackened by smoke and dust, met Alec and Jimmy by a WVS van which was dispensing hot drinks and sandwiches to the workers. 'Mornin', girls,' the two young men chorused. They were as black as Kathy and Jane, but grinned wearily, their teeth flashing white in their filthy faces.

Jimmy handed the cup of tea he was cradling to Jane, and took another from the counter. 'I guess it's about time you two went home and got cleaned up. Then you can both have a few hours in bed. There's no point in me goin' back home. I'm so tired, I doubt if I could sleep a wink.'

'We've been at that shelter under the Co-op, the one we tried to get you to use,' Alec said, reaching for a cup of tea and handing it to Kathy. 'It's terrible; the worst yet, I should say. The building next door collapsed on to the shelter and the roof caved in. There were little kids . . .' He shuddered. 'Well, no point in talking about it but we've got to go back as soon as we've finished this cuppa. I don't suppose we'll be more than an hour or two, but by God, when we saw it, we could only be thankful you'd refused to go below.'

'I am *not* going home to sleep until you do,' Kathy said firmly. She drank her tea and handed the mug to a grey-haired WVS worker whose eyes were red-rimmed with tiredness, but who wore a bright smile as though it were a part of her uniform. 'Come on, you two, let's be gettin' back to the Co-op. Jane and I may not be able to heave concrete blocks about but we can help shift the smaller stuff.' There was a token attempt from both men to get the girls to go home but when they saw it was not going to be successful they gave up and the four of them returned to do what they could to help those still trapped. Eventually, some of the workers gave a cheer and began to help people from the wreckage. Many were injured but others were unhurt and reported, as they scrambled out through the tiny gap, that there were a number of dead.

'One of the fellers were real good, brave as a lion,' an elderly woman told Kathy as she was heaved free of the ruin. 'He were a seaman, only home on leave, but he were that cheerful and jolly, he kept us all laughin'. My daughter, Effie, and her five littl'uns really took to him, so they did. He were badly injured when the roof come in but he still kept cracking jokes and mekkin' the kids laugh. When he went quiet, we thought he'd dropped to sleep but he were dead as a doornail.'

Kathy said how sorry she was and wondered whether the woman, or anyone else in the shelter, knew who the sailor was and presently, when the bodies were being brought out, asked another survivor, a grizzled man in his sixties, whether he knew anything about the seaman who had died. The old man shook his head. 'No, queen, only what he told us,' he said. 'He come back to Liverpool on leave because his ship were torpedoed but he came to this shelter because he told us his young lady had said she would come here. Only it seems she'd not arrived – and a good thing too, for if she'd been below she'd ha' been wi' her young man and he was sittin' where the roof collapsed.' He glanced around as he spoke and pointed. 'They're just bringin' him up, queen. If it's someone you know . . .'

Kathy murmured that she was sure the sailor would be a stranger to her but went over to the stretcher and glanced down at the still figure lying upon it. For a moment she could only stare, disbelief warring with pity. It was Mr Philpott.

Kathy could not believe it at first. He had been afraid of enclosed spaces, had hated the thought of being entombed in a shelter because of the great weight of earth around and building above. But she guessed that he found it even more daunting being alone in the house in Daisy Street. The docks were so near and Kathy knew that they had been a target many times that night. She imagined Mr Philpott, in his small room in Daisy Street, yearning for the companionship that he had known aboard his frigate. He would have waited, hopefully, for her to return, as she had half promised to do, and would probably have been driven out to the shelter simply to find someone – anyone – with whom to share the hours of terrifying noise and danger which lay ahead.

Then she remembered what the old man had said.

Mr Philpott had told people that he had chosen the Co-op shelter because he believed his young lady would be there. Kathy was not a conceited girl but she thought it very probable that poor Mr Philpott had been referring to her. She knew that he rather liked her, but because she thought him such a wet week she had never given him the slightest encouragement and in fact had denied, even to herself, that she was anything to him apart from his landlady's daughter.

'Kathy? Wharron earth are you doin' . . .?' Jane's voice broke off as she saw the still figure on the stretcher. 'Oh, my God, it's Mr Philpott, isn't it? Oh, the poor feller! But wharrever were he doin' here? I thought you said he were goin' to kip down in Daisy Street.'

Kathy found that she was crying and wiped her eyes with the backs of both hands. 'He was, but I think he got lonely,' she said. 'An old feller who chatted to him in the shelter told me that Mr Philpott came down looking for – for a girl he knew. I – I'd said we'd probably use this shelter . . . oh, Jane, if I'd gone home like I'd said I might, Mr Philpott would still be alive!'

'You don't want to go blaming yourself . . .' Jane was beginning, when an arm slid round Kathy's waist and Alec's voice said in her ear: 'What's all this, then? Why's my brave girl piping her eye?' Alec's gaze must have followed the direction of Jane's glance, for he stiffened suddenly. 'Dear God, is that the feller who was sitting in your kitchen when we called for you? Oh, Kathy, no wonder you're crying. You know him well, of course. I am so sorry.'

Kathy sniffed and knuckled her eyes again, then straightened her shoulders and gently pushed Alec away from her. It seemed wrong to be looking down on Mr Philpott, who had said he only wanted to talk to her, whilst being cuddled by Alec. 'Yes, I did know him well, though not well enough to even know what his first name was,' she admitted. 'I did tell you he was our lodger. It seems he – he came down the shelter looking for me, because I said we'd use the Co-op one if we got caught in a raid. But I never dreamed . . . he said he hated shelters!'

'It's easy to hate shelters when you don't need 'em,' Alec said wisely. 'And judging by his uniform, he were a sailor, probably on convoy duty. I've a friend doing that and the stories he tells make me powerful glad I joined the Junior rather than the Senior Service.'

The two of them began to walk back towards Daisy Street, following Jane and Jimmy along the rubble-strewn pavement. One had to pick one's way but it was impossible not to crunch on glass at practically every step and Kathy began to fear for her shoes. It would not do to let a shard pierce the sole and enter her foot. 'Yes, he was on convoy duty,' Kathy admitted. 'When I think about it, Alec, I feel really bad. We got along with him all right – Mam, Billy and myself – but we were never truly friends, not like we are with Mr Bracknell, our other lodger. Poor Mr Philpott never really joined in and you couldn't tease him because he took everything so seriously. I – I don't think he was a very happy man and I don't think he had much of a life, either, and in a way that makes his being killed even more unfair. You see, if he'd had a future, it might have been a happy one with a wife and kids and a home of his own instead of lodging with strangers. Oh, how I hate the bloody Jerries! They stole his future away from him!'

By this time they were turning into Daisy Street and

Alec took her hand and gave it a gentle squeeze. 'Oh, that weren't nothing to do with you,' he said firmly. 'There's misfits in every walk of life, girl Kathy, and if they don't choose to try to help themselves then, believe me, no one else can do it for 'em.' They had reached the Kelling house and Jane had already opened the front door. Alec gave Kathy's arm a little shake. 'Go indoors and get some sleep while you can,' he advised. 'Jimmy an' me are going to do the same and when we wake we'll come and call for you, because I dare say you'll want a hand with funeral arrangements.'

'Funeral arrangements?' Jimmy said in an astonished tone. 'Mam and meself have done all that – I *telled* you, it's all arranged for two o'clock tomorrow afternoon.'

Kathy passed him, then turned in the doorway. She was feeling quite light-headed from lack of sleep but had understood at once what Alec had meant. 'No, not your dad, Jimmy,' she said gently. 'It's Mr Philpott; there's only me now to do the arranging for that funeral.'

When she got into bed, Kathy was haunted by Mr Philpott's sad fate. It was a shame that she had not really liked him very much, had considered him to be wishy-washy and without character, because somehow this made his death seem even more pitiable. Who would go to his funeral? In normal circumstances she was sure that the inhabitants of the flower streets would have rallied round, but knew that was unlikely to happen when so many deaths had occurred in the raid which had crushed the shelter. She thought, guiltily, that few people even remembered him, and those who did remember would not think to support her as they would have supported her mother.

Outside the window, the life of the street went on, making it difficult for Kathy to fall asleep, though Jane seemed to find it no problem. Little snorts and snores emanated from her and Kathy envied her, wishing that she herself could forget the still figure on the stretcher and sink into a deep and peaceful sleep.

In fact, she had almost done so when something Mr Philpott had said the previous evening popped into her head. *All I want, I swear it, is just to talk to you.* She could not remember anything else that he said, but this particular sentence seemed not only innocuous but pretty pointless. After all, why should he have to swear that he just wanted to talk to her? And what *else* had he said? She was sure he had said something important, though she could not quite remember . . .

She was at the warm, delicious stage when sleep is only seconds away when she remembered some fragments of his conversation . . . *lovely hair, lovely an' smooth an' shiny. I been watchin' you wi' that yaller-headed girl* . . .

It doesn't make sense, Kathy thought dreamily, pulling the blankets up a little higher and burrowing into the pillow, it really doesn't make . . . and she was asleep.

Some time later she awoke, her spine prickling. I must be going mad, she thought; Mr Philpott never said those things, it was the feller who grabbed me on the North Dingle that night. *He* said he only wanted to talk to me, and then went on about my lovely shiny hair and seein' me with the yaller-headed girl. How could I possibly confuse that man with poor Mr

Philpott? But then she heard again the voice in her head and knew that she was not mistaken. It had been Mr Philpott who had grabbed her on Christmas Day almost five years earlier!

The realisation banished sleep. Kathy lay there, staring at the ceiling and going over everything Mr Philpott had said to her, both on that Christmas Day and on the previous evening, and the more she thought, the more certain she became that Mr Philpott and her attacker were one and the same. At first she felt indignant, truly angry with him for having scared her so badly, but the more she considered it, the more she realised just how desperately unhappy and lonely Mr Philpott had been. He must have received many rebuffs to make him so scared that he could not even tell a young girl he admired her. His only friend was Mr Bracknell and Kathy imagined that his enormous shyness and lack of self-confidence would have backed down at once before Mr Bracknell's cheerful, outgoing personality. He would not have dreamed of trying to compete with the older, more experienced man.

Kathy lay on her back, staring up at the ceiling. She could not blame herself for not understanding Mr Philpott, for wanting to be with Alec whilst she had the chance, but one thing she could do; she could join the WAAF – she had intended to do so anyway, she reminded herself ruefully – and do her best to see that the Allies won the war. And she would never tell a soul, not her mother, not Jane, not Alec, that it had been Mr Philpott who had grabbed her so long ago.

Having made up her mind, she turned on her side to prepare for the sleep which she needed so badly, and suddenly realised that she was crying in good earnest now, crying for the sad and ineffective young man who had put up such a brave front in the shelter and whose death was all the more tragic because he would be so little missed.

Chapter Thirteen

August 1941

'Right, young ladies, quick march!' The sergeant's voice was strident and Kathy felt perspiration beginning to trickle down her forehead. She glanced sideways at Jane and saw her friend flick a hand across her brow and then continue to march across the great concrete swath of the parade ground. It was a fortunate thing that she and Jane were of a similar height since it meant that they could pair up for drill without receiving any adverse comment from officers or other Waafs. There was supposed to be no opportunity for idle chat but she and Jane usually managed to exchange, if not a few words, then at least speaking looks. Basic training had been invented, Jimmy had told them, to turn everyone into replicas of each other. Uniform helped, of course, and very soon the girls began to realise that life in the WAAF was a good deal easier if you conformed totally to what the officers and NCOs wanted and kept your own personality completely hidden, though it would emerge quickly enough once basic training was over.

'Right . . . wheel!' A silent snigger passed between Jane and Kathy. Only the previous evening, as they polished their buttons to gleaming whiteness and shined their shoes until the leather mirrored their faces, they had wondered aloud what would happen if, on reaching the end of the parade ground, the sergeant forgot to give the order to right wheel. 'We'd all march straight into the chain-link fencing and pile up like a traffic accident,' Jane had giggled. 'No one would dare disobey and wheel right of their own accord – we'd probably get jankers if we did!'

Kathy and Jane had not believed that Waafs would ever be given jankers, but they soon realised their mistake. Punishment and threats of punishment surrounded the Waafs as surely as chain-link fencing surrounded the camp. There was a kit inspection several times a week and woe betide you if one article of your uniform was missing, or unpolished, or even placed in the wrong order upon your bed. Jane, who had lived a pretty casual life in her mother's house, Kathy knew, found the business of unmaking one's bed every morning and making it up each night particularly trying. The beds consisted of an iron bedstead and a mattress which was in three parts. These parts were called biscuits and had to be piled neatly at the foot of one's bed each morning whilst one's blankets and sheets were folded in a certain way and placed on top of the biscuits. When there was a kit inspection, one's entire uniform had to be laid out, again in a certain order. Dreadful punishments awaited anyone who lost anything, even if the loss was only temporary, and the girls in Hut 5 had soon learned what every experienced Waaf knew – that one stuck by one's friends and helped them in time of adversity. If someone three beds up was a pair of stockings short, then she whose kit had been examined and found to be correct would wait until the officer moved on and then pass her stockings along to the unfortunate who had mislaid hers.

'It's a good thing the officers are all such mean old bitches because it teaches us to stick together and stand up for one another,' Jane had observed the first time she had seen equipment being moved about during the kit inspection. 'Why, if there's one person I really hate it's that Ellen Morris. She's so common – I don't believe she's washed once since we started basic training – and as for her hair . . . yuck! But she passed her ground sheet along when she saw someone had borrowed mine just as though we were real pals, so I suppose she isn't so bad after all.'

'I admit she isn't the cleanest Waaf on the station but she does wash now, you know,' Kathy had pointed out. 'A good few of them are from large families where washing's a luxury and it takes time before they begin to see it has its advantages. Ellen washes her hair now whenever she can get hold of a bit of soap. And anyway, I'd rather have her than Pauline Whittle. I heard her telling everyone that the Section Officer had told her she was officer material and ought to put in for a training course, but I bet the SO says that to everyone – she certainly said it to me!'

'And me,' Jane had agreed. 'She asked me whether I'd be interested in barrage balloons, so I said I was but to tell the truth I didn't know what she were talking about. Do they want clerical workers or something on the balloon sites? Only men fly the buggers, don't they? I've seen 'em on the balloon sites around Liverpool an' they're all fellers.'

'Squad . . . halt! Stand – at – ease!'

The drill sergeant's loud voice sounded almost as fed up with drill and the sun-drenched parade ground as Kathy felt. She was hot, tired and heartily sick of drill. It was a sweltering August day and she longed for nothing so much as a cool drink and a sit down, but knew she was unlikely to get either until they were dismissed to go to the cookhouse for their dinner. And, knowing the RAF, it won't be salad, or cold meat, it'll be stew and spuds, Kathy thought, unconsciously mimicking the head cook, a big beefy man who disliked all Waafs and had been known to fling mashed potato on to one's plate with such force that the gravy splattered someone a couple of feet away. You'd think the air force would have realised by now how simple it was to make a Spam salad, but their main aim in life seems to be to fatten us up. She glanced at Jane, unable to help noticing that her friend looked a good deal sturdier than she had when they were both in Civvy Street. Somewhat smugly, Kathy glanced down at her own front. Despite a diet of potatoes, stews and boiled puddings, she was still as slim as ever and intended to remain so. Other girls might hold their plates out hopefully for a second spoonful but Kathy was not one of them.

'Squaaad . . . dismiss!'

This time the sergeant's voice sounded far happier and as the girls broke ranks and headed for their huts, Kathy thought that she would give herself a good strip-down wash before going along to the cookhouse. Jane, hurrying along beside her, was of the same mind and they both entered their hut, tore off their tunics and caps and headed for the ablutions which were at the far end of the room.

'What are we doing this afternoon?' Jane asked presently.

'There's a lecture on barrage balloons,' Kathy said. 'I wonder if I'll have time after dinner to write to that feller I met back in Liverpool?' She glanced rather guiltily at her friend. 'I did tell you we were going to write to one another, didn't I?'

Jane, who had been combing out her hair and trying to subdue its exuberance with a great many hairgrips, turned to Kathy, eyes rounding. 'I suppose you mean Alan Grimshaw? Well, if you ain't a dark horse! You never said a word! Whenever I've seen you scribblin' away, I've thought how good you were to write to your mam and Billy so often.' She turned back to the mirror once more, bending towards it to check that the last frond of hair was neatly in place. 'Jimmy's a grand letter writer – better than I am meself. But what with writing to Mam and Dad and the kids . . . well, you've only got one life an' writin' borin' letters is no way to spend half of each day.'

'I quite like writing letters,' Kathy said. She did not add that Jane was mistaken; that it was Alec Hewitt to whom she wrote, and not Alan Grimshaw. The fact was, she could not forget that Jane had seemed to like Alec rather too much, so Kathy had decided to keep their relationship a secret. Now she said, as casually as she could: 'I meant to write to that pal of your Jimmy's, but I've not got round to it, so if you've seen me scribbling the letter will certainly have been to Mam or Billy. But I thought Alec was rather nice – you liked him, didn't you?'

'Oh aye, he were all right as fellers go,' Jane said indifferently. 'The trouble with war is that you meet someone once and then never again. Jimmy tells me they're always movin' aircrews around, though they usually keep them together. So it'll be barrage balloons, will it? Well I just hope I don't fall asleep, that's all. Poor ACW Davidson got kitchen duty for a week when she fell asleep in map reading, and I'm sure I didn't blame her. That woman's voice was so flat and borin' she might as well have read out o' the telephone directory. Wonder what's for grub?'

Despite their fears, the balloon lecture proved to be enthralling. Kathy suspected it was partly because the air force officer giving the lecture was young and handsome, with a pair of twinkling brown eyes, a tiny blond moustache and a ready smile. He made flying a balloon sound fascinating and explained carefully that the air force had decided to give Waafs a chance to enter this unusual trade in order to release men for more important work.

'Though flying the balloons is extremely important,' he added hastily. 'As you must have realised, balloons prevent the Luftwaffe from coming in low and strafing civilians in the streets. They can bring down enemy aircraft if a Jerry should happen to fly into the guide wires, and of course keeping the enemy at a height means their bombing is less accurate. Yes, Aircraftwoman?'

ACW Whittle's hand had shot up halfway through the officer's explanation and now she stood up. She was a thin, raw-boned girl with very large hands and feet and a smug expression and now she smiled ingratiatingly at the officer on the platform. 'Please, sir, people feel better when they see the balloons up there in the sky even though it means there are enemy aircraft in the vicinity. The balloons look so fat and comfortable, and you can see the Jerries don't like flying near them. I'm from Liverpool, an' the balloons do a grand job of keeping the bombs away from the docks.'

'Yes, the balloons make people feel safer,' the officer agreed. 'But flying them is no sinecure. We intend replacing our seven airmen and two NCOs with twelve Waafs and two NCOs because men are both stronger and heavier than the fair sex.' He grinned engagingly at them. 'Oh, I forgot to mention that WAAF balloon operatives will get paid a good deal more than Waafs in other trades and will also have special rations.'

'And a good deal more freedom,' someone muttered in the row behind Kathy. 'You get far fewer officers snooping around a balloon site and I've heard the fellers say that no one interferes with you. How about it, girls?'

'So if any of you are interested in becoming balloon ops – or Bops as we call them – then, when your basic training is over, you can apply to go to Number One Balloon Training Unit at Cardington,' the young man said. 'We are putting the word about to Waafs in other trades that they can remuster but it is amongst the new entrants that we shall be hoping for the most support. Good afternoon, ladies.'

After he was gone, the buzz of quiet conversation became louder and more general. 'He said you've gorra be strong and very fit,' Jane said musingly as she and Kathy made their way out of the large Nissen hut in which the lecture had been held. 'I dunno what to do for the best. I've gorra fancy to work on a station; I'd like to drive an officer around in a car or mebbe a blood wagon, only that might be a bit depressin'. But it would be nice to get more money and have a bit more freedom.'

'But Jane, you can't drive,' Kathy pointed out. 'So whatever you do, it looks as though you'll be in for another training course. Do you think they'd take me on balloons? I know I'm not very heavy but I reckon I'm just as strong as you.'

'From what the feller said and the way he smiled at us, they'd be willin' to take a monkey provided it could learn to fly a balloon,' Jane commented. 'Oh, come on, we might as well apply. And even if you are too thin, we'll all have the same medical and it won't be like the FFI, because we've all had that and got cleared or we wouldn't be in the WAAF at all.'

'I suppose they'll want us to lift heavy weights and heave on ropes, like in a tug-o'-war,' Kathy said as they made their way over to the mess. 'Well, I'm willing to have a go if you are because the WAAF wouldn't be any fun at all if we got separated.'

'Well, they've finished their basic trainin', so Jane says,' Jimmy remarked to Alec as the two of them lounged on their beds, both reading the post which had arrived in the early morning, whilst they were still sleeping off the effects of a raid over Germany. 'Jane says she and Kathy have put in to be balloon operatives, but they haven't heard yet whether they've been accepted or not. I thought that was a trade for men only.' He peered curiously at Alec, also reading a letter. 'Who's that one from? It ain't your mam; she always uses white paper and that's blue.'

'It's from one of my great circle of admiring women,' Alec said loftily, spoiling the impression by adding, 'D'you remember that skinny little kid who came out with us a couple of times when I was staying with you in Liverpool? It's her.'

Jimmy sat up and ran both hands through his soot-black hair, making it stand comically on end. 'You don't mean Kathy Kelling?' he asked incredulously. 'I didn't know you liked her. Nor I didn't know she liked you,' he added thoughtfully. 'Give us the letter, then – I've known Kathy all me life so she's got no secrets from me.'

'Read your own damn letters and leave me to read mine,' Alec growled. He folded the letter and shoved it into his pocket, feeling the hot blood rush to his cheeks. He was all too conscious that if Jimmy knew Jane was writing to him there would be one hell of a fuss and that was the last thing he wanted. In fact, he had been half shocked and half delighted when Jane's first letter had arrived. Being as aware as he that Jimmy would not take kindly to seeing her handwriting on a letter to his best pal, she had got another girl to write the address for her. Alec thought it a pity that the other girl was clearly almost illiterate, but agreed with Jane that it was a good deal safer that Jimmy should not find out.

The letter he had just shoved into his pocket, however, actually did come from Kathy. It was a nice letter, bright and intelligent and full of gossipy and amusing bits of news. He had known very little about the WAAF, but now he knew a good deal for Kathy pulled no punches in her description of life at the basic training camp. She described her feelings on being forced to spend a day in the cookhouse, peeling mounds and mounds of spuds simply because she had mislaid an item of her equipment. On another occasion, she had been late for drill and had been ordered to do twenty laps of the perimeter track, with a great heavy kitbag filled with bricks across her shoulders, whilst the sun poured down and she longed, passionately, for a nice cold bath.

Jane had written to him twice and he had destroyed the letters as soon as he had read them, thinking it a good deal safer than keeping such explosive material, for Jane's letters were neither funny nor chatty. They were somewhat basic, telling brief scraps of her life at the training camp but concentrating more on how much she wanted to see him again. Alec wanted to see her – well, he thought he did – but was certainly not going to say so in a letter which might, if one were careless, be read by almost anyone. Another subject on which Jane had touched had been Paragraph Eleven. Alec had not known what this implied but had asked a young Waaf on the station and she had gone cherry red before informing him, in an embarrassed mutter, that Paragraph Eleven dealt with Waafs who 'got in the family way' whilst still in the service.

Alec had been rather shocked and wondered whether he had misunderstood; Jane had been talking about a friend who was miserably unhappy in the WAAF and meant to 'work her ticket out of the service' by using Paragraph Eleven as a reason for quitting. Surely, no one in their right mind would consider having a baby, which was a lifetime's responsibility, just to avoid remaining in the air force?

Still, he did not know the girl in question; she might be married for all he knew, though Jane's laconic comment had not seemed to apply to a married woman. Anyway, he guessed that Jane did not find letters easy to write, was not good at communicating her feelings and had no ability to make events in her life sound either interesting or amusing. But what did it matter, after all? When one looked at Jane's beautiful face and perfect figure, conversation – or letter-writing ability – would be the last thing on one's mind.

'Oh, come on, Alec, don't be so bleedin' mean!' Jimmy's voice brought him back to the present with a jolt. 'It ain't as if Kathy's your girl or anything like that an' I'm so bored! If there's a gharry going into town, we might see a flick, only we're on call, aren't we?' He glanced out of the tiny window nearest his bed. 'It's a clear afternoon so mebbe it'll be a clear night, and if so we'll be scrambled again later.'

'Tell you what, I'll show you Kathy's letter if you'll show me Jane's,' Alec said, causing Jimmy to give a crack of laughter.

'Oh, all right, keep your letter to yourself. Did Kathy say anything about this balloon business when she wrote?'

'Yes. She said they were applying but she didn't think she'd get accepted, and if not she's going for R/T Operator.' He grinned across at his friend. 'She might end up here! R/T Ops go all over the country so she could be posted anywhere.'

'Yeah,' Jimmy said thoughtfully. 'Alec . . . you were so rude about Kathy, calling her a skinny little kid, that I never thought you might really have liked her. *Do* you? Only she's a very bright girl and I suppose that's made her a bit standoffish. It's easy to tell when a girl like Jane likes you – she nearly lands in your lap – but with Kathy it 'ud be a lot more difficult. It ain't that she's shy exactly, but she's been brought up to keep her feelings to herself. I didn't use to like her; I thought she was stuck up – but once she and Jane were both in the factory together, I realised she were a grand girl really. So there's no reason why you shouldn't be serious about her.'

'Serious?' Alec's voice rose to a squeak. 'I'm not serious about anyone, not with a war on. Besides, I'm writing to other people as well as Kathy, you know. There's a girl who live in our village, Bella, and that kid what I took out from Watton . . . it were just good luck that the couple we took out in Church Broughton weren't the letter-writing kind.'

Jimmy gave a hoarse laugh. 'Not the letter-writin' kind . . . that's puttin' it nicely! If Jane knew about them two . . . if me mam knew, come to that . . .'

'Yes, well,' Alec said awkwardly. He still felt ashamed of the episode, which had happened on the last night they had spent at the training centre. The girls had been a couple of little floozies, eager for fun and willing to do whatever was asked of them, and – and Jimmy and me were both a trifle bosky, Alec thought now; what you might call market peart. Still an' all, we shouldn't have done it.

Jimmy must have guessed Alec's thoughts because he leaned over and punched his friend lightly on the shoulder. 'You're a right little puritan, you are,' he said mockingly. 'I reckon a feller's entitled to a bit of lovin' when the girls are as keen as them two were. Oh, come on Alec, don't look so Friday-faced. They was beggin' for it.'

Alec couldn't help grinning but he still felt uncomfortable whenever the last night at Church Broughton was mentioned. And if I feel bad about it, Jimmy should feel a lot worse, he reminded himself. He says he's going to marry Jane just as soon as they can afford it, yet he went off quite happily with that little tart. It's different for me, I've never had a real girlfriend, just pals like.

But whenever he tried to tell himself that his behaviour had been acceptable, he was forced to remember that Jimmy would kill him if he knew that Alec was encouraging Jane to play fast and loose. And I am encouraging her every time I reply to one of her letters, Alec told himself miserably now. Only – only she's so beautiful and warm and loving, and she's never known any feller but Jimmy . . . oh, hang it, I can't help myself. I do believe that this time I'm in love.

It was a windy October day when Kathy and Jane, with their kitbags packed and their hearts high, set off for Cardington and the No. 1 Training Unit for barrage balloon operatives. They arrived there with a great many other girls straight from basic training.

Despite an early start, it was already dark by the time they reached their destination. They were sent straight to the cookhouse, though it was far too late for the kitchen staff to be serving proper meals.

The train journey had been a long drawn out affair with waits on draughty platforms for connections prolonging it still further, but the girls were glad to get into the warm, even though all they were served with was wads and cocoa. Jane pulled her wad apart to peer at the contents and announced, gleefully, that at least it were corned beef and brown sauce, which was a good deal tastier than the bread and jam they had feared. Kathy, hunched up exhaustedly on her deal chair, had scarcely the energy to eat her own sandwich but drank two cups of strong cocoa eagerly and began to feel more alive.

'I don't know which is worse, to be so warm your chilblains itch, or so cold your feet might as well not be there,' she told Jane. She glanced up at the clock over the counter. 'Dear God, it's half past ten already and we've still not made up our beds or been assigned to huts either, for that matter. It'll be morning before we get between the sheets at this rate.'

They had already been told that, as balloon operatives, they would be issued with additional items of uniform but were astonished – and peeved – to be told presently, by the officer who escorted them to their tents, that this temporary accommodation would have to suffice since the number of Waafs taking over from men on balloon sites had taken everyone by surprise.

'Fortunately, it isn't snowing,' he said, grinning at them. 'But there'll be a uniform parade in the building we just passed at 0730 hours so you'd best get your heads down as soon as you can.'

'They might give us a chance to get ourselves some breakfast,' Jane grumbled as soon as the middle-aged warrant officer had left the tent. She glanced round her and gave a shudder. 'By God, queen, I never thought they'd purrus in a bleedin' tent – and this is a four month course, ain't it? Why, we'll die of the perishin' cold once winter sets in.'

'They'll move us into proper Nissen huts in a few weeks,' Kathy said reassuringly. 'A tent full of frozen Waafs won't be flyin' balloons for anyone! Don't worry about it. They're not daft, you know.'

'I hope to God you're right because I hate being cold,' Jane said crossly. 'And anyway, why on earth do we need extra uniforms so soon?'

Kathy shrugged. 'You know the WAAF,' she said resignedly. 'I don't suppose we'll wear the new stuff we're issued with for weeks, but they like to get everything done as soon as possible.' She glanced around her at the exhausted girls. Most of them were making up their beds but one or two, still fully dressed, had simply climbed between the blankets, removing only cap and shoes, and were settling themselves to sleep. 'No use worrying about it, Janey. If we get a move on, we might actually fall asleep before reveille.'

Despite the fact that every draught known to man – or woman – seemed to whistle under the tent flaps, the exhausted girls slept well and woke reluctantly when a voice from the tannoy reminded them that it was 0600 hours and time to get up. Because it was a new station and they did not yet know what lay ahead, everyone hurried. No one washed, apart from a quick dabble with what little water was available, and those who had not undressed the previous night stared with some horror at their creased and crumpled uniforms. Lucy, in the bed next to Jane, brushed herself briskly, twisted her hair into a hard little knob on the back of her head and jammed her hat down low over her eyes.

'Will I pass, do you reckon?' she asked Jane anxiously. 'I ain't never slep' in me gear before but I was so bleedin' tired I never give a thought to wharr' I'd look like in the mornin'.'

'We all look terrible, queen,' Jane said comfortingly. 'Kathy and me took off our skirts and battledress, but my skirt fell on the floor during the night and it's got pretty creased.' She peered out of the tent flap. 'Anyroad, it's so bleedin' dark outside that they probably wouldn't notice if we trooped to the uniform parade in our pyjamas.' As she spoke, she jammed her cap on her tousled curls and winked at Kathy, and the three of them set off in the direction of the outside world. As it happened, Jane was right. At this hour of the morning no one seemed particularly interested in the new intake. The NCO who had come to call for them took them along to the cookhouse where they had tea and porridge before being escorted to a large hangar. They formed into a queue at the counter and were issued with trousers, overalls, thick seamen's jumpers and socks, gloves and woolly hats, as well as short boots and thick mufflers. With their arms full of their new acquisitions, they made their way back to the tent and changed at once into the overalls, since the NCO had told them that the work they would be doing might well be dirty.

They were taken to the classroom where their training began immediately with recognising cordage, which meant rope from the very fine sort to the very thick ones so far as Kathy could see. Then they moved on to knot tying, learning a variety of both simple and complex knots which, their instructor informed them, they would be using constantly once they were on a real balloon site.

Over the days and weeks which followed the girls learned to know the workings of a barrage balloon more intimately than they had ever known anything before. Because a great deal of their work would be done in the dark and often in adverse weather conditions they were taught to recognise ropes, wire and cable and the many and complicated knots by feel, for they might well be controlling the balloon and unable to use their torches.

They were told that they must know enough about the winch engine to service it and keep it in good repair and, naturally, to put it right when it broke down. They must also be able to mend the balloon if any part of their enormous charge became worn or ripped, and were shown how to use a cobbler's palm and a great curved sailmaker's needle to patch canvas.

As well as all these things, there was aircraft recognition, so that if friendly aircraft looked like approaching too close to the balloons they could bring the balloon down. And they had to learn to use naval terms, for as far as the air force was concerned the barrage balloon was an airship and the girls were no longer a flight but a crew, so port and starboard and bows and stern were used rather than left and right and front and back.

At the end of six weeks, Kathy and Jane were given leave to go into the nearest town and relax for a few hours. It was an extremely cold day but the streets were busy with people and, though shop windows had little on display, there was a pleasantly festive spirit abroad for Christmas was not far off. The girls wandered round the shops, buying small gifts to send to the folk back home. Jane bought coloured pencils and a pad of rough grey wartime paper for her young brothers and sisters to share and Kathy bought a pair of grey woollen gloves for her mother and a monkey on a stick for Billy, although she told Jane he was far too old for it really, but she knew it would give him a laugh.

Having exhausted the charms of shopping they went into a small tearoom, ordered cheese on toast and a pot of tea, and leaned back in their chairs feeling wonderfully free of the WAAF for once. However, their talk speedily turned to barrage balloons and the training they were receiving.

'It's so bleedin' technical! If I'd known from the start that I were goin' to have to learn how engines work, how to recognise aircraft just from the sound of their engines, how to tie and untie knots in total darkness and all that, I'd have quit on the first day,' Jane said, taking a long drink of her tea. 'To tell you the truth, queen, I didn't know I were capable of understandin' such stuff and when I write to Jimmy and tell him what I've done, I feel right proud of meself.'

'The air force knows what it's doing. They teach you little bit by little bit, and the instructors make sure that each little bit gets well and truly dinned into our heads before they start on something else,' Kathy said, cutting a wedge off her toasted cheese and dipping it into the puddle of red sauce on the side of her plate. 'It is extremely technical, of course, and we're obviously going to have to be really strong and pretty quick when we're working with real balloons, but by the time we leave here I'm certain sure we'll be able to cope. They aren't hurrying us because they realise how important it is that we know exactly what we're doing, and the reason they want us to know is because a barrage balloon is bloody important to the war effort and bloody expensive too,' she ended.

Jane laughed and took a large bite of her own toasted cheese, speaking rather thickly through her mouthful. 'You're right there, queen. According to the NCOs, every bit of our equipment and every stitch of our uniform has gorra be treated like gold dust 'cos it costs a fortune to replace. But that doesn't apply to us; we're just bodies so far as they're concerned. We get bawled at and punished and put on jankers for the least little thing and if we get a hole in a stocking and don't mend it before one of the old cows comes round on an inspection, then we'll be spud bashin' for a week. Still, we won't get none of that when we're on a permanent site, they say.'

'Yes, I know what you mean,' Kathy acknowledged. 'But, you know, the stuff our uniform's made of is first class, really durable, I mean. Those black waterproofs may not be glamorous – well, they're not – but they'd keep you dry in a thunderstorm, and now that I've broken them in I really love my lace-up boots. And the woolly jumpers and gloves and things are ever so warm – ever so cosy when you compare them with the ordinary WAAF uniform.'

'And I suppose our black-outs and twilights are really sexy, really pretty,' Jane said with a giggle. 'And them lisle stockings – are they cosy an' all?'

Kathy had to laugh as well, although she shook her head reprovingly at her friend's descriptions of the black and grey issue knickers. 'This is a smart tearoom full of civilians but, in any event, it's no place for discussing knickers,' she said severely. 'I agree with you that our underwear isn't very glamorous, but it isn't supposed to be. It's practical, warm and pretty comfortable. What more can one ask?'

'One can ask a helluva lot more,' Jane grumbled. She had recently been punished for wearing a piece of frivolous red ribbon to tie back her hair and was still full of resentment against the spiteful spinster officer who had penalised her. 'Still an' all, I know what you mean, an' the blue uniform looks well on me; I can't count the number of fellers who've told me it brings out the colour of me eyes.'

Kathy sighed, knowing full well that blue did nothing for her; but then who would care on a balloon site manned by women? What mattered there would be efficiency and the speed with which you obeyed orders. She said as much and Jane smiled at her, affection and smugness mingling. 'Oh you, Kathy Kelling,' she said. 'If you don't know how good you look in your bleedin' uniform then I don't intend to swell your head by tellin' you!'

As the weeks went on, both Jane and Kathy were aware that they were growing stronger, nimbler and more self-confident. They understood the workings of flying the balloons even though they had not yet actually done so, and could have named every part of the huge charges so soon to be theirs. When, in their turn, they went to the old airfield and actually flew a balloon, they could scarcely wait for the end of the course. They had been promised a week's leave and after that would be posted to a balloon site 'somewhere in England', though they had no idea, as yet, where it would be.

'But we're bound to be together,' Kathy told Jane joyfully. 'I was talking to the Wing Officer this morning and she said that when they have a good crew they don't want it split up.'

'That's grand,' Jane said absently. She was trying to persuade her curls into a pompadour and having very little luck. 'Are you goin' home for your leave, Kath? Because if so, I s'pose you'll go to Rhyl.'

'I think I'll come back to Liverpool for part of the week,' Kathy said at once. 'I don't know a soul in Rhyl apart from me mam and Billy, so I wouldn't want to spend the whole week there. But what about you, Jane? Don't you want to go and see Jimmy? If you do, I thought I might come along. I'd – I'd like to see Alec again.'

'Oh aye,' Jane said, settling her cap on her curls and regarding her reflection anxiously. 'I wonder if I oughter have me hair cut? Only it's too curly to wrap round a ribbon and me cap looks silly sittin' on top of it, like a cat on a gorse bush.'

Kathy laughed but considered the question seriously. 'I think you're right, you'd find it a lot easier to deal with if it was short,' she said, 'but you didn't answer my question – aren't you thinking of going over to see Jimmy? A week's leave is long enough, you know.'

'Oh, I dunno,' Jane said. She headed for the door. 'Do stop chatterin', queen. One thing about being a Bop is that you're always ready for your dinner.'

Kathy followed her friend along to the cookhouse; Jane had certainly given her considerable food for thought, even though she was clearly unaware of it. Kathy had never known her to prevaricate in the way she so often did now and she had certainly avoided Kathy's question with all the adroitness at her command, which wasn't much, Kathy concluded ruefully. She had noticed that Jane had several times

flirted with some of their instructors but soon realised
that showing disapproval merely annoyed her friend.
After all, flirting meant nothing, not really. Jane had
told her so often that she was in love with Jimmy and
meant to marry him that it had not occurred to Kathy,
until very recently, that time and experience could
change not just one's attitude, but also one's feelings.
Jane was a good girl, a loving sister to her siblings, an
excellent friend to Kathy herself and a very good
Waaf. But all around her, she was seeing other pretty
girls falling in and out of love, going out with a
different young man every two or three weeks and
generally enjoying themselves whilst she, Jane, who
was prettier than all of them, could only write letters
and have an occasional phone call.

So when Jane had announced that she was going to
the flicks with Sergeant Cripps or AC2 Taylor, Kathy
could not find it in her heart to blame her. She was
pretty sure that Jimmy probably talked and flirted
with other girls, so why should not Jane do the same?
She decided that Jane needed experience before
settling down and salved her conscience by telling
herself that Jane would turn back to Jimmy in the end.

At this point in her musings, she and Jane reached
the long counter where the cooks were dispensing
today's rations. Kathy held out her plate and had
mince and onions ladled on to it by one man and two
huge scoops of mashed potato added to it by another.
A third spooned cabbage into the mixture and then
she and Jane made for the table where other members
of their crew were already sitting. Kathy wondered
whether to pursue the question of where Jane meant
to spend her leave, then decided against it. It was a
mean thing to do, to force her best friend into telling
her lies, but that, she sadly acknowledged, was what

would happen if she persisted. For some reason, Jane did not want her company if she did go to meet Jimmy, and Kathy supposed that this was fair enough. After all, they were together twenty-four hours a day, seven days a week and would continue to be so for the foreseeable future. So she changed the subject to wonder where their posting would send them, and by the time they had finished their meal she had banished Jane's strange behaviour from her mind.

That evening, however, when they returned to their mess, a surprise awaited them. She and Jane went straight to the bulletin board, hoping for letters from home. Instead, to their dismay, they saw a large notice announcing that all leave for balloon operatives had been cancelled and that the girls were to report to their new sites at the beginning of the next week. Beneath that was a list of postings and another girl began to read them out loud, lists of names and destinations, then suddenly Kathy realised something was wrong and pushed her way nearer the bulletin board. 'Oh, Jane,' she said, almost unable to believe what she was about to say. 'You're going to a dock site near Liverpool . . . but I'm being sent to Nottingham as acting corporal in Betty Miller's place!'

It was a disappointment not to have leave, but later that night as she lay in her bed, Kathy concluded that perhaps a separation from Jane, which she had thought so dreadful, might be the best thing for both of them. She was uneasily aware that she had begun to rely on Jane always backing her up and this had given her a good deal of confidence; now she would have to manage the girls in her crew without Jane's familiar presence. In other words, had the two of them been together she would have had no fear of a rebellion in the ranks when she began to tell the rest of the crew what to do. Jane would have backed her up and if anyone had tried to bully her, or disobey her commands, Jane would have sorted them out. Now, Kathy would be truly in command and on her own; she would just have to hope that the girls in her new crew would be as helpful and friendly as those in her previous crew had been.

The girls were given rail warrants late on Sunday night and on Monday morning, early, they found themselves jostling amongst a huge crowd of Waafs on the station platform. The crowding eased as trains arrived for various destinations and the Waafs, each one with her two kit bags, clambered aboard. You could always tell a Bop by her kit bags, since they were the only people in the air force who had so much clothing and equipment that two kit bags were necessary. Jane and Kathy grinned at each other but had no opportunity for a proper farewell. Kathy was marshalling her crew, trying to make sure that they all got into the same carriage since they would only be on this train for a few stops and would then have to change. As her train pulled out, she let the window down and poked her head through but could see no sign of her friend, so settled back on her kit bags – every seat had already been taken before the Waafs climbed aboard – to get what rest she could. She guessed that the day ahead of her was going to be a long and trying one and said as much to the ACW1 who was her second-in-command. The other girl, Paddy O'Toole, nodded in agreement. She was a fair-haired, blue-eyed Irish girl whose rose-petal complexion and apparent frailty were deceptive. In fact, she was as strong as an ox and was a great comfort to Kathy as they sat on their kit bags in the corridor and chatted. Kathy gathered that Paddy was determined to rise in the air force and was anxious to do well, and since this was exactly how Kathy regarded her own future they might help one another to attain higher rank.

The girls arrived in Nottingham without incident and climbed aboard the gharry which would take them to their site. Kathy had taken care to get to know the members of her crew, though she had not needed Paddy to point out the two troublemakers, ACWs Stutton and Wintersett. They were large, masculine-looking girls with short haircuts and loud cockney voices. But they were evidently waiting until they reached the site to see whether they could push their new acting corporal around, and once there, Kathy decided, I shall make sure they toe the line. I must begin as I mean to go on, even if it makes me unpopular. I can, after all, make their lives pretty miserable if I choose to do so. I don't think they'll like it much if they find themselves always called upon for extra duty, or turned out of their beds to peel mounds of spuds. Yes, if they're going to be difficult, I shall have to show them it doesn't pay.

Having made up her mind on her future strategy, Kathy settled down on the uncomfortable metal boxes which passed for seats in the gharry and watched the suburbs of Nottingham gradually give place to countryside. I'll write to Mam tonight, give her my new address and tell her all about the site, she thought to herself. And after that, I'll write to Alec, because Nottingham's a good deal nearer to Lincoln than Cardington was.

*

In fact, it was a full week before Kathy had the opportunity to write to anyone. They arrived at the site and found a draughty Nissen hut standing on a hill with an ancient churchyard to the left of it and a huge expanse of ploughed field to the right. Kathy cast a quick glance around, checking for hazards such as church towers, well grown mature trees or any buildings tall enough to interfere with the balloon in bad weather, but saw nothing which looked potentially dangerous. She had been congratulating herself on getting a good site when Paddy remarked that it was bloody exposed, so it was, and would mean that half the time they would be fighting strong winds both when flying the balloon and when bringing her down again.

This remark had proved to be all too true. On that first evening, Kathy had organised some of the girls into a domestic party, who would cook and serve the food they found waiting in the kitchen, and had then taken the rest of the crew out to examine the balloon, accompanied by the sergeant in charge. He was a stocky, middle-aged man with a Black Country accent so strong that the girls had difficulty in understanding him at first. The men, who had departed only that morning, had left the blimp on close haul with everything ready so that it could be flown at a moment's notice and Kathy decided, after a discussion with the sergeant, that they would take it up to two thousand feet as soon as it grew dark. None of them, except for the cheerful sergeant himself, had ever flown a balloon in the dark before, and they had been strongly advised by their instructors at Cardington to practise just as much as they were able, so that the real thing, when it came, did not end in hopeless confusion.

By the time they had had a meal they were all ready for their beds and Kathy felt a secret sympathy with her crew as they stumbled out of the makeshift cookhouse and headed, uncertainly, for the balloon. There was a moon, but because the wind was quite strong the clouds scudded across its face constantly, making it difficult to see what one was doing. The sergeant climbed on to the winch and Kathy, at his suggestion, shouted the orders to bring the balloon lower so that they might add the armaments to the main cable. Since this was only a practice, she did not actually attach any of the explosive devices which stood ready to hand, but merely pretended to do so.

Fortunately, she had disposed her whole team and presently one of the guards came puffing up to shout that the telephone had rung. 'I answered it and some feller on the other end just snapped "Fly five thousand feet" and slammed the phone down,' she said breathlessly. 'What did he mean, Corp?'

Before Kathy could answer, the sergeant began to work the winch and to shout orders. The balloon was brought to the correct height for Kathy to add the armaments in cold fact, and from then on the night became memorable indeed.

They got the balloon up to five thousand feet, fully armed and prepared, but the winds up there were very strong and they could see the blimp behaving more like a ballet dancer than a balloon, rearing and tugging on her cable as though she longed for nothing more than to be free. Then they heard the familiar sound of throbbing engines and the knowledge they had gained so painfully at Cardington became useful at last. 'Here come the Luftwaffe,' someone said urgently. 'I hope they ain't goin' to drop no bombs here.' But on this particular night, they were in luck, for the bombers passed away to the north, well clear of both balloons and the ack-ack, whose batteries kept up a steady fire even though, Kathy suspected, the enemy were well out of range.

Getting the balloon down again when the second phone call came from HQ was a tricky business, with the crew not used to night flying and lacking the experience of the men they had replaced. They managed it, however, and when Kathy saw them back to their hut at last she told them that she was proud of them and meant every word.

The next day, she and the sergeant discussed how they could best prepare the crews for more such events and Sergeant Jackson said they would practise every night for a week so that the girls might become experienced without risking the safety of the blimp.

'Barrage balloons is tricky beasts,' he told her. 'If everyone takes a turn on the winch, then they'll get the feel of it. It's a bit like drivin' a team of four great strong horses, all tryin' to pull in different directions, and a bit like landin' a huge salmon when you've only got a trout rod, but you gets used to it. I reckon, after three or four months, you will know as much about your blimp as a mother knows about her new babby. But we'll practise during the day as well, 'cos her needs a deal of understandin'. Have you worked out a rota so's everyone gets a go at everything? I know you've done the guard rota and the kitchen one, but you'll want one for the blimp as well.'

So for the first week on site, Kathy was far too busy to write letters. Indeed, for six weeks she scarcely dashed off more than short notes. She had looked up Lincoln on the map and had seen that it would be perfectly possible to reach Waddington and Alec when she got the forty-eight hours' leave they had been promised, but so far everyone had been much too busy to even think about leaving the site. Here, everything was geared to the balloon. When a WAAF officer came to do a kit inspection, she was chiefly concerned to see that the girls' clothing was in good repair and capable of keeping them warm, or dry, or both. Since the clothing depot was actually several miles away, it would have been quite an outing to go there for new boots, gloves or woolly hats, but so far there had been no necessity for such a journey. As Kathy had told Jane, that day which now seemed so far away, the quality of their garments was first rate. It would probably be years, rather than months, before it became necessary to issue anything new.

In fact the only real outing, if you could call it such, was taken when the girls were marched to the nearest bus stop in order to visit the municipal baths. There was only cold water on site and each night one of the girls was detailed to fill half a dozen large, enamel jugs with water at the kitchen sink and to disperse them among the beds in the Nissen huts. Each girl had been issued with a small tin basin and though everyone did their best to keep clean, the weekly visits to the municipal baths became an urgent necessity, particularly in wet weather, when the site became a morass of churned up mud and the girls grew used to being constantly dirty.

At the end of six weeks, just when Kathy was thinking that she really might take a forty-eight, she was told to report to HQ; it appeared the powers that be had decided she was doing well as acting corporal and wanted her to take the examination which would give her the full rank. Kathy had grown used to command and knew that she would really miss it if she had to go back to being 'just one of the crew' again. So she went off at the appointed time and came back successful. She and Paddy had worked hard, swotting up all they would need to know for the examinations, and Paddy had been delighted to be told that she, too, would sit the exam and, if she passed, would eventually be given the rank of corporal and a crew of her own.

'It's all change in the WAAF,' Kathy said dolefully, when Paddy's posting came through. The two girls had been close throughout the bitterly cold winter and it seemed sad that, with the coming of spring, they should be parted.

'But we'll see quite a lot of each other, so we shall, because I'm only posted to Number Two Balloon Site and that's just a couple of miles up the road,' Paddy pointed out. 'I'm going to buy an old bike so I'll be able to cycle over to Site 21 whenever I get a few hours off and you can come over to me sometimes, even if you have to walk. Or you might be able to buy a bike, too,' she added craftily. 'We could go for rides together – there must be some of Nottingham which isn't flat as a pancake and covered with plough.'

Chapter Fourteen

1942

By the time Paddy left, March was well advanced and evenings were pulling out. Kathy decided that she would speak to HQ about the possibility of taking her forty-eight, and the next time the gharry went into Nottingham she went with it to enquire about rail fares to Lincoln, for she had decided that she really would make the effort to see Alec once more. They were still exchanging letters, sometimes as often as once a week, and she thought that the tone of Alec's correspondence was becoming friendlier with every week that passed. She knew that the bomber crew were on standby, as indeed were the balloon operatives, but hoped that he might manage a few hours in her company at least. She did not intend to tell him of her plans in advance in case he thought she was being fast or forward, but meant to pretend she had come to Lincoln to see a WAAF friend stationed nearby and had rung him up on the off chance of a meeting. A forty-eight started at midnight and ended exactly forty-eight hours later, but if one were lucky, and off duty, one's actual leave could start the evening before and not end until parade the morning after, so that a forty-eight could be 'stretched' into a sixty-hour absence. She would need several hours to reach Lincoln and the same amount of time to get back, but that would still leave her a nice chunk of time in which to meet up with Alec once more. She had seen too many Waafs posted from site to site for no apparent reason to believe that she herself would be immune. At present, the journey to Lincoln was possible – in fact, relatively easy – but if she were to be posted to the north of Scotland . . . she must seize the opportunity while it existed.

So as soon as the girls were dismissed that evening, Kathy handed over to her replacement NCO and trudged to the nearest bus stop. She caught the train in reasonable time and, to her surprise and delight, reached Lincoln in the early hours of the following morning. A friendly porter advised her that there were few hotels yet open but unlocked the ladies' waiting room for her. It was neither warm nor particularly comfortable, but at least it was quiet and out of the wind, and Kathy was extremely tired. She lay down on one of the long benches, using her kit bag as a pillow, and slept soundly until other people began to come on to the station platform and the sound of trains and general bustle woke her.

For a moment, she wondered where the devil she was, then remembered and got, somewhat groggily, to her feet. She had the remains of a headache and the nasty, frowsty feeling of one who has slept in her clothes, but a cup of railway coffee and a round of toast cleared her head and a quick, though cold, wash in the Ladies' woke her up properly.

She had not meant to ring the station until perhaps halfway through the morning, in case the crew of Wellington BN1543 had been on a raid the night before, but the trouble was, she had no idea where she would find digs in the city. She did not want to go to a hotel because she guessed that it would cost a good deal, and thought that if she could consult Alec he might be able to advise her. She left the railway station and found a telephone box, but just as she was about to take down the receiver from its rest and ask for the number of Alec's mess, it struck her that he was unlikely to be able to help her. After all, he lived on the camp and would have no need of digs. Stepping out of the box, Kathy glanced around her and saw a line of taxis, presumably waiting for the arrival of the next train. She picked out a car with a fatherly-looking driver and went over to his cab, tapping on the window. The man immediately climbed out and opened the back door for her; an action that Kathy might have expected, though in fact she had not. 'Where to, miss?' he said briskly. 'Out to one of the airfields, is it? Been on leave, have you?'

'No, I don't want the airfields, I'm here to visit a friend,' Kathy said, knowing that she was going scarlet but powerless to stop herself. 'I've only got a forty-eight so I shan't be staying more than the one night. I suppose . . . do you happen to know . . .?'

'Oh aye, your best bet will be Tentercroft Street,' the driver said at once. 'It ain't far from the station and there's several houses lets rooms along there.' He looked her assessingly up and down. 'Mrs Bridges will suit you,' he announced with a triumphant air. 'Her house is clean and comfortable, though she won't stand no nonsense, no hanky panky. But you don't look like the sort of young person who'd – er . . .'

'Mrs Bridges sounds fine,' Kathy said quickly. 'Is her house fairly near the station? Only I don't want to miss my train back.'

'It's two minutes away,' the driver said cheerfully. 'Hop in.' He started the engine and drove along the main road for a few hundred yards before swinging his vehicle into a narrow street lined with neat terraced houses. Several of them had boards outside their front doors announcing rooms to let, but the taxi took her past these to a larger house where two dwellings had been knocked into one. The garden was hedged with forsythia, already bursting into yellow bloom, and there were spring bulbs – daffodils, pheasant-eye narcissus, grape hyacinths and crocuses – blossoming in the beds that surrounded a small, circular lawn.

The driver jumped out and helped Kathy to alight, saying as he did so: 'I always say, if someone takes care over a garden, then likely they'll take care of the house an' all. I'll hang around till you're took in, but it's a quiet time of year; I don't reckon you'll have no trouble.'

He was right. Mrs Bridges, a comfortably plump woman of forty or so, with brown hair tied back from her face and her body enveloped in a floral wraparound apron, said immediately that she had plenty of rooms empty at present and took Kathy up to what she described as her 'small back', which was a pleasantly furnished room with pink patterned curtains and a matching bedspread. The room overlooked a tiny cobbled yard and on to the backs of a great many similar terraced houses. Mrs Bridges announced that it cost seven and six a night, though if Kathy intended to stay a second night, the price would drop to five shillings. 'Because a second night in the same sheets means less laundering,' she explained. 'And the seven and six includes breakfast and a cup of cocoa and sandwiches, which I serves at eleven; a late supper like. I can do a proper evening meal but that's an extra half crown and if you're only here for one night you'll likely not want to waste time coming back here from the town centre since I serve it at half past six. And I don't suppose I need to tell you that you mustn't bring young men up to your room.' She cast a glance, half shy, half defiant, at the younger woman. 'I've got me reputation to consider, you see,' she finished.

Kathy agreed to abide by these rules since she had not the slightest intention of asking anyone back to her room and paid immediately, then placed her kit bag carefully on the single chair and asked to be shown the bathroom and lavatory. 'I've been travelling all night and only had a cold wash in the Ladies' in the station,' she explained rather shyly. 'I'd like to have a hot wash, if that's all right, and then lie down on my bed for an hour. My – my friend is aircrew and if his squadron were out last night he won't welcome a call much before lunchtime. Is that all right?'

Mrs Bridges agreed that this was fine, and when Kathy left the house again at noon, she knew she was looking her best. She was in uniform, of course, but she had brushed her hair until it gleamed before rolling and pinning it under her cap and her uniform was spotless, her brass shining whitely and her collar so stiff and well starched that it threatened to cut her neck whenever she turned her head sideways. Mrs Bridges had told her which bus to catch to get into the city centre and had advised her to ring her friend from a telephone box on the way to the bus stop rather than returning to the station.

'There's usually a queue at the station once the London train gets in,' she explained. 'But the one down the road should be empty; you'll be able to ring from there without a queue of people starin' at you and banging on the glass if you take too long.'

Kathy took her advice and rang the number Alec had given her, for they had begun the habit of an

342

occasional phone call, perhaps once a month, as well as their letters. She was in luck. The cheerful young man who answered the phone in the mess shouted Alec at once and in no time at all Kathy heard the familiar voice. 'Hello? Alec Hewitt speaking.'

Kathy's relief was so great that her voice rose by several octaves. 'Alec? It's Kathy. Oh, I'm so glad I've got you; I kept worrying that you might still be sleeping. I'm – I'm in Lincoln; they've given me my forty-eight at last and I didn't really want to go home until my long leave, so I thought – I thought I might as well see a bit of the country – and see you at the same time. Is there – is there any chance of you getting into Lincoln? If so, we could meet up . . . if you'd like to, that is.'

Kathy swallowed nervously. She hadn't meant to admit that she'd come to Lincoln in the hope of seeing Alec. She had planned to say she had WAAF friends on one of the stations but somehow, as soon as she had heard his voice, the truth had come tumbling out. And anyway, was it so awful? There was nothing wrong with wanting to see a friend, was there? And Alec's reply soon put any doubts to rest.

'Kathy!' There was no mistaking the genuine pleasure in Alec's voice. 'I can't believe it! Of course we must meet up, and as soon as possible. How long are you here for? I know you said you'd got a forty-eight but getting here must have taken a good deal of it. There'll be a gharry going into town in an hour. Will that be soon enough? I could send for a taxi but they cost an arm and a leg, because we're a fair way from Lincoln. Where are you staying? Is it an hotel? If so, we can meet in the foyer. Well, this is a wonderful surprise and the last thing I expected. Oh, Kathy, I can't wait to see you!'

Kathy laughed rather breathlessly. Her heart was singing; she had been right to come and it was clear that Alec's only reaction had been surprise and pleasure. She explained quickly that she had digs in the suburbs and meant to make her way to the centre by bus, and he said at once that she must find the Saracen's Head, a pub everyone knew because it was a sort of unofficial headquarters for the bods from RAF Waddington. 'At least we shan't have to wear red roses in our buttonholes, because I'd know you among a thousand other Waafs,' he told her. 'Buy yourself an orange squash and wait for me in the bar; I'll pay you back when I arrive. And don't go getting picked up by any feller who happens to shoot you a line,' he added. 'See you soon, sweetie.'

Kathy put the phone back on its rest with trembling fingers, adjusted her cap in the small mirror, and headed for the bus queue. She was so happy she could have sung aloud, and climbed aboard the bus feeling confident that the day ahead would be a delightful one. How nice Alec was! It was the first time he had used an endearment towards her and she found it set her nerves jangling, though in a very pleasant sort of way. She sat in the bus, watching the passing scene and scarcely seeing a thing. In her mind's eye she saw Alec greeting her as in a romantic film and, though she scolded herself, it was with considerable excited anticipation that she sat down in the bar of the Saracen's Head with her orange squash and stared at the door.

The door had swung many times but only twenty minutes had passed before she saw Alec's figure approaching her. He had tilted his cap to the back of his head and was grinning widely, holding out both hands towards her. Kathy jumped to her feet and for once did not wonder what was the right thing to do. Instinct sent her straight into his arms and if he was surprised he did not show it. He simply folded her in his embrace, then held her back from him, his eyes twinkling. 'Did I see you salute me, Aircraftwoman?' he asked teasingly. 'Behaviour like this is frowned upon by the top brass, you know. Oh, but it's grand to see you, Kathy – aren't you the prettiest thing? And there's more of you than there was when last we met.' He stepped back a pace, the wicked twinkle much in evidence. 'You always did have a pretty face but now you've got a gorgeous figure as well.'

'You cheeky beggar!' Kathy said with pretended wrath. 'It isn't that I've changed, not really. The truth is, I look better when Jane's not around.'

Now it was Alec's turn to scoff. 'Just because you're best friends, that don't mean to say you're anything alike,' he assured her. 'In fact, you're chalk and cheese, so don't go getting an inferiority complex, for goodness' sake. Now, what are we going to do with our day?'

'It really isn't a whole day,' Kathy pointed out. She glanced shyly up at him. 'I – I suppose there's no chance of you being free tomorrow? Only my train doesn't go until six and if you were free we really could have a whole day to explore. But I don't suppose you'll be allowed off the station two days running,' she finished despondently.

Alec, however, gave her hand a little shake. 'In the ordinary way you'd be right, but it just so happens that we shan't be doing ops for another couple of days. Last night we were badly shot up over Germany – there's a lot of damage to be put right before old Bare Nell will be operational again.'

Kathy happened to be looking at him as he spoke

and was secretly appalled and even a little frightened by the sudden change in his expression. He no longer looked like handsome, carefree Alec Hewitt; he looked very much older and very much grimmer too, but she knew that it would not be tactful to say so and merely said how sorry she was. 'I know an awful lot about balloons but I'm afraid I'm extremely ignorant about aircraft,' she admitted.

'Most people are, unless they're aircrew,' Alec assured her. 'But there's no point talking about it. Would you like to walk up to the cathedral and take a look around? You get a marvellous view from up there. Or do you think I'm a dull dog to suggest such a thing? Tomorrow we could take a boat on the river.'

Kathy agreed with considerable eagerness because it was impossible to ignore the cathedral, which reared above the town, higher even than the castle and a good deal more impressive. It was equally impossible not to wonder, however, whether Alec had suggested the cathedral because he thought her a studious type of girl who would prefer church visiting to other, more exciting, pastimes. If, for instance, he had been entertaining Jane, he would undoubtedly have taken her to the flicks so that they could cuddle in the dark, safe from the eyes of any senior officers who might be about.

However, Kathy was well aware that this was a stupid thing to start thinking. She knew that Alec had written to Jane once or twice – Jane had made no secret of it – but she did not think for one moment that Jane would want to carry the intimacy beyond friendship. Neither did she think that Jane would be such a fool as to do the enormous cross-country trek from Liverpool to Lincoln in order to see Alec, who was in the same aircrew as Jane's long-time official boyfriend. So she squared her shoulders and the two of them set off towards the distant tower of the cathedral.

Kathy soon discovered that reaching the cathedral was a tough business. In Steep Street, there was a handrail running along the side of the pavement and she was very soon glad of its aid and wondering how old people managed. After all, there was, presumably, some sort of cathedral close up here where elderly and retired clergy lived, and they would have to make their way up and down Steep Street every time they visited the shops.

She put the question to Alec, but not until they had climbed the hill and were actually about to enter the cathedral. It made him laugh but he said he supposed that a lifetime of hauling themselves up the hill must have toughened the inhabitants of the Close, since he had never seen anyone collapse by the wayside yet, and he often came up here to enjoy the quiet and beauty of the place. He proved his point by giving her a tour of the cathedral and showing how familiar he was with every nook and cranny of the place. Kathy was impressed and delighted with the beauty of it and entranced by the Lincoln Imp, though she nearly broke her back as Alec manoeuvred her into a position whence she could look up at the elaborately carved rafters and see the Imp's small face peering down at her, seeming as amused at her strange position as she was by his.

By the time they left the cathedral they were both hungry, and Alec suggested that they should have a sort of high tea at a café he knew. It was at the bottom of Steep Street and soon they were ensconced in a dark little tearoom, eating their way through baked beans on toast, a plateful of bread and margarine and some fancy cakes which Kathy decided, after one bite, were probably made of sawdust. And whilst they ate, they talked. Kathy felt that she was getting to know Alec for the first time, know what made him angry and what made him sad; what gave him satisfaction and what made him laugh. He told her about bombing raids over Germany, trying to relate incidents which were funny, or even scary, but had turned out all right in the end. It was at this point that Kathy noticed how often he put his left hand to his face, shielding his eye almost as though the light hurt it. She pretended to be concentrating on her food but watched him covertly with quick little glances until she realised that his left eyelid kept fluttering uncontrollably and that every now and then the left side of his face was forced into a spasm so severe and prolonged that she could scarcely fail to notice it. Hastily, Kathy began to talk about Site 21. She told him about ACW Smith, who had got in the way of one of the new concrete bollards one windy night and had broken her foot as a result. She told of other girls riding the tail guy, despite its being strictly forbidden, whilst she worried herself sick in case someone became too scared to let go and got carried away by Betty Blimp up to four thousand feet. It hadn't happened – she hoped it never would – but it was a magnificent feeling being swept giddily into the air provided you let go when you were only six feet or so above the ground. She told him of Annie, the cook, who was petrified of mice and who had screamed the place down and demanded an armed escort when one of the girls had put a pink and white sugar mouse just inside the flour barrel. There was the night in their Nissen hut when an NCO had stripped the blankets off ACW Shaw to find an embarrassed airman in the bed with her, and another night when someone had poured too much Brasso into the recalcitrant tortoise stove and five Waafs had ended up looking like a Black and White Minstrel Show.

Her talk relaxed him, she could see, and when she suggested a visit to the cinema he agreed gladly. They went to the Odeon, simply because it was nearest, but it turned out to be an unfortunate choice. A war film – *Target for Tonight* – was showing and halfway through the performance Kathy glanced at her escort's face, so near her own since he had his arm about her shoulders, and saw, with real distress, that tears were rolling silently down his cheeks.

She said nothing but leaned up and gently kissed his jawline and was astonished, and even a little frightened, by his reaction. He turned in his seat, putting both arms about her and hugging her so tightly that she could scarcely breathe. He muttered that no one knew . . . no one understood . . . he couldn't explain how he felt at the thought of doing another op.

Kathy found herself comforting him as though she, and not he, were the older. 'Never mind, never mind,' she whispered softly, for the film was still continuing and other members of the audience would have been quick to shush her had she spoken out loud. 'Why, you and Jimmy are the best navigator and rear gunner in the service, and your pilot is first rate – you said so.'

Alec did not answer but continued to clutch her convulsively, only gradually relaxing as the scene changed to a romantic shot of two young people, immaculately uniformed and hand in hand, strolling through a field of standing corn in a way which, Alec told her afterwards, would cause any self-respecting farmer to mow them down with a machine gun, if one were handy.

When the film ended, they left the cinema, still entwined, and Alec said he would walk her back to her digs. 'We'll meet up first thing in the morning, as soon as there's transport going into Lincoln,' he said eagerly. 'Oh, Kathy, it's been a grand day; the best I've had since the war started. And the forecast is good for tomorrow so I'll buy us a picnic and we'll take that boat on the river. I've had enough of war for a bit and there's nothing I'd like better than to see fields and hedgerows, cows and ponies. If we hire the boat for the whole day, then we can moor up somewhere pretty and take a look at the countryside. Would you like that?'

Kathy admitted that she would like it very much indeed and for a while the two of them strolled on in silence, but when they reached Mrs Bridges's house and Kathy turned to bid Alec goodnight he clutched her fiercely, murmuring into her hair: 'Do you *have* to go in? I wish – I wish we could spend the night together. Oh, not together in that sense,' he added hastily, as Kathy stiffened a little, 'but just together, beside one another, holding hands, that sort of thing. Somehow, contact, even just holding hands, stops me thinking about . . . about . . .'

'Oh, Alec, I wish we could,' Kathy said wistfully. 'I'm sure it would all be perfectly innocent, but Mrs Bridges is ever so strict and I had to promise not to bring young men in when I paid for the room.' She glanced at her wristwatch, which had once belonged to her father and looked very masculine on her small wrist. 'It's after midnight, too, but I'm sure she'll still be awake listening.'

'Well, I'll have to get myself kipped down on a

350

bench somewhere,' Alec said ruefully, 'because the last transport went at eleven. Never mind, it's a fine enough night, though I dare say it'll get mortal cold towards dawn.'

Kathy hesitated, looking up into his face. She hated to abandon him but could see no alternative. Mrs Bridges was not the sort of woman to see her rules flouted and Kathy remembered tales told by other Waafs of landladies listening for a telltale footfall which meant that more than one person was quietly climbing her stairs. But another look at Alec's face made her decide to be brave. Poor Alec had suffered enough. He had told her how hellishly difficult he found it to sleep at night when they were not due to go on a bombing raid. The raids turned one's life upside down, he explained, so that one got used to sleeping during the day and being active at night. When a break in routine occurred and the crew of Bare Nell got four or five days off, they all had great difficulty in sleeping and when they did, at last, get to sleep towards morning, they suffered from frightful nightmares in which they had fallen asleep whilst the great Wellington roared over France and Germany and was shot up by enemy aircraft before they could do anything about it. Such dreams usually ended with them jumping out of the plane, realising too late that they had failed to strap on their parachutes and plunging sickeningly towards the ground. They would wake, drenched in sweat and terrified, quite unable to return to sleep.

'If you like . . . if you want to take the risk . . . you can come up with me,' she said, her voice trembling only a little. 'It's almost bound to rain before morning, judging by the clouds . . . oh, but Alec, if she catches us, she'll turn me out! Not that it matters, because two can share a park bench as well as one, I suppose.'

Alec laughed, put both arms round her and began to kiss her. This was not the gentle, friendly kiss of earlier in the day, but a fierce and much more exciting one. When he held her back from him, Kathy was aware that she was not only breathless, but rather disappointed. That kiss had been the beginning of something and she found herself resenting the fact that he could stop without any apparent distress, whereas she felt as though she had been abruptly drenched in cold water. Like when they chuck a bucket of the stuff over two dogs who've been fighting, or making love, she told herself with an inward grin. Oh well, at least I'm not trying to be all romantic!

But now Alec was pushing her gently towards the front door. 'I can't risk you getting into trouble and being turned out,' he murmured in her ear. 'Is there a shed round the back? I see there's a little lane leads round to something. I'll be all right there.'

But having made her decision, Kathy was determined. She shook her head chidingly at him. 'We've had a lovely day, Alec, and I won't have either of us made miserable when we could be happy together. I'll make a tiny crack in the blackout curtains, just for a minute; there's a sort of outbuilding below my window, and I'm sure you could scramble up on it and get in that way. If not, then I'll call out to Mrs Bridges that I've left something in the downstairs hall and I'll let you in the front door and you can come in and sneak up the stairs after me.'

For the first time since he had wept, the wicked twinkle was back in Alec's eyes. 'I can climb up by a drainpipe if it's near your window,' he said exultantly. 'Oh, Kathy, you're a princess – and much prettier than Jane, whatever you may think.'

Kathy was beginning to laugh, to tell him that the moonlight must have gone to his head, but he put a finger across her lips, unlocked the door and pushed it open, and gave her back the key. He reached out and drew a hand lovingly down the side of her face and across her chin and then, soft-footed, made his way down the path and into the darkness.

Kathy went as quietly as she could up the stairs and into her room. Mr and Mrs Bridges – she assumed that there was a Mr Bridges – must be asleep since there was no light under any of the doors on the upper landing. She let herself into her room, closed the door softly behind her and switched on the light. She crossed the room quietly and made a tiny crack in the blackout curtains, then retreated to the door and switched off the light. The small room was stuffy, smelling slightly of mothballs and cooked cabbage, and she opened the window wide, reflecting that whether Alec came or not she would be glad of the fresh air.

It was odd, standing there in the dark with the lighter square of the window before her, wondering what would happen next. She thought it quite likely that, in fact, nothing would occur; Alec would go off and find himself a bench somewhere and she would be left wondering whether he had changed his mind because she did not sufficiently attract him or because he liked her too much to want to get her into trouble.

After a few minutes, she began to undress, smiling to herself at the contradiction in her thoughts. She was used to getting changed in the dark so it presented few problems, but just as she was beginning to put on her regulation pyjamas she heard the slightest of slight scrapings from the direction of the open window. She turned towards it, suddenly aware that her heart was thumping uncomfortably. Whatever was she doing? She, cool, level-headed Corporal Kathy Kelling, who was proud of her record in the air force, was about to behave like any of the little sluts at No. 21 Balloon Site, who would crawl into bed with anyone and boast about sleeping with a different fellow every night of the week.

But this isn't like that, Kathy thought wildly as she did up the last button of her pyjamas, and saw Alec step neatly over the sill. This is due to him missing the last transport and he's in a pretty bad state because his kite was shot up and, anyway, we're not going to do what the bad girls do, we just want to be together.

Standing awkwardly beside the undisturbed bed, she waited for Alec to speak or to take her in his arms but to her astonishment he shot straight past her, a finger to his lips, and stood in the shadows beside the door. Kathy was about to speak, to ask him what he was doing, when she, too, heard the footsteps. Someone was approaching her door along the landing.

She had no time to wonder what was happening before the door shot open. Mrs Bridges stood there, the light behind her emphasising her large and bulky figure. Before she had thought, Kathy had said angrily: 'Put off that bloody light! Don't you know there's a war on? What on earth's the matter, Mrs Bridges? Is it a raid? I've only just come in but I'm sure I haven't heard the siren.'

This full frontal attack seemed to take Mrs Bridges by surprise. She stepped back with a mutter of apology and clicked off the landing light, though she did not go away. In fact, she came a little further into the room, saying grudgingly: 'I'm sorry, miss, I'm sure, if I've been mistook, but I could have sworn I heard something . . . it sounded like someone clambering about on the lean-to kitchen roof.' She glared around the room by the light of the moon coming through the window, at the still unrumpled bed, at the tiny curtained-off area where Kathy was, presumably, to hang her clothes, and then actually bent and peered under the bed.

Kathy felt as furious as though she was not indeed guilty of precisely the crime Mrs Bridges suspected. She felt a tide of heat invade her cheeks and turned towards her landlady. 'Just what do you thing you are doing, Mrs Bridges?' she enquired frigidly. 'Not that I need to ask, because it's pretty damned obvious. Here, let me help you.' She crossed the small room in a couple of strides and whipped back the curtain, revealing only her uniform hanging in the tiny space provided. Then she seized the only chair and turned it upside down, letting its legs clang against the still wide open door. 'And I assure you that if anyone comes through that window you'll hear a scream loud enough to wake the dead. All right?'

Mrs Bridges began to back down so fast, Kathy thought, that her heels must have smoked. 'I'm that sorry, Miss Kelling,' she gabbled, 'but you don't know what it's like, trying to run a respectable house in wartime. Once I get a name for laxness, then the real bad types will be the only ones who'll come here. I hopes I'm not a killjoy but there's right and wrong and I won't have goings-on under my roof.'

Kathy knew a wild desire to say *or on your roof, apparently*, but bit the words back. Instead, she accepted Mrs Bridges's apology gracefully and ushered the older woman out of the room, saying: 'I must admit, I thought I heard something myself, but thought it was a cat. I was looking out of the window when you burst in, but I didn't see anything. Probably the noise you made – and the light streaming out – scared it off. Is there a key to my room, Mrs Bridges, because I hope you won't be offended, but I've no desire to be shocked out of my sleep by another surprise visit.'

Kathy saw Mrs Bridges begin to bridle and then change it into an understanding nod. 'Aye, I know what you mean, but I honestly thought . . . still, enough of that. There ain't a key, miss, but there's a bolt about halfway down. And now I'll bid you goodnight.'

She went out, shutting the door firmly behind her. Kathy immediately shot the bolt across, then turned to Alec. She had wondered whether he had taken the opportunity of escaping from the house whilst Mrs Bridges was searching the room in the half dark, but he was still there, grinning ruefully at her.

'Are you OK?' Kathy whispered.

Alec took her in his arms, then kissed her gently on the mouth. 'When she threw that bloody door open, she nearly broke my nose,' he whispered. 'I'm sure it's twice the size it was when I came through the window. God, what a harridan! But you were marvellous, Kathy. I'm sure most girls would have broken down in tears and admitted everything, but not you! I nearly died laughing when you picked the chair up and hurled it against the door, although it didn't do much to improve my nose, I can tell you.'

Kathy sniggered, but quietly. 'I'm just so thankful we got away with it. But Alec darling, what'll happen in the morning? I guess she probably gets up as soon as it's light, and even if she doesn't hear anything I reckon she'll nip out and take a look at the tiles, just to see if there are any signs.'

'I'll leave before she's even thinking of getting up,' Alec promised. 'I'll go as far as Frank's Cabin and get myself some breakfast there. It's a sort of workman's caff, but he does a goodish spread, for wartime that is. It's on Rosemary Lane, so I suggest you come and pick me up there at nine o'clock. We'll go along to the railway station and dump your kit bag in the Left Luggage and then we'll have a lovely day, OK?'

'That sounds wonderful,' Kathy said. She climbed into her bed and held the covers up so that Alec could squiggle in beside her. 'I say, it's a narrow bed, isn't it? Don't go falling out or the old horror will be along here before you can say knife.'

'The door's locked, and anyway I think you've spiked her guns. She won't dare to interfere again,' Alec said drowsily. He put both his arms round her and kissed the back of her neck. 'Oh, Kathy, it's grand to be with you.'

His hands, which had rested lightly round her waist, suddenly began to do a bit of exploring and Kathy pinched him as hard as she could. 'Stop that!' she hissed. 'You know what we said; just you stick to it, Alec Hewitt, or you'll find yourself sailing through that window a lot quicker than you came in.'

Alec's hands returned meekly to her waist and Kathy, not sure whether to be pleased or sorry, patted him approvingly. 'Thanks, Alec,' she murmured. 'And now let's see if we can both get a good night's sleep.'

'Good God, Al, what the devil's happened to your nose? I'd never have thought you were the fightin' kind but I see I were wrong. And is that the beginnin'

357

of a black eye? But I suppose you'll say that the other feller's still in hospital!'

Two days had passed since Alec had said goodbye to Kathy on the platform of Lincoln station, but this was the first time he had seen Jimmy since Bare Nell had gone in for repairs. Now Alec turned and grinned, a trifle lopsidedly, at his friend. He had not been kidding when he told Kathy that he feared his nose was broken, and now, standing in the ablutions hut with his towel slung round his neck, clad only in his underpants, he looked curiously at his reflection in the small, tin mirror which was all the RAF considered it necessary to provide. Jimmy was right; his nose was swollen and a fiery red and his left eye had a purple bruise across the cheekbone. But it had been worth it, he thought contentedly now. He had had the best night's sleep for many months and though Kathy had woken him while the stars still pricked the dark sky, he had understood her anxiety and had dressed and slid quietly down to ground level without making a sound.

They had met, as arranged, in Frank's Cabin where Alec had been finishing off an unlikely breakfast of sausage, chips and baked beans, accompanied by great doorsteps of bread and marge. Kathy had sat down beside him, accepting a large tin mug of strong tea and giving him a sweet, conspiratorial smile. In response to his hand squeeze and raised eyebrows, she had said softly: 'Everything was fine, honest it was. Mrs B was friendly as anything, kept saying what a nice sort of girl I was and how she hoped I'd stay with her again next time I was in Lincoln. She never alluded to what happened last night and I was glad of it because I still feel a bit guilty.'

'Well, you weren't guilty; you're as pure as the

driven snow,' Alec said, somewhat gloomily. 'I did hope you might fall asleep and go all lovin' and cuddly on me, or perhaps have a nightmare so I had to comfort you. But all you did was snore like a motor bike all night.'

'I never did!' Kathy had squeaked indignantly. 'I *never* snore! If I did, I'd know all about it because there's twenty-eight of us in our hut who'd be only too happy to chuck things at me or moan that I lost them sleep if I did snore. Mind you, O'Haggerty snores,' she added reflectively. 'We've told her over and over and the girl next to her gives her a shove whenever she's lying on her back, but O'Haggerty still maintains it's just heavy breathing.'

Alec had laughed and kissed her again, then picked up a sausage from his plate and offered it to her. 'I was having you on, seeing if I could get a rise out of you,' he admitted. 'Here, have my last sausage to show there's no ill feeling; though it is only "bread-crumbs in battledress" and not a real, meaty sausage.'

Kathy had giggled but refused his kind offer. 'Mrs B gave me a good breakfast: a sausage which was almost real, a great pile of dried egg – yuck – and some delicious bottled tomatoes,' she said. 'And lots of toast – she makes her own bread – as well as plum jam or marmalade, which she also makes herself.' She had smiled up at him, an expression of great sweetness on her small face, and Alec thought that there was an austere beauty in Kathy now which transcended Jane's more obvious prettiness. 'Well, we couldn't have a lovelier day, Alec, so what have you planned for us?' She had glanced up at the sky-light above her head, blue and gold with sunshine.

Alec had told her that even now Frank was putting them up a packed lunch, so it seemed sensible to go straight to the Brayford Pool, where they could hire a boat. Kathy had agreed enthusiastically and presently the two of them had set off into the sunny morning, gleefully aware that they had the whole day before them.

'Hey, Hewitt! I axed you a question, so don't you go off into a dream afore you've answered. Who biffed you on the nose . . . and come to that, where the devil have you been these past two days? I know the Wingco said that we could make ourselves scarce for the next four or five days, but I didn't know you meant to light out for Norfolk!'

'I didn't,' Alec said briefly. 'I fancied a bit of time to myself, you know how it is, and the weather was bootiful, so I just made myself scarce. Come to that, where have *you* been? I was back on the station a couple of days ago but I saw no hide nor hair of you.'

'*I* went home to me folks,' Jimmy said righteously. 'And of course, I went and saw Jane 'cos her site's so handy. The first thing she said – after she'd kissed me till I nearly fainted, of course – was, "Where's Alec?" I might have took offence but I decided to forgive her because I were wonderin' where you were an' all. I went into the mess to suggest you might come home with me, but someone said you'd had a phone call and caught the next gharry into town. I waited till after five,' he continued aggrievedly, 'but there were no sign of you so I went off meself, gorra train in Lincoln headin' for home and rang the mess from there. Twice I rang,' he went on, 'but all they could tell me was that you hadn't come back, so of course I guessed you'd gone back to Norfolk.'

'Well, I didn't,' Alec said again. He was tempted to tell Jimmy that he had spent the two days with Kathy, and was not quite sure why he did not do so. They had had such a wonderful time, had shared so many laughs, that it seemed ridiculous not to tell his best friend that he had a girlfriend at last, and one who meant a great deal to him.

The truth was, he did not want the fact that he had spent two days with Kathy to get back to Jane. The first time he and Jane had agreed to rendezvous at a town roughly midway between Lincoln and Liverpool, they had booked in as Flight Lieutenant and Mrs Hewitt. Jane had done the booking since she had arrived at the King's Head first but, Alec reminded himself grimly, you went along with it. Jane had been both willing and eager and, when he had proved uneasy, had assured him that he was by no means the first. 'Jimmy and me has shared a bed whenever we got the chance since he joined the air force,' she had told him. 'I takes precautions, of course, because I don't want no baby messin' my life up – I seen what it done to my mum – but honest to God, Alec, what's so perishin' special about it? Kissin' and cuddlin's grand fun and it leads on to the other. So what? If you make sure there won't be babies, then it's only a tiny little step further than kissin', wouldn't you say?'

Alec had understood what she meant, though he found he did not agree with her; going to bed with a girl was a great deal more intimate than just kissing her. But though he told himself he did not approve of Jane's moral stance, he had made love to her because she expected it (he also told himself) and he had thoroughly enjoyed the experience. Yet now, comparing the nights he had spent with Jane to the time with Kathy, he knew, to his own secret astonishment, which one he would rather repeat. He had revelled in Kathy's innocent acceptance of his promise not to do anything further, and had enjoyed the soft yet subtle feel of her in his arms even more than he had enjoyed Jane's uninhibited gymnastics. He was pretty sure that if Jane wanted to get in bed with him again, he would repulse her. Well, fairly sure.

On the other hand, he hoped very much that the next time he and Kathy got together, she would be less shy, more willing. He saw himself asking her to marry him, giving her an engagement ring, because he was already fairly sure that he liked her better than any other girl he had ever dated. But was this love? He honestly could not say. He just knew that when he put his arms round Kathy, something moved in his heart and an enormous tenderness took possession of him. He was certain that if they eventually married, he would be gloriously happy and fulfilled in a way he had never been before.

Still, one did not ask a girl to marry in wartime. A bride one day, a widow the next, he thought ruefully. No, it was better for both of them not to get entangled. He knew that everybody in his squadron thought that the war had a long way to go yet, and he agreed with them. Only – only it would be awful to die without ever having made love to Kathy. She was sweet as honey and sharp as a lemon, bright as sunshine yet deep, deep as the ocean. Beside her, Jane was shallow as a mountain stream, and the fact that she could sleep with him and with his best friend – and possibly with several others – simply went to prove his point. Kathy was worth wooing and winning, and he should not hesitate but should make up his mind not to see Jane again, and tell Jimmy at once how he felt about Kathy and where he had spent the first two days of his leave.

He and Jimmy strolled back to their beds, Jimmy chattering inconsequentially as they went. Alec found himself wishing that he could be absolutely frank, could tell Jimmy all about Kathy and what had happened at Mrs Bridges's, but he told himself that if he did so, Jimmy would either disbelieve him, in which case he would think Kathy no better than she should be, or assume that Alec had gone off his rocker to let such an opportunity pass him by. As for Jane, what did she really matter? He truly believed she was a nice girl who had let the excitement of war go to her head. In normal circumstances, she would have flirted with him a little – and probably with other fellows too – and would then have returned to her beloved Jimmy without a stain on her character. They would have married and had a family and lived happily ever after. It was all the fault of this terrible, bloody war which taught girls – and young men – that if they did not act today, it might be too late tomorrow.

'Well, if you won't tell me what you done to get that swollen nose, then I'm bound to think the worst,' Jimmy grumbled, as the two of them set off for the cookhouse. He grabbed Alec's arm, bringing his friend to an abrupt halt. 'I say, I s'pose it weren't a judy, were it? Don't tell me my solemn, self-righteous, priggish pal has gone and got fresh with one of the WAAF Wing Officers!'

For a moment, Alec was honestly tempted to say something outrageous. Something like, *No, not a Wing Officer. It were your girlfriend, Jane. Her foot caught me in the nose at an intimate moment*; that would teach Jimmy not to call him a self-righteous prig. Fortunately, common sense came to his aid. It would not do even to tell Jimmy the truth: that his wound had been inflicted by an irate landlady. He would simply have to grin and act mysterious. 'Never you mind,' he said airily, therefore. 'But it were worth it, I'm telling you.'

PART III

Chapter Fifteen

1943

It was an icy cold day in February when Kathy lugged her two kit bags down off the train in Liverpool Lime Street and made for the exit. This would be her fifth posting since she had joined the WAAF and the first time she had ever been so near home. She was doubly glad to be back in her home town – or near it – because her mother and Billy had moved back into the house in Daisy Street several months before. Sarah had explained, half apologetically and half defiantly, that with Billy growing up so fast and becoming so independent, the lure of her own home had finally proved too strong. Although there had been odd raids on Liverpool since the May blitz, almost two years earlier, they had been no worse than one might expect anywhere, and besides, Dorothy's Tearooms was flourishing once more and in desperate need of staff.

Kathy's last posting had been way up in the north, near Newcastle upon Tyne, and because of the distance which had to be travelled she had only seen Alec once since that memorable leave in Lincoln. She had felt mean telling her mother that she was spending her one week's leave – the only proper leave she got all year – with her young man, but Sarah, already engaged to Sam Bracknell and plotting to return to Daisy Street, had been both sweet and understanding. *War can tear your life apart*, she had written, *and when it's over, you are the only one who can* *pick up the pieces. I shall have Sam, God willing, and though you'll be welcome to share the house in Daisy Street, you are going to want a man and house of your own. If you have a stable relationship with a nice young man, then you'll find that that's half the battle, so I'm happy for you to live your own life and spend your leave with your young fellow, so long as you're careful. Dear Kathy, it would be a great mistake to get yourself into trouble, but I'm sure you won't do that. By the way, Jane and Jimmy had a week's leave in Daisy Street a while back, and came down to Rhyl to pay us a visit; a right pair of love-birds they were, billing and cooing! So just you enjoy your leave, queen; and don't worry about Billy or myself.* The letter had then gone on to speak of other things; her mother rejoicing in the fact that Billy had not had a single fit since they had left the city.*

Looking back on it now, as she lugged her kit bags to where the gharry waited to take her to Balloon Site 7, Kathy remembered the week's leave she had shared with Alec. It had been absolutely wonderful, better than anything that had happened in her life before. They had gone to the Peak District and had had a walking holiday, stopping at a different inn or guesthouse each night, buying any food available for picnic lunches and booking into the accommodation as Flight Lieutenant and Mrs Hewitt, though at first this had terrified her, despite the fact that Alec had assured her everyone did it. 'A double room's half the price of two single ones,' he had pointed out earnestly. 'And you know how self-controlled I can be. In fact, you've only got to look at my nose to be convinced that you're in no danger. I'm telling you, the battering I took at Mrs Bridges's hands has unmanned me for life.'

They had both laughed at the recollection and had

gone off for the first day's hike in complete accord. Kathy had been determined not to let Alec 'mess her about' as she put it, but this resolve proved impossible to keep. He was so sweet to her, so loving and understanding, that when they were ensconced in a large feather bed, with the curtains drawn back and the stars twinkling in the dark blue of the night sky, it seemed churlish not to lie in his arms. She had meant to fall asleep at once, had not been prepared for the excitement which coursed through her as his hands caressed her back, and by next morning they were lovers.

From that moment on, Kathy knew she was different. The girls at the balloon site knew too, though they were not aware of the reason for such a change. Her friend and fellow corporal, Rosie Butler, said wisely that the complete relaxation of a walking holiday had done her a world of good, eased off all the tensions and made her more approachable. Kathy had smiled and agreed, not realising until much later that all the girls had taken it for granted that she and Alec had been lovers for months. And when she did realise it no longer bothered her; in fact, she decided she had been a fool in Lincoln, and selfish too, because one only had to see the difference it made to Alec to realise that she had given him something precious – not only herself, but also peace of mind. He had told her, on their last night together, that he now felt he had a future. 'We'll marry just as soon as this damned war is over,' he had said. 'Or we might make it earlier; what do you think, sweetheart? In a way, it seems daft to wait, but there's no chance of us being together, not while we're still in the service. In a way, I wish I hadn't spent all my money the way I have, because I can't even buy you an engagement ring, not a real one. But I could run to a wedding ring, if that's what you'd like.'

Kathy had been lying with her head on his shoulder, their bodies warm and comfortable together, and she had turned her head and kissed the soft spot where neck and shoulder joined before replying. 'I don't think we ought to marry yet, Alec,' she had murmured. 'You've met my mam and my brother but I've never met your parents. It's only fair that they should at least see us before we take such a big step.'

At the time, Alec had agreed, but in his later letters he was beginning to suggest more and more that they might spend their next leave getting to know one another's family properly, and Kathy was sure that this was a prelude to the wedding for which they both now longed. If they were married, they would not have to skulk about; she could go to his airfield and he could come to her balloon site and they could be together openly for a few wonderful hours, instead of having to hide away and pretend that they were 'just good friends' as the saying went.

Crossing the familiar pavement, seeing St George's Hall up on its plateau, battered but unbowed, she thought of Jane and herself on these very streets with Jane chattering inconsequentially of boys, cinema heroes and old friends. Like herself Jane had had to endure a good many postings and was now on a site in Southampton, whence she sent ill-written – and extremely short – letters to her friend, complaining about the hard work and commenting on films, friends and allied subjects, much as they had done when they were young girls.

There were three gharries drawn up alongside the pavement. The first two contained RAF personnel, but Kathy glimpsed WAAF uniforms in the last one and headed for it. She had no idea where Site No. 7 would prove to be and hoped that there might be someone aboard the gharry who could give her some information. Accordingly, she went straight to the driver, a pretty blonde Waaf who looked no more than eighteen or nineteen, showed her papers and identity card and was told to, 'hop into the back, 'cos you're me last pick-up today and I wanna get back so's I can see the flick at the Electric Palace this evenin'.'

Kathy hopped, selected an empty space on the metal bench and was disposing of her kit bags when someone squeaked: 'Kathy!' and she found herself being violently hugged.

It was truly odd. She had not set eyes on Jane since they had gone their separate ways after Cardington and now her friend was hugging her so tightly that she could not actually see her face at all. Yet from that one word and from the feel of her, she had known Jane at once. 'Steady on, you idiot,' Kathy said, trying to straighten her cap and her No. 1 uniform whilst struggling out of Jane's octopus-like embrace. 'What on earth are you doing here? Last time you wrote, it was from Southampton!'

Jane let her go and sank down on the metal bench opposite, staring at Kathy incredulously, and grinning from ear to ear. 'I *was* in Southampton . . . and you was in Newcastle,' she rejoined. 'I were posted, o' course; you know what the WAAF's like, they never let you stay in one place for long. But wharrabout you, queen? Oh, I s'pose I should call you Corp.'

'I've been posted too,' Kathy said briefly. 'To Number Seven Site. Where are you going?'

Jane was already grinning like a Cheshire cat but at

Kathy's words the grin actually appeared to widen, making Kathy fearful that the top of her friend's head might fall off. 'I'm for Number Seven an' all . . . in fact everyone on this gharry is. Did you clock me stripes? I passed me exams five months ago an' I've been acting corporal ever since, but on this site I'm made up to full, pay an' all. So you an' me's goin' to be workmates as well as best buddies.'

Kathy was delighted. It would have been difficult to order her old friend about, as she would have had to do had she and Jane not shared the same rank. Now they could revert to the friendship which had once been so dear to them both. She was about to say something of the sort when the gharry started with a jerk. It was an elderly vehicle and fearfully noisy, making conversation impossible, but it was not long before the WAAF driver came round to the rear and lowered the tail-gate, saying cheerfully: 'Site Number Seven, ladies, out you come!'

Kathy and Jane, along with the rest of their fellow passengers, caught hold of the rope and swung themselves to the ground.

Kathy had been shocked, as they drove through the city, at the amount of bomb damage on every side, but now she looked curiously about her. The site was a pretty decent one, not far from the docks, with the waters of the Mersey gleaming like steel beneath the clouded sky. Kathy's eye checked for trees; nearer at hand, there should have been a Nissen hut or two and a squat block of ablutions, but she could see nothing of the sort, only a huge house and, in the distance, a long, low hut with a pitched roof and various impedimenta strewn around it.

She was about to ask Jane whether she thought the hut in the distance was their eventual destination when a voice spoke almost in her ear. 'Come along, girls. I'll just show you round, and then leave you to settle into your quarters. I'm Sergeant Jim Fazakerley, an' I'm stayin' on site till you've settled in and know the ropes. After that I'm goin' to take up me old trade of motor mechanic, so the quicker you settle in, the sooner I'll be off.'

Jane and Kathy turned towards the speaker. He was a grizzled man, probably in his mid-forties, his face so tanned by the wind and weather that it looked like leather. He had twinkling pale blue eyes, a friendly grin and a slight London accent, but there was something in the way he marshalled them into line and strode off ahead of them which told Kathy, plainer than words could, that he would stand no nonsense and would make everyone toe the line.

Balloon Site No. 7 had once been a private boarding school, and to the girls' joy the sergeant explained they would not be sleeping in a Nissen hut but in the school itself. 'There's plenty of bed space so you'll only need to sleep four to a room,' he informed them. 'There are several bathrooms, though hot water will only be available a couple of times a week, and, of course, you can eat in the kitchens, which are pretty well equipped, better than usual, I'd say. The grounds are quite extensive so you won't be cramped, but you'll find the fellers in the searchlight battery have the games pitch and the pavilion, so no straying over the boundary line; you know the rules. Fraternisation is probably a court martial offence.'

He led them towards the big, old-fashioned red brick house that Kathy had already noticed. She caught up with him just before they entered. 'I thought I was the only new entrant to this site, but the whole lot are new, aren't they, Sarge?' she said, a trifle breathlessly. 'I know the air force are always posting Bops from one side of the country to another, but they don't usually go a whole crew at a time – two crews, really – do they?'

'Not usually, but the girls on this site have been sent to relieve crews on the inner ring around London,' the sergeant explained. 'They're still being raided, night after night, and the top brass decided it was time they had a bit of a break. Any more questions?'

'No, I don't think so,' Kathy said. 'Thanks for the info, Sarge. Me an' Corporal O'Brien are local girls, you know, so we'll be able to see our folks from time to time, which will be a nice change. It's a good site, as well, so it shouldn't be long before you're off.'

And so it proved. Within a week, the crews had mastered the art of flying the blimp from this particular site, and at the end of three weeks Sergeant Fazakerley shouldered his kit bag, wished them luck and left them, assuring them that he had seldom been attached to a more efficient crew. 'He's only saying that because he's desperate to get away,' Kathy said, but though Jane pretended to agree, they were both secretly pleased with such praise from a man who demanded the best and knew when he was getting it. Just before he left, the sergeant informed them that though their Section Officer would be doing an inspection some time in the next few days, this was the exception rather than the rule.

'I'm not saying she don't do her job – mebbe it's because she trusts the girls on Number Seven Site – but if she does an inspection a couple of times a month, you'll be lucky,' he said. 'I won't tell you what I think of her because you must form your own opinions, but I dare say she's fair enough.'

Jane and Kathy soon settled into life on the new site. Their chief difficulty was caused by the sea winds coming off the Mersey, often gusty because of the quantity of buildings, warehousing and so on which surrounded the docks. It made the blimp difficult to launch and extremely difficult to bring down to the deck, but the girls were used to the various antics of other balloons they had flown and soon became relatively competent with this one. The bitter cold did not ease when the month ended and despite the fact that raids – and the presence of enemy aircraft – had slowed to a tiny trickle, they were still called upon to get their balloon up whenever raiders neared the coast and seemed likely to pass near enough to the city for an alert to be sounded.

As was usual on the sites, the girls soon sorted their crews into who was best suited for which particular job. Jane and Kathy were both extremely good on the winch, having a 'feel' for the great creature tethered only by a slender steel cable, quiet and seemingly compliant one moment and making desperate attempts to escape or to come crashing down on the nearest buildings the next. But at such times, when the wind was high and conditions hellish, both crews were turned out, and then either Jane or Kathy would go to the winch whilst the other acted as No. 1.

It was a great comfort to them both to be together. They shared a small room at the head of the stairs, where they could be easily fetched by the guard when Balloon Centre rang to tell them there was an alert. To Kathy's pleasure, Jane seemed to have abandoned her free and easy ways and to have settled down with Jimmy as the only man in her life once more. Despite the convenient closeness of 'Cupid's Cavalry', as the searchlight boys were called, Jane steadfastly refused all invitations to go to the flicks, out dancing or to some other form of entertainment. Kathy also refused such advances. She had told Jane she had a boyfriend to whom she wrote regularly but had never revealed that it was Jimmy's greatest friend. She felt superstitiously certain that if she did so something awful would happen. The plane would crash and she and Jane would lose their lovers in one blow, or Alec and Jimmy would fall out and have a fearful row, which would make life aboard their Wimpey both difficult and dangerous. At best, one or other of them might be posted, and she would feel it was her fault for having let Jane – and the fates – know of the strange coincidence. For it was a strange coincidence that two best friends, in the same aeroplane, were going out with two Bops, also best friends, working on the same balloon site.

It was tempting, of course, to tell Jane about Alec, to share the fact that they meant to marry when the war was over, if not before, but for the first three weeks on site, at any rate, she had managed not to do so. She and Jane were getting on so wonderfully well, slipping back into their old intimacy, that she hesitated to do anything which might spoil it. And it was impossible not to remember that Jane had once liked Alec very much indeed, had even seemed to think him better looking than her beloved Jimmy.

The icy cold weather continued and the girls were delighted to have proper quarters instead of a draughty Nissen hut and the horrors of air force ablutions which, on a balloon site, usually meant a small basin of cold water beside one's bed and a lengthy route march to the municipal baths once a week. Instead, the girl who had been detailed to do the cooking and cleaning of the house, Norah Brown, got up early and boiled a huge preserving pan full of water in the kitchen. The girls trooped in and took turns to have a really good wash over the sink, finding it a good deal more satisfactory than trying to cart a basin of hot water back to their own rooms. Any shyness about stripping naked in front of their friends had been dissipated years before in chilly Nissen huts all over the country, so removing their garments in the warmth of the kitchen was nothing to them.

But though the weather continued cold and flying the balloon was made, if possible, more difficult by gusty March winds, the crew on Balloon Site 7 were settling in and were not displeased to be told, by telephone, that their officer would be visiting them that very same day and would expect a complete turn out. This meant that anyone hoping to sneak off home for half an hour or so, or to have an extra sleep to make up for the fact that they had been working in the early hours, would be disappointed. However, it gave them time to get everything ready. The balloon was on close haul; the balloon bed itself had recently been painted during a lull in activities and looked first rate, the blimp had been 'topped up' with hydrogen the day before so that she looked as fat and sleek as a pig about to give birth, and the girls themselves laid out their kit in readiness on their beds, and then helped Norah to black lead the cooking stove, polish the kitchen floor and whiten every step in the place. The officer was supposed to arrive at eleven o'clock, but it was noon before she put in an appearance. Jane saw her first and raced back to warn the others. 'They said she'd be on a bicycle, and so she is, but it's an awful smart one,' she said breathlessly. 'Norra bit like the old boneshakers officers mostly use. She's ever so tall and haughty looking. She's one of them what pushes her cap forward so she has to raise her chin to see daylight even. She saw me and beckoned me over, then shoved the bike at me and told me to get the crews lined up around the balloon bed. We'd better gerra move on. I reckon she's one of them what enjoys finding fault.'

'She won't find much fault with us today,' Kathy said with satisfaction. 'Everyone's present, there's no kit missing, and for once the blimp is behaving herself. What's more, we're all old hands so we know the balloon drill backwards. Let's get out there!'

The girls drilled without even the smallest mistake and then Kathy, as the senior NCO present, went over to the officer to accompany her on her tour of inspection. 'All present and correct . . . ma'am,' Kathy said, lifting her gaze as she did so, to look squarely into the officer's eyes, though these were deeply shadowed by the peak of her cap. 'Would you like to do the kit inspection first or the kitchens?'

Such was Kathy's preoccupation that, for a moment, she stared at the officer without really seeing her. Then, as the woman said coldly: 'Kit inspection first, corporal,' she had to strangle a gasp. The officer was Marcia Montgomery!

Two hours later, sitting in the kitchen at the long wooden table and eating the hot meal that Norah and her helpers had prepared, Kathy told Jane who their officer actually was. Jane's eyes rounded and she gave vent to an incredulous whistle. 'Oh, Kathy, there's your sergeant's stripes gone for a burton,' she said. ''Cos if you reckernised her, she'll have known you, 'course she would. Didn't she give no sign? I thought she were extra specially nasty in the bedrooms, pullin' the girls' kit about and sayin' she'd seen brighter brasswork on a new recruit, but I thought it were just her way, like.'

'If I'd thought she had recognised me, I'd be a gibbering wreck,' Kathy admitted. 'But I'm bloody sure she didn't. She's the type who never really looks at anyone she considers her social inferior, and after I'd realised who she was I pulled my cap down myself and never said a word more than I had to.'

'Ye-es, I did notice that, 'cos it ain't like you to keep shtum,' Jane teased, grinning. 'Now you've told me, I remember the name an' all. Ain't she the one you punched on the nose in Paddy's market?'

Kathy gave a groan and buried her face in her hands. 'Yes, you're right. I'd forgotten that. I wonder if I ought to put in for a posting? But why the blazes should I? I really like this site; it's grand having a house of our own instead of Nissen huts and we've got a first-rate crew without a single troublemaker aboard. What's more, I can visit Mam and Billy easily from here, now that they're back in Daisy Street.' She squared her shoulders, smiling at her friend. 'No, that settles it. Marcia bloody Montgomery isn't going to scare me away; I mean you never know where I might get sent. It could be miles away and I'd hate that.'

'You're right there,' Jane said. 'I suppose your best bet is to do everything so bleedin' perfectly that she can't complain and go on keeping your head down. Good thing she ain't like some officers, prowlin' round the sites two or three times a week. The sarge said once a month was more her style and he's been right so far. C'mon, let's get down to the kitchen and give Norah a hand with the dinner.'

*

It was inevitable, of course, that Marcia should recognise Kathy, but when she did so her only response was to be haughtier than ever. She completely ignored Kathy and talked to Jane instead, and if Jane was not present, she talked to a point about three inches above Kathy's cap, seldom giving the younger girl a chance to speak at all. Accordingly, the weeks passed pleasantly enough. Kathy and Jane were both swotting in the hope of passing their sergeant's examinations by the end of the summer, since this would mean more pay and they felt their present responsibilities could scarcely be more onerous; after all, they were in charge of the site and managing it as well as anyone could, or so they thought. Certainly, the flight sergeant, who was in charge of a good many balloon sites, told them on his weekly visit that they were streets ahead of the other sites, getting the balloon up quicker, when necessary, and running the site without fuss or arguments, so that a happy atmosphere prevailed. It was clear that their Section Officer, despite her dislike of Kathy, had never complained about them at Balloon Centre and had sent in reports which, while they may have damned with faint praise, certainly brought no adverse reaction from their masters.

It was almost June before Marcia came to the site one morning to tell them, in her coldest and most off-hand manner, that No. 7 Balloon Site had been chosen for an inspection by the Top Brass. 'You have two full weeks to make sure that your balloon drill is perfect and the site itself the same,' she said. 'The Air Commodore will go everywhere, examine every-thing, including the entire house, so I, or Flight Sergeant Griffiths, will be visiting the site daily from now on. I know you must feel that because you have your own bedrooms you have the right to some privacy . . .' here she glared straight at Kathy, '. . . but this is not the case. All traces of your personal possessions must be out of sight, is that understood?'

Jane and Kathy agreed that it was, and immediately began on the enormous task of making a practical working site look like a model in which every length of rope was meticulously coiled and every tool neatly hung in its place. The balloon bed itself was whitewashed, with the bricks picked out in red ochre, and the blimp was topped up with hydrogen and checked down to every tiny patch to make sure that nothing untoward would catch the official eye.

The girls played up magnificently, even Norah allowing her kitchen to be cleaned and polished until it was impossible to imagine that a meal had ever been cooked there, let alone eaten. On the morning of the inspection itself, Kathy and Jane did a hasty last minute tour of the bedrooms and were actually in their own room when Jane, looking out of the window, gave a squeak and turned so quickly that she banged her knee on the bedstead. 'They're here!' she exclaimed. 'Oh, Kathy, we'd best get down before that hateful Marcia starts complaining about us.'

She flew out of the room as she spoke and Kathy was about to follow her when something on the floor caught her eye. It was a letter, written in familiar handwriting. Kathy swooped on it with an inward curse and crammed it into the pocket of her boiler suit. As commanded, she had put all her personal possessions, including Alec's letters, neatly away into the small locker one was allowed for such things but, clearly, she had been a bit careless, since this page had escaped. But this was no time to worry about a moment's inattention; Kathy flew for the stairs and tumbled down them, and by the time Marcia and the Top Brass arrived the crews were ready to start balloon drill.

'Well, that went off a treat!' Jane remarked, sitting down on her bed with a sigh of relief. Kathy and Jane were in their room, getting ready for an evening's relaxation after the strain of the inspection. They meant to leave their two senior Bops in charge whilst they paid a hasty visit to Daisy Street and since they were still wearing their crisply starched boiler suits – one always wore boiler suits for a balloon drill inspection – they would have to change into their No. 1s.

'Yes, we did bloody Marcia proud,' Kathy said, beginning to struggle out of her boiler suit. 'Can you come round to mine after about an hour, Jane? Only I told Mam we'd be coming home after the inspection and she said she'd bring enough meat and potato pie back from the tearooms to make a decent tea for four.'

Because the girls both now had bicycles, it only took about ten minutes to reach Daisy Street from the balloon site, so it was a regular thing for either Kathy or Jane to bicycle home and arrange their next visit. Sometimes, of course, they combined a visit home with a trip to the cinema or a session at the nearest dance hall, but on this occasion, at least, they wanted to tell their families how the inspection had gone.

'Course I can,' Jane said briefly. She had stripped off her own boiler suit and was already fastening her skirt. 'Your mam's meat and potato pie is one of me all time favourites.'

'Me too,' Kathy was beginning to reply, when a rustling from the pocket of her boiler suit made her remember the letter. Swinging round with her back to

Jane, she plunged a hand into the pocket and pulled it out. She was about to put it in her locker when something about it caught her attention. It was Alec's writing all right, but he had not started the letter in his usual way. Of late, his letters began *My darling Kathy*, but this one . . . Kathy sat down heavily on her bed. This one started *Dear Jane*!

For a moment Kathy was quite literally devoid of speech; she could not so much as open her mouth but simply sat, staring at the page spread out before her. Jane, blissfully unconscious that anything untoward had happened, continued to prattle about the inspection whilst Kathy tried to gather her wits. It was not one of her letters, it was one of Jane's . . . but the writing was still Alec's, which meant . . . which meant . . . just what did it mean, exactly?

'Kathy? Wharron earth are you starin' at? Oh, I guess it's a letter from your feller. Well this is no time to be readin' old letters or we'll be late for your mam's meat and potato pie and we don't want—'

'Shut up a moment,' Kathy said. Her tone was peremptory but not, as yet, particularly unfriendly. 'I've got to read this, it won't take me a minute.'

Jane shrugged and began to polish her nails and Kathy, taking a deep, steadying breath, started to read.

Dear Jane, Yes it would be grand to meet you again, you beautiful thing, you! I can get a forty-eight but I agree with you we shouldn't meet anywhere near the station. We'll rendezvous somewhere a bit of a way off, then everyone will assume I've gone back to my folks and you've gone back to yours. There's a rather good hotel called the Feathers in a town not . . .

The words were like a dagger through Kathy's heart. So it had all been pretence. He had been in love

383

with Jane all the time and simply making use of Kathy.

'Kathy, you must have read that letter a dozen times over.' Jane's voice was edged with impatience now. She got up and peered curiously at the page held so stiffly before her friend. 'Ooh, you cheeky bugger! It's addressed to *me*! Wharron earth d'you think you're doin', readin' me letters?' It was said half jokingly but, nevertheless, Kathy crumpled the letter in her hand, still not sure precisely what she was going to do.

'Yes, it is your letter,' she said slowly, rising to her feet. 'But it's not from Jimmy. It's from – a friend of his.' She was watching Jane's face as she spoke and saw the expression of guilt and unease which flickered across it, though Jane only said airily: 'And what's wrong wi' that, may I ask? I've as much right to exchange letters wi' a feller as you have! Why, I remember you used to write to that Alec – d'you remember him? He come home wi' Jimmy for one leave and we went out in a foursome – oh, Kathy, you must remember him.'

'Yes, I remember him,' Kathy said through gritted teeth. 'I've been writing to him for over a year now. But just what have you been doing, Jane? This is from Alec . . .' She waved the letter almost in Jane's face, then snatched her hand back as Jane tried to grab it. 'No you don't, my lady. This is a letter from Alec to you, planning a meeting. You were going to some hotel together . . . and don't try to tell me it was just for a friendly chat or you wouldn't have minded meeting him in Lincoln, with your Jimmy along as well.'

'Give me my letter,' Jane said, the colour suddenly flooding her face. 'I didn't know you were still writing to him but that's because I've not been in touch with him for ages and ages. C'mon, give me that letter!'

'You slept with him, didn't you?' Kathy said baldly. 'C'mon, admit it, because I know it's the truth. When we first joined the WAAF, you went out wi' all sorts and I suppose you slept with several of them, but . . . Alec and me . . . I thought we had a future together. I thought he were going to marry me. But if he thinks I'm taking your leavings, Jane O'Brien, he can think again. And if you think I won't tell Jimmy what a nasty little slut you are, then you're much mistaken.'

She turned on her heel and would have left the room but Jane grabbed her shoulder, pulling her round. 'Kathy, do stop it! I didn't mean . . . didn't know . . . it were ages ago! I promise you on me mother's life that it were only the once! Oh, I must have been mad . . . just let me explain . . .'

But Kathy was past explanations. She struck out blindly and in two seconds both girls were fighting in good earnest, Kathy trying to keep the letter and to punish Jane for the pain she had caused her and Jane trying to grab the letter and to make Kathy listen.

In the end, they stopped fighting because they were both exhausted. The letter, now in three pieces, lay disregarded on the floor. Kathy, panting heavily, made for the door. 'Don't bother to come round to my place this evening, Corporal,' she said coldly. 'Because you'll have the door slammed in your face if you do. I've seen enough of you to last me a lifetime.'

Jane had slumped on to her bed but now she got to her feet. 'Kathy, for God's sake, listen!' she said, her voice breaking. 'You're going to ruin your life and mine 'cos you found out I did a foolish thing – oh, ages ago. Please, Kathy . . .'

But the slam of the door was the only answer she got, as Kathy ran down the stairs. Feeling aghast at what had happened, she mounted her bicycle and cycled shakily away, not stopping until she reached the nearest telephone box. From there, she telephoned Waddington and managed to speak a few words to Alec, though her voice was so choked with tears that he must have been hard pressed to recognise it. 'It's over,' she said thickly. 'I . . . I know about you and Jane . . . I found a letter. You and she had an affair . . . she's admitted it.'

Alec began to speak, trying to explain, trying to make her understand that it was not an affair, but Kathy cut across him. 'Oh, Alec, how could you? She were me best friend and Jimmy were yours!' And then, before he could speak another word, she had slammed the receiver back on to its rest and had gone out into the wild and windy afternoon.

Alec had not had a good day. He and the rest of the crew had shared the cost of an elderly motor car, an Austin 12, and had intended to spend the afternoon in Lincoln since they would not be flying that night. It was a big old car and, if necessary, all five of them could cram into it somehow, but when Jimmy went to start it, it made desperate groaning sounds and the engine refused to fire. The rest of the crew, secure in the knowledge that they actually had fuel and meant to spend a relaxing day in the city, were as disappointed as Alec himself when they realised that their doughty vehicle was about to let them down. However, they were all mechanically minded and never averse to getting their hands dirty so, in two minutes, the bonnet was up and various spare parts strewn around on the grass. But despite their best efforts, it was not until two in the afternoon that they discovered the fault – discovered too that they needed a new part and could not merely botch something together.

'That's our day in Lincoln,' their skipper Frank said resignedly, trying to clean oil off his hands with a bunch of grass. He glanced at his watch. 'Is there a gharry going into town, anyone know? If so, at least we could see a flick.' But there had been no gharry available. The only one had left at noon. Sighing, Jimmy said that one of the bods had a motor bike and would probably lend it for a few bob, in which case he could at least try to buy the part they needed. The crew had agreed this seemed the only answer and, cheated of their day out, had returned to their mess to discuss the probable acquiring of the spare part and how they would, in future, try to get spares for 'the old girl' before the car actually broke down on them again.

Alec had been particularly sore because he had been saving up to buy Kathy a real little engagement ring, not a Woolworth's one, such as she had worn on their week's holiday, but a proper gold one with a ruby and two tiny diamonds. He had seen it in a jeweller's shop in Lincoln which had a small section of the window set aside for second-hand goods. Alec had liked it and was sure it would suit Kathy, so he had been putting aside as much money as he could afford, every week, for its purchase. Today was to have been the great day and he had planned to take it to Liverpool the next time he got some leave and make their relationship official.

Still, life in the air force had taught him the impossibility of planning ahead so he tried to make the best of his disappointment. He was sitting with a group of young men, the crew of another Wellington, when his skipper shouted out to him. 'Alec, are you busy? Reggie here was asking if I knew anyone who could lend him a navigator, just for one night. Only their chap's got a bad case of the squits and he doesn't fancy flying over Germany with some kid straight out of Navigation School. I told him you were the best and that we weren't flying tonight, but if you've other plans . . .'

A nasty, superstitious fear curdled Alec's guts. He did not want to fly tonight. One was supposed to have a break from operational flying after so many ops and Frank and his crew were nearing their limit. Yet it sounded bad to say no to a friend of the skip's. He was opening his mouth to prevaricate, to ask a question or two, when he heard his name.

'Hewitt? Is Flight Lieutenant Hewitt here? You're wanted on the phone.'

Alec got to his feet, his heart lifting. His parents considered the telephone an instrument that should only be used in dire emergencies; they had only once rung him and then his mum had shouted so loudly that the telephone had seemed unnecessary. Now he approached the instrument sure that it would be Kathy on the other end of the line.

Nevertheless, it did not do to take too much for granted. 'Flight Lieutenant Hewitt here,' he said briskly, and then, his voice warming: 'Kathy, my darling, is that you? Your voice sounds very small and distant. I hoped it was you when I was called to the phone, because I wanted to tell you—'

Her voice cut across his and he could tell she had been crying, probably still was. 'It's over,' she said thickly. 'I . . . I know about you and Jane . . . I found a letter. You and she had an affair . . . she's admitted it.'

Alec could not believe his ears. Whatever was the matter with his love? It was true that he had once slept with Jane – he was still deeply ashamed of the fact – but it had been long ago, before he had really known Kathy. He tried to tell her so, tried to explain. He began to say that it had meant nothing, that he was ashamed of his behaviour, but she cut across him ruthlessly, her voice cold even though it was still thickened by tears.

'Oh, Alec, how could you? She were me best friend and Jimmy were yours!' There was a crash as her receiver went down but Alec continued to stand where he was, unable to believe what had happened. Then the operator's voice said briskly: 'The other party has cut the connection, caller; would you please replace your receiver. I have another incoming call for your number.'

Slowly and carefully, like a man in a dream, Alec replaced the receiver. He walked back to the chair he had vacated and slumped into it, staring sightlessly ahead of him. His sweet and gentle Kathy seemed to have gone mad. He thought about ringing No. 7 Balloon Site but the girls were not supposed to take personal calls and he was pretty sure Kathy had rung him from a public call box. She would not have risked anyone overhearing what she had just said to him. After a few moments he shook himself and decided that he must write a letter immediately, trying to explain. Only . . . only a letter seemed so final, somehow; after all, what could he say that he had not already said? It had happened a long time ago; he sincerely regretted it. He knew that he had behaved badly but could not accept that he had hurt anyone. Of course, if Jimmy knew, their friendship would be over. But then Jimmy had not acted so very well himself. When they had first been posted to Watton he had behaved like a man with no ties. Alec knew his friend had slept with two or three of the Waafs on the station and had clearly not considered himself bound to be faithful to Jane. That had all changed, of course; Jimmy had matured, grown more serious, and now would not dream of so much as kissing another girl.

'Hey, Alec! Are you going to oblige my old pal? Only they'll be flying in an hour – it's a long way to Germany!'

For a moment Alec simply stared up at Skip, unable to make sense of the words. Then he remembered and his brow cleared. Some people might not consider a bombing raid over Germany to be preferable to writing a letter but Alec thought, with grim humour, that in this particular case a bombing raid would be a piece of cake compared to writing to Kathy.

'Oh, tell him I'm on,' he said easily. 'I'll just go over to the cookhouse and get some char and a wad. Then I'll be with him.'

On the other side of the room, Skip's friend raised both thumbs in the air and gave a subdued crow of pleasure. 'Tell them to pack you sandwiches while you're in there,' he called. 'The briefing's in an hour.'

By the time Kathy returned to the balloon site, the weather had taken a turn for the worse. The wind had risen to gale force and the dark clouds massing overhead showed occasional flashes of lightning. Despite the wind, it was by no means cold and Kathy thought that there was probably a storm on the way. She pushed her bicycle into the shed and hesitated by it for a moment. She was still in her best blues and decided to go straight back to her room and get to bed, hoping against hope that Jane would not return to the site until late. Kathy had gone home, but had not stayed long and knew she had been poor company. Sarah Kelling had shot one shrewd glance at her daughter's face and had not reproached her for being later than she had planned. Instead, she had got the food on the table and told Billy to run round to the O'Briens' and tell Jane that her grub was ready.

'Jane isn't coming,' Kathy had said shortly. 'The inspection went well, Mam, but it's left me with a deal of paperwork. I'll just eat up and then get back.'

She had done just that, giving her mother an extra specially affectionate hug because she had asked no awkward questions, but now, climbing the stairs to her room, she wondered if she had been foolish. She would have to meet Jane before she was really ready to do so; if she had stayed in Daisy Street, she would have had a couple of hours to think things through, decide what she had best do. It was tempting to apply for a posting but she told herself that such a move would be a cowardly act. She and Jane had a problem and they must solve it, for better or worse.

She opened the bedroom door cautiously but there was no one in there, so she took off her uniform and put on her striped pyjamas. I have done the right thing, she comforted herself as she slid between the sheets. Now I can think things through sensibly and decide just what to do. Hopefully, there won't be a raid tonight – I need all the sleep I can get after the shock of this afternoon.

She had hoped to fall asleep immediately, worn out by the events of the day, but two hours later she was still lying awake in the dark, staring wide-eyed at the lighter patch of window. The sky had cleared, partially at least, but the wind still howled round the old building.

Lying there in the dark, Kathy faced up to things for the first time since she had seen the letter. Jane and Alec had both behaved badly but they had not injured her by so doing. She suspected that Jimmy had been a one for the girls – Jane had said so – so perhaps you could not altogether blame Jane for following suit, even though Kathy still thought it a dirty trick for a girl to have an affair with her young man's best friend.

But you only found out, Kathy Kelling, by reading a letter which wasn't addressed to you and you were never meant to see, she reminded herself sternly. And would you have felt as bad if it had been someone else Alec had slept with and not Jane? If you ask me, you've always been jealous of Jane . . . well, no; jealous was not really the word. She had envied Jane her pretty looks, her lovely, bouncy golden hair, and her total ease with the opposite sex. Jane flirted deliciously whilst Kathy's relationships had been plodding and pedestrian in comparison.

And as for Alec – oh, poor Alec! She had told him that it was all over but she knew now that this was not true. She loved him and knew he loved her and though his affair with Jane had hurt and deeply upset her, he had only spoken the truth when he had said that it had all been over a long time ago. What was more, she knew, none better, how very important it was that men on active duty were not anxious or upset over their personal lives. Many a tale was told about pilots whose wives sent them 'Dear John' letters and who subsequently flew their aeroplanes into tall buildings or were too preoccupied to take proper precautions and crashed on landing.

The thought made Kathy sit up in bed, sweat prickling out all over her. She threw back the covers and went to the window. She must get in touch with him! She would go down to the office and telephone Waddington, never mind the rules; then she would tell him it was all a horrible mistake, that she hadn't meant what she said, that she was sure their love could transcend one little fall from grace. She had grabbed her boiler suit off its hook and was scrambling into it, telling herself that it was only ten o'clock, that he was probably still sitting miserably in the mess, when she heard feet flying up the stairs and someone banged on the door, then threw it open. 'Corp, a call just came from the centre to bring all balloons down to storm bedding. The Met Office has said that the atrocious weather will actually worsen towards dawn and they want all the balloons storm bedded as soon as poss. Oh, I see you've guessed. Right, I'll go and wake the rest.'

It was ACW Ellis, one of the two girls on guard duty. Kathy struggled into her oilskins and in a couple of minutes she was out on the site and climbing aboard the winch. The rain was driving into her face and she had no time now to think about her own troubles. She was even glad to see Jane, wearing her heavy duty oilskins with her woolly cap pulled well down over her curls, ordering the girls into position. She did not look at Kathy so Kathy kept her own eyes averted, but presently, when the balloon was down to a hundred feet, Kathy called ACW Gibbons, a large and placid girl who could be relied upon not to act hastily, to take over the winch.

It had been hard work getting the balloon down to a hundred feet, but lower than that it became next to impossible. The wind was so gusty that the balloon yawed and ducked and tugged towards the sea one minute and the hills the next, like a mad thing.

Kathy fought her way across to the balloon bed where the girls were preparing for the most difficult part of the descent.

The balloon was almost on the deck and the last and worst stage of hauling it down had arrived. Because of the violence of the wind, the girls had great difficulty in attaching the concrete blocks, and even when they were attached the blimp refused to be bedded but continued to yaw and heave, lifting the blocks two or three feet off the ground and crashing them down unexpectedly hard so that the girls were constantly having to change position. Kathy got four girls to go to the tail-guy, leaving only a couple to watch the blocks. Jane was No. 1, which meant that she should go under the balloon, now a bare four or five feet from the ground. She would take in the straw mattress that would be thrown over the wires to stop the blimp rubbing itself into holes. This was the trickiest of all the very dangerous jobs connected with storm bedding and Kathy usually did it herself since she was small and light and therefore had a better chance of getting in under the blimp's belly – and out again – without being hurt.

In normal circumstances, Jane would have handed her the mattress, taking it for granted that the smaller girl would do the honours; indeed, Jane did give her a fleeting glance, but when Kathy made no move to respond she squared her shoulders, doubled up and disappeared amongst the tangle of ropes, cables and wires which were the chief impediment to her escape.

As soon as Jane had disappeared, Kathy felt absolutely awful. Had she deliberately let the other girl take on a dangerous job because of what had happened earlier? Anxiously, she dragged her big torch out of the pocket of her oilskins and began to play it around the balloon, searching for a safe path so that Jane could get out again without having to cross the many moving wires and ropes with which the blimp was surrounded. It was difficult to see through the pouring rain, now driving sideways and obscuring what was happening, but she found the best place at last and steadied her torch, shining the beam in under the blimp's bloated form. It seemed an age and there was still no sign of Jane, so Kathy went forward, picking her way delicately amongst the stretched and twisting ropes and wires, and peered at the balloon bed. Jane was lying in a puddle of mud, her arms flung out and her golden hair spilling across her shoulders, and Kathy remembered, belatedly, that Jane had not been wearing a tin hat. Her first impulse was to dive under the balloon, but she was in charge and must not act in any way which might endanger the rest of her crew. She stepped back and grabbed the nearest girl, who was trying to control one of the concrete blocks. 'O'Brien's hurt,' she screamed above the roar of the wind. 'I'm going in, so you'll have to take charge and light me out.' She handed her the torch and then, doubled up, Kathy crawled under the balloon. Once there, it was too dark to see much but she managed to assure herself that the mattress was in position as the girl who was lighting her out flashed her torch a couple of times. She knew the most important thing now was to drag Jane to safety; it was useless trying to discover what had happened to her friend, or if moving her could do more harm than good, for move her she must. Kathy seized Jane's wrists and began to pull, wishing devoutly that the other girl had been a good deal slimmer and the mud a good deal less clingy.

As she began to haul, Jane's eyes flickered open.

Kathy stopped pulling for a second to get her breath and, to her great relief, Jane sat up. 'Is that you Kathy? I'm awful sorry, queen, but something whacked me on the head. I dunno what.'

'Yes, it's me; it should have been me who went under in the first place,' Kathy said grimly. 'Head for the light, Jane – you go first and I'll come after you.'

Halfway out, Kathy began to giggle. There were the two of them, both on all fours, plodding along like a couple of elephants in a circus, with their long oilskins hampering their movements and the mud clinging to everything. If I had a trunk and Jane had a tail, then I'd grab hold of her and we really would look a right stupid pair, Kathy thought, still giggling. But as they emerged, following the beam of the torch, she was infinitely relieved when Jane stood upright and began to walk, slowly but carefully.

Kathy was about to follow her example when something struck her a hefty blow. She heard screams and a sound as of sticks snapping, then felt a terrible pain in her legs, and plunged into darkness.

Chapter Sixteen

Kathy was unconscious for two days, during which time Jane spent every available minute by her friend's bed, all unpleasantness and arguments forgotten. But because she was now the only NCO on No. 7 Balloon Site she could not take a great deal of time off, so it was Sarah Kelling who was sitting by Kathy's bed when her daughter eventually regained consciousness. Kathy's eyelids fluttered open and she gazed about her in a bemused fashion for several moments whilst Sarah watched, her heart in her mouth. She had seen Kathy appear to wake before and then sink once more into unconsciousness without a word, but this time was different, for presently Kathy's head moved ever so slightly on the pillow and, as Sarah leaned forward, a tiny smile touched the pale lips.

'Mam,' she whispered huskily, 'oh, Mam, where am I? What's happened? I feel ever so weird, as if I was going to float away. Am I still on the site? Only my arm's that tired of holding the cable . . . and my mouth's ever so dry.'

Sarah looked pityingly down at the small figure between the crisp white sheets. Her head was heavily bandaged and one arm was strapped to a board with tubes leading out of the strapping. Sarah gently stroked the damp hair off her daughter's brow and lifted a cup from the bedside locker, pouring some water into it. 'Of course your mouth is dry; you've been unconscious for two whole days so you haven't been able to eat or drink anything. Now let me give you a sip or two of water – will it hurt if I pull you up the bed a little?'

'I don't know,' Kathy said doubtfully. 'But it might be better not to try. I hurt all over, Mam, as if I've been run over by a bus. And me legs are just agony if I even move them the tiniest bit.' She glanced sideways at her mother. '*Was* I? Run over by a bus I mean.'

Sarah tried to give a reassuring chuckle but it was a poor effort. 'No, nothing like that; don't you remember anything, queen?'

Kathy frowned doubtfully, then winced and closed her eyes. 'I think I remember working the winch in a fearful gale,' she said. 'But – but I thought it was Jane who was hurt. She was lying on the ground in a pool of mud, her hair was all straggly, and – and . . .' She heaved a sigh and fell silent. Sarah looked wildly around the ward. If only the nurse would come!

But one of the other patients, who had been listening interestedly, leaned out of bed and said comfortably: 'I've gorra feedin' cup, missus. I doesn't' need it no more, so you're welcome to it for that poor gal.' She held out a small beaker-like object with a spout. 'It's been cleaned so you needn't fear I'll pass me broken hip on to your kid,' she added, grinning broadly as Sarah took the cup.

Kathy was able to take a couple of sips of water but her eyes were so anxious that Sarah decided it would be better to tell her what had happened rather than wait for her memory to return. Besides, the doctor had already warned her that it was quite possible the memory would not return and Kathy would never know exactly what had happened on that fearful and stormy night. 'It were Jane who were hurt to start with; she'd gorra bump on the head from that there balloon of yours. It knocked her out for a moment, but o' course you didn't know how badly she'd been hurt. So you went in under the balloon to fish her out. You did that all right because Jane came round and was able to crawl out ahead of you. The trouble came, Jane tèlled me, when she stood upright and someone called out: "Thank God, they're OK, now we can storm bed the blimp." Apparently, the young woman on the winch started to lower the balloon again, the wind caught it and it caught you a terrific thump, knocking you to the ground. Before anyone knew what was happening, the balloon gave a great jerk and one of the concrete bollards, which Jane tells me anchored the thing to the deck, was pulled several feet off the ground and – and . . .'

'Did it get me on the head?' Kathy asked fearfully. 'If so, I'm perishin' lucky not to have been killed.'

'No, no, it didn't hit your head. It was the balloon what banged you on the head. The concrete block fell across your legs. Oh, Kathy, my love, I know it could have been worse, we could have lost you, Billy and me, but it ain't too good, queen. The doctors reckon it'll be a – a long while before you're able to get around.'

'Oh, I see,' Kathy said quietly. 'But – but I will walk again, won't I, Mam? I'll go back to the site in a few weeks and do my normal work, won't I?'

Sarah sighed. Perhaps, in this case, truth was better than fiction. 'I don't know as they'll let you fly balloons again,' she said. 'It's a hard physical job, me love, and there's plenty of girls who have not suffered the way you have who can do work like that. But the WAAF won't let you down; they'll find you a good job somewhere, I'm sure of it.' She waited a moment and then asked, tentatively: 'Is there anyone I should write to, queen? You've gorra feller, haven't you? Alec? He's air force, isn't he? Wouldn't it be a kindness to drop him a line, or is Jane letting him know?'

Kathy sighed again and closed her eyes. 'We had a quarrel the night I was knocked down,' she said wearily. 'But I'll let him know somehow, don't worry, Mam.' And very soon Sarah tiptoed away from the bed. Her daughter needed all the sleep she could get and she wanted to find the sister and tell her that Kathy had come round.

Two weeks after Kathy had been sent to hospital, Jane was having her breakfast with the rest of the crew when the post was delivered. Norah had dished out the porridge and she was now piling scrambled eggs – dried, of course – on to toasted slices of her own homemade bread when an airman from Balloon Centre came into the kitchen. 'Letters, ladies,' he bawled cheerfully, slinging a dozen envelopes on to the table. 'I say, is there a cup o' tea goin' for a poor feller what's already cycled ten miles this mornin'?'

Norah gave him a cup of tea and doled out some eggs on toast whilst Jane picked up her letters and examined the writing. One was from Mrs Kelling, who visited Kathy every single day and kept Jane informed of her progress, and the other – oh bliss – was from Jimmy. His letters were never long but quite often he told Jane when he would be available to receive a telephone call, and the pair of them enjoyed their conversations almost as much as a meeting.

Jane felt the envelope; this was a thicker letter than usual, so she was in for a treat. But she decided to open Mrs Kelling's letter first to see how Kathy was.

Ever since that awful night, Jane had been miserably aware that most of Kathy's injuries, if not all, were her, Jane's, fault. If she had worn her tin hat, if they had not quarrelled, if she had been faithful to Jimmy all those years ago . . . but Jane was too practical a person to believe that vain regrets would help anyone. So she had decided to do everything in her power to help Kathy to get well again and she had dashed off a letter to Alec, admitting everything. She told him how she had not even realised that one crumpled page of his letter had been stuck down the side of her kit bag. It had been the page on which Alec had suggested rendezvousing some way from his station and, unfortunately, Kathy had found and read it. Jane apologised humbly to Alec both for the way she had behaved in the past and for her carelessness in holding on to a letter which she should have destroyed ages ago. Then she had explained that, as a result of their subsequent quarrel, Kathy had been badly injured and was now in the Stanley Hospital.

I've known Kathy for years and she were in a rare old temper after the row we had, she had written, *so I guess her first act was to ring you up and tear you off a strip. I know she spoke to you, Alec, because I were sitting by her bed one night, before she'd regained consciousness properly, and she kept mumbling on about saying horrible things to you and how she wished she hadn't.*

This had not been strictly true because Kathy's mumblings had been wild and fragmented, but Jane had got the gist of what her friend meant to say. The writing of the letter had done a good deal to ease Jane's conscience about the whole affair since she had ended with a desperate plea to Alec to come as quickly as he possibly could so that her friend would know he bore her no grudge.

Jane had realised, even in her distress, that if Jimmy saw her writing on an envelope addressed to Alec he might naturally demand to be allowed to read what she had written and that would never do, so she had got Acting Corporal Ellis to do the necessary and, ever since, had been awaiting Alec's arrival with mixed feelings.

Jane scanned Sarah's letter, which was brief. It said her friend was very depressed and miserable and in a great deal of pain, though she was trying to do without the tablets the doctors had prescribed for her since she said they made her feel 'sleepy and stupid'.

Jane decided that she would visit Kathy in her lunch break, then thrust Sarah's letter into the pocket of her boiler suit and began to read Jimmy's. It was, as she had suspected, a long letter but, far from being a treat, with every word she read Jane's sense of foreboding grew. Jimmy would not go on like this, telling her all about how Skip had asked Alec to do an extra op as a favour to another pilot, unless something had happened. And sure enough, on the next page, Jimmy had written it all down.

I thought Alec was sure to refuse, Jimmy had written. *It's bad luck to go changing your plane – and your crew – in most men's eyes, same as the fellers don't like doing an op on a wedding anniversary or a special birthday. In fact, Skip was pretty sure he'd refuse as well and had already started asking around amongst other crews. Alec had been playing cards or something, but he was called away to the telephone, and when he came back Skip's pal asked him again if he were on and Alec said he were.*

I thought he looked odd; ill almost, but when I asked him if there were anything up, he just stared at me for a moment and then said, 'No, why should there be?' and walked away. It's not like Alec to act unfriendly so I guessed he'd got a belly-ache, or maybe it were a premonition because that Wimpey never come back after the raid and the whole crew, including Alec, is posted as missing.

I asked and asked everyone who was on ops that night whether the kite had been shot down and whether any of the crew had got out, but it seems it were a big raid – masses of ack-ack and searchlights everywhere, so you were lit up like on a stage – and Jerry fighters coming at you from every angle. We had heavy losses that night. We'll miss Alec like the very devil. He were the best, you know, and I'm not just saying that because he were me pal. He were a first class navigator, got us safe there and back, night after night. Well, we were a good team, to tell you the truth. Skip's a steady sort of pilot, not like some of these young ones, all talk and no do, so as I said, we'll miss Alec. There's been no word of his ditching coming home, but you never know; they might have used their 'chutes and got down safe somewhere. I hope to God they have.

Jane sat back in her chair and let the tears rain unchecked down her cheeks. She kept getting a mental picture of her dear Kathy lying crumpled and broken in her hospital bed. She would have to tell her what had happened because otherwise she would be watching the doors at the end of the ward, hour after hour, day after day, expecting Alec to come bursting through them, with a grin on his face and a straggly bunch of flowers in one hand. Jane had heard girls in the crew whose boyfriends had been killed saying that by far the worst time had been the waiting, the not knowing. The girls said they could not take up their lives afresh when they did not know whether they had lost their lovers or whether the missing one would walk through the door one day and give them a big hug. Oh yes, Jane thought, not knowing, and being able to imagine unimaginable horrors, is by far the worst.

Kathy was sitting up in bed trying to read a book, though the letters kept blurring and then doubling up as she strove to concentrate. The crack on the head she had received from the balloon had not affected her too badly, but as soon as she grew tired her eyes refused to focus, so now she laid her book down on the coverlet and glanced, hopefully, towards the swing doors, through which a figure was coming, accompanied by Sister, who was chattering away to the newcomer and gesturing up the ward as though pointing out a bed.

Kathy had been in hospital now for two weeks. She had not heard a word from Alec but told herself, resolutely, that the fault was hers. She had been absolutely horrible to him the last time they had spoken and though she longed to write and apologise, explain that she had had no right to blame him for something long past, she had not yet managed to do so. She had broken her right wrist in the fall, and in any case this was the arm into which the tubes led, so it was strapped to a board and pretty well useless. As she was right-handed, letters were an impossibility, and though several people had offered to take one down at her dictation, her pride simply would not let her make her feelings so public. She had toyed with the idea of simply agreeing to let her mother write to Alec, explaining that she was in hospital and would very much like to see him. But she hesitated to do so. She was such a mess! Two badly broken and painful legs, now hoisted up on a pulley contraption and terminating in permanently icy cold feet, a broken wrist which made even feeding herself difficult, a memory which was unreliable to say the least, and a tendency to splitting headaches did not make her much of a companion. Besides, for all she knew, Alec might have been so upset that he had gone out and got himself another girl, and who could blame him? So, on the whole, it would be wiser to wait until she was well enough to pen her own apologies, though in her secret heart she was sure Alec would be in touch long before then.

The woman coming down the ward was getting closer and Kathy realised she looked familiar. What was more, Sister was leading her straight to Kathy's bed and the woman was smiling at her, though it was a sad, lop-sided smile.

'I've a visitor for you, Miss Kelling,' Sister said. She was a brisk and businesslike woman, but today her voice was gentle. She drew the curtains round the bed, saying as she did so: 'I think you might like some privacy and because you're on traction I can scarcely offer you the loan of my office.' She left them, but not before giving Kathy's shoulder a squeeze.

Kathy stared apprehensively up at her visitor. She had reddish-brown hair and eyes that matched exactly and a strong, handsome face. She held out her hand to Kathy, then shook her head at her own foolishness and sat down on the end of the bed.

'I see you can't shake hands, and whass more, you don't know me from Adam,' she said rather gruffly. 'I'm Betty Hewitt, Alec's mum. I've had a letter, thass from my son's squadron leader. I think you should read it. I'm that sorry to be bringing bad tidings but, if it were me, I'd rather know than not.'

She held out a thin sheet of blue paper but Kathy did not take it immediately. As soon as she had heard the woman speak, she had known that this must be Alec's mother, for they shared the same accent, the same way of turning a sentence. She looked steadily across at her visitor and saw that her eyes were bright with unshed tears.

'I guessed who you were; you're so like Alec,' she said huskily. 'I don't need to read it,' she went on, her own voice unsteady. 'Alec has been killed, hasn't he? Was it a car crash? Only I've a friend whose boyfriend flies with Alec and if anything had happened to him, she'd have told me.'

Mrs Hewitt looked puzzled but continued holding out the letter so Kathy took it and began to read, through tear-blurred eyes.

Dear Mr and Mrs Hewitt, I'm sorry to have to tell you that your son, Flt Lt Hewitt, took the place of a sick navigator in the crew of another Wellington bomber some days ago and the whole crew have now been posted as missing. This does not mean that he is presumed killed since it takes time before the authorities let us know if an airman has been taken prisoner. However, since neither he nor the rest of the crew has returned to the station, I thought it best to let you know. I have taken charge of all Alec's personal possessions and will forward them to you in due course. Everyone who knew Alec liked him; he was a grand, cheerful chap and one of our top navigators. He will be sadly missed. Yours sincerely . . .

Kathy handed the letter back to her visitor and used the sheet to wipe her eyes. Then she fished the handkerchief out from under her pillow and blew her nose. For a few minutes she stared down at the bedclothes; then she looked up and the eyes that met Mrs Hewitt's were no longer tear filled. 'Do you *believe* that?' she asked, in a cold, almost accusing voice. 'Because I do not! It's – it's just the sort of letter they write to people when they're not sure what has happened to their boys. I'm sure Alec's still alive, I'm sure I'd have known if – if something awful had happened. To tell you the truth, I've been lying here wondering why he'd not got in touch, but it never occurred to me for one moment that he might be dead and I don't believe it now – I *won't* believe it!'

Mrs Hewitt leaned across the bed and took Kathy's good hand. 'You're right and that's what Bob and I keep telling ourselves and each other. But Alec had written to us a while back, telling us that he'd met the most wonderful girl and meant to marry her. He said he was going to bring her home next time he had a leave so's we could meet up. And on the bottom of the letter, he'd scribbled your name and number and your address on the balloon site. And under that, he said if anything happened to him, he trusted us to get in touch with you and see you right.'

Kathy smiled ruefully. 'Well, I wouldn't say you were seeing me right. I'm in a real mess, but I expect they told you what happened when you visited Site Seven.'

'Aye, they did an' all,' Mrs Hewitt confirmed. 'And Sister told me you'd be stuck here for weeks and weeks, until they got you sorted out. But I wondered whether you might come back to Norfolk, to Father and me, when they let you out of hospital? It's quiet country living but tha' int like living in a city. We've all the fruit and vegetables we can eat, we make our own butter and cheese and there's always someone killing a pig or pulling the necks of a few chickens who'll be happy to sell a bit to a neighbour. I know Alec would want . . .' her voice wobbled dangerously, then righted itself '. . . Alec would want us to do everything we could to get you well again,' she finished firmly.

When her visitor had gone, Kathy allowed her fear and grief full reign, but only for ten minutes or so. She told herself again that she was sure Alec was still alive, and in any case she would no longer believe him to be angry with her. It had been impossible not to worry when the days passed and he did not get in touch. But because of Jane's attachment to Jimmy, she had not dreamed that Alec might be posted as missing. She realised, of course, that Jane must have been aware of the substitution, must have realised that Alec had not returned from his last op, but could not find it in her heart to blame her friend for keeping such news to herself. However, when Jane arrived to visit her later that day, Kathy told her about Mrs Hewitt's visit and the news the older woman had brought.

Jane looked relieved. 'I didn't know what to do,' she confessed. 'I only found out myself yesterday what had happened. As soon as I heard, I rang Jimmy in the mess. I told him you and Alec were going steady – he *was* surprised – and asked if I should break the news to you. But he said the Groupie was sending out letters and it was better that you heard official like.' Jane leaned across the bed and took her friend's good hand in a gentle clasp. 'I can't tell you how sorry I am, queen! He was one of the best, was old Alec, and you're another. If – if it were Jimmy who'd been killed . . . but it don't do to think like that.'

Kathy sat up a little straighter, though a dreadful pain shot through her legs as she did so. 'If Alec had been killed I don't think my life would be worth living,' she said almost savagely. 'But he hasn't been killed, Jane. OK, he's been posted as missing, but that isn't the same thing at all and I'll thank you not to speak of him in the past tense because I'm *sure* he's still alive.'

Jane looked at her doubtfully for a moment, then her face cleared and she beamed. 'That's the spirit, queen,' she said joyfully. 'D'you remember how, when we were kids, your da' would tell us to stop meetin' troubles halfway? Well, that's just what I was doin', but I won't do it no more. If you're sure he's alive, then he bleedin' well is and we'll look forward to his coming home as soon as the war is ended.'

Kathy stood shakily on Stanley Road, gazing up and down as though she could not believe she was free from her prison at last. She was on two crutches and behind her, pushed by her mother, was the wheelchair which the authorities had insisted she would need to use for distances of more than a few feet until her legs grew stronger. But she was out, breathing the fresh December air, feeling the nip of cold and hearing the hum of the traffic and the chatter of passers-by in a way she had not done for many months.

For a great deal of time had passed – six months, in fact – since Kathy had been struck down. This was because her legs had refused to heal straight and strong and she had had three operations on them before the hospital finally decided they had done all they could. Now, as she finally emerged from the hospital, Christmas was almost upon them. She meant to go straight home for a week's much needed rest because a great many of the balloon sites had been closed down and those that remained were once more to be run by men. Nevertheless, she would still have insisted upon returning to Balloon Site 7 had there been a balloon site to return to. The Air Ministry, acting with hindsight as usual, and far too late, announced that the work was too heavy for Waafs, that too many serious injuries had resulted from flying the blimps and that, in any event, their presence around northern and eastern England was no longer as necessary as it had once been. In the order informing the Bops of the fate of their sites, the girls were also told that they would be remustered. Jane had gone off to Scampton to be a waitress in the officers' mess there and was happy with her lot since it brought her within a dozen miles of Jimmy at Waddington, but Kathy had no idea what fate – and the WAAF – had in store for her.

'Kathy love, you know what the doctor said. You ain't supposed to walk more'n a few yards and you've come all the way from the ward without so much as a sit-down. Why not let me wheel you the rest o' the way?'

Kathy was tempted to tell her mother that she did not intend to use the wheelchair, that it might as well be left at the hospital, but already her legs were aching dreadfully and she knew it was only a matter of time before they simply gave way under her. Clearly, she would have to be sensible and use the chair when her strength failed her. Accordingly, she turned and took a couple of shaky steps backwards, then sank into the hard leather seat. It felt soft as a feather pillow after the strain of her short walk and she laid her crutches across her knee, then smiled up at Sarah Kelling.

'Tell you what, Mam,' she said cheerily, 'if you'll push me halfway down Daisy Street, then maybe I can walk the last few yards. Only – only I feel like a perishin' cripple in the wheelchair, honest to God I do.'

'Oh, you,' her mother said, but she spoke lovingly. 'You know very well your legs will get strong again, because the doctor said so. Why, you'll be skippin' about like young Billy does by the time summer comes. Anyway, them there legs of yours is war wounds and you've no call to be ashamed of *that*.'

As the two of them entered Daisy Street, doors shot open and neighbours came on to the pavement to congratulate them on Kathy's safe return, their breath puffing clouds of steam into the frosty air. 'You've been stuck in that bloody hospital, you poor little bugger,' Mrs O'Brien said bracingly. 'But you're goin' to be awright, queen. Once you're on your feet, you'll find yourself a nice feller and get married . . .' she laughed heartily at her own words '. . . and then your happiness will be at an end, 'cos marriage ain't no picnic, and havin' half a dozen kids to bring up ain't exactly a bed o' roses either. Still, it's what the fellers say women want and we've none of us got the gumption to tell 'em that marriage is only fun for the feller.'

The small crowd of women surrounding Kathy all laughed but told Mrs O'Brien that 'she were a terrible woman, to try to scare the poor little gal and her only just out of 'orspital', but Kathy had her own answer ready.

'I agree with every word, Mrs O'Brien,' she said, her own voice sounding brittle. 'I've always meant to have a career with a steady wage; it's so much more reliable than a husband.'

The women dispersed, laughing, and Kathy, who had stood up on her crutches as soon as the first door opened, sank thankfully back into the seat once more.

'That told 'em,' she muttered as her mother pulled the wheelchair backwards into the house. 'If I can't have Alec, Mam, I'd sooner be a spinster for the rest of my days, and that's God's truth.'

Her mother wheeled the chair into the front room and helped Kathy out of it and on to the sofa. 'Now that's foolish talk,' she scolded fondly. 'If you've told me once that you were sure Alec was alive, you've told me a thousand times. Why, for all you know, he could be back here by Christmas. And since that other feller, what was his name, the one who was in the same plane as Alec, appeared on a list of RAF personnel in a German POW camp . . . you must have been surer than ever that Alec was safe; so let's have no defeatist talk in this house, as old Winnie used to say,'

'Sorry, Mam,' Kathy said humbly. She did not add that the quotation was usually attributed to Queen Victoria, or that learning one of Alec's companions was a POW had depressed her most dreadfully, for surely if Alec had escaped from the plane at the same time as the rear gunner he, too, would have been taken prisoner by now? So the dogged hope which had helped her through the worst and most painful months in hospital was beginning to fade.

However, Kathy was coming to terms with what had happened. The dreadful nightmares which had haunted her ever since she had heard that Alec was missing had begun to diminish; they came less often and were less terrible, less explicit. In the early days, her nights had been made hideous by dreams of Alec being horribly injured as his 'chute failed a hundred feet from the ground. Then there were the dreams of the kite's catching fire and Alec's being badly burned. In other dreams he was captured by the Nazis and tortured, so that she woke screaming, unable to share her fears with other patients, yet equally unable to dispel them even in the clear light of day.

One good thing to come out of Alec's being missing was Kathy's friendship with Betty Hewitt. It was a wonderful bonus to find Alec's mum so bright and humorous, so brave and honest, and, above all, so like Alec. Of course, the Norfolk burr which enriched her speech was so reminiscent of Alec that Kathy had had to fight back tears at first, every time Betty opened her mouth. But this had passed and the two of them had become really friendly. They did exchange telephone calls but these were rare as the only telephone box near the Hewitts' farm was a three-mile walk away, and even had Mrs Hewitt been at ease with the instrument it would have been a lengthy and expensive business, since she had to telephone first to the main reception of the hospital, then get the call put through to Sister's office and then wait while Kathy was fetched. But Mrs Hewitt had made the long cross-country trek from Norfolk to Liverpool twice. On the first occasion she had put up at a guesthouse but on her second visit Sarah Kelling had insisted that she spend the night in Kathy's old room in Daisy Street. Kathy did not know what the two women had talked about after they returned from their hospital visiting, but she did know that friendship had blossomed between the two mothers as well as between herself and Betty, and was glad of it. She meant to accept Betty's invitation to visit as soon as she was well enough, but looking ruefully at her thin, wasted legs, she doubted that she would manage it for a good few months to come. Still, now she was home, she could practise her walking skills, with and without the crutches, five or six times a day;

surely if she did that, she would begin to improve more rapidly?

Her mother, popping back into the room, put an end to her musings. 'It ain't time for dinner yet, but I baked last night so if you could fancy a cup of Bovril and a nice thick round of me homemade bread, that should keep you satisfied for the next hour or so,' Mrs Kelling said cheerfully. 'Oh, queen, it's grand to have you home, so it is. I didn't say a word to Billy so it'll be such a wonderful surprise to find you here when he comes in from school. I know he's a big feller now and he's not had a fit . . . oh, for years, but I reckon he'll be chuffed to bits to have his sister home.'

'I love being home, of course I do, but I'm hoping that I shan't be here all that long,' Kathy said presently, sipping her Bovril. 'There must be jobs I can do in the WAAF as soon as my legs are strong enough. Oh, I know that balloons are out of the question now, but there must be *something* I can do!'

For Kathy, the months that followed seemed to last for ever, but at the end of May she was on leave at the Hewitts' farm in Norfolk, having her first taste of country living. She had started work with the WAAF once more, though she was doing a desk job which suited her physical condition better than a more active role would have done. She had been posted to Coltishall, which was a bare twenty miles or so from Horsey, and had been grateful for the warm welcome the Hewitts offered her whenever she had leave which was not long enough for the return trip to Liverpool. Their warmth and friendliness was such that she no longer felt she had to let them know when she would be arriving but simply turned up, sure of her welcome and knowing that Betty, in particular, loved to have her company and her help around the house.

Now, the Hewitts and Kathy were having their elevenses when the door opened and the postman came in, chucking three or four letters on to the table but refusing the cup of tea which Mrs Hewitt offered. 'I'm suffin' awful late,' he said apologetically, 'so I dussn't stop, do I'll get wrong. See you tomorrow, missus.' The door swung noisily shut behind him.

Kathy's eyes were turned, irresistibly, towards the letter on the top of the pile. It bore a foreign stamp and looked as though it had spent many months on its journey, and the writing on the front was strange and spiky.

'That come from abroad, judging by the stamp,' Bob said, eyeing the envelope. 'Go you on and open that 'un first, my woman, do I'll be out of the place afore you're halfway through the post.'

Betty obediently picked up the envelope, slit it open and pulled out the single sheet which it contained. She glanced at it and her face turned first red and then white, her hand going to her throat. 'Thass from our Alec,' she whispered, and Kathy saw that tears were running down her cheeks. 'He's alive! He's alive and being helped by a marvellous family, though he daren't say no more than that in case the letter gets intercepted. He say he's going to give the letter to a chap who's travelling to Spain and could post it there for him, just to let us know he's still alive. He say we're to tell Kathy.' She smiled tremulously at the younger woman, tears quivering on her lashes, then turned back to her husband. 'Oh, Bob, oh, Bob, I know I always said he weren't dead, but there's been times . . .'

Kathy sat there like a statue whilst husband and

wife hugged and Betty wept and Bob tried to grin, though his mouth trembled. She felt tears slide down her own cheeks but was aware of a tremendous glow of happiness which seemed to warm her all through. He was alive! Nothing mattered but that fact.

Betty turned to her and gathered her into her arms and Bob hugged the pair of them, saying thickly that this was the best thing that had happened in his whole life. 'I never knew no one could cry for joy,' he said gruffly. 'Well, I've heered as folk do but I never believed it afore today.'

Later, of course, when they had sobered down, it occurred to them to look at the postmark, for the letter itself was undated. The letter had, indeed, been a long while on its travels but no one was pessimistic enough to mention all the things which could have happened to Alec in the interim. They simply rejoiced that he was safe and would, in due course, return to them.

After their first excitement was over, everyone returned to work. Kathy was still on her crutches, but did not need them inside the house provided she could hang on to the furniture. This very morning, she had concocted and carried out to the pigsty, one by one and with considerable difficulty, two buckets of pigswill. It had meant frequent stops as she manoeuvred herself along, on her crutches, the bucket of pigswill swaying dangerously. But six months ago I wouldn't have been able to reach the sty empty-handed, let alone carrying the swill, she reminded herself, watching the two enormous sows, Sandra and Belinda, guzzling the food as though they had not eaten for a week. I am getting better; in fact, if it wasn't for the way my legs ache after I've done a bit of walking, you'd never know they'd both been broken. She glanced down at them, hating their thinness and the shape of them. I don't suppose my shin bones can possibly straighten, she thought ruefully, but I don't mind that if only they'll let me walk normally one day.

Having fed the pigs, she turned back to the house. Her left leg dragged a bit – it was the weaker of the two – but she was sure this particular affliction would pass in time. She was longing for Alec to come home, of course she was, but she was determined to stay away from him until she was completely fit. She was well aware that in the time which had passed since they had last met, his feelings towards her might have changed. After all, she had done her best to alienate him completely when they had last spoken. If he chose to find himself another girl – a strong and healthy one – then she could scarcely blame him. Yet he had asked his mother to let her know that he was safe. Surely that must mean something?

But right now, she was so full of the wonderful news that he was still alive that nothing else seemed to matter much. Even if he were only a friend, she would rejoice wholeheartedly to hear he was safe. Going indoors once more, she smiled across the kitchen at Betty, then took down her gas mask case from where it hung behind the back door and fished out paper and writing materials.

'I'm going to write to Jane and me mam,' she announced, beginning to smile. 'I just can't wait to tell them the news.'

Within two weeks of the Hewitts' receiving Alec's letter, news of the Normandy landings was on everyone's lips. Kathy followed the Allies' gradual incursion into France with her heart in her mouth.

She had assumed that Alec's 'friendly family' must be in eastern France and, naturally, this would be the last part of the country the Allies would reach, yet she could not help hoping. Surely he would hear news of the advance and would try to meet his compatriots – unless he was injured, ill, unable to travel . . .

But that way lay madness and Kathy resolutely refused to consider that anything bad could have befallen her lover. Waiting was hard but when the waiting was over she and Alec would be together once more and that was all that mattered, she told herself constantly as the weeks passed.

Being on opposite sides of the country as they were, she and Jane had only exchanged letters of late but, to Kathy's pleasure, Jane had recently been posted to a Norfolk airfield. This meant that the girls could meet up in Norwich when the gharries dumped them there for a few hours of comparative freedom. Kathy was able to discuss with Jane what had happened to make Alec go as navigator in a different plane on that fateful night.

'I've asked Jimmy why Alec went off in the other kite,' Jane had told Kathy. 'Apparently, the two skippers were big pals and it would have been very difficult for Alec to say he wouldn't go. So don't you go thinkin' he went off on the raid that night because he were upset by what you said. Refusing would have made things awkward, see?'

Kathy did see but she thought, privately, that she would blame herself for that dreadful telephone call for as long as she lived. If only she had been able to explain to Alec, to write a letter taking back all the bitter things she had said, but it had not been possible then and was impossible still.

Meanwhile, she had to continue with her life. Other

people had lovers in German POW camps, or simply missing. Aircrew risked their lives every time they took their kites over Germany and you could tell by the haunted eyes of wives and girlfriends that they suffered every bit as much as Kathy was doing. After all, one bit of bad luck and an aircraft could crash, 'chutes could fail to open or a stray bullet might find its mark.

So Kathy appreciated that Jane and many other women suffered from the same restless, gnawing anxiety as she did herself and determined to show a cheerful face and an optimistic attitude, both at work and at play.

By mid-September, it became clear to everyone that the whole of France would soon be liberated. The Third Reich was tottering. To be sure, the hated doodlebugs had taken their toll and the V2s, immensely powerful rockets which came soundlessly overhead and caused enormous damage when they landed, were dreaded, but they were reputed to be the last horrible surprise in Hitler's armoury. The fear that he might try to use biological warfare had gradually faded as both sides, presumably, realised that it was a two-edged weapon which could twist in the hand and attack the very forces who were using it.

Harvest time came. Everyone on the stations was urged to help the farmers and gharries full of RAF personnel took them round to neighbouring fields where they worked with a will alongside land girls, elderly farm workers and the many Italian prisoners of war who had ended up in Norfolk. Kathy, however, made her way to the Hewitts' whenever she could. Betty and Bob were always delighted to see her, for though she still needed her crutches at times there were many jobs with which she could cope comfortably.

Kathy was actually at the farm, perched on top of a load of straw which Clark, the shire horse, was about to pull back to the rickyard, when Betty came running down the lane. She had a yellow envelope in one hand and a piece of paper in the other and even from her lofty perch Kathy could see the excitement on the older woman's face. 'It's a telegram – a telegram from Alec!' Betty shrieked. 'He's back in England! He has to report to some board or other – he don't say which – but he'll be coming home next Thursday. Oh, Bob, Bob, I couldn't believe my eyes when I first opened the envelope. Our boy's safe and we'll be seeing him in less than a week!'

Bob had been pitching sheaves of straw up to Kathy but now he held up his arms and caught her as she slithered down from the laden wagon. To Kathy's amazement, for Bob had never been a demonstrative man, he gave her a quick, hard hug and planted a kiss on her forehead before turning round to lift Betty off her feet with a shout of triumph. 'Our lad's back in England,' he shouted to the assembled workers. 'Oh, thank the good Lord, the boy Alec is coming home.'

By dusk, the field was finished and the workers scattered, the Hewitts and Kathy to return to the farmhouse. They had had a large tea, but Betty had boiled the kettle and baked some potatoes in the oven, and though Kathy protested that she could not eat a thing she soon found she was able to do so and despatched two cups of tea and a large potato before settling back in her chair to discuss what celebrations should be planned for the returning hero.

It was then that Kathy realised she simply could not face the thought of meeting Alec for the first time in the bosom of his family whilst still struggling about on crutches. To be sure, she was a great deal better than she had been, and did not need the crutches at all in the house. But it might put Alec in a terribly uncomfortable position since he had no idea that she was not still on a balloon site outside Liverpool; no idea that she had met his parents, knew them quite well in fact. He had never been told about her accident, knew nothing of her change of work and might well be flabbergasted to find her comfortably ensconced in his mother's kitchen. After all, he had been in France for more than a year and, as a result, his whole life must have changed. The family who had hidden him – she assumed that this was what must have happened – might have a daughter with whom he was madly in love. She could picture his dismay upon seeing her, perhaps remembering their friendship as something which had happened long ago, in another life, a friendship that he now wanted to forget.

But it was not possible to say any of this to dear kind Betty and Bob, who had made her so wonderfully welcome and were taking it for granted that the Alec who was coming home to them would be the selfsame one who had gone away. She had never told either Bob or Betty of the telephone conversation – if you could call it that – she had had with their son last time they had spoken. It would scarcely have been possible without causing deep distress and even offence, but it did mean that they would expect her to fall into Alec's arms and vice versa. They could not possibly realise how hurt and angry Alec must have been, how easy it would have been for him to fall in love with another woman, believing Kathy to have turned from him.

She could say none of these things, would have to invent a reason why she could not be back at the farm next Thursday . . . and at this point she began to wonder why Thursday was so significant. Surely there had been something . . . something . . .

'Don't forget, though, I shan't be around next Thursday. I've got my medical board in London, and that's something I simply must attend. But I'm sure Alec will understand; he knows the RAF.'

Betty stared at her, her eyes rounding with dismay. 'I'd forgotten the medical board,' she said slowly. 'Oh, but surely, love, if you explain . . . it'll be his first day home and for all we know the air force might post him to the highlands of Scotland or even abroad! Surely, if you explained . . .'

Kathy laughed but shook her head. 'It doesn't work like that, Betty. A medical board is an important business. As you know, I've wanted to remuster as something a bit more exciting than an office worker; this medical board may be my one chance. R/T Operatives have to be able to climb stairs and get around in the R/T office room without crutches getting in everyone's way; or I might be a driver – I'd love that, you know.'

'Well I think if you really tried . . .' Betty was beginning, when Bob interrupted her, leaning across the table to give her shoulder a little shake.

'The girl's right, Bet. If this here medical board give her the go-ahead, then she'll mebbe get a decent job and a bit more money. And besides, I reckon mebbe it'll be easier on Alec if he gets his meetin's and greetin's over one at a time, so to speak. Of course, it'll be Kathy he'll want to see most, 'cos thass human nature, thass is, but think on, my woman; Kathy told us she got a nice little bit o' leave fixed up for after her medical board, so if she catch the milk train from Liverpool Street Station, even if she can't catch an earlier one, they can have their own private reunion in the early hours o' Friday mornin' and then come back here all lovey-dovey.' He turned to Kathy, giving her the wide, innocent grin which was the only physical resemblance between him and Alec. 'Thass what you're plannin', int it, my woman?'

'Well, something like that,' Kathy said guardedly. The moment Bob had mentioned her leave, she had decided what she would do. She would have her medical board and then send the Hewitts a telegram. She would say something like *Called home unexpectedly due to illness* and would then go straight to Euston Station and catch the next train home to Liverpool. Her mam would be delighted to see her and it would put off the evil hour for as much as a week, since she had seven days' leave owing. Furthermore, it would put the ball in Alec's court. If he wanted to cut the connection, all he had to do was . . . nothing! He could spend whatever leave he had with his parents and then go wherever the RAF posted him. He would not need to get in touch with her or send her his address; he could simply treat their relationship as a thing of the past, best forgotten.

That's the best plan, Kathy told herself resolutely as she got ready for bed that night in the Nissen hut at Coltishall, for the gharries had picked the harvesters up by moonlight and taken them back to their own beds. On the other hand, if Alec hasn't changed his mind, really does still love me, then he knows very well that I live in Daisy Street and can come to me there.

Satisfied that she was doing the right thing, Kathy undressed and slid between the sheets, and, rather to her own surprise, slept soundly till morning.

*

Thursday came. Kathy was up very early indeed and went straight to the cookhouse where she ate a hearty breakfast of porridge, toast and dried egg accompanied by a large tin mug of tea. Then she heaved herself aboard the gharry in the pearly morning light. She was the only passenger so sat beside the driver and chatted idly to him as the lorry thundered along the winding country roads, depositing her at last outside Thorpe railway station.

'Good luck, Corp,' the driver shouted and Kathy turned into the station forecourt. She was trying very hard to keep her mind on her medical board but found the only thing she could think of was Alec. He was coming home! In three hours or so she would be in London, and probably a couple of hours later he would be on the very station platform on which she now stood. She could imagine him so clearly; his cap pushed to the back of his curly chestnut hair, his eyes bright and eager, his kitbag – if he had one – slung over one shoulder whilst he looked around anxiously to see whether anyone was meeting him. But it was no use thinking about Alec's arrival and, anyway, she was sure the decision she had made was the right one.

The train came in and she was lucky enough to get a corner seat. She settled into it, sighed and glanced around her. The carriage was filling up but she recognised nobody, though there was a Waaf in the far corner and two young airmen in uniforms so new and shiny that she guessed they had been in the service weeks rather than months.

Presently, the train slid out of the station and Kathy let her attention be drawn to the beautiful day which was unfolding outside the carriage. The sun shone from a pale blue sky and in the meadows she saw the workers bringing in the harvest and knew that back in Horsey, Bob and Betty would be doing the same, for the harvest stops for no man, not even a son from the war returning.

Kathy glanced around the carriage again. The other Waaf was reading a paperback and several travellers had bought newspapers or magazines, but she had been far too preoccupied to think of such a thing. Anyway, she had always found enough entertainment in the passing scene to keep her happily occupied, no matter how long the journey. Today, however, was different. She felt herself staring, unseeingly, at meadows, woodland, streams and country cottages, whilst her mind dwelled on Alec. It occurred to her, not for the first time, that he might have been injured when jumping from the Wellington bomber. Of course, she knew he could not be seriously hurt or the people who had hidden him would, she assumed, have had to hand him to the authorities for hospital treatment. But he could have broken an ankle or an arm. Suppose he, like herself, was limping, or carried an arm awkwardly? But at that point she gave herself a resolute shake and told herself not to be an absolute fool if she could possibly help it. Neither of them knew what had happened to the other during the long months they had been apart. Her first plan had been a wise one. She was giving him space and time to settle back into a normal life. Once that period was over, then they would either meet or not, according to how he felt; more than that she could not offer him.

So it was strange that the further the train got from Norwich, the more thoroughly uncomfortable and unsettled she felt. She found herself getting out of her seat and looking desperately up and down the platform every time the train stopped at a station.

Other travellers came and went but the Waaf with the paperback and the two airmen stayed, though no one addressed her or so much as glanced in her direction.

As soon as she had settled herself in the train, Kathy had put her crutches and her kit bag up on the overhead rack. This meant a good deal of disruption if she wanted to extract the packet of sandwiches with which the cookhouse had provided her. Kathy turned her attention to the bustling station outside her window as they drew to a halt. There was a fat old woman pushing a trolley up and down the platform and shouting her wares. Of course she could get out and pursue her but she would feel safer with her crutches. Yet getting them down would be such a business because now they were underneath all the possessions of other travellers who had joined the train after herself.

Sighing, Kathy decided to resign herself to her lot and pressed her nose wistfully to the window, watching others queuing at the trolley. She wondered whether she might lean out of the window and persuade someone to fetch her some tea but at that moment the train began to move and she realised she was too late. She sank back in her seat and then leaned forward, a hand flying to her throat. There was someone walking along the platform, heading for the trolley. His cap was on the back of his head and he wore an aggressively new uniform, yet the very way he wore it – as well as the wing on his chest – proclaimed that this was no lad joining up for the first time, but a seasoned campaigner.

Kathy jumped to her feet with a shriek which rivalled the whistle with which the train had announced its departure. She jerked the window down, snatched at the door handle and fell out on to the platform. She heard cries and shouts, saw an official bearing down upon her, his face red with anger, heard the slam as someone pushed the door she had opened vigorously closed. Then she was running, running, dodging passengers, swerving round the tea trolley, and hurling herself into Alec's welcoming arms.

Chapter Seventeen

For a long moment, Kathy thought of nothing but Alec. Her arms were up round his neck and her cheeks were wet with tears; it was several moments before she realised that the tears were his as well as hers. Then she tried to stand back, stammering that she had glimpsed him from the train window and had wanted so desperately to be with him that she had simply run to him.

'I can't believe it,' Alec was saying huskily. He put his arm round her and led her into the station buffet, sat her down at a table and then wiped the palms of his hands across her wet cheeks. 'I've been dreaming of this moment for months and months and then you're in my arms and the pair of us are crying like the great boobies we are. But, sweetheart, what were you doing on that train? Oh, there's so much I don't know! I've been in London seeing the Top Brass at Adastral House but my leave starts today. Oh, Kathy, Kathy, I can't tell you how wonderful it is to be with you again.'

He had sat down opposite her and Kathy leaned across the table and touched his cheek gently. It was seamed by a ragged scar which ran from the corner of his eye to his jawbone. 'Oh, darling Alec, you *were* hurt! What happened?'

'We've got an awful lot to tell one another,' Alec said contentedly, getting to his feet. 'But if we're going to occupy this table, I'd better buy a couple of mugs of tea and some buns – I only got off the train to get a cup of tea! Did you know I was coming home today?'

Kathy nodded. 'Yes, I knew, but I was on my way to Adastral House as well.' Her hand flew to her mouth. 'Oh, dear God! I've got a medical board later this morning and of course I've missed my train and you've missed yours . . . oh, oh, oh, and my crutches and kit bag are still on the luggage rack! Oh, Alec, what a fool I've made of myself, and I dare say I'll be in the most awful trouble when I don't turn up on time.'

'Crutches?' Alec looked flabbergasted. 'What on earth do you want with crutches? Why, you fell out of the train and tore along the platform like an Olympic runner. I've never seen anyone move so fast!'

Kathy giggled but stood up and gave him a push towards the counter. 'It's too long a story to tell in a couple of sentences,' she said. 'Go and get the tea and buns and then I'll tell you everything. Oh, Alec, it's so good to be with you again!

The explanations could have taken several hours, but once Kathy had explained about her accident Alec decided to take matters into his own hands. He said that they would both catch the next train to London together and explain that Kathy had got out of the first train in order to buy a cup of tea and it had left without her. 'Of course, the real story is a lot more romantic,' he said, grinning down at her. 'But this version will be easier for the air force to swallow. I'm afraid your crutches may never be seen again, nor your kit bag, but that's a loss we shall have to face. And honestly, sweetheart, if you can run like that, I don't really think the crutches are a great loss. Do your legs still give you very much pain?'

Kathy leaned her head against his shoulder and squeezed his hand. 'Hardly any,' she said truthfully. 'In fact, Alec, I think it's been fear of falling and making a fool of myself which caused me to cling to the crutches, rather than a real need. But when I saw you through the train window, my one thought was to reach you before you disappeared. Now I've explained what happened to me, you can tell me all about France after your plane was shot down, and getting back to dear old Blighty in one piece.'

Alec remembered the horrors of those first few days in France, before he had been found and hidden by the Vitré family. His 'chute had opened and he had been blown over the top of a wood or forest for what he thought was some way before the gust had dropped him. He had crashed through the branches of a tree, one of which had ripped his cheek open. He had done his best to keep the wound clean but it had festered and by the time Louis Vitré had found him he had been in a sorry state. The man had been wonderful, burying Alec's parachute and helping him to reach the farm which he and his wife and his old father were endeavouring to run between them, since the Vitré boys had escaped to England when France fell and were now, their parents assumed, fighting with the Free French under de Gaulle.

But it was not necessary to go into much detail, Alec decided, and dwelled more on the kindness of his hosts than on the horrors of those first few days or the rigours of his trek through occupied France, for the moment news of the Allied landings had come to his ears he had set off for the Channel ports. It would not have been fair to let the Vitré family risk more than they had done already, for the German army would take revenge, if they could, on anyone who had harboured their enemy.

For his own part, he was intrigued by Kathy's friendship with his parents and by the coincidence of her being posted to Coltishall, so near his own home. And when she suddenly began to apologise for the things she had said to him on his last evening in England, he silenced her with kisses, assuring her truthfully he had known all along that it had been surprise and disappointment which had caused her fury and not lack of love for him.

By the time the train reached Liverpool Street, all the necessary explanations had been made and the two of them were looking as smart and serene as was possible in the circumstances. Alec insisted on getting a taxi to take them to their destination, but there he had to leave Kathy. 'I'll be back in a couple of hours to pick you up, so don't you dare leave without me,' he instructed her. 'But I'm going to send a telegram to my ma and pa explaining that I've been held up and won't be home until tomorrow. I won't tell them that you'll be coming home with me,' he added, smiling down at her, 'because that can be a pleasant surprise. I take it that you'd planned to go back to Norfolk after your medical?'

'Well, I thought I'd give you a couple of days to settle in at home first,' Kathy said. 'And it's about time I went back to Daisy Street for a bit, too. Would – would you come with me, Alec? Only I can't bear the thought of being apart from you.'

Alec groaned softly. 'I want to give you a great big hug, but right here with the Top Brass coming and going all the time I dare not even squeeze your hand,' he said remorsefully. 'OK, we'll go home to Honeywell Farm tomorrow morning and tell my parents we're going to be married just as soon as we can arrange it. Then we'll go back to Daisy Street and tell your mam and young Billy. How does that suit you?'

'Oh, Alec, it sounds wonderful,' Kathy said. 'But suppose they post me miles away from you? If I pass the medical board they could remuster me . . . come to that if I fail it they could do the same! And you . . . you could go anywhere, too.'

'Yes, I know, but that's war for you. And we might find ourselves on the same station, even. I'm going to be training chaps to navigate Wimpeys for a bit, anyway. They've already said they won't put me back on active service for some time. And, sweetie, if you fail your medical board . . . well, they might decide you should leave the WAAF and then you could come and live near where I was stationed.'

'If we got married and I began to make a baby, then they would kick me out,' Kathy said longingly. How strange it was, to actually long to leave the WAAF, where she had been so happy! But that was love, she told herself; the true love sort which turns your whole world upside down.

Alec grinned down at her and squeezed her hand, then began to lead her along the pavement, away from Adastral House and the Top Brass which inhabited it. 'Well, if making a baby is the only way to stay together, I think we might manage that,' he said thoughtfully. They rounded a corner and he pulled her to a halt once more. 'What really worries me is what will happen when the war's over – which won't be long now – and we both go back to Civvy Street. Darling Kathy, I couldn't ever live in a city, you know. I'm a countryman, and once I get out of the RAF all I'll want to do is farm. But you . . . well, you can't deny you're a city girl. Have you ever considered actually spending all your time in Horsey? No cinemas, only one pub and that a good walk away, no theatres, teashops, clubs, dance halls. No pals living cheek by jowl with you, like in Daisy Street – no real neighbours, come to that. And though I love my home, I'm bound to admit that there's one helluva lot of plough and pasture, a great deal of hard and mucky work and very few diversions. Of course, there's the sea just over the marram bank, and the mere . . . but it int the sort of life many city girls would want.'

Kathy thought of the farm. Of the salt marshes which stretched between the good pasture lands and the sea, the remoteness of the house, the way it seemed to squat amidst the farm buildings, pulling its tiles down low as a farm labourer pulls down his cap in bad weather. She thought of the hustle and bustle of Stanley Road, the warmth of Daisy Street, where there was always someone on hand to mind a child, give a hand, share a trouble or a laugh.

But then she thought of other things, things which mattered, though Alec had not mentioned them. The wild beauty of the coastline where the great white-topped breakers came roaring on to the pale, shell-studded sand, the quiet of the ancient church surrounded by the gently leaning gravestones, the mighty oaks and elms which separated it from the country lanes in heavy, luxuriant leaf. The lanes themselves with their rich hedgerows and flowering verges. The new orchard at Honeywell, which had been replanted in '39, whose trees were taller than herself now and fruiting well. The hens which came bustling to the back door whenever Betty beat their food bucket with the big wooden spoon, and the pigs, standing on end in the sty in order to see who was bringing what in their direction.

And there was beauty there too, despite the flatness of the land and the practicality of the farm and its buildings. She saw, in her mind's eye, a group of winter-bare trees, starkly black against a lemon-coloured sky. The early mists of autumn lying across the water meadows so that the cattle seemed to be wading through milk. The mere in high summer, reflecting the blue of the sky so that it was hard to see where one began and the other ended.

'Well, my woman?' Alec's voice was suddenly worried. 'Being a tenant farmer's no picnic, but it's – well, it's what I was born to be. Only you. . . it's different for you. You wanted a proper career, a university education, all sorts of things I can't offer you. So – so I'm not sure if I'm being fair to ask you to marry me right now. . . or at any time, perhaps,' he finished gloomily. 'Only – oh, Kathy, I want you so!'

Kathy smiled up at him. 'Are you trying to put me off? Because if so, you're going the wrong way about it. Alec, I've been happier helping your parents at Honeywell than I ever thought I would be again. I think the country's beautiful, I don't even mind the mud! Of *course* I'll miss Daisy Street and all my pals, and of *course* I'll have a lot to learn, but don't you see? A proper career and a university education don't mean a thing to me. It's you who matters. I'd live in – in a pigsty if that was the only way we could be together.'

Alec's face cleared and he smiled at last, gently pulling her to him. 'I think we can do better than a pigsty; how about a stable?' he said. 'Now let's get away from here, because if I don't kiss you soon I'll burst!'

'Ditto,' Kathy said dreamily. 'Lead on, MacDuff!'

To find out more about Katie Flynn why not join the Katie Flynn Readers' Club and receive a twice yearly newsletter.

To join our mailing list to receive the newsletter and other information* write with your name and address to:

Katie Flynn Readers' Club
The Marketing Department
Arrow Books
20 Vauxhall Bridge Road
London
SW1V 2SA

Please state whether or not you would like to receive information about other Arrow saga authors.

*Your details will be held on a database so we can send you the newsletter(s) and information on other Arrow authors that you have indicated you wish to receive. Your details will not be passed to any third party. If you would like to receive information on other Random House authors please do let us know. If at any stage you wish to be deleted from our Katie Flynn Readers' Club mailing list please let us know.

ALSO AVAILABLE IN ARROW

Orphans of the Storm

Katie Flynn

Jess and Nancy, girls from very different backgrounds, are nursing in France during the Great War. They have much in common for both have lost their lovers in the trenches, so when the war is over and they return to nurse in Liverpool, their future seems bleak.

Very soon, however, their paths diverge. Nancy marries an Australian stockman and goes to live on a cattle station in the Outback, while Jess marries a Liverpudlian. Both have children; Nancy's eldest is Pete, and Jess has a daughter, Debbie, yet their lives couldn't be more different.

When the Second World War is declared, Pete joins the Royal Air Force and comes to England, promising his mother that he will visit her old friend. In the thick of the May blitz, with half of Liverpool demolished and thousands dead, Pete arrives in the city to find Jess's home destroyed and her daughter missing. Pete decides that whatever the cost, he must find her . . .

From the rigours of the Australian Outback to war-ravaged Liverpool, Debbie and Pete are drawn together . . . and torn apart . . .

arrow books

ALSO AVAILABLE IN ARROW

Darkest Before Dawn

Katie Flynn

The Todd family are strangers to city life when they move into a flat on the Scotland Road; their previous home was a canal barge. Harry gets a job as a warehouse manager and his wife, Martha, works in a grocer's shop, whilst Seraphina trains as a teacher, Angela works in Bunney's Department Store and young Evie starts at regular school.

Then circumstances change and Seraphina takes a job as a nippy in Lyon's Corner House. Customers vie for her favours, including an old friend, Toby.

When war is declared the older girls join up, leaving Evie and Martha to cope with rationing, shortages, and the terrible raids on Liverpool which devastate the city. Meanwhile, Toby is a Japanese POW, working on the infamous Burma railway and dreaming of Seraphina . . .

arrow books

A Long and Lonely Road

Katie Flynn

Rose McAllister is waiting for her husband, Steve, to come home. He is a seaman, often drunk and violent, but Rose does her best to cope and sees that her daughters, Daisy, 8, and Petal, 4, suffer as little as possible. Steve however, realises that war is coming and tries to reform, but on his last night home he pawns the girls' new dolls to go on a drinking binge.

When war is declared Rose has a good job but agrees the children must be evacuated. Daisy and Petal are happy at first, but circumstances change and they are put in the care of a woman who hates all scousers and taunts them with the destruction of their city. They run away, arriving home on the worst night of the May Blitz. Rose is attending the birth of her friend's baby and goes back to Bernard Terrace to find her home has received a direct hit, and is told that the children were seen entering the house the previous evening. Devastated, she decides to join the WAAF, encouraged by an RAF pilot, Luke, whom she has befriended . . .

arrow books

The Cuckoo Child

Katie Flynn

When Dot McCann, playing relievio with her pals, decides to hide in Butcher Rathbone's almost empty dustbin, she overhears a conversation that could send one man to prison and the other to the gallows – and suddenly finds herself in possession of stolen goods.

Dot lives with her aunt and uncle, the cuckoo in the nest, abandoned to these relatives after her parents died. She feels very alone . . . until she meets up with Corky who has run away from a London orphanage. They join forces with Emma, whose jeweller's shop has been burgled, and with Nick, a handsome young newspaper reporter who is investigating the crime. The four of them begin to plot to catch the thieves . . .

But Dot and Emma have been recognised, and soon both are in very real danger . . . .

arrow books

ALSO AVAILABLE IN ARROW

Little Girl Lost

Katie Flynn

It is a cold night and Sylvie Dugdale is weeping as she walks by the Mersey. A figure approaches and, dodging aside to avoid him, she falls into the river.

Constable Brendan O'Hara, just coming off duty, sees the girl's plight and dives in to rescue her. He is dazzled by her beauty, but Sylvie's husband is in prison and the closeness that Brendan soon longs for is impossible.

Sylvie has to escape from Liverpool, so Brendan arranges for her to stay with his cousin Caitlin in Dublin until it is safe to return. There she meets Maeve, a crippled girl from the slums, who will change all their lives when a little girl is lost . . .

arrow books